I0643000

THE LONDON OF SHERLOCK HOLMES

OVER 400 COMPUTER GENERATED STREET LEVEL PHOTOS

By

Thomas Bruce Wheeler

First edition published in 2011
© Copyright 2011
Thomas Bruce Wheeler

The right of Thomas Bruce Wheeler to be identified as the author
of this work has been asserted by him in accordance with the
Copyright, Designs and Patents Act 1998.

All rights reserved. No reproduction, copy or transmission of this
publication may be made without express prior written permission.
No paragraph of this publication may be reproduced, copied or
transmitted except with express prior written permission or in
accordance with the provisions of the Copyright Act 1956 (as
amended). Any person who commits any unauthorised act in
relation to this publication may be liable to criminal prosecution
and civil claims for damage.

All characters appearing in this work are fictitious. Any
resemblance to real persons, living or dead, is purely coincidental.
The opinions expressed herein are those of the authors and not of
MX Publishing.

Paperback ISBN 9781780922096
ePub ISBN 9781780922102
PDF ISBN 9781780922119

Published in the UK by MX Publishing
335 Princess Park Manor, Royal Drive, London, N11 3GX
www.mxpublishing.com
Cover design by www.staunch.com

"It is my business to know what other people don't know."

— Sherlock Holmes: *"The Blue Carbuncle"*

-To My Wife-
For reasons she knows best

USING GOOGLE MAPS TO SEE STREET VIEWS OF OVER 400 SHERLOCK HOLMES SITES

The e-book version of this book will generate over 400 street level photographs of the places Sherlock Holmes knew.

The latitude and longitude of each site (in blue) is hyperlinked to Google Maps.

A Pegman is shown in the upper left of each generated Google Map.

Click and drag the Pegman to the marked Sherlock Holmes site. This will open a street level photograph. All surrounding streets marked in blue, can also be viewed.

A control button in the upper left hand corner provides 360-degree control of the picture. Your mouse wheel will allow you to zoon in and out.

The upper right hand corner of each photo has two control buttons. One will expand the picture to full monitor size, and one will close that picture.

Using a large computer monitor or a HD internet TV will enhance the experience.

There are some excellent tube maps to give you the broad picture at the www.tfl.gov.uk website.

London 43 have a great London Tube Map .

CONTENTS

SHERLOCK HOLMES ADVENTURES (IN CHRONOLOGICAL ORDER) – Page 27

THE CARDBOARD BOX (1889?)

HOUND OF THE BASKERVILLES (1889)

A CASE OF IDENTITY (1889?)

THE BLUE CARBUNCLE (1889?)

THE COPPER BEECHES (1890?)

SILVER BLAZE (1890?)

THE SECOND STAIN (1890?)

THE RED-HEADED LEAGUE (1890)

THE BERYL CORONET (1891?)

WISTERIA LODGE (1891?)

THE FINAL PROBLEM (1891)

THE EMPTY HOUSE (1894)

THE GOLDEN PINCE-NEZ (1894)

THE NORWOOD BUILDER (1895?)

THE SOLITARY CYCLIST (1895)

THE THREE STUDENTS (1895)

ADVENTURE OF BLACK PETER (1895)

THE BRUCE-PARTINGTON PLANS (1895)

THE VEILED LODGER (1896)

THE SUSSEX VAMPIRE (1896?)

THE MISSING THREE-QUARTER (1897?)

THE DEVIL'S FOOT (1897)

ABBEY GRANGE (1897)

THE DANCING MEN (1897)

THE RETIRED COLOURMAN (1898?)

CHARLES AUGUSTUS MILVERTON (1899?)

THE SIX NAPOLEONS (1900?)

THE PROBLEM OF THOR BRIDGE (1900?)

SHOSCOMBE OLD PLACE (1901?)

THREE GABLES (1902?)

THE RED CIRCLE (1902?)

THE THREE GARRIDEBS (1902)

THE DISAPPEARANCE OF LADY FRANCES CARFAX (1902?)

THE ILLUSTRIOUS CLIENT (1902)

THE BLANCHED SOLDIER (1903)

THE PRIORY SCHOOL (1903?)

THE CREEPING MAN (1903?)

THE MAZARIN STONE (1903?)

THE LION'S MANE (1907)

HIS LAST BOW (1914)

SIR ARTHUR CONAN DOYLE'S FAVORITE ADVENTURES:

THE SPECKLED BAND

THE RED-HEADED LEAGUE

THE DANCING MEN

THE FINAL PROBLEM

A SCANDAL IN BOHEMIA

THE EMPTY HOUSE

THE FIVE ORANGE PIPS

THE SECOND STAIN

THE DEVIL'S FOOT

THE PRIORY SCHOOL

THE MUSGRAVE RITUAL

THE REIGATE SQUIRE

LONDON UNDERGROUND & DOCKLAND LIGHT RAIL STATIONS

UNDERGROUND STATIONS – Page 241

FARRINGDON (FOUR SITES)

FULHAM BROADWAY (ONE SITE)

GLOUCESTER ROAD (TWO SITES)

GOODGE STREET (TWO SITES)

GREEN PARK (TEN SITES)

HAMMERSMITH (THREE SITES)

HAMPSTEAD HEATH (THREE SITES)

HARROW & WEALDSTONE (THREE SITES)

IGH STREET KENSINGTON (SIX SITES)

HOLBORN (SIX SITES)

HOLLAND PARK (ONE SITE)

HYDE PARK CORNER (TWO SITES)

ISLAND GARDENS (DLR) (ONE SITE)

KENNINGTON (FIVE SITES)

KENSINGTON (OLYMPIA) (ONE SITE)

KILBURN PARK (ONE SITE)

KINGS CROSS / ST. PANCRAS (FOUR SITES)

LAMBETH NORTH (ONE SITE)

LANCASTER GATE (THREE SITES)

LIMEHOUSE (DLR) (TWO SITES)

LIVERPOOL STREET (ONE SITE)

LONDON BRIDGE (TWO SITES)

MANSION HOUSE (ONE SITE)

MARBLE ARCH (THIRTEEN SITES)

MARYLEBONE (ONE SITE)

MOORGATE (ONE SITE)

NOTTING HILL GATE (ONE SITE)

OVAL (SEVEN SITES)

OXFORD CIRCUS (NINETEEN SITES)

PADDINGTON (TWO SITES)

PICCADILLY CIRCUS (TWENTY SITES)

PIMLICO (FIVE SITES)   *

PUTNEY BRIDGE (ONE SITE)

REGENTS PARK (FOUR SITES)

RUSSELL SQUARE (FIVE SITES)

SHADWELL (DLR) (ONE SITE)

SOUTH KENSINGTON (1 SITE)

STAMFORD BROOK (1 SITE)

ST JAMES'S PARK (4 SITES)

ST JOHNS WOOD (1 SITE)

STOCKWELL (THIRTEEN SITES)

ST PAUL'S (ONE SITE)

TEMPLE (FIVE SITES)

TOTTENHAM COURT ROAD (NINE SITES)

TOWER HILL (THREE SITES)

VAUXHALL (FIFTEEN SITES)

VICTORIA (SEVEN SITES)

WARREN STREET (ONE SITE)

WATERLOO (THREE SITES)

WESTBOURNE PARK (ONE SITE)

WESTMINSTER (EIGHTEEN SITES)

RAIL STATIONS – Page 341

ANERLEY (TWO SITES)

BECKENHAM HILL (TWO SITES)

BLACKHEATH (FOUR SITES)

BLACKWALL (ONE SITE)

CLAPHAM JUNCTION (ONE SITE)

CRYSTAL PALACE (ONE SITE)

DENMARK HILL (FOUR SITES)

DEPTFORD (ONE SITE)

EAST CROYDON (TWO SITES)

ESHER (FOUR SITES)

HERNE HILL (TWO SITES)

LEE (ONE SITE)

LIVERPOOL JAMES STREET (ONE SITE)

LOUGHBOROUGH JUNCTION (FOUR SITES)

MADEN MANOR (ONE SITE)

NORBURY (THREE SITES)

NORWOOD JUNCTION (SIX SITES)

QUEENS ROAD PECKHAM (TWO SITES)

SHOREDITCH HIGH STREET (TWO SITES)

STREATHAM (FOUR SITES)

STREATHAM HILL (ONE SITE)

WALLINGTON (ONE SITE)

13

WANDSWORTH COMMON (ONE SITE)

WESTCOMBE PARK (ONE SITE)

WEST CROYDON (ONE SITE)

WOOLWICH ARSENAL (THREE SITES)

WOOLWICH DOCK (TWO SITES)

SHERLOCK'S LONDON ON THE BAKERLOO LINE (104 SITES):

HARROW & WEALDSTONE

KILBURN PARK

PADDINGTON

BAKER STREET

MARYLEBONE

REGENTS PARK

OXFORD CIRCUS

PICCADILLY CIRCUS

CHARING CROSS

EMBANKMENT

WATERLOO

LAMBETH NORTH

SHERLOCK'S LONDON ON THE CENTRAL LINE (75 SITES):

HARROW & WEALDSTONE

KILBURN PARK

PADDINGTON

14

MARYLEBONE

BAKER STREET

REGENTS PARK

OXFORD CIRCUS

PICCADILLY CIRCUS

CHARING CROSS

EMBANKMENT

WATERLOO

LAMBETH NORTH

SHERLOCK'S LONDON ON THE CIRCLE LINE (94 SITES):

BAKER STREET

PADDINGTON

NOTTING HILL GATE

HIGH STREET KENSINGTON

GLOUCESTER ROAD

SOUTH KENSINGTON

VICTORIA

ST JAMES'S PARK

WESTMINSTER

EMBANKMENT

TEMPLE

BLACKFRIARS

MANSION HOUSE

CANNON STREET

TOWER HILL

ALDGATE

LIVERPOOL STREET

MOORGATE

BARBICAN

FARRINGDON

KINGS CROSS / ST. PANCRAS

EUSTON SQUARE

FINDING SHERLOCK'S LONDON ON THE DISTRICT LINE (70 SITES):

PADDINGTON

NOTTING HILL GATE

HIGH STREET KENSINGTON

KENSINGTON (OLYMPIA)

FULHAM BROADWAY

PUTNEY BRIDGE

GLOUCESTER ROAD

STAMFORD BROOK

EARLS COURT

SOUTH KENSINGTON

VICTORIA

ST JAMES'S PARK

WESTMINSTER

EMBANKMENT

TEMPLE

BLACKFRIARS

MANSION HOUSE

CANNON STREET

TOWER HILL

ALGATE EAST

SHERLOCK'S LONDON ON THE DLR (6 SITES):

SHADWELL

LIMEHOUSE

ISLAND GARDENS

CUTTY SARK

SHERLOCK'S LONDON ON THE HAMMERSMITH & CITY LINE (35 SITES):

HAMMERSMITH

PADDINGTON

BAKER STREET

EUSTON SQUARE

KINGS CROSS / ST. PANCRAS

FARRINGDON

BARBICAN

MOORGATE

LIVERPOOL STREET

ALGATE EAST

SHERLOCK'S LONDON ON THE JUBILEE LINE (65 SITES):

ST JOHNS WOOD

BAKER STREET

BOND STREET

GREEN PARK

WESTMINSTER

WATERLOO

LONDON BRIDGE

CANARY WATER

SHERLOCK'S LONDON ON THE METROPOLITAN LINE (33 SITES):

BAKER STREET

WARREN STREET

EUSTON SQUARE

KINGS CROSS / ST. PANCRAS

FARRINGDON

BARBICAN

MOORGATE

LIVERPOOL STREET

ALDGATE

SHERLOCK'S LONDON ON THE NORTHERN LINE (89 SITES):

EDGWARE

HAMPSTEAD HEATH

CAMDEN TOWN

KINGS CROSS / ST. PANCRAS

EUSTON

WARREN STREET

GOODGE STREET

TOTTENHAM COURT ROAD

CHARING CROSS

EMBANKMENT

WATERLOO

MOORGATE

LONDON BRIDGE

KENNINGTON

OVAL

STOCKWELL

SHERLOCK'S LONDON ON THE PICCADILLY LINE (71 SITES):

HAMMERSMITH

EARL'S COURT

GLOUCESTER ROAD

SOUTH KENSINGTON

HYDE PARK CORNER

GREEN PARK

PICCADILLY CIRCUS

COVENT GARDEN

HOLBORN

RUSSELL SQUARE

KINGS CROSS / ST. PANCRAS

CALEDONIAN ROAD

SHERLOCK'S LONDON ON THE VICTORIA LINE (84 SITES):

EUSTON

KINGS CROSS / ST. PANCRAS

WARREN STREET

OXFORD CIRCUS

GREEN PARK

PIMLICO

VAUXHALL

STOCKWELL

BRIXTON

WALKING TOURS —IN HOLMES AND WATSON'S FOOTSTEPS – Page 357

NAMED CHARACTERS – Page 364

NAMED CHARACTER STATISTICS – Page 389

STAY AT ONE OF THE DELUXE VICTORIAN HOTELS SHERLOCK HOLMES KNEW

CHARING CROSS—WC2: [Latitude / Longitude: 51.50872,-0.125144]. Tel. 44-845-305-8125

CLARIDGE'S—W1: [Latitude / Longitude: 51.512846,-0.148169]. Tel. 44-20-7629-8860

THE GRAND—WC2: [Latitude / Longitude: 51.506939,-0.124715]. Tel. 44-866-539-0036

THE GROSVENOR—W1: [Latitude / Longitude: 51.496002,-0.145335]. Tel. 44-845-305-8337

THE LANGHAM—W1: [Latitude / Longitude: 51.518077,-0.143875]. Tel. 44-20-7636-1000

RENAISSANCE ST. PANCRAS—W1: [Latitude / Longitude: 51.529407,-0.125712]. Tel. 44-20-7841-3540

About the author

Thomas Bruce Wheeler is a retired senior civil service executive and Sherlock Holmes enthusiast. He discovered the Great Detective as an undergraduate, and has retained his interest for over sixty years. Although he and his wife have been frequent visitors to the UK, he did not have time to share his interest with other enthusiasts until after retirement. Since then he has written *London Secrets* (2004) and *The New Finding Sherlock's London* (2009).

Wheeler and his wife live in Memphis Tennessee. He is a member of the Sherlock Holmes Society of London, former president of The Giant Rats of Sumatra (the Memphis Sherlock Holmes Club), and founder life member of Memphis's Crescent Club.

ACKNOWLEDGEMENT

I wish to thank Roger Johnson and Jean Upton, of the Sherlock Holmes Society of London, for their suggestions. I was also greatly assisted by two authors: Bernard Davies' two volume set *HOLMES & WATSON COUNTRY, Travels in Search of Solutions,* Sherlock Holmes Society of London – 2008, and Arthur M. Alexander's book, *HOT ON THE SCENT*, *A Visitor's Guide to the London of Sherlock Holmes*, Calabash Press – 1999.

INTRODUCTION

In the Sherlock Holmes adventures, Sir Arthur Conan Doyle formed our image of Victorian London. In our mind's eye, we still see the sinister, fog-bound city that was the center of the Empire.

Holmes and Watson traveled all over Greater London. Time, the Blitz, and urban redevelopment have taken their toll, but many of the places Sherlock "saw" are still there. Conan Doyle was unusually precise in his London locations, only occasionally disguising a site. However, many times he gave enough clues to help us find these locations.

The task of writing this book was further complicated by street name changes and renumbering. However, with humble detective skills, and the help of those who have researched The Canon before me, I was able to identify over four hundred Sherlock Holmes sites in Greater London. The first part of the book places these sites in adventure context, and with hyperlinked map coordinates in the e-book, allows you to access Google Map Street Views.

In the second part of the book, I have grouped the sites by their nearest underground or train station. With map coordinates and a hand-held GPS device, London visitors can get turn-by-turn walking directions to the various Sherlock Holmes sites.

Six walking tour maps are also included. These are not the usual rambling tours, but walks that Holmes and Watson took in one of their adventures.

Finally, for those with a statistical bent, I have listed the 454 characters named in this book, and statistically analyzed their titles and occupations.

THE "GLORIA SCOTT" - 1874

No. 31 "221B" BAKER STREET—W1: [Latitude / Longitude: 51.517932,-0.155587]. The *Gloria Scott* was Sherlock's first published adventure, and occurred before he met Watson. Watson learned of the case one winter evening at Baker Street, when Holmes handed him some papers and said, "These are the documents in the extraordinary case of the *Gloria Scott*, and the message which struck Justice of the Peace Trevor dead with horror." The note read, *"The supply of game for London is going steadily up. Head-keeper Hudson we believe has been now told to receive all order for fly-paper and for preservation of your hen-pheasant's life."* Watson said the note made no sense. **Underground Station: Marble Arch**

BISHOPSGATE TERMINUS (site)—E1: [Latitude / Longitude: 51.523399,-0.077453]. During Holmes's first two years in college, Victor Trevor was his only close friend. Victor invited Holmes to spend a month at Donnithorpe, the elder Trevor's estate in Norfolk. In 1874, Holmes probably left London on a Great Eastern Line train, from the old Bishopsgate Terminus located at the junction of Shoreditch High Street and Bethnal Green Road. **Rail Station: Shoreditch High Street**

Young Trevor told his father of Holmes's power of observation and inference. The old man said, "I am an excellent subject, if you can deduce anything from me." Having noticed that Mr. Trevor had added lead to the head of his walking stick, Holmes replied, "I might suggest that you have gone about in fear of some personal attack." When Holmes reeled off other observations, the old man fainted. When he recovered, he told Holmes, "That's your line of life, sir, and you may take the word of a man who has seen something of the world."

MONTAGUE STREET—WC1: [Latitude / Longitude: <u>51.519069,-</u> <u>0.12463</u>]. After Holmes's observations, the old man felt uneasy around Holmes. To keep from embarrassing Victor, Holmes returned to his Montague Street rooms in London. There, Holmes received a telegram from Trevor, imploring him to return to Donnithorpe. **Underground Station: Russell Square**

When Holmes arrived, Trevor said his father was dying from Apoplexy and nervous shock. Victor said Hudson, an old acquaintance of his father, had arrived at Donnithorpe, and was given the butler's position. One evening, when Hudson made an insolent reply to his father, Victor grabbed him by the shoulders and threw him out of the room. Mr. Trevor asked his son to apologize, and when he refused, Hudson left. He said he was going to stay with Mr. Beddoes in Hampshire.

Shortly thereafter, a letter arrived from Hampshire that caused the elder Trevor to have a stroke. Victor said that the letter was absurd and trivial, but when Holmes read it, he saw that if you read every third word, the message was clear. *"**The** supply of **game** for London **is** going steadily **up**. Head-keeper **Hudson** we believe **has** been now **told** to receive **all** order for **fly**-paper and **for** preservation of **your** hen-pheasant's **life**."*

On his deathbed, Mr. Trevor told his doctor about, "the papers in the back drawer of the Japanese cabinet." They told the whole story. The elder Trevor's real name was James Armitage. As a young man, he had embezzled money, and was sent to Australia on the convict ship *Gloria Scott*. In addition to Armitage and thirty-seven other convicts, the ship carried a crew of twenty-six: eighteen soldiers, a captain, three mates, and four warders. There was also a doctor and chaplain onboard.

One convict, Jack Prendergast, bribed the chaplain, some of the crew, and two of the warders. His scheme to take over the ship was successful. When Prendergast said, he was going to kill everyone who could testify against him, Armitage, another young convict named Evans, two other convicts, and three bribed sailors objected. They did not want to see men killed in cold blood.

Prendergast said those who objected could take a lifeboat and go. He gave them "a suit of sailor togs each, a barrel of water, two casks, one of junk and one of biscuits, and a compass." Prendergast also threw them a chart, saying that when rescued, they should say they were shipwrecked mariners whose ship had sunk at Latitude 15° and Longitude 25°. After the lifeboat cleared the ship, the *Gloria Scott* exploded. One of the doomed sailors fled to the gunpowder room, and blew up the ship. When Armitage and the others rowed back, the only person they found was a young sailor named Hudson. The next day, the brig *Hotspur*, bound for Australia, picked up those in the lifeboat. The captain had no difficulty in believing they were survivors of a floundered passenger ship.

ADMIRALTY HOUSE, Whitehall—SW1: [Latitude / Longitude: 51.505557,-0.126826]. The Old Admiralty Offices in Whitehall are where it was set down that the convict ship *Gloria Scott* was lost at sea. No word ever leaked out as to her true fate. **Underground Station: Charing Cross**

After the *Hotspur* landed in Sydney, Armitage changed his name to Trevor, and Evans changed his to Beddoes. Both men prospered in Australia, and returned to England as rich men. The only man, who could incriminate them, without incriminating himself, was Hudson.

Victor Trevor was heart-broken when he learned of his father's deception, and left England to work on a tea plantation in India. Hudson and Beddoes disappeared. Holmes thought it likely that Beddoes killed Hudson and fled the country, with as much money as he could lay his hands on.

No. 31 "221B" BAKER STREET—W1: [Latitude / Longitude: <u>51.517932,-0.155587</u>]. Watson learned of the Musgrave Ritual when he commented on Holmes untidy habits. Holmes kept "his cigars in a coal-shuttle, his tobacco in the toe end of a Persian slipper, and his unanswered correspondence transfixed by a jack-knife into the very center of his wooden mantelpiece." When Watson suggested they needed to tidy up, Holmes went into his bedroom and pulled out a large tin box. In it were items and papers from his early cases. One item was a small wooden box. Inside was "a crumpled piece of paper, an old-fashioned brass key, a peg of wood with a ball of string …, and three rusty old discs of metal." Holmes said, "These are all I have…to remind me of the adventure of the Musgrave Ritual". **Underground Station: Marble Arch**

MONTAGUE STREET—WC1: [Latitude / Longitude: <u>51.519069,-0.12463</u>]. In his early days in London, Holmes had rooms in Montague Street. He was just out of college, and wanted quarters near the British Museum's Reading Room. One morning, he received a visit from Reginald Musgrave. Musgrave had been at Sherlock's college, and after his father's death, had taken over the family estate. Musgrave said he needed Holmes's help. **Underground Station: Russell Square**

Author's note: There is no indication that Holmes's Montague Street rooms were at the same location in 1879, as they were in 1874. In fact, since it is likely that he finished college between these dates, and given the state of his finances, it does not seem logical that he would have retained London quarters.

RUSKIN PRIVATE HOTEL, No. 23-24 Montague Street—WC1: [Latitude / Longitude: <u>51.519614,-0.125197</u>]. Author's note: On one of my trips to London, I talked to the owner of the private Ruskin Hotel. He claimed his modest Bed & Breakfast was the location of Sherlock's Montague Street rooms. I do not know where he got the idea, but it makes a good story, and is probably good for business. **Underground Station: Russell Square**

BRITISH MUSEUM, Great Russell Street—WC1: [Latitude / Longitude: 51.518406,-0.12584]. The Museum's famous Reading Room contains an enormous collection of scientific works. This is where young Sherlock studied those branches of science, which would later make him so efficient in his chosen profession. **Underground Station: Tottenham Court Road**

Author's note: In *A Study in Scarlet*, Watson summarized the extent of Holmes's knowledge:

>   Knowledge of <u>Literature</u> —Nothing.
>
>   Knowledge of <u>Philosophy</u> —Nothing.
>
>   Knowledge of <u>Astronomy</u> —Nothing.
>
>   Knowledge of <u>Politics</u> —Feeble.
>
>   Knowledge of <u>Botany</u> —Variable. Well up in <u>belladonna</u>, <u>opium</u> and <u>poisons</u> generally. Knows nothing of practical <u>gardening</u>.
>
>   Knowledge of <u>Geology</u> —Practical, but limited. Tells at a glance different soils from each other. After walks, has shown me splashes upon his trousers, and told me by their colour and consistence in what <u>part of London</u> he had received them.
>
>   Knowledge of <u>Chemistry</u> —Profound.
>
>   Knowledge of <u>Anatomy</u> —Accurate, but unsystematic.
>
>   Knowledge of <u>Sensational Literature</u> —Immense. He appears to know every detail of every horror perpetrated in the century.

Knowledge of <u>Musical Instruments</u> —plays the violin ` well.

Knowledge of the <u>Martial Arts</u> —Expert singlestick player, boxer and swordsman.

Knowledge of the <u>Law</u> —Good practical knowledge of British law.

HOUSES OF PARLIAMENT—SW1: [Latitude / Longitude: <u>51.500945,-0.123661</u>]. After his father's death, Reginald Musgrave began managing the Hurlstone estate, and became a Member of Parliament. **Underground Station: Westminster**

Hurlstone, Musgrave found his butler, Richard Brunton, going through the family papers. These included an ancient observance called the "Musgrave Ritual." The ritual was a series of questions and answers that each male Musgrave had to memorize:

Whose was it? His who has gone.
Who shall have it? He who will come.
Where was the sun? Over the oak.
Where was the shadow? Under the elm.
How was it stepped? North by ten and by ten, east by five and by five, south by two and by two, west by one and by one, and so under.
What shall we give for it? All that is ours.
Why should we give it? For the sake of the trust.

Musgrave fired Brunton, and gave him one week to leave. On the third day, Brunton disappeared, but left his clothes, watch and money behind. The servants checked all through the old house, but could not find the missing butler. Rachel Howells, the housemaid, became hysterical. Later, when she also disappeared, they dragged the pond for her body, but found only an old linen bag, containing discolored metal, and several colored pebbles.

LONDON BRIDGE RAILWAY STATION—SW1: [Latitude / Longitude: 51.505848,-0.086521]. When Holmes left London to visit Hurlstone, in western Sussex, he took the train from the London Bridge Station. **Underground Station: London Bridge**

After Holmes arrived at Hurlstone, he felt that the Musgrave Ritual was the key to the mystery. The Ritual mentioned landmarks, directions and distances on the old estate. Using mathematical calculations, Holmes and Musgrave were able to find the place described in the Ritual. They also found that the Butler had been there before them. His body was in a pit in an old unused section of the house. A heavy stone lid covered the pit. By putting himself in Brunton's place, Holmes realized that he would have needed help to lift, and prop-open the stone lid. Brunton had enlisted Rachel's help. After Brunton jumped into the pit, and handed up the linen bag, Rachel let the heavy stone slip shut. Later, in remorse, she threw the bag into the pond, and fled.

By examining the dates on coins found near the pit, and learning that Musgrave's ancestor, Sir Ralph Musgrave, was a prominent cavalier, Holmes understood the significance of the items in the old linen bag. They were the remnants of the Ancient Crown of England. The Musgrave's had guarded the treasure, and tried to pass down the knowledge of its secret hiding place. Over the generations, the ritual's meaning was lost. It took Sherlock Holmes (and the butler) to unlock the mystery.

STUDY IN SCARLET - 1881?

UNIVERSITY COLLEGE, LONDON (Former University of London), Gower Street—WC1: [Latitude / Longitude: 51.524369,-0.1345]. In 1878, Watson received his medical degree from the University of London. The primary buildings for medical studies were on Gower Street. **Underground Station: Euston Square**

MUSEUM OF MANKIND (Former University of London offices), Burlington Gardens—W1: [Latitude / Longitude: 51.509889,-0.140459]. When Watson was studying for his medical degree, the University of London used Burlington Gardens for administrative offices. **Underground Station: Green Park**

UNIVERSITY COLLEGE HOSPITAL (site), Gower Street—WC1: [Latitude / Longitude: 51.524369,-0.1345]. In addition to St. Bartholomew's Hospital (St. Bart's), Watson could have learned his surgical skills at the old University College Hospital. The new hospital, built between 1897 and 1906, is on the same spot. **Underground Station: Euston Square**

After getting his medical degree, Watson went to Netley, near Southampton, for an Army surgeon course. He then joined the Fifth Northumberland Fusiliers in India as an assistant surgeon. After being wounded at the battle of Maiwand, he was sent back to England.

THE STRAND—WC2: [Latitude / Longitude: 51.509577,-0.123639]. Having neither "kith nor kin" in England, Watson moved to London, "That great cesspool into which all the loungers and idlers of the Empire are irresistibly drawn." At first, he stayed at a small private hotel in The Strand. Watson soon found that his "wound pension" of eleven shillings and sixpence a day could not support his London life style. He made up his mind to leave the hotel, and take up less expensive quarters. **Underground Station: Charing Cross**

CRITERION GRILL, No. 224 Piccadilly—W1: [Latitude / Longitude: 51.510162,-0.134436]. The day Watson made up his mind to move out of his Strand hotel, he went to The Criterion Bar. There, he met young Stamford. Stamford had been a dresser under Watson at "St. Bart's." Watson asked Stamford to have lunch with him at The Holborn Restaurant. **Underground Station: Piccadilly Circus**

Author's note: The Criterion has reopened. The spacious and ornate dining room is in the Criterion Theatre Building at Piccadilly Circus. Ask if they still have the good-value pre-theater dinner. Also, look for the wall plaque that commemorates the event that resulted in Watson meeting Holmes.

HOLBORN RESTAURANT (site), Holborn—WC2: [Latitude / Longitude: 51.517467,-0.120574]. The Holborn Restaurant was located on the southwest corner of today's Holborn and Kingsway. During lunch, Watson mentioned that he was looking for "comfortable rooms at a reasonable price." Stamford said that was strange because, "You are the second man today who has used that expression to me." The other person was Sherlock Holmes. **Underground Station: Holborn**

When Watson said he would like to meet Holmes, Stamford said, "You don't know Sherlock Holmes yet, perhaps you would not care for him as a constant companion." Watson insisted, and he and Stamford made their way to St. Bartholomew's Hospital, where Holmes was "sure to be at the laboratory."

ST. BARTHOLOMEW'S (ST. BART'S) HOSPITAL—EC1: [Latitude / Longitude: 51.518033,-0.10098]. Stamford introduced Watson and Holmes in St. Bart's chemical laboratory. Holmes told Watson, "You have been in Afghanistan, I perceive." This was the first time Holmes astonished Watson with his special abilities. **Underground Station: Farringdon**

Author's note: St. Bart's has an excellent small museum, just inside the Henry VIII Gate. Among the items displayed, is the plaque commemorating the first meeting of Holmes and Watson.

Holmes said, "It's just as well for two fellows to know the worst of one another." He mentioned his use of strong tobacco, his chemical experiments, and his moods. Watson said he kept a bull pup, objected to confrontations, got up at ungodly hours, and was extremely lazy. Holmes said, "I think we may consider the thing settled—that is, if the rooms are agreeable to you."

No. 31 "221B" BAKER STREET—W1: [Latitude / Longitude: 51.517932,-0.155587].

The day after they met, Holmes and Watson went to inspect the rooms at Mrs. Hudson's 221B Baker Street. They consisted of "A couple of comfortable bedrooms and a single large airy sitting room, cheerfully furnished, and illuminated by two broad windows." In later adventures, we learn that Watson's bedroom was on the floor above, and Sherlock's bedroom eventually had three doors: one leading to the sitting room, a second exiting into the hallway, and a third hidden door, added later, which opened behind the sitting room curtains. **Underground Station: Marble Arch**

Author's note: In the late nineteenth century, the name "Baker Street" applied only that section of the modern street, south of Paddington Street. The portion of the street north of Paddington was known as York Place. In addition, the highest house number, on nineteenth century Baker Street, was 85. This means that Conan Doyle hid the true location of 221B, until he revealed it as today's No. 31 Baker Street in *The Adventure of the Empty House*.

During their first week at Baker Street, Watson learned that Holmes had acquaintances from all classes of society. When people arrived, Holmes would beg for use of the sitting room, and Watson would retire to his bedroom. Holmes explained that these were his clients, and he was the world's only "consulting detective."

One morning, Holmes received a note from Tobias Gregson, and showed it to Watson. The note said, "There has been bad business during the night at 3 Lauriston Gardens, off Brixton Road." Enoch J. Drebber of Cleveland, Ohio was murdered. Holmes told Watson, "Gregson is the smartest of the Scotland Yarders", and that, "He and Lestrade are the pick of a bad lot." Holmes asked Watson to get his hat. This was the first time Holmes asked Watson to accompany him on one of the adventures.

LAURISTON GARDENS (site), Brixton Road—SW9: [Latitude / Longitude: 51.466777,-0.11309]. On the way to Lauriston Gardens, Holmes and Watson traveled along Brixton Road. When they arrived, Inspector Gregson asked Holmes to examine the murder site. **Underground Station: Brixton**

Author's note: Bernard Davies identified Lauriston Gardens as a group of four detached, double-fronted houses on the East side of Brixton Road, between Villa Road and St John's Crescent. Today, Max Roach Park occupies the site.

As the police lifted the body, a woman's ring rolled across the floor. It was a plain gold wedding band. In addition to the ring, the police found men's jewelry and a Russian leather card case with the cards of Enoch J. Drebber of Cleveland. There was "no purse, but loose money to the extent of seven pounds thirteen, a pocket edition of Boccaccio's 'Decameron' with the name of Joseph Stangerson upon the flyleaf, and two letters—one to E. J. Drebber and one to Joseph Stangerson."

BRIXTON ROAD POLICE STATION, corner of Brixton & Cresham Roads—SW9: [Latitude / Longitude 51.464754,-0.114193]. Holmes asked Gregson if he and Lestrade had taken a cab to Lauriston Gardens. He already knew they had not, but he wanted to confirm his observations. This meant that the two Scotland Yard men walked from the Brixton Road Police Station, just a quarter of a mile away. **Underground Station: Brixton**

AMERICAN EXCHANGE, The Strand—WC2: [Latitude / Longitude: 51.508624,-0.125379]. The two letters were addressed to the American Exchange, The Strand. The letters were from the Guion Steamship Company, and referred to the sailing of their boats from Liverpool to New York. In the 1880's, the American Exchange was located at 449 The Strand, with a kiosk style booth on the south side of the street, between the two exit gates of the Charing Cross Railroad Station. **Underground Station: Charing Cross**

In an adjoining room at Lauriston Gardens, Lestrade discovered the word *RACHE*, written in blood. Lestrade thought the murderer had meant to write the female name Rachel, but had been disturbed before finishing. Holmes examined the whole room with a tape measure and, his now famous, large round magnifying glass. He also asked for the name and address of the constable who found the body. On his way out, Holmes told Lestrade, "don't lose your time looking for Miss Rachel...'Rache' is the German word for "revenge"."

SUB-DISTRICT POST, MONEY ORDER AND TELEGRAPH OFFICE, No. 304 Brixton Road—SW9: [Latitude / Longitude: 51.469866,-0.112588]. Having determined that Gregson wired Cleveland, but did not ask the correct questions, Holmes and Watson walked to the nearby telegraph office to dispatch their own wire. The building that contained the telegraph office is marked as the home of The Eagle Printing Works. **Underground Station: Stockwell**

AULTON PLACE, "Audley Court"—SE11: [Latitude / Longitude: 51.486117,-0.109459]. Holmes and Watson then went to see the constable, who found Drebber's body. His name was John Rance, who lived at No. 46 Audley Court, Kennington Park Gate. Bernard Davies identified the address as Aulton Place, a narrow alley off Stannary Street. **Underground Station: Kennington**

Constable Rance was asleep when Holmes and Watson arrived, but a gold half-sovereign soothed his irritability. He said his shift was from ten at night to six in the morning. At eleven, there had been a fight at the White Hart Tavern, but other than that, he said it was a quiet night.

HENRY "HENRIETTA" STREET—SW9: [Latitude / Longitude: 51.477458,-0.108383]. Constable Rance said it began to rain at one o'clock, when he met Constable Harry Murcher, "him who has the Holland Grove beat" at the corner of "Henrietta Street". Henry Street is no longer there, but it entered the north side of Vassall Road, just west of the Holland Grove. **Underground Station: Oval**

Rance said he continued his patrol down Brixton Road, when a glint of light from the empty Lauriston Gardens house caught his eye. When he pushed open the door, he found a candle burning on the mantelpiece, and the dead body on the floor. As he went outside to summon other constables, he saw a drunk by the front gate. Rance said the man had a reddish face and wore a brown overcoat. Holmes thought the "drunk" might be the murderer, who had come back to retrieve the ring.

WHITE HART TAVERN, Lilford & Loughborough Roads— SW5: [Latitude / Longitude: 51.470575,-0.106884]. **Holmes** placed an ad in the evening paper. It read, ***"In Brixton Road, this morning. A plain gold wedding ring, found in the roadway between the White Hart Tavern and Holland Grove. Apply Dr. Watson, 221B Baker Street, between eight and nine this evening."*** Holmes apologized to Watson for using his name. **Underground Station: Brixton**

WHITE HORSE PUB (site), No. 1 Loughborough Road—SW9: [Latitude / Longitude: 51.470491,-0.112181]. **Author's note:** The ad, as written, makes no sense. It says that the ring was "In Brixton Road, but the White Hart Public House is 400 feet away. It is more likely that Watson wrote "White Hart" instead of "White Horse", the latter pub was on the corner of Loughborough & Brixton Roads. The building is still there, but it is no longer a pub. **Underground Station: Stockwell**

No. 13 CAMPERDOWN "DUNCAN" STREET—E1: [Latitude / Longitude: 51.514275,-0.071154]. A few minutes after eight, an old woman arrived in response to the ad. Holmes had expected a man. The woman said her name was Mrs. Sawyer, and that she lived on Duncan Street near Houndsditch. She said the ring belonged to her daughter Sally. Later, when Holmes went to the Duncan Street address, he found it belonged to a respectable paperhanger named Keswick, who had never heard of Mrs. Sawyer. Holmes surmised that "Mrs. Sawyer" must be an active man, and an incomparable actor. Duncan Street is now Camperdown Street. **Underground Station: Aldgate East**

PECKHAM—SE15: [Latitude / Longitude: 51.476218,-0.06404]. "Mrs. Sawyer" said that her daughter Sally Dennis lived in Peckham with her husband Tom. **Rail Station: Queens Road Peckham**

THE HIGHWAY "RATCLIFF HIGHWAY"—E1: [Latitude / Longitude: 51.509666,-0.054955]. The papers were full of the Brixton Murder, and the Daily Telegraph compared it to, "The Ratcliff Highway murders." The Ratcliff Highway, in Wapping, had a sinister reputation. Watson began saving the press clippings, putting him on the road to becoming Holmes's "Boswell". **Dockland Light Rail Station: Shadwell**

No. 129 CAMBERWELL ROAD—SE5: [Latitude / Longitude: 51.48108,-0.094332]. After his arrival in London, Enoch Drebber bought a hat from John Underwood, a haberdasher at No. 129 Camberwell Road. Drebber gave Mrs. Charpentier's boarding house as his London address. **Underground Station: Kennington**

After reading the newspapers, Watson heard the scrambling of steps in the hall. Holmes said that it was "The Baker Street division of the detective police force." They were a rag-tag bunch of dirty Street Arabs who Holmes called his "Baker Street Irregulars." Holmes used them, and their lieutenant "Wiggins," for his eyes and ears. They could travel unnoticed, all over London.

After the "Irregulars" left, Gregson arrived, and said he had solved the case. He had arrested Arthur Charpentier, a sub-lieutenant in Her Majesty's Navy. Gregson had traced Drebber through the hat he bought on Camberwell Road, and found that he was staying at Madam Charpentier's boarding house. When Gregson went to see Mrs. Charpentier, he found her daughter Alice with her. Alice pleaded with her mother to tell the whole truth.

DOVER "TORQUAY" TERRACE, Coldharbour Lane—SE5: [Latitude / Longitude: 51.467149,-0.099714]. The newspapers mentioned that the deceased, Edward Drebber, was an American gentleman. He and his private secretary, Joseph Stangerson, stayed at Mrs. Charpentier's boarding house in Torquay Terrace, Coldharbour Lane. Keeping the nautical theme, Watson substituted the word "Torquay" for Dover. Bernard Davies suggests Mrs. Charpentier's house was the first house in Dover Terrace, on the east side of Coldharbour Lane, at the corner of Harbour Road. **Rail Station: Loughborough Junction**

EUSTON RAILWAY STATION—NW1: [Latitude / Longitude: 51.528401,-0.131943]. At about half-past eight on Tuesday, Enoch Drebber and Joseph Stangerson had been seen on a Euston Station platform, where they were waiting for the 9:15 Liverpool Express. **Underground Station: Euston**

Mrs. Charpentier said that Drebber and Stangerson had left to catch the 9:15 train to Liverpool, but Drebber returned alone, saying he had missed the train. He had been drinking, and proposed to Alice, trying to drag her towards the door. Mrs. Charpentier's son, Arthur, entered, and with the help of a stout oak cudgel, chased Drebber out of the house. The next morning, Mrs. Charpentier heard about Drebber's death, and feared her son had something to do with it. As Gregson finished telling how he solved the case, Lestrade arrived. Gregson said, "Have you managed to find…Joseph Stangerson"? Lestrade replied, "Stangerson was murdered at Halliday's Private Hotel about six o'clock this morning."

LITTLE GEORGE STREET (site)—NW1: [**Latitude / Longitude:** 51.527987,-0.13656]. Halliday's Private Hotel was located in Little George Street. The word *RACHE*, written in blood, was above Joseph Stangerson's body. A milk delivery boy had seen someone using a ladder to enter, or exit, the room's open window. The boy said the man was tall, had a reddish face, and was dressed in a long brown coat. **Underground Station: Euston**

Author's note: Little George Street no longer exists. In 1881, it ran east west between Hampstead Road, and Cardington Road, on the south side of St James Gardens. The nearby Exmouth Arms Pub was open for business in 1881. As for its location of Halliday's Hotel, there were no hotels, private or otherwise, in Little George Street. Bernard Davies has identified the one hotel in the neighborhood that matches the Canon's description --- Emms' Private Hotel at No. 56 Drummond Street, near the corner of Cardington Street, along the side of Euston Station.

EMMS' PRIVATE HOTEL, No. 56 Drummond Street (site)—NW1: [**Latitude / Longitude:** 51.527731,-0.135227]. Emms' was the only private hotel in the neighborhood that fits Watson's description. Emms' no longer exists, and was located where the modern Hotel Ibis sits today. **Underground Station: Euston**

Lestrade said he had found a month-old telegram in Stangerson's pocket. It read, "J. H. is in Europe." In addition to the telegram, Lestrade had found a small pillbox with two pills. With this information, Holmes jumped up and shouted, "The last link, my case is complete." To prove his theory, he had Mrs. Hudson's ailing terrier brought up. The dog had been in bad shape for some time, and Mrs. Hudson had begged Watson to put him down. Holmes cut one of the pills in half, and fed it to the dog, which "gave a convulsive shutter, and lay as lifeless as if it had been struck by lightning."

At this point Wiggins, the Street Arab's leader, arrived, and told Holmes, "I have the cab downstairs." Holmes said, "Just ask him to step up." When the cabman came into the room, Holmes slapped him into handcuffs, and introduced him to Gregson and Lestrade as Mr. Jefferson Hope, the murderer of Enoch Drebber and Joseph Stangerson. With that, Hope tried to break free and escape through the front window. It took the four of them to subdue him.

Hope did not resist when they placed him in the cab. On his way to Scotland Yard, he explained to Watson that he had an aortic aneurism, and had only a few months to live. As it turned out, he beat the gallows by dying the night before he was to appear before the Magistrates.

ADVENTURE OF THE SPECKLED BAND - 1883

No. 31 "221B" BAKER STREET—W1: [Latitude / Longitude: 51.517932,-0.155587]. One April morning, in 1883, Holmes woke Watson, saying, "Mrs. Hudson has been knocked up, she retorted upon me, and I on you." An excited young lady had arrived at Baker Street, and insisted on seeing Holmes. Her name was Helen Stoner, and she lived with her stepfather, the last survivor of the Roylotts of Stoke Moran. **Underground Station: Marble Arch**

WATERLOO RAILWAY STATION—SE1: [Latitude / Longitude: 51.503943,-0.11391]. Helen Stoner left Leatherhead on the first train to Waterloo Station. She wanted to consult Holmes on the strange events at Stoke Moran. Later in the day, Holmes and Watson left London from Waterloo Station. **Underground Station: Waterloo**

The Roylotts had been one of the wealthiest families in England, but over the years, they lost most of their property. Now, the only thing left was a few acres and a two-hundred-year-old, heavily mortgaged house, near Leatherhead.

Dr. Grimesby Roylott, Helen's stepfather, had been a medical doctor in Calcutta. In a fit of anger, he beat his native servant to death, and served a long imprisonment in India. Before returning to England, he married Mrs. Stoner, the young widow of Major General Stoner. Mrs. Stoner had twin daughters, Helen and Julia, and an annual income of not less than £1,000 a year. After her accidental death in 1875, she provided that each of her girls receive their own income when they married. Until then, the income went to Dr. Roylott.

Two years ago, within a fortnight of her engagement announcement, Julia Stoner died a mysterious death. The night Julia died; Helen heard her cry out and rushed to her side. As she did, Helen heard a low whistle, and a clanging metal sound. As she died, Julia said, "Oh my God! Helen! It was the band! The speckled band!" Since Julia had been secure in her locked room, and there was no trace of poison, Helen believed her sister died of pure fear.

Recently, Helen announced her own engagement. Two days ago, repairs on the west wing of the house forced Helen to move into her sister's old room. Last night, she heard the low whistle again, and could not sleep. In the morning, she took the first train to London, to consult Holmes.

Holmes wanted to see Helen's bedroom without Dr. Roylott's knowledge. Helen said he would be in London today, and she could arrange to get the housekeeper out of the way. Holmes promised to come to Stoke Moran that afternoon. After Helen left Baker Street, Dr. Grimesby Roylott stormed in, and demanded to know what Helen had said. Holmes was not intimidated, and told him nothing.

After breakfast, Holmes told Watson he was going to Doctors' Commons, where he hoped to get some helpful data. He said they would take an early afternoon train from Waterloo Station to Leatherhead.

DOCTORS' COMMONS (site), Godliman Street—EC4: [Latitude / Longitude: 51.512072,-0.099838]. On the Faraday Building, at the north side of Queen Victoria Street, on the corner of Godliman Street, there is a blue plaque saying that this was the site of the Doctors' Commons, demolished in 1867. The Doctors' Commons was the old ecclesiastical court that had jurisdiction over marriage licenses; divorce documents, and wills, etc. They ceased to operate in 1858-59, when wills and divorces passed to the civil authorities, and the records moved to Somerset House. In 1883, the term "Doctors' Commons" remained in common usage. **Underground Station: Mansion House**

SOMERSET HOUSE, The Strand—WC2: [Latitude / Longitude: 51.511834,-0.117642]. Built on the site of the mansion built for Edward VI's uncle, Somerset House contains the national archives of wills. In 1883, this is where Holmes would have come to examine Mrs. Stoner's will. Sherlock used the vernacular, "Doctors' Commons".
Underground Station: Temple

As agreed, Holmes and Watson took the train from Waterloo Station to Leatherhead, and a trap to Stoke Moran. Helen Stoner was waiting, and showed them her new bedroom. There, Holmes found a dummy bell-rope, attached to the ceiling near a small ventilator opening. Both the bell-rope and the ventilator were modern changes. Holmes also noted that the bed was bolted to the floor, and could not be moved. In Dr. Roylott's adjoining room, Holmes found an iron safe, with a small bowl of milk on top. The seat of the wooden chair, and the footprint upon it, caught Holmes's attention, as did a small dog lead on the corner of the bed.

As they left the house, Holmes gave instructions to Helen. When her stepfather retired for the night, she was to open her window shutters, and put a lamp there. Then, she was to move back into her old room. Holmes and Watson went to the nearby country inn, where they could see the signal lamp. At the stroke of eleven, Holmes and Watson saw the lamp, and went across the lawn to the open window. They slipped off their shoes, crept in, and waited. After three in the morning, there was movement in Grimesby Roylott's room. Then, they heard a sound like steam escaping from a kettle. Holmes lashed out at the bell-rope with his long thin cane. Responding to a cry, they entered Dr. Roylott's room and found him dead. Around his head was a speckled swamp adder, the deadliest snake in India. Roylott had sent the snake through the ventilator to kill Helen, as it had her sister. When Holmes struck the snake with his cane, it retreated through the ventilator, and bit Roylott.

Holmes and Watson told Helen of the plot, and sent her to her aunt at Harrow. The official inquiry found that Dr. Roylott died from indiscreetly playing with a dangerous pet.

FIVE ORANGE PIPS - 1885

No. 31 "221B" BAKER STREET—W1: [Latitude / Longitude: 51.517932,-0.155587]. On a blustery and rainy September night in 1885, Holmes and Watson were enjoying a quiet evening. Although Watson was now married, his wife was visiting her mother, and he was spending the night at Baker Street. There was a knock at the door and a young John Openshaw entered. **Underground Station: Marble Arch**

Author's note: As a puzzle for Sherlock Holmes fans, Conan Doyle indicated that Watson was married in 1885, two years before he met Mary Morstan. Was this an earlier marriage, or a typographical error?

Openshaw lived in Sussex, near Horsham. He said that his late uncle Elias, as a young man, had immigrated to America, and became a planter in Florida. He served in the Confederate Army, and rose to the rank of Colonel. Several years after the war, he returned to England and bought a small estate in Sussex. Having no sons, Elias asked John to come live with him. On March 10, 1883, Colonel Openshaw received a letter with an Indian postmark. He was greatly agitated when he saw that the envelope contained five dried orange pips. He shrieked, "K.K.K....my sins have overtaken me!" On the night of May 2, 1883, he was found dead outside his house. The coroner's jury brought in a verdict of 'suicide'.

The estate was left to Joseph Openshaw, John's father. In 1884, Joseph came to live at Horsham. On January 4, 1885, a letter signed K.K.K. arrived. Inside were five orange pips, and a note that read, ***"Put the papers on the sundial".*** John and his father did not know which papers, but assumed they were the ones Elias had burned before he died. Only one small remnant remained. Several days later, Joseph Openshaw was found murdered. With the deaths of his uncle and father, John Openshaw came into his inheritance. He too received a K.K.K. note demanding that the papers be placed on the sundial. The envelope was postmarked London—Eastern Division. John came to see Holmes, with the letter in hand. Holmes advised him to return home, and put the remnant on the sundial.

WATERLOO RAILWAY STATION—SE1: [Latitude / Longitude: 51.503943,-0.11391]. John Openshaw had arrived in London at Waterloo Station. After Openshaw visited Holmes, he tried to catch the late train back to Horsham, but on the way to Waterloo Station, he was attacked and killed. **Underground Station: Waterloo**

WATERLOO BRIDGE—WC2: [Latitude / Longitude: 51.509534,-0.117613]. John Openshaw drowned in the Thames, near Waterloo Bridge. Holmes and Watson read about the tragedy in the morning newspaper. Holmes told Watson that K.K.K. were not initials, but an acronym for the Klu Klux Klan. **Underground Station: Temple**

VICTORIA EMBANKMENT—WC2: [Latitude / Longitude: 51.509637,-0.118543]. Holmes wondered how members of the Klan decoyed John Openshaw from Waterloo Bridge to the Victoria Embankment. **Underground Station: Embankment**

LLOYD'S REGISTER OF SHIPPING, No. 71 Fenchurch Street—EC3: [Latitude / Longitude: 51.512593,-0.078943]. After John Openshaw's murder, Holmes spent the day at Lloyd's, going over ship files. When he returned to Baker Street, he placed five orange pips in an envelope, with "S. H. for J. O." written under the flap. He addressed the envelope to, "Captain James Calhoun, Bark *Lone Star*, Savannah, Georgia". Holmes told Watson that the *Lone Star* was the only ship of American registry, that matched the dates and places of the case. **Underground Station: Aldgate**

KING GEORGE V (ALBERT) DOCK—Liverpool L3: [Latitude / Longitude: 53.400581,-2.991006]. After his day at Lloyd's of London, Holmes went to King George V Dock, now called Albert Dock. The *Lone Star* had left London by the early tide, bound for Savannah, Georgia. Holmes determined that the Captain and two mates were the only native-born Americans on the ship, and that the three of them had been away from the boat on the night John Openshaw was murdered. Holmes sent his envelope with the five orange pips, so that it, and the police, would be waiting for Captain Calhoun when he docked in Savannah. **Rail Station: Liverpool James Street Rail**

Unfortunately, the ship never arrived. Watson said, "We did…hear that somewhere far out in the Atlantic a shattered stern-post of the boat was seen swinging in the trough of a wave,…and that is all which we shall ever know of the fate of the *Lone Star*".

ADVENTURE OF THE NOBLE BACHELOR - 1886

No. 31 "221B" BAKER STREET—W1: [Latitude / Longitude: 51.517932,-0.155587]. One rainy October afternoon in 1886, Holmes received a letter from Lord St. Simon, concerning his missing bride. Inspector Lestrade had referred St. Simon to Holmes. **Underground Station: Marble Arch**

GROSVENOR SQUARE—W1: [Latitude / Longitude: 51.511792,-0.150194]. Lord St. Simon's letter to Holmes came from Grosvenor Mansions, Grosvenor Square. St. Simon was the second son of the Duke of Balmoral. **Underground Station: Bond Street**

Before St. Simon arrived at Baker Street, Holmes and Watson reviewed the society papers. St. Simon was engaged to Miss Hatty Doran, the daughter of the California millionaire. The papers also said, "It is an open secret that the Duke of Balmoral had been compelled to sell his pictures in the last few years, and…Lord St. Simon has no property of his own, save the small estate of Birchmoor".

ST. GEORGE'S, HANOVER SQUARE, No. 2A Mill Street—W1: [Latitude / Longitude: 51.512486,-0.143133]. The society papers said the wedding would take place at St. George's, Hanover Square. After the ceremony, a wedding breakfast was held at Lancaster Gate, where Aloysius Doran, the bride's father, had taken a furnished house. **Underground Station: Oxford Circus**

LANCASTER GATE—W2: [Latitude / Longitude: 51.513667,-0.175915]. Hatty disappeared from her Lancaster Gate wedding breakfast, and St. Simon and the bride's father went to the police. Their first line of inquiry was to find Flora Millar. She had tried to force her way into the wedding breakfast, indicating she had some claim on Lord St. Simon. **Underground Station: Lancaster Gate**

St. Simon told Holmes that Hatty had seemed happy before the wedding, but at the ceremony, she dropped her bouquet into the front pew, and a gentleman there had handed it back to her. After that, she seemed agitated.

HYDE PARK—W2: [Latitude / Longitude: 51.512036,-0.172305]. After bolting from her wedding breakfast, Hatty Doran was seen walking in Hyde Park with Flora Millar. Flora had been on "very friendly footing" with Lord St. Simon, and had created a disturbance outside the Lancaster Gate house. **Underground Station: Lancaster Gate**

THE SERPENTINE (LAKE), Hyde Park—W2: [Latitude / Longitude: 51.511582,-0.175781]. In a futile effort to find Hatty, Inspector Lestrade began dragging The Serpentine, in Hyde Park. **Underground Station: Lancaster Gate**

Author's note: This Hyde Park boating lake dates from 1730 when Queen Caroline, wife of George II, ordered the damming of the River Westbourne.

TRAFALGAR SQUARE FOUNTAIN—WC2: [Latitude / Longitude: 51.508061,-0.127214]. When Inspector Lestrade told Holmes about dragging the Serpentine, Holmes laughed and asked if he was also dragging the Trafalgar Square Fountain, "Because you have just as good a chance of finding this lady in the one as in the other". **Underground Station: Charing Cross**

Lestrade found Hatty's wedding dress in Hyde Park. In its pocket was a note that read, *"You will see me when all is ready. Come at once. F.H.M".* Lestrade was convinced that this implicated Flora Miller. Holmes was more interested in the paper on which the note was written. It was a fragment of a hotel bill that read, *"Oct. 4ᵗʰ, rooms 8s, breakfast 2s. 6d., cocktail 1s., lunch 2s., 6d".* As Lestrade was about to leave, Holmes said, "Lady St. Simon is a myth, There is not, and there has never been, such a person". Lestrade thought Holmes was crazy.

METROPOLE HOTEL (site), Northumberland Avenue, between Great Scotland Yard and Whitehall Place—WC2: [Latitude / Longitude: 51.506873,-0.124315]. On the West side of Northumberland Avenue, south from Great Scotland Yard to Whitehall Place, was the site of The Metropole Hotel. The Metropole is a likely candidate for being "The...select London hotel," where Francis Hay Moulton stayed. "Eight shillings for a bed" gave Holmes a clue. Holmes said, "There are not many (hotels) in London which charge at that rate". **Underground Station: Embankment**

GORDON SQUARE—WC1: [Latitude / Longitude: 51.52473,-0.130552]. Holmes went to Moulton's hotel, and found he had left, but was having his mail forwarded to No. 226 Gordon Square. There, he found the young couple. He offered them a chance to come to Baker Street, dine with St. Simon, and explain the situation. **Underground Station: Euston Square**

No. 31 "221B" BAKER STREET—W1: [Latitude / Longitude: 51.517932,-0.155587]. To explain the situation, Holmes arranged for a catering firm to lay on a late supper at Baker Street for St. Simon and the young couple. He ordered, "Cold woodcock, a pheasant, a *pâté de foie gras* pie with a group of ancient and cobwebby bottles". **Underground Station: Marble Arch**

Francis Hay Moulton and Hatty had been secretly married in California two years earlier. When Francis was prospecting in New Mexico, Hatty read that Apache Indians had killed him. Actually, he was taken prisoner. When he escaped and returned to San Francisco, he found that Hatty had gone to London. Francis followed, and when he read about the wedding to St. Simon, he entered the church and sat in the front pew. He passed her the note when returning her bouquet. St. Simon was ungracious about losing his newfound wealth, and would not dine with the young couple.

THE RESIDENT PATIENT - 1886?

THE STRAND—WC2: [Latitude / Longitude: 51.509577,-0.123639]. At seven o'clock one humid and rainy October evening, Holmes and Watson grew weary of their Baker Street sitting room, and took a three-hour ramble through the West End. On their walk, they watched the ebb and flow of life on The Strand. **Underground Station: Temple**

FLEET STREET—EC4: [Latitude / Longitude: 51.51381,-0.111419]. Having walked as far as Fleet Street, if was ten o'clock before Holmes and Watson returned to Baker Street. A brougham was waiting at their door. From the instruments inside, Holmes surmised their visitor was a medical doctor. **Underground Station: Temple**

BROOK STREET—W1: [Latitude / Longitude: 51.512949,-0.1472]. Their guest introduced himself as Dr. Percy Trevelyan. He lived at No. 403 Brook Street, in the Cavendish Square quarter. **Underground Station: Bond Street**

UNIVERSITY COLLEGE, LONDON (Former University of London), Gower Street—WC1: [Latitude / Longitude: 51.524369,-0.1345]. When Trevelyan received his medical degree from the University of London, the primary buildings for medical classes were on Gower Street. **Underground Station: Euston Square**

UNIVERSITY COLLEGE HOSPITAL (site), Gower Street—WC1: [Latitude / Longitude: 51.524369,-0.1345]. Trevelyan would have learned some of his surgical skills at the old University College Hospital. The 'new' hospital was built between 1897 and 1906, on the same site. **Underground Station: Euston Square**

MUSEUM OF MANKIND (Former University of London offices), Burlington Gardens—W1: [Latitude / Longitude: 51.509889,-0.140459]. In the 1880's, the University of London used the Burlington Gardens for administrative offices. **Underground Station: Green Park**

KING'S COLLEGE HOSPITAL, Denmark Hill—SE5: [Latitude / Longitude: 51.468641,-0.091889]. After graduation, Trevelyan devoted himself to research, and obtained a small position in King's College Hospital. There, he won the Bruce Pinkerton prize, and was thought to have a distinguished career ahead of him. However, a lack of capital prevented him from finding proper quarters. **Rail Station: Denmark Hill**

CAVENDISH SQUARE—W1: [Latitude / Longitude: 51.516888,-0.14598]. Percy Trevelyan said, "A [medical] specialist who aims high is compelled to start in one of a dozen streets in the Cavendish Square quarter". This is still true today. **Underground Station: Oxford Circus**

One day, a man named Blessington came to Trevelyan's modest quarters and made an unusual offer. He would set up Trevelyan in Brook Street, furnish the house, and pay the maids. For this, Blessington would become a resident patient, and keep three quarters of what Trevelyan earned. Trevelyan agreed, and moved in on Lady Day.

Blessington was a hypochondriac with strange, but regular, habits. One day, after Dr. Trevelyan had seen a new patient, Blessington returned from his daily constitutional and demanded to know who had been in his bedchamber. He saw fresh footprints on the bedroom carpet. Blessington was greatly agitated, and asked Dr. Trevelyan to seek Sherlock's help. After hearing Trevelyan's story, Holmes and Watson accompanied him back to Brook Street.

OXFORD STREET—W1: [Latitude / Longitude: 51.514658,-0.146878]. Holmes and Watson crossed Oxford Street, as Holmes pondered Blessington's attitude. **Underground Station: Bond Street**

HARLEY STREET—W1: [Latitude / Longitude: 51.517653,-0.146323]. When Holmes questioned Blessington, he refused to say why he was afraid. Holmes said he could not help unless he did. When Blessington still refused, Holmes and Watson left. They were halfway down Harley Street before Watson could get a word out of Holmes. **Underground Station: Oxford Circus**

Early the next morning, Trevelyan sent his brougham for Holmes and requested they come at once. When they arrived, they found Inspector Lanner of Scotland Yard waiting for them. Blessington was dead, hanged from a hook in the center of his bedroom ceiling. By looking at the clues in the room, Holmes was able to ascertain that three men had entered the house, probably with the aid of the missing pageboy. The three crept up to Blessington's room, picked the lock, and entered. They tied up Blessington, and after holding a conference, hanged him.

No. 31 "221B" BAKER STREET—W1: [Latitude / Longitude: 51.517932,-0.155587]. Inspector Lanner started the hunt for the missing page, while Holmes and Watson returned to Baker Street. After breakfast, Holmes went out to get answers for a few remaining questions. He asked Lanner and Trevelyan to come to Baker Street at three. When they arrived, Lanner said he had found the page. Holmes said he knew the identity of the three men. They were Biddle, Hayward, and Moffat. The inspector cried, "The Worthingdon bank gang". That meant that Blessington must be Sutton, the man who had turned informer. Biddle, Hayward and Moffat had been sent to prison for fifteen years, and had just been released. **Underground Station: Marble Arch**

The three suspects fled the country, and were never brought to justice. However, there were reports that they were among the passengers on the steamer *Norah Creina*, which was lost with all hands on the Portuguese coast. The case against the page was dropped because of lack of evidence.

THE REIGATE SQUIRES – 1887

No. 31 "221B" BAKER STREET—W1: [Latitude / Longitude: 51.517932,-0.155587]. In April 1887, Holmes was exhausted from the strain of dealing with the colossal schemes of Baron Maupertuis in the Netherland-Sumatra Company Case. Watson received a telegram from France, saying that Holmes was lying ill in the Hotel Dulong in Lyons. Watson hurried to Lyons and brought Holmes back to Baker Street to recover. Watson was delighted when Colonel Hayter invited them to visit his home near Reigate in Surrey. Watson accepted, knowing that a week of country springtime was what Holmes needed. **Underground Station: Marble Arch**

On the evening of their arrival, Colonel Hayter told them of a recent local break-in. Mr. Acton, a county magistrate, had his house burgled. The curious thing was that the thieves had ransacked the library, but only took, "an odd, volume of Pope's Homer, two plated candlesticks, an ivory letter-weight, a small oak barometer, and a ball of twine". This oddity caught Holmes's interest, as did Colonel Hayter's comment that Acton had earlier initiated a legal action against Justice of the Peace Cunningham, another neighbor.

The next morning, Hayter, Holmes and Watson, heard that there had been another break-in, and a murder. This time it was at the home of Mr. Cunningham. His coachman, William Kirwan, had been shot. Inspector Forrester arrived and asked for Sherlock's help. Forrester showed Holmes a portion of a note that had been found in the dead man's hand. In addition to being the torn corner of a larger letter, the writing seemed to be from more than one person. Holmes thought that the murderer had snatched the letter from Kirwan's hand after murdering him.

Holmes and Inspector Forrester went to examine the crime scene. It was in a fine, eighteenth century, Queen Anne house. There they met Mr. Cunningham the elder, and his son Alec. When asked about clues, Inspector Forrester was about to tell about the torn note, when Holmes fainted, and had to be carried into the house. When he recovered, he questioned the Cunninghams, and asked to see the rooms from which they had witnessed the murderer's escape.

Holmes also recommended that Mr. Cunningham offer a reward, which he did in a hand written note. Holmes had noticed discrepancies in the stories of the two Cunninghams, and wanted a sample of Old Mr. Cunningham handwriting. Through a ruse, Holmes gained access to Alec Cunningham's dressing room. There he recovered the rest of the missing letter. When the Cunninghams realized what was up to, they rushed into the dressing room and tried to kill Holmes. Watson and Inspector Forrester heard the struggle, and came to the rescue. The Cunninghams burgled Mr. Acton's house in an attempt to recover the legal papers that would support Acton's legal claim. William Kirwan saw the burglary, and blackmailed the Cunninghams. They sent a letter to Kirwan, asking him to come to their house. When he did, they murdered him, and recovered the incriminating invitation. Unfortunately, a piece of the letter was left in the dead man's hand. .

Holmes suspected the Cunninghams, and had to feign the fainting spell to keep Inspector Forrester from revealing that they had a portion of the letter. Holmes thought that the rest the letter had been stuffed into the dressing gown that Alec Cunningham's wore the night of the murder. The Cunninghams, father and son, had jointly written the letter, so that they each would be a party to the murder.

THE YELLOW FACE - 1887?

HYDE PARK—W2: [Latitude / Longitude: 51.51083,-0.157821].
Holmes and Watson took an early spring walk in the Park. Their two-hour stroll could have been in Regent's Park, but I think it was more likely to be in Hyde Park. When they returned at five, they found they had missed a client. The pageboy said the visitor had waited half an hour, and said he would return. **Underground Station: Marble Arch**

Their guest had left his expensive pipe behind. Using his usual methods, Holmes said he was a muscular man, left handed, with an excellent set of teeth, careless in his habits, with no need to practice economy. Then, Holmes heard their visitor on the stairs. It was Grant Munro, an agitated young man, who said he needed Holmes' help and advice. Munro had been married for three years. Recently, something from his wife Effie's past had come between them. He did not know what it was. When they first met, she was a young widow whose husband and daughter had died in the Atlanta, Georgia's yellow fever epidemic. After their deaths, she left the United States, and came to England to live with a maiden aunt at Pinner in Middlesex. There, she met Munro, fell in love, and remarried.

NORBURY—SW16: [Latitude / Longitude: 51.410601,-0.117806].
Grant Munro was a hop merchant in the City. With the addition of Effie's income, they took a nice eighty-pound-a-year villa at Norbury. Recently, a nearby cottage was let, and Munro saw a face in the upper window. He could not tell whether the face belonged to a man or woman, but its color was a chalky yellow. **Rail Station: Norbury**

LONDON BRIDGE RAILWAY STATION—SW1: [Latitude / Longitude: 51.505848,-0.086521]. In the 1880's, the train service from the City to Norbury would have used the London Bridge Railway Station. **Underground Station: London Bridge**

When they married, Effie assigned her money to her husband. Later, she asked for a hundred pounds, but would not say why she needed it. One night, at three in the morning, he woke to see his wife leaving the house. When she returned, he asked where she had been. She said she went outside to get a breath of fresh air, but he did not believe her.

CRYSTAL PALACE—SW20: [Latitude / Longitude: 51.422494,-0.07714]. Disturbed by the actions of his wife, Munro did not go into the City the next day. He walked as far as the Crystal Palace before returning home. **Rail Station: Crystal Palace**

Author's note: In 1851, the Crystal Palace was built in Hyde Park for the Great Exhibition. After the exhibition, the Crystal Palace moved to Sydenham Hill in South London, and was re-opened by Queen Victoria on June 10, 1854. It was destroyed by fire in 1936.

On the way home, Munro stopped by the cottage to see if he could see the face again. To his surprise, the cottage door opened and his wife stepped out. When he tried to enter, she pleaded with him not to do so. She said, "Our whole lives are at stake in this, If you come home with me all will be well. If you force your way into the cottage all is over between us". As she led him home, Munro looked back and saw the yellow face watching them from the upper window. The next day, Grant went to the City and returned on the 2:40 train, instead of his usual 3:36. At home, he found his wife gone. She was at the cottage, and her maid ran to warn her. When Grant forced his way into the cottage, he found it empty. The occupants had fled.

NORBURY RAILWAY STATION—SW16: [Latitude / Longitude: 51.412056,-0.123618]. The next day Munro went to see Holmes, who advised him to return to Norbury. If he found the cottage occupied, he was to notify Holmes, but not enter. Holmes received a message, that the cottage was occupied and that Munro would meet him at the train station. **Rail Station: Norbury**

Although Effie and the housekeeper tried to stop him, Grant followed by Holmes and Watson, forced his way into the cottage. In an upper-room, they found a little girl in white gloves and a full-face yellow-white mask. Holmes, with a laugh, peeled off the mask and revealed a little coal-black Negress. Effie's late husband was a Negro, and this was their daughter. Effie said, "dark or fair, she is my own dear little girlie, and her mother's pet". Effie had used the hundred pounds to bring her daughter to England. She had not told her husband about her past, because she did not know if he would accept it. The mask and gloves were an attempt to hide the girl's race from the neighbors. After a long pause, Grant Munro broke the silence. He lifted the child, kissed her, and held out his hand to his wife. He said, "I am not a very good man, Effie, but I think I am a better one than you have given me credit for being".

GREEK INTERPRETER - 1887?

WHITEHALL—SW1: **[Latitude / Longitude:** 51.503534,-0.126218]. *The Greek Interpreter* is the adventure in which Watson first met Mycroft, Sherlock's older brother. Mycroft worked at the government offices in Whitehall. According to Sherlock, Mycroft had a better analytical mind. Sherlock thought their abilities came from their grandmother, who was a sister of Vernet, the French artist. Holmes took Watson to the Diogenes Club, where Mycroft was a founding member. **Underground Station: Westminster**

Author's note: In *The Adventure of the Bruce-Partington Plans*, we learn that Mycroft was one of the most indispensable men in the British government. To paraphrase Holmes: "He has the tidiest and most orderly brain, with the greatest capacity for storing facts. The conclusions of every department are passed to him. All other men are specialists, but his specialism is omniscience. Again and again his word decided the national policy".

TOWARD OXFORD "REGENT" CIRCUS—W1: [Latitude / Longitude: 51.514592,-0.147661]. On their way from Baker Street to the Diogenes Club, Holmes and Watson walked east on Oxford Street toward "Regent" (Oxford) Circus. They must have turned south before reaching the Circus, because they entered the west end of Pall Mall from St. James's Street. **Underground Station: Oxford Circus**

BOND STREET—W1: [Latitude / Longitude: 51.514418,-0.146685]. On their way from Baker Street to the Diogenes Club, Holmes and Watson probably walked south on Bond Street. **Underground Station: Bond Street**

PICCADILLY—W1: [Latitude / Longitude: 51.507968,-0.140226]. Holmes and Watson crossed Piccadilly, between Bond Street and St. James's Street, on their way south to Pall Mall and the Diogenes Club. **Underground Station: Green Park**

ST. JAMES'S STREET—SW1: [Latitude / Longitude: 51.506383,-0.139174]. On their way to Mycroft's club in Pall Mall, Holmes and Watson walked south from Piccadilly on St. James's Street. **Underground Station: Green Park**

Author's note: As Holmes and Watson reached the south end of St. James's Street, they passed the old St. James's Palace **[Latitude / Longitude: 51.505293,-0.137727]**. Built between 1531 and 1536, the palace was the official residence of English Sovereigns for over 300 years. Foreign ambassadors are still accredited to the Court of St. James's.

PALL MALL—SW1: [Latitude / Longitude: 51.505938,-0.136213]. Mycroft Holmes lived in Pall Mall chambers. His Diogenes Club was just opposite. Holmes said that the Diogenes Club was the queerest club in London, and Mycroft was one of its queerest members. He was at his club every day from quarter to five to twenty to eight. **Underground Station: Piccadilly Circus**

After they arrived at the club, Mycroft told them of a "singular problem". He asked Mr. Melas, who lived on the floor above Mycroft's in his Pall Mall chambers, to join them. Mr. Melas was an interpreter of Greek extraction.

CARLTON CLUB (site)—SW1: [Latitude / Longitude: 51.506577,-0.134204]. Watson said that the Diogenes Club was, "Some little distance from the Carlton". The Carlton Club, formed in 1832, moved to their then new Pall Mall building at Carlton Gardens four years later. **Underground Station: Piccadilly Circus**

NORTHUMBERLAND AVENUE—WC2: [Latitude / Longitude: 51.50697,-0.124991]. Mycroft told Sherlock and Watson that Mr. Melas often acted as a guide to the wealthy Orientals who stayed at the Northumberland Avenue hotels. The three luxury Northumberland Avenue hotels were The Metropole Hotel, The Hotel Victoria, and The Grand Hotel. All of them were new in 1887. **Underground Station: Embankment**

METROPOLE HOTEL (site), Northumberland Avenue, between Great Scotland Yard and Whitehall Place—WC2: [Latitude / Longitude: 51.506873,-0.124315]. One of the three luxury Northumberland hotels was The Metropole, located on the west side of Northumberland Avenue, between Great Scotland Yard and Whitehall Place. **Underground Station: Embankment**

HOTEL VICTORIA—WC2: [Latitude / Longitude: 51.506939,- 0.124715]. One of the three luxury Northumberland hotels was The Hotel Victoria, located at 8 Northumberland Avenue. It is now confusingly called The Grand Hotel. **Underground Station: Embankment**

THE GRAND HOTEL—WC2: [Latitude / Longitude: 51.50738,- 0.127255]. One of the three luxury Northumberland hotels was The Grand Hotel, located in the curved front building on the east side of Northumberland, across from Trafalgar Square. **Underground Station: Charing Cross**

CHARING CROSS—WC2: [Latitude / Longitude: 51.507347,- 0.128016]. One night, a Mr. Latimer called on Paul Melas and said he needed a Greek interpreter. He asked Melas to accompany him to Kensington. They left in a four-wheeled carriage, and set off from Pall Mall, through Charing Cross. Melas was alarmed to see that Latimer carried a lead weighted bludgeon. **Underground Station: Charing Cross**

HAYMARKET—WC2: [Latitude / Longitude: 51.50943,- 0.132619]. From Charing Cross, Latimer and Melas probably traveled up Haymarket to Shaftesbury Avenue. **Underground Station: Piccadilly Circus**

SHAFTSBURY AVENUE—WC2: [Latitude / Longitude: 51.51203,-0.131965]. The carriage with Melas and Latimer continued up Shaftsbury Avenue towards Oxford Street. **Underground Station: Piccadilly Circus**

OXFORD STREET—W1: [Latitude / Longitude: 51.517022,-0.125903]. When the carriage reached Oxford Street, Mr. Melas commented that this was a roundabout way to Kensington. At that point, Mr. Latimer covered the windows. When they arrived at their destination, the trip had taken an hour and thirty-five minutes. Obviously, they were not in Kensington. **Underground Station: Tottenham Court Road**

Wilson Kemp was waiting for Melas and Latimer when they reached their destination. He told Melas to get answers from an emaciated Greek gentleman. Melas was shocked to see the man's face covered with sticking plaster. By secretly getting additional information during questioning, Melas learned that the prisoner's name was Kratides. He had been held prisoner and starved for three weeks to get him to sign a document. At one point in Melas's questioning, a young lady burst into the room and called the man Paul, and he called her Sophy.

WANDSWORTH COMMON—SW17: [Latitude / Longitude: 51.455692,-0.168786]. Latimer and Kemp paid Melas five sovereigns for his services, and warned him to tell no one of his experience. They took Melas to Wandsworth Common. **Rail Station: Wandsworth Common**
CLAPHAM JUNCTION—SW11: [Latitude / Longitude: 51.4655,-0.170749]. After walking across Wandsworth Common to Clapham Junction, Mr. Melas was just in time to catch the last train to Victoria Station. **Rail Station: Clapham Junction**

VICTORIA RAILWAY STATION—SW1: [Latitude / Longitude: 51.496697,-0.144058]. After his strange experience, Mr. Melas was just able to return to Victoria Station on the last train from Clapham Junction. The next day, he related the story to Mycroft Holmes, who knew that Sherlock would be interested. **Underground Station: Victoria**

BECKENHAM—BR3: [Latitude / Longitude: 51.425491,-0.021286]. After hearing Melas's story, Sherlock asked Mycroft if he had taken any action. Mycroft said he had placed an advertisement in all of the London dailies, asking for information on Paul and Sophy Kratides. Sherlock warned Melas to be on his guard, because the ads indicated that he had talked about his experience. J. Davenport, from Lower Brixton, answered the ad. He said he knew Sophy, and that she lived at The Myrtles in Beckenham. **Rail Station: Beckenham Hill**

When Sherlock learned where Paul Kratides was being held, he enlisted the aid of Inspector Gregson. Before going to Beckenham, Sherlock, Mycroft, Watson, and Gregson went to Pall Mall to pick up Melas, and found he had been abducted

LONDON BRIDGE RAILWAY STATION—SW1: [Latitude / Longitude: 51.505848,-0.086521]. It took an hour for Inspector Gregson to get a warrant to enter the house in Beckenham, and an additional forty-minute train ride from London Bridge Station. **Underground Station: London Bridge**

BECKENHAM HILL RAILWAY STATION—BR3: [Latitude / Longitude: 51.425491,-0.021286]. Proceeding from the Beckenham Railway Station, they found The Myrtles dark. Melas and Paul Kratides were upstairs, poisoned from the fumes of a charcoal fire. Kratides was dead but Melas survived. **Rail Station: Beckenham Hill**

They learned from Mr. Davenport that Paul was Sophy's brother, and that they were from a wealthy Greek family. Sophy had fallen under the spell of Latimer and his evil associate, Wilson Kemp. They tried to get Paul to sign away his and his sister's inheritance. Months later, a curious newspaper clipping reached Holmes from Budapest. It told of two Englishmen, traveling with a woman, who had met a tragic end. The police thought they had killed each other. Holmes thought a Grecian girl had exacted her revenge.

SIGN OF FOUR - 1887

No. 31 "221B" BAKER STREET—W1: [Latitude / Longitude: 51.517932,-0.155587]. September 1887 was the month that Mary Morstan, Watson's future wife, came to Baker Street. Before she arrived, Holmes amazed Watson by deducing he had been to the Wigmore Street Post Office to send a telegram. **Underground Station: Marble Arch**

WIGMORE STREET POST OFFICE (supposed site), No. 132 Wigmore Street—W1: [Latitude / Longitude: 51.515784,-0.152761]. Holmes amazed Watson by saying that he had been to the Wigmore Street Post Office to send a telegram. Holmes deduced the Wigmore Street location from the reddish dirt on Watson's shoe. They were taking up the pavement squares across the street from the Post Office, and the reddish color of the earth there was unique in the neighborhood. The fact that Watson had been with Holmes most of the morning, and had not written a letter, indicated that the only reason for his going to the post office was to send a telegram. **Underground Station: Marble Arch**

Author's note: In 1887, there was no post office on Wigmore Street, and there was a perfectly good post office at No. 66 Baker Street: **[Latitude / Longitude: 51.519292,-0.15619].** Placing an imaginary post office on Wigmore Street creates a quandary. For a complete explanation of this puzzle, read Bernard Davies' paper, *"Dr Watson's Deuteronomy"*.

CAMBERWELL—SE5: [Latitude / Longitude: 51.470762,-0.086861]. Mary Morstan came to see Holmes on the advice of Mrs. Cecil Forrester of Lower Camberwell. Mrs. Forrester employed Mary as a governess. **Rail Station: Denmark Hill**

THE LANGHAM HOTEL, Portland Place—W1: [Latitude / Longitude: 51.518077,-0.143875]. Mary Morstan said that her father had been a senior captain in an Indian regiment. When Mary's mother died, her father sent Mary to live in Edinburgh. In 1878, Captain Morstan obtained leave, and telegraphed Mary from London's Langham Hotel, saying that he had arrived safely. When Mary went to see her father, he was not there. The hotel said he had gone out the night before and did not return. His luggage, and curiosities from his service on the Andaman Islands, were in his room. Mary contacted the police and advertised in the newspapers, but to no avail. Mary did find a strange note in her father's papers. It had the notation, *"The Sign of the Four—Jonathan Small, Mahomet Singh, Abdullah Khan, Dost Akbar".* **Underground Station: Oxford Circus**

UPPER NORWOOD—SE25: [Latitude / Longitude: 51.402958,-0.088041]. When Captain Morstan disappeared, the police contacted Major Sholto, the Captain's only known London friend. Sholto and Morstan had served in the same regiment. Sholto had retired to Upper Norwood, and said he did not know Morstan was in London. **Rail Station: Norwood Junction**

Almost four years after the disappearance of her father, on May 4, 1882, an advertisement appeared in the *Times* asking for the address of Miss Mary Morstan. At the time, Mary was working for Mrs. Forrester, who advised Mary to answer the advertisement. When she did, she received a large lustrous pearl. Every year since, on May 4, she received an additional pearl.

LYCEUM THEATER, No. 21 Wellington Street—WC2: [Latitude / Longitude: 51.511641,-0.11952]. The morning of her visit to Baker Street, Mary Morstan received a strange letter. It instructed her to be, *"At the third pillar from the left outside the Lyceum Theatre tonight at seven o'clock".* Holmes compared the handwriting on the letter, to the handwriting on the boxes that contained the pearls. They were from the same person. **Underground Station: Covent Garden**

Author's note: The Lyceum Theater is a London landmark. After several fires in the 19th Century, it reopened in 1904. Originally known for Victorian melodramas and lavish Shakespearean productions, the Lyceum became a dance hall after World War II, and converted to a legitimate theater in 1996.

The letter to Mary said she could bring two friends, so she asked Holmes and Watson to accompany her. She said she would return to Baker Street at six, and depart for the Lyceum from there. Holmes went out that afternoon, to review newspaper files. It was half past five before Holmes returned. He discovered that Major Sholto had died on April 8, 1882, just two weeks before Mary Morstan started receiving the pearls. Holmes thought this was significant.

THE STRAND—WC2: [Latitude / Longitude: 51.509577,-0.123639]. Mary Morstan arrived at Baker Street in a four-wheeler. She, Holmes, and Watson, drove down The Strand toward the Lyceum. It was a damp, foggy, September evening, and "the lamps were but misty splotches of diffused light". **Underground Station: Charing Cross**

Williams, a coachman, approached them when they arrived at the theater. After Mary assured him that Holmes and Watson were not policemen, they entered a waiting four-wheeler, and started their journey. At first, Watson was familiar with their route. In those days, Wellington Street was open to The Strand, so they probably traveled back down The Strand towards Charing Cross. On the left they passed Simpson's, "their Strand Restaurant", followed by the Charing Cross hotel, and Train Station. On the right, Watson could see Trafalgar Square.

Author's note: In chronicling their journey, Watson mentions ten streets or locations: Rochester Row, Vincent Square, Vauxhall Bridge Road, Vauxhall Bridge, Wandsworth Road, Priory Road, Larkhall Lane, Stockwell Place, Robert Street and Coldharbour Lane, in that order. He failed to mention earlier and later streets in their journey. With the help of Bernard Davies, I suggest that the following is the route they took.

WHITEHALL—SW1: [Latitude / Longitude: 51.503534,-0.126218]. From Trafalgar Square, Holmes, Watson and Mary's most likely route was down Whitehall and through its Parliament Street lower end. There may have been too much fog to see Downing Street on the right, but surely, Watson saw the Houses of Parliament and Big Ben. **Underground Station: Westminster**

PARLIAMENT STREET—SW1: [Latitude / Longitude: 51.501425,-0.126205]. As they continued down Whitehall, the street's name changed to Parliament Street. **Underground Station: Westminster**

Author's note: Parliament Street had been a small side road alongside Westminster Palace. When the palace was destroyed, Parliament Street was widened to match Whitehall and became its lower end. The present appearance of the street is largely the result of 19th century redevelopment.

VICTORIA SQUARE—SW1: [Latitude / Longitude: 51.500245,-0.126676]. To continue their journey, Holmes, Watson and Mary Morstan must have traveled around Victoria Square to Victoria Street. **Underground Station: Westminster**

VICTORIA STREET—SW1: [Latitude / Longitude: 51.497612,-0.135099]. As they traveled down Victoria Street, with the fog, and his limited knowledge of London, Watson lost his way. Holmes, on the other hand, had a map of London in his head, and began muttering names as they rattled through squares and streets. **Underground Station: St. James's Park**

ARTILLERY ROW—SW1: [Latitude / Longitude: 51.496864,-0.135625]. To reach Vauxhall Bridge from Victoria Street, Williams probably turned South on Artillery Row. **Underground Station: Victoria**

GREYCOAT PLACE—SW1: [Latitude / Longitude: 51.496416,-0.135303]. From Artillery Row, Williams turned left on Greycoat Place to reach Rochester Row. **Underground Station: Victoria**

ROCHESTER ROW—SW1: [Latitude / Longitude: 51.494218,-0.136794]. As Holmes, Watson, and Mary Morstan continued their journey to Lambeth, Holmes muttered Rochester Row. **Underground Station: Pimlico**

VINCENT SQUARE—SW1: [Latitude / Longitude: 51.494218,-0.136794]. On their way down Rochester Row, they passed near Vincent Square. If it had been a sunny day, they could have seen it through Vane Street. **Underground Station: Pimlico**

VAUXHALL BRIDGE ROAD—SW1: [Latitude / Longitude: 51.490553,-0.133427]. From Rochester Row, they turned left on Vauxhall Bridge Road, toward the river. **Underground Station: Pimlico**

VAUXHALL BRIDGE—SE8: [Latitude / Longitude: 51.487371,-0.126473]. As they crossed the Thames, Holmes remarked that he could catch glimpses of the river through the fog. **Underground Station: Vauxhall**

WANDSWORTH ROAD—SW8: [Latitude / Longitude: 51.478425,-0.12922]. On the Lambeth side of the river, Holmes, Watson and Mary were driven south on Wandsworth Road. **Underground Station: Vauxhall**

Author's note: For some reason, American texts persist in calling this "Wordsworth" Road.

PRIORY ROAD—SW8: [Latitude / Longitude: 51.475304,-0.1301]. From Wandsworth Road, they turned left on Lansdowne Way. In Sherlock's day, the Western section of Lansdowne Way was called Priory Road. **Underground Station: Stockwell**

LANSDOWNE WAY—SW8: [Latitude / Longitude: 51.474903,-0.127943]. Williams continued on Priory Road as its name changed to Lansdowne Way. **Underground Station: Stockwell**

LARKHALL LANE—SW8: [Latitude / Longitude: <u>51.474689,-0.126774</u>]. As they were driven east on Lansdowne Way, Holmes, Watson and Mary passed Larkhall Lane on the right. Watson called it "Lark Hall" Lane. **Underground Station: Stockwell**

BINFIELD ROAD—SW4: [Latitude / Longitude: <u>51.473498,-0.124798</u>]. From Lansdowne Way, the coachman turned right on Binfield Road toward Stockwell Place. **Underground Station: Stockwell**

STOCKWELL PLACE (site)—SW8: [Latitude / Longitude: <u>51.472362,-0.122137</u>]. Thanks to Bernard Davies, we now know that Stockwell Place was not a street, but rather a group of Victorian houses on the east side of Clapham Road, just north of the Stockwell Road junction, opposite Binfield Road. At least one of the old houses remains. **Underground Station: Stockwell**

STOCKWELL ROAD—SW9: [Latitude / Longitude: <u>51.47019,-0.12042</u>]. After Williams traveled through the Binfield / Clapham Road junction, I think he drove Holmes, Watson and Mary Morstan down Stockwell Road. **Underground Station: Stockwell**

STOCKWELL LANE—SW9: [Latitude / Longitude: <u>51.469769,-0.119069</u>]. To get to Robert Street, I think Williams turned right on Stockwell Lane to Sidney Road. **Underground Station: Stockwell**

SIDNEY ROAD—SW9: [Latitude / Longitude: <u>51.47005,-0.117116</u>]. The coach with Holmes, Watson and Mary continued down Sidney Road to Robert Street. **Underground Station: Stockwell**

ROBERT STREET—SW9: [Latitude / Longitude: <u>51.470584,-0.115185</u>]. Holmes, Watson and Mary were getting close to their destination as they were driven down Robert Street, now called Robsart Street. **Underground Station: Stockwell**

BRIXTON ROAD—SW9: [Latitude / Longitude: <u>51.470664,-0.11261</u>]. The coachman had to take a short jog to the right on Brixton Road, to continue his journey from Robert Street to Loughborough Road. **Underground Station: Stockwell**

LOUGHBOROUGH ROAD—SW9: [Latitude / Longitude: 51.469461,-0.106409]. Then, as today, Loughborough Road turns south on its path from Brixton Road to Cold Harbour Lane. **Rail Station: Loughborough Junction**

COLDHARBOUR LANE—SW9: [Latitude / Longitude: 51.469461,-0.106409]. From the Lyceum Theatre, Holmes, Watson, and Mary were driven through a labyrinth of Lambeth streets, to Coldharbour Lane. Watson called it Cold Harbour. Holmes remarked that, "Our quest does not appear to take us to very fashionable regions". **Rail Station: Loughborough Junction**

Author's note: Watson noted, "We had reached a questionable and forbidding neighborhood...long lines of dull brick houses". Then came rows of two-storied villas, each with a fronting of miniature garden, and...lines of new...brick buildings". This indicates that Thaddeus Sholto's house was in a brand-new terrace, and could not have been in Coldharbour Lane, which was fully developed in 1887. Williams must have continued on past Coldharbour Lane.

HINTON ROAD—SW9: [Latitude / Longitude: 51.465352,-0.102532]. As Loughborough Road crossed Coldharbour Lane, the name changed to Hinton Road. After 500 feet, they bore right on Milkwood Road, and continued their southward journey. **Rail Station: Loughborough Junction**

MILKWOOD ROAD—SE24: Latitude / Longitude: 51.456966,-0.103405]. After continuing about half a mile on Milkwood Road, Holmes, Watson and Mary turned left on Gubyon Avenue and its line of new terrace houses. They stopped at No. 13. **Rail Station: Herne Hill**

No. 13 GUBYON AVENUE—SE24: Latitude / Longitude: 51.455184,-0.101516]. Watson said, "At last the cab drew up at the third house in a new terrace". Bernard Davies identifies the house as No. 13 Gubyon Avenue. As they entered the house, a Hindu servant led them to a room outfitted in Oriental splendor. There they met Thaddeus Sholto, the son of the late Major Sholto. Thaddeus told Mary of their fathers' involvement in finding Indian treasure. Thaddeus said that he wanted justice for Mary, and was going to see that she got it, regardless of what his brother Bartholomew thought. Bartholomew was living in Pondicherry Lodge, their father's old house in Upper Norwood. **Rail Station: Herne Hill**

"PONDICHERRY LODGE", Kilravock House, 103-105 Ross Road, Norwood—SE25: [Latitude / Longitude: 51.402958,-0.088041]. When the late Major John Sholto retired from the army, he returned from India with a large fortune. He and his two boys, Thaddeus and Bartholomew, lived in luxury at Pondicherry Lodge in Upper Norwood. Major Sholto lived in constant fear, and hired two prizefighters as porters. Thaddeus said that his father also had a marked aversion to men with wooden legs. **Rail Station: Norwood Junction**

Author's note: The Cannon offers several clues to describe "Pondicherry Lodge", and its location. Bernard Davies describes the Lodge as, "a very large square house of unusual height, with a plain, gentle sloping roof having dormer windows. It was almost certainly built before 1870, and stood in its own spacious grounds on a high road or street, surrounded by a high wall. It stood on a steep hillside so that its back appears much higher than its front. Mr. Davies suggests the house must be on the extreme southern borders of Upper Norwood and, must not be too far from the railway yet not too close to a police station. After an extensive search, Mr. Davies identified Kilravock House on Ross Road as the true "Pondicherry Lodge". Today, eight flats occupy Kilravock. Its roofline has been modified, the surrounding wall torn down, and the extensive grounds sold off.

Early in 1882, Major Sholto received a letter from India. He told his two boys about his ill-gotten wealth. He said that half of the treasure belonged to Captain Morstan's daughter. He also said that Captain Morstan had come to Pondicherry Lodge to claim his half of the treasure. There was an argument, and Captain Morstan had a heart attack. Major Sholto and one of his Indian servants disposed of the body. Before he revealed the treasure's location, Major Sholto saw a face at the window, and died from fright. For six years, Thaddeus and Bartholomew searched the house and grounds without success. Finally, Thaddeus moved to Gubyon Avenue. He also began sending Mary a pearl each year, so that, "she might never feel destitute". Yesterday, Thaddeus learned that Bartholomew found the treasure. He wanted to go to Norwood with Mary, and force his brother to give Mary her share.

Pondicherry Lodge stood in its own grounds. A very high masonry wall, covered with broken glass, surrounded it. When they arrived, McMurdo, the prizefighter, confronted them. He wanted to admit only Thaddeus, but Sherlock reminded him of the three rounds he fought with an amateur named Holmes. The housekeeper said that Bartholomew had locked himself in his room, and would not answer. When they broke open the door, they found him dead, with a long, dark thorn stuck just above his ear. The treasure had been hidden in the attic, and was gone. A note was left that read, *"The Sign of the Four"*.

SOUTH NORWOOD POLICE STATION, No. 83 High Street—**SE25: [Latitude / Longitude: 51.39861,-0.076153]**. The police were summoned from the nearby South Norwood Police Station. Before Athelney Jones and his police squad arrived, Holmes spent half an hour examining the crime scene. He determined that a small agile man had gained access to the room through the attic. He had lowered a rope out the window, where a man with a wooden leg hauled himself up. In the attic, Holmes found small naked footprints. A further examination showed that the small, bare-footed man had stepped in creosote. Holmes said he knew, "A dog that would follow this scent to the world's end". **Rail Station: Norwood Junction**

Author's note: The substantial brick station building is still there, but is now a bank.

Athelney Jones arrested Thaddeus for the murder. Holmes promised to clear him, but Athelney Jones told Holmes to not promise too much. Holmes also told Jones that one of the men he was looking for was Jonathon Small, a name on the document Mary had shown Holmes.

BLACK PRINCE ROAD, "No. 3 Pinchin Lane"—SE1: [**Latitude / Longitude: 51.492446,-0.121568**]. After escorting Mary Morstan back to Lower Camberwell, Watson stopped at No. 3 Pinchin Lane, an address in the "lower quarter of Lambeth, "down near the water's edge". Black Prince Road then called Princes Road, fits the description. Watson told Sherman, the old bird stuffer, that Holmes needed Toby. **Underground Station: Vauxhall**

Author's note: The east was gradually getting light as Holmes, Watson and Toby started their trek from Pondicherry Lodge. Bernard Davies suggests the following conjectural "Creosote Trail". Their quarry occasionally used parallel side roads on their six-mile trek.

WHARNCLIFFE ROAD—SE25: [**Latitude / Longitude: 51.404738,-0.088041**]. From Pondicherry Lodge on Ross Road, Toby led Holmes and Watson up Wharncliffe Road. **Rail Station: Norwood Junction**

GRANGE ROAD—SE19: [**Latitude / Longitude: 51.409891,-0.089028**]. On their northward journey, Toby led Holmes and Watson into Grange Road. **Rail Station: Norwood Junction**

BEULAH HILL—SE19: [**Latitude / Longitude: 51.417011,-0.09804**]. At the junction of Grange Road and Beulah Hill, Toby led Holmes and Watson northwest on Beulah Hill. **Rail Station: Norbury**

CROWN LANE—SW16: [Latitude / Longitude: 51.423247,-0.111923]. When they came to Crown Lane, Toby indicated that their quarry had taken a westward jog. **Rail Station: Streatham**

LEIGHAM COURT ROAD—SW16: [Latitude / Longitude: 51.426445,-0.114133]. From Crown Lane, Toby followed the creosote scent north on Leigham Court Road. **Rail Station: Streatham**

STREATHAM HILL—SW2: [Latitude / Longitude: 51.44,-0.125749]. Leigham Court Road ended at the rail station. Toby led Holmes and Watson north on Streatham Hill. **Rail Station: Streatham Hill**

BRIXTON HILL—SW2: [Latitude / Longitude: 51.452972,-0.121064]. Toby, Holmes and Watson continued north as Streatham Hill's name changed to Brixton Hill. **Underground Station: Brixton**

BRIXTON ROAD—SW9: [Latitude / Longitude: 51.462635,-0.115077]. Near Brixton Station, Toby, Holmes and Watson continued northward on Brixton Road. **Underground Station: Brixton**

CAMBERWELL NEW ROAD—SE11: [Latitude / Longitude: 51.481672,-0.111625]. Holmes, Watson and Toby found themselves east of The Oval, where Brixton Road meets Kennington Park. There, they turned left on Camberwell New Road, continued across Kennington Park Road, as the name changed to Harleyford Street. **Underground Station: Oval**

HARLEYFORD STREET—SE11: [Latitude / Longitude: 51.482187,-0.112621]. Watson remarked that the men they were pursuing had certainly taken a zigzag path. **Underground Station: Oval**

KENNINGTON OVAL—SE11: [Latitude / Longitude: 51.48283,-0.115038]. Toby led Holmes and Watson around the south side of The Oval on Harleyford Road. **Underground Station: Oval**

HARLEYFORD ROAD—SE11: [Latitude / Longitude: 51.484768,-0.118579]. In my opinion, it must have been at the junction of Harleyford Road and Durham Street where Toby picked up a false creosote scent. He followed this false trail up Harleyford Road to Kennington Lane. **Underground Station: Oval**

KENNINGTON LANE—SE11: [Latitude / Longitude: 51.486291,-0.122956]. On the wrong trail, Toby led Holmes and Watson on Kennington Lane toward Vauxhall Bridge. **Underground Station: Vauxhall**

BONDWAY—SE8: [Latitude / Longitude: 51.483164,-0.12557]. From Kennington Lane, Toby led Holmes and Watson down Bond Street, now called Bondway, to Miles Street. **Underground Station: Vauxhall**

MILES STREET—SE8: [Latitude / Longitude: 51.483311,-0.126772]. Holmes, Watson and Toby continued west on Miles Street, to Wandsworth Road. **Underground Station: Vauxhall**

WANDSWORTH ROAD)—SW8: [Latitude / Longitude: 51.483699,-0.127033]. Toby led Holmes and Watson north on Wandsworth Road, pass Knights Place, to Nine Elms Lane. **Underground Station: Vauxhall**

KNIGHT'S PLACE (site)—SW8: [Latitude / Longitude: 51.483365,-0.127183]. Knight's Place was a terrace of houses on the west side of Wandsworth Road between Miles Street and Nine Elms Lane. **Underground Station: Vauxhall**

NINE ELMS LANE—SW8: [Latitude / Longitude: 51.484794,-0.127995]. Toby had followed the wrong trail along Nine Elms Lane to Broderick and Nelson's timber yard. After reaching a false end, the dog "waddled around in circles...as if to ask for sympathy in his embarrassment". Holmes and Watson had to backtrack to find their quarry. **Underground Station: Vauxhall**

BELMONT PLACE (site)—SW8: [Latitude / Longitude: 51.484273,-0.126046]. In backtracking to the place they lost the true scent, Holmes, Watson and Toby passed Belmont Place, a terrace of houses located on the east side of Wandsworth Road, across from Knight's Place. **Underground Station: Vauxhall**

DURHAM STREET—SE11: [Latitude / Longitude: 51.485708,-0.118865]. If Toby had not followed the false scent, he would have led Holmes and Watson up Durham Street to Kennington Lane. **Underground Station: Vauxhall**

KENNINGTON LANE—SE11: [Latitude / Longitude: 51.486436,-0.119208]. Toby had been misled when the scent trail split. Holmes and Watson may have backtracked to Durham Street, and followed it to where their quarry had crossed Kennington Lane. **Underground Station: Vauxhall**

TYERS STREET—SE11: [Latitude / Longitude: 51.488258,-0.119294]. Tyers Street is across Kennington Lane from Durham Street. The true trail led Toby, Holmes and Watson north on Tyers Street. **Underground Station: Vauxhall**

BLACK PRINCE ROAD—SE11: [Latitude / Longitude: 51.491386,-0.117953]. Toby led Holmes and Watson down Tyers Street to Princes Street now called Black Prince Road. **Underground Station: Vauxhall**

BROAD STREET—SE1: [Latitude / Longitude: 51.490967,-0.116969]. The river end of Black Prince Road was called Broad Street. Today, it is Black Prince Road, West. Toby led Holmes and Watson to Mordecai Smith's boatyard. There, their quarry had hired the *Aurora*. Mrs. Smith said the boat was the fastest steam launch on the river, a claim that would later be tested. **Underground Station: Vauxhall**

MILLBANK PENITENTIARY (site)—SW1: [Latitude / Longitude: 51.492464,-0.125291]. At the end of their long walk, Holmes and Watson returned Toby and took a wherry to the north side of the river, near Millbank Penitentiary. **Underground Station: Pimlico**

79

Author's note: In 1887, Millbank Penitentiary was the largest prison in London, and contained men only. They could not communicate with each other for the first half of their sentence. The prison closed in 1890 and was demolished in 1903.

GREAT PETER STREET POST OFFICE, Great Smith Street—SW1: [Latitude / Longitude: 51.496944,-0.129382]. On their way back to Baker Street, Holmes wired ahead from the Great Peter Street Post Office to mobilize the "Baker Street Irregulars". Holmes instructed Wiggins, their dirty little lieutenant, to search the riverside for the *Aurora,* but to do so without raising suspicion. **Underground Station: St. James's Park**

Author's note: The Great Peter Post Office was on a corner, and actually fronted on Great Smith Street.

No. 31 "221B" BAKER STREET—W1: [Latitude / Longitude: 51.517932,-0.155587]. At Baker Street, as Watson napped, and dreamed about Mary Morstan, Holmes researched the identity of the strange little man who murdered Bartholomew Sholto. Everything pointed to a small savage, but there were no people like that on the Indian subcontinent. Then Holmes read about the cannibal natives of the Andaman Islands in the Bay of Bengal. They fit the description. All that day, and the next, there was no word on the location of the *Aurora.* Holmes even went out himself to search. After the Irregulars found the *Aurora,* Holmes sent a telegram to Athelney Jones, asking him to come to Baker Street if he wanted to be in at the finish. Jones was there when Holmes returned. **Underground Station: Marble Arch**

WESTMINSTER PIER (STAIRS)—SW1: [Latitude / Longitude: 51.501036,-0.123811]. Holmes asked Athelney Jones to have a fast police steam launch at the Westminster Stairs at seven o'clock. As it turned out, the police launch was just fast enough. **Underground Station: Westminster**

TOWER OF LONDON—SE1: [Latitude / Longitude: 51.507313,-0.074308]. Holmes told the police launch to go downstream to the Tower of London. **Underground Station: Tower Hill**

JACOBSON'S BOAT YARD (site)—SE1: [Latitude / Longitude: 51.50553,-0.075306]. Holmes told the police launch to go downstream to the Tower of London, and stand off opposite Jacobson's boat yard, on the Surrey (south) side of the river. **Underground Station: London Bridge**

TOWER BRIDGE—E1: [Latitude / Longitude: 51.50553,-0.075306]. As the police launch continued downstream, they passed the construction site of the new Tower Bridge. **Underground Station: Tower Hill**

POOL OF LONDON—E1: [Latitude / Longitude: 51.50553,-0.075306]. After Holmes saw the signal from one of his "Baker Street Irregulars", the police steam launch started after the *Aurora* as she sped downstream into the Pool of London. **Underground Station: Tower Hill**

Author's note: The term "Pool of London" generally refers to the stretch of the River Thames between London Bridge and Rotherhithe. This was the farthest point upstream that could accommodate a tall ship.

WEST INDIA DOCKS—E14: [Latitude / Longitude: 51.503098,-0.025744]. When the police launch raced after the *Aurora*, they sped through the Pool of London, and past the West India Docks. To keep up, it took every bit of speed they had. **Dockland Light Rail Station: Limehouse**

DEPTFORD REACH—SE10: [Latitude / Longitude: 51.48275,-0.01884]. The police launch sped through the Pool of London, past the West India Docks, and down the long Deptford Reach. They were gaining on the *Aurora*. **Rail Station: Deptford**

ISLE OF DOGS—E14: [Latitude / Longitude: 51.488125,-0.022495]. In their attempt to catch the *Aurora*, supposedly "The fastest boat on the river", the police steam launch sped past the Isle of Dogs. **Dockland Light Rail Station: Island Gardens**

GREENWICH—SE10: [Latitude / Longitude: 51.484491,-0.004463]. At Greenwich, the police launch was about three hundred paces behind the *Aurora*. **Dockland Light Rail Station:**

BLACKWALL REACH—E14: [Latitude / Longitude: 51.501276,-0.008801]. When they reached Blackwall, the police launch was only two hundred and fifty paces behind the *Aurora*. **Dockland Light Rail Station: Blackwall**

BARKING LEVEL—RM9: [Latitude / Longitude: 51.504495,0.089049]. The two boats were flying at a tremendous pace as they passed Barking Level on the left and Plumstead Marshes on the right. **Rail Station: Woolwich Dock**

PLUMSTEAD—SE28: [Latitude / Longitude: 51.504495,0.089049]. As the police steam launch continued downstream, Barking Level was on the left and Plumstead Marshes on the right. Today, this area is upstream from the Thames Flood Barrier. **Rail Station: Woolwich Dock**

When the two boats were just a boat-length apart, the hideous dwarf raised a blowgun to his lips. Holmes and Watson both fired, hitting the dwarf, and knocking him into the river. Later, they found that the poisoned dart had just missed them. Jonathan Small threw himself on the tiller forcing the boat to the southern shore. He tried to escape in the marsh, but his wooden leg sank in the mud. After Small's capture, they transferred the treasure chest to the police launch,

MILLBANK at VAUXHALL BRIDGE—SW1: [Latitude / Longitude: 51.48907,-0.128814]. Holmes, Watson and Jones made their way back upstream. They used their searchlight to look for the Islander, but there was no sign of him. The police launch landed at Vauxhall Bridge, and Watson, accompanied by an inspector, took the treasure box to Mary Morstan. **Underground Station Pimlico**

When she and Watson opened the box, it was empty. Jonathan Small had thrown the treasure into the river, piece by piece. Watson said, "Thank God...you are within my reach again". Mary said, "Then I say Thank God, too".

VALLEY OF FEAR – 1887?

No. 31 "221B" BAKER STREET—W1: [Latitude / Longitude: 51.517932,-0.155587]. On January 7, at the end of the 1880's, Holmes received a letter from Porlock, the nom-de-plum of an associate of Professor Moriarty. Porlock sent Holmes a coded message. It read, *"534   C2   13   127   36   31   4   17   21   41   Douglas   109   293   5   37   Birlstone 26   Birlstone 9   47   171"*. **Underground Station: Marble Arch**

Holmes said, "It is clearly a reference to the words in a page of some book. Until I am told which page, and which book, I am powerless". He hoped that the key would arrive in the next post. Unfortunately, when Billy delivered the next letter, Porlock said he had come under suspicion, and could not send additional information. Holmes said, "Let us consider the problem in the light of pure reason". Since the cipher begins with the number 534, "we may take it as a working hypothesis that 534 is the particular page to which the cipher refers". This means the book is a large one. The next code, 'C2' cannot mean chapter because if a page number is given, the chapter number is immaterial. 'C2' must mean column 2.

From this analysis, Holmes assumed he was looking for a large book printed in double columns of considerable length, since one of the words in the cipher was the 293rd word. The fact that Porlock intended to send the key in a letter, means that it was a common book. The clues suggested Whitaker's Almanac, but page 534 did not yield a message. Then, Holmes realized that his almanac was the new version. Using page 534 in the previous year's almanac yielded a message. It indicated danger was coming soon to a rich country gentleman at somewhere called Birlstone.

At that point, Inspector Alec MacDonald arrived. He was stunned when he read the scratch paper Holmes and Watson had used to solve the cipher. He said, "Where in the name of all that is wonderful did you get these names? Mr. Douglas of Birlstone Manor House was horribly murdered last night!"

CAMBERWELL—SE5: [Latitude / Longitude: 51.475257,-0.092291]. After Holmes explained, the exercise they had just gone through, MacDonald wanted to lay his hands on Porlock. MacDonald noticed that Porlock's letters came from Camberwell, and Holmes sent him money there. **Rail Station: Denmark Hill**

VICTORIA RAILWAY STATION—SW1: [Latitude / Longitude: 51.496697,-0.144058]. MacDonald asked Holmes and Watson to join him on the trip to Birlstone Manor. They had to leave Baker Street in five minutes in order to catch the train from Victoria Station. **Underground Station: Victoria**

Word of the murder had reached MacDonald from White Mason, a rural police officer. Mason specifically asked MacDonald to bring Holmes, saying, "He will find something after his own heart…It is a snorter". Birlstone was a moated Manor. The only access was over a drawbridge. By tradition, the bridge was raised every evening, and lowered every morning. Mr. John Douglas and his wife had owned the Manor for five years. Rumor was he made his money in the California gold fields. Mrs. Douglas was a beautiful English lady, twenty years younger than her husband was. The other residents of Birlstone Manor were Ames, the butler, Mrs. Allen, the housekeeper, and six other servants.

HAMPSTEAD—NW3: [Latitude / Longitude: 51.558825,-0.172446]. Cecil James Barker, of Hales Lodge Hampstead, was a frequent visitor to Birlstone Manor. Although Barker was English, he had known Douglas in America. Ames, the butler, described Barker as, "An easy-going…gentleman…But, my word! I had rather not be the man that crossed him". **Underground Station: Hampstead**

The first alarm of the murder was at eleven forty-five when Cecil Barker woke up Sergeant Wilson of the Sussex Constabulary. After alerting the county authorities, Wilson went to the Manor. The drawbridge was down, and the whole house was in a state of confusion. Only Barker seemed to be in control.

When Dr. Wood, the local doctor, arrived, he found Mr. Douglas's face horribly mutilated from a shotgun blast. Across his chest was a double barrel sawed-off shotgun. The triggers had been wired together, to make the discharge more destructive. Sergeant Wilson allowed nothing to be touched until his superiors arrived. Barker assured him that he had not touched anything after he heard the gun shot, and found the body at half-past eleven. On the table, beside the body, Barker said he saw an extinguished bedroom candle.

At first, Wilson thought that Douglas had killed himself, but Barker showed him a bloody footprint on the windowsill. It seemed to indicate that someone escaped by wading across the three feet deep moat. However, the question remained, how did they arrive, if the drawbridge had been up since about six o'clock? There was no sign of muddy footprints in the room. This seemed to indicate that the killer arrived before six, waited in the house until after eleven, before shooting Douglas as he made his nightly rounds. Wilson also found where someone had been behind the curtains. The interrogation of Ames, the butler, and Mrs. Allen, the housekeeper, provided little information. However, Mrs. Allen said she heard a sound at least a half and hour before the body was found. She thought it was a door slamming.

Beside the body, Wilson found a rough cardboard card with the initials V.V. and the number 341. Dr. Wood also noticed that Douglas had a strange mark on his right arm. It was a triangle inside a circle. It looked like brand, the kind they use on cattle. The butler said he had previously noticed the mark on his master. The butler also mentioned that Mr. Douglas' wedding ring was missing from the body. He wore it behind a nugget ring, which was still on his finger. Sergeant Wilson said, "Then the murderer…took off this…nugget ring, then the wedding ring, and afterwards put the nugget ring back on again". Wilson said, "Seems to me that the sooner we get London on this case the better".

Inspector MacDonald, Holmes and Watson arrived at noon. White Mason arranged rooms at the Westville Arms. Mason relayed Sergeant Wilson's observations, and added a few of his own. He had examined the hammer found near the body, and found no signs of violence. When he examined the shotgun, he found the letters *P-E-N* on the fluting between the barrels. Holmes said it was, "Pennsylvania Small Arms Company", a well know American firm. Mason also said that the butler had been with the Douglas's for five years, but had never seen the gun. White Mason said he did not find signs of anyone exiting the house through the moat.

When they arrived at the house, Holmes noticed one dumb-bell under the table, it was one of a pair, but the other was missing. Holmes and MacDonald questioned Mrs. Douglas. They learned that she felt her husband was in fear of something, or someone, from his past. He did not explain his fear, but told her, "I have been in the Valley of Fear; I am not out of it yet". Once, when he had a high fever, he mentioned a name: "McGinty, Bodymaster McGinty".

While Cecil Barker was out of the house, Holmes examined the bedroom slippers Barker was wearing when he discovered the body. Naturally, they were stained with blood, but the slipper exactly matched the footprint on the windowsill. Barker had marked the sill himself! While Holmes continued his investigation, Watson walked back to the Westville Arms. On the way, he explored the manor grounds and the adjoining ancient village. Behind a yew hedge, he heard a man's voice and feminine laughter. It was Cecil Barker and Mrs. Douglas. When they saw Watson, their lighthearted attitude changed. When they saw the suspicion on his face, Mrs. Douglas asked for Watson's advice. She wanted to know if Holmes would pass on all information to the police. Watson replied, "Mr. Holmes is an independent investigator. He is his own master, and would act as his own judgment directed". When Watson told Holmes of this encounter, Holmes said, "I wish none of their confidences". He also indicated that the solution to the whole affair might hang on the missing dumb-bell.

After high tea at the Westville Arms, Holmes told Watson, "The whole story told by Barker is a lie. Nevertheless, Mrs. Douglas corroborates Barker's story. Therefore she is lying also". To untangle the lies, Holmes, with Ames the butler's help, developed a plan for Holmes to spend the night alone in the manor house study. MacDonald and Wilson went to Tunbridge Wells to identify an abandoned bicycle found near Birlstone Manor. The hotel manager identified the bicycle as belonging to an American guest named Hargrave, who had not returned.

Holmes asked Inspector MacDonald to send a note to Barker, saying they planned to drain the moat the next morning. MacDonald was to have the note hand delivered at four o'clock. Holmes, Watson, MacDonald, and Wilson proceeded to a hidden spot facing the manor's drawbridge. They saw the window in the study open, and someone retrieve something out of the moat. They rushed across the drawbridge, burst into the study, and found Cecil Barker with a sodden package weighted with a dumb-bell. Holmes had retrieved the same package the night before, examined it, and put it back in the water. In addition to the dumb-bell, the package contained a pair of American boots, a sheathed knife, and clothing. The clothing matched those belonging to the missing Hargrave. The coat had a label from Vermissa, U. S. A. Holmes surmised that the V. V. on the card found near the body, stood for Vermissa Valley, one of the best known coal and iron valleys in the United States. Holmes thought this was the "Valley of Fear" to which Douglas referred. Mrs. Douglas entered the room as Barker refused to explain his actions; When Holmes pressed them for their explanation, a man appeared out of one of the room's ancient hiding places. It was John Douglas!

John Douglas said there were men in his American past who wanted him dead. A few days ago, in Tunbridge Wells, Douglas spotted one of his old enemies. Douglas was on his guard when he returned to Birlstone, but felt safe when the drawbridge was up. On the night of the killing, while making his rounds, he spotted a boot under the window curtain. As the man sprung at him with a knife, Douglas hit him with a hammer that lay nearby. The assailant then pulled out his sawed-off shotgun. As the two men struggled, the gun went off and struck the assailant in the face. Barker and Mrs. Douglas heard the shot and rushed into the room. They waited for other members of the household to arrive, but when they did not, they came up with the plan to fake John Douglas's death.

The dead man and Douglas had the same general appearance, and the damage to the face made the deception possible. In addition, both men had the same brand on their arms. They placed Douglas's nightclothes and jewelry on the dead man, and threw the dead man's clothes in the moat. Barker placed his footprint on the sill to indicate how the murderer escaped. After Douglas hid in the ancient hiding place, Barker reloaded the shotgun, fired, and rang the bell. The "door slamming" that Mrs. Allen heard was the first discharge. After hearing the tale, Holmes said, "The story is not over yet, I fear, you may find worse dangers than the English law…take my advice and still be on your guard".

SCANDAL IN BOHEMIA - 1888

No. 31 "221B" BAKER STREET—W1: [Latitude / Longitude: 51.517932,-0.155587]. After Watson's marriage, Holmes remained at their old quarters in Baker Street. One evening—it was March 20, 1888—Watson was passing through Baker Street and decided to stop by and see his old friend. Holmes showed him a note that had come that day in the last post. It said that Holmes would receive a masked visitor at quarter to eight. This visitor wanted to consult him on, "matters which are of an importance which can hardly be exaggerated". The note was written on expensive Bohemian paper. Holmes also noted, because of the sentence construction, that the writer's native language was German. **Underground Station: Marble Arch**

When the richly dressed guest arrived, he said he could be addressed as, "Count Von Kramm, a Bohemian nobleman". Holmes saw through the subterfuge and knew he was addressing, "Wilhelm Gottsreich Sigismond von Ormstein, Grand Duke of Cassel-Felstein, and hereditary King of Bohemia". The King acknowledged his identity, and asked for Holmes's help. Years earlier, as Crown Prince, he had an affair with Irene Adler, the contralto Prima Donna. Irene was now retired, living in London. She had kept a photograph of the two of them together. In three days, the King was going to announce his betrothal to the second daughter of the King of Scandinavia, and could not afford a scandal. Irene had threatened to send the picture to the bride's family the day the betrothal was announced.

THE LANGHAM HOTEL, Portland Place—W1: [Latitude / Longitude: 51.518077,-0.143875]. The King said he was staying at the Langham Hotel, under the name Count Von Kramm. **Underground Station: Oxford Circus**

ST. JOHN'S WOOD—NW8: [Latitude / Longitude: 51.53237,-0.173582]. Irene Adler lived in Briony Lodge, at the fictional Serpentine Avenue, St. John's Wood. Holmes devised a plan to find where she hid the picture. **Underground Station: St. John's Wood**

After the King's visit, Holmes asked Watson to come back the next day at three. When he arrived, he found that Holmes had left early that morning. It was nearly four when Holmes returned. He had spent the day in St. John's Wood, disguised as a drunken out-of-work horse groom. In the mews, he learned quite a bit about Briony Lodge and Irene Adler. For example, she only had one regular male visitor—Godfrey Norton.

INNER TEMPLE—EC4: [Latitude / Longitude: 51.513806,-0.110968]. Godfrey Norton practiced law in the Inner Temple. At first, Holmes did not know if Irene Adler was Norton's client, friend, or mistress. "If the former, she had probably transferred the photograph to his keeping. If the latter, it was less likely". **Underground Station: Temple**

The next day, in his horse groom disguise, Holmes observed Godfrey Norton leaving Briony Lodge. As he left, he shouted to the cab driver, "Drive like the wind...first to Gross & Hankey's in Regent Street, and then to the Church of St. Monica in the Edgware Road". Godfrey Norton and Irene Adler were to be married.

REGENT STREET—W1: [Latitude / Longitude: 51.511142,-0.138904]. Godfrey Norton rushed into Gross and Hankey's in Regent Street, before going to the Church of St. Monica. Because of the last minute nature of the wedding, we can assume that Gross and Hankey's was the jewelry store, where he bought the wedding ring(s). **Underground Station: Piccadilly Circus**

CHURCH OF ST. MARK "CHURCH OF ST. MONICA", Old Marylebone Road—NW1: [Latitude / Longitude: 51.518481,-0.167137]. Godfrey Norton and Irene Adler were married in The Church of St. Monica, Edgware Road. The most likely candidate is the Church of St. Mark, located on Old Marylebone Lane, near Edgware Road. **Underground Station: Edgware Road**

Holmes managed to get to the church just after the couple arrived. They needed a witness for the marriage, and the idle horse groom at the back of the church, was just the man. Later, Holmes told Watson that he, "found himself mumbling responses…and vouching for things of which I knew nothing, and generally assisting in the secure tying up of Irene Adler, spinster, and Godfrey Norton, bachelor". Holmes went on to say, "The bride gave me a sovereign, and I mean to wear it on my watch-chain in memory of the occasion".

That evening, Holmes and Watson went to Irene's house. They wanted to be there when she arrived home at seven. Holmes had devised a plan to make her reveal where she had hidden the picture. Holmes, disguised as a non-conformist clergyman, feigned an injury, and gained access to the house. Watson then threw a plumber's smoke rocket into the sitting room, and raised the call of fire. Everything went as planned, and when Irene attempted to save the picture, Holmes saw the secret hiding place. When Holmes and Watson returned to Baker Street, a slim young man passed by and said, "Good-night Mister Sherlock Holmes". Holmes thought he had heard that voice before. It was a disguised Irene Adler, who had seen through the ruse.

Holmes sent a wire to the King, asking him to return to Baker Street early in the morning. Using the King's brougham, the three of them hurried to Briony Lodge. On the way, Holmes told the King that Irene had been married the day before. When they arrived, the couple had fled, and left a message for Sherlock. The elderly housekeeper said, "My mistress told me that you were likely to call. She left this morning with her husband by the 5:15 train from Charing Cross for the Continent". Inside the secret hiding place was a new photograph of Irene, and a letter addressed to "Sherlock Holmes, Esq.". The letter said she loved her husband, and would not interfere with the King's marriage. She also said she would keep the incriminating picture to guarantee her future safety. The King saw that his reputation was safe, and in gratitude, offered Holmes his emerald snake ring. He was amazed when Holmes said that he would prefer Irene's picture instead.

CHARING CROSS RAILROAD STATION, The Strand—WC2:
[Latitude / Longitude: 51.508497,-0.125551]. Irene and her new husband, Godfrey Norton, left for the Continent from Charing Cross Station on the 5:15 train. They were trying to escape from the King of Bohemia's agents, Holmes included. Later, whenever Sherlock referred to Irene Adler, he always used the honorable title of *The Woman*. Watson said "There was but one woman to him, and that woman was Irene Adler, of dubious and questionable memory". **Underground Station: Charing Cross**

THE CROOKED MAN – 1888

WATERLOO RAILWAY STATION—SE1: [Latitude / Longitude: 51.503943,-0.11391]. One summer night, a few months after his marriage, Watson was staying up late. His wife and the rest of the household had gone to bed, when there was a knock at the door. It was Holmes, who had just come from Waterloo Station. He had arrived from Aldershot, and asked Watson to accompany him when he returned the next day. **Underground Station: Waterloo**

Holmes briefed Watson on the situation in Aldershot. The Royal Munsters Regiment was billeted there. Their commanding officer, Colonel James Barclay, had been killed. Major Murphy, the adjutant, had requested Sherlock's assistance because Nancy Barclay, the colonel's wife, was the chief suspect. Colonel Barclay had risen from the ranks, and at one time had been a private in the regiment he now commanded. Nancy had grown up in the regiment, having been the daughter of the colour-sergeant. As a young enlisted man, James Barclay competed with, Corporal Henry Wood for Nancy's hand. When Corporal Wood was captured, and presumably killed, by Indian rebels, James Barclay married Nancy, and rose to be the regiment's commanding officer

The Barclays lived at Lachine, their villa in Aldershot. Nancy was Roman Catholic, and active in the Guild of St. George. The Guild supplied clothing to the poor. The evening of the colonel's death, Nancy attended a guild meeting with Miss Morrison, a lady from the neighboring villa. When Mrs. Barclay returned, she seemed agitated, and ordered Jane Stewart, the maid, to bring her a cup of tea in the morning room. Hearing her return, the Colonel joined her.

When the maid came with the tea, she found the morning-room door locked, and her master and mistress arguing. Although she could not hear every word, she heard, "You coward! Give me back my life. I will never so much as breathe the same air with you again!" The maid also heard the name, 'David.' Then, there was a cry, a crash, and the sound of Nancy crying. Unable to force the door, a coachman ran outside, and entered through the French windows. He found the Colonel dead on the floor, with a wooden club nearby. Nancy Barclay had collapsed, and was lying on the coach. When the coachman tried to unlock the door, he found the key had disappeared.

When Holmes arrived, he examined the morning room and found the footprints of a small carnivorous animal. It had climbed up the curtains in an attempt to get at a caged canary. Since Mrs. Barclay was in good terms with her husband when she left the house, it was obvious that something had happened while she was out. Her companion, Miss Morrison, told Holmes of the strange misshapen man they had met on the street that night. Nancy recognized him as Corporal Henry Wood. He told her the story of his capture and torture at the hands of the Indian rebels, and that her husband was the one who betrayed him.

Holmes assigned Simpson, one of his Baker Street Irregulars, to keep an eye on Henry Wood. Later, when Holmes and Watson interviewed Henry Wood, he told his story. As a young soldier in India, his unit was surrounded, and he volunteered to warn General Neill's column. When he slipped out at night, the rebels were waiting for him. James Barclay, through his native servant, had alerted them. It was Barclay's way of ridding himself of a rival for Nancy's affection.

After years of slavery and torture, Wood managed to escape and return to England. He was a broken man, and only managed to live by performing tricks with Teddy, his pet mongoose. After Nancy recognized him, he followed her to the villa, and saw her and her husband arguing. When Wood thought she might be in danger, he entered the room through the French windows. Colonel Barclay recognized him, and died of apoplexy. When the Colonel fell, he struck his head on the fireplace fender. The club they found was Henry's walking stick, which he had dropped trying to assist Nancy. Henry started to unlock the inside door, but thought better of it, put the key in his pocket, and fled.

Holmes told Watson, "It was quite a simple case, after all". Watson said, "If the husbands name was James, and the other was Henry, what was this talk about David"? Holmes reminded Watson of the Biblical story of King David, Uriah, and Bathsheba, in the Book of Samuel.

STOCK-BROKER'S CLERK - 1889?

PADDINGTON—W2: [Latitude / Longitude: 51.514567,-0.173905]. Shortly after his marriage, Watson bought a Paddington medical practice from old Mr. Farquhar. For three months he worked hard to increase the number of patients, and saw very little of Holmes. Watson was surprised when Holmes arrived in Paddington early one morning, and asked if Watson could accompany him to Birmingham. **Underground Station: Paddington**

THE CITY—EC2: [Latitude / Longitude: 51.512589,-0.087011]. Outside, a cabby was waiting to take them to the train station. Inside was Hall Pycroft, "A well-built…young fellow, with a frank, honest face and a slight, crisp yellow moustache". He dressed like a smart young City man, but could not hide his cockney beginnings. On the train, Pycroft repeated his story to Watson. **Underground Station: Bank**

Author's note: Traditionally, to qualify as a Cockney, a person has to be born within earshot of "The Bow Bells" – that is the bells of the Church of St. Mary le Bow, **[Latitude / Longitude: 51.514111,-0.09392]**.

EUSTON RAILWAY STATION—NW1: [Latitude / Longitude: 51.528401,-0.131943]. In the 1880's, as it does today, trains to Birmingham leave from London's Euston Station. **Underground Station: Euston**

DRAPERS' GARDEN—EC2: [Latitude / Longitude: 51.516189,-0.087805]. Pycroft said he "used to have a billet at Coxon & Woodhouse's, of Draper Gardens". He and twenty-six other clerks were let go after the Venezuelan loan problem. Although Pycroft wore out his boots trying to find a new position, he was near the end of his tether when he saw a help wanted ad. **Underground Station: Moorgate**

Author's note: Drapers Garden is at the junction of Throgmorton and Copthall Avenues. The land had been used by the Drapers' Company for gardens, but was later used for offices buildings, including Coxon & Woodhouse.

LOMBARD STREET—EC3: [**Latitude / Longitude:** 51.512589,-0.087011]. The advertised position was with Mawson & Williams's, the great stock-broking firm in Lombard Street. The ad specified a response by letter only. After he sent in his application, Pycroft was surprised to receive a reply by return mail. He had the job and was to report the next Monday. **Underground Station: Monument**

HAMPSTEAD—NW3: [**Latitude / Longitude:** 51.558825,-0.172446]. Hall Pycroft lived in Hampstead, at the fictitious Potter's Terrace. Before reporting to his new position at Mawson & Williams's, he received a visit from Arthur Pinner, whose card said he was a "Financial Agent" for a Birmingham hardware company. **Underground Station: Hampstead**

Pinner questioned Pycroft on his knowledge of the current stock market, and said he was, "Much too good to be a clerk at Mawson's". Pinner offered him a position with a starting salary of five hundred pounds a year with the Franco-Midland Hardware Company, Ltd. of Birmingham. Pycroft reported to Birmingham the next day, and was given an advance of one hundred pounds. He also wrote and signed a paper that said, "I am perfectly willing to act as business manager to the Franco-Midland Hardware Company, Limited, at a minimum salary of £500".

In Birmingham, Pycroft met Arthur Pinner's "brother", who gave Pycroft a task that kept him in Birmingham. When Pycroft returned the completed paperwork, he noticed that the "brother", had the same "badly stuffed" gold tooth as Arthur. Pycroft suspected that the two men were the same person, and returned to London to seek Sherlock's advice. The next day, when Holmes, Watson and Pycroft returned to Birmingham, Pycroft was going to introduce Holmes and Watson as two friends who were also looking for a billet.

When Holmes, Watson and Pycroft entered the "Offices of Franco-Midland Hardware Company", they found Pinner reading a newspaper, with a look of grief and horror on his face. He excused himself and went into the adjoining room. When he did not return, Holmes, Watson, and Pycroft broke down the locked door, and found Pinner in a closet, trying to hang himself. When they read the newspaper, they learned the reason for his distress. It said that the robbery had failed, and that his brother was charged with the murder of a watchman.

Arthur Pinner's real name was Beddington. He and his real brother were famous forgers and safe crackers. They had been recently released from prison, and planned to rob Mawson & Williams. The plan was for one of them to impersonate Hall Pycroft, when he reported for work. Once one of them was on the "inside", he could burgle the safes. To impersonate Pycroft, they needed a sample of his handwriting, hence the "employment" note. The other brother got Pycroft out of London, with the fake job offer, and kept him there with busy work. With only two of them in on the plot, one had to play both "outside" roles.

ADVENTURE OF THE ENGINEER'S THUMB - 1889

PADDINGTON RAILWAY STATION—W2: [Latitude / Longitude: 51.515637,-0.175678]. In the summer of 1889, shortly after his marriage, Watson set up private practice near the Paddington station. Early one morning, two men came from the Station. One was a station guard, and the other was Victor Hatherley. Hatherley had previously departed from Paddington to meet Colonel Lysander Stark in Eyford, near Reading. When he returned, he had lost his thumb, and needed medical attention. **Underground Station: Paddington**

No. 16A VICTORIA STREET—SW1: [Latitude / Longitude: 51.49666,-0.144314]. When Watson examined Hatherley's card, he saw that he was a hydraulic engineer, with professional chambers in a third floor walkup at No. 16A Victoria Street. **Underground Station: Victoria**

No. 31 "221B" BAKER STREET—W1: [Latitude / Longitude: 51.517932,-0.155587]. After hearing how Hatherley lost his thumb, Watson suggested that they go to Baker Street, before going to the police. After giving them a hearty breakfast of streaked rashers and eggs, Holmes invited Hatherley to tell his story. **Underground Station: Marble Arch**

GREENWICH—SE10: [Latitude / Longitude: 51.478097,-0.016748]. For seven years, Victor Hatherley had apprenticed with Venner & Matheson, the well-known engineering firm in Greenwich. In 1887, he went into practice for himself, but the business had not done well. **Dockland Light Rail Station: Cutty Sark**

The day before, Hatherley received a visit from Colonel Lysander Stark, who spoke with a German accent. He said he needed a hydraulic engineer, who was "capable of preserving a secret". Stark also said that he knew that Hatherley was an orphan, a bachelor, and resided alone. Stark offered Hatherley a commission that paid fifty guineas for one night's work. The job was in Eyford, near Reading. Hatherley took the train from Paddington Station, and arrived in Eyford about 11:15 that night.

Colonel Stark met Hatherley when his train arrived. At the end of a long carriage journey, they arrived at an old house. Hatherley did not know where it was. Based on the travel time, he thought it was about ten miles from Eyford, but did not know if it was north, south, east, or west. A beautiful young woman met them. When they were alone, she told Hatherley in broken English, that he should go, "Before it is too late". Colonel Stark returned with another man, who he introduced as Mr. Ferguson. Stark led them to a small room that was within a large hydraulic press. After Hatherley diagnosed and fixed the problem, Stark locked him in the room and started the press. Luckily, Hatherley found another doorway and escaped. This time, when the young woman asked him to flee, he did so. To escape from the house, Hatherley had to jump out of an upper floor window. As he hung from the windowsill, Stark cut off his thumb with a butcher's cleaver.

While making his escape, Hatherley fainted from the loss of blood. When he woke, he was amazed to find himself near the Eyford Station. Because of his weakness, he decided to return to London and have his wound attended to there, before contacting the police. After hearing the story, Holmes showed them a year-old newspaper clipping. It told the story of Mr. Jeremiah Hayling, a young hydraulic engineer who had disappeared. Holmes thought this disappearance represented "The last time that the colonel needed to have his machine overhauled".

After going to Scotland Yard, Holmes, Watson, Hatherley, Inspector Bradstreet, and a plain-clothes man, left Paddington for Eyford. Bradstreet said that they had been looking for the counterfeiters who had been turning out half-crowns by the thousands, but that the trail always ended in Reading. After arriving in Eyford, they saw a nearby house on fire. The long carriage ride the night before had been a ruse. The oil lamp that Hatherley had left in the press had started the fire. The stationmaster said that the house belonged to Dr. Becher, an Englishman, who had a German guest that matched Colonel Stark's description. Becher, Stark and the young woman had fled.

BOSCOMBE VALLEY MYSTERY - 1889?

One morning in June, while having breakfast with his wife, Watson received a telegram from Holmes. It read, *"Have you a couple of days to spare? Have just been wired for from the West of England in connection with Boscombe Valley Tragedy - Leave Paddington by the 11:15".*

PADDINGTON RAILWAY STATION—W2: [Latitude / Longitude: 51.515637,-0.175678]. Watson arrived at Paddington Station, and found, "Sherlock Holmes…pacing up and down the platform, his tall gaunt figure made even gaunter and taller by his long grey traveling-cloak and the close-fitting cloth cap" **Underground Station: Paddington**

Author's note: This may be the first mention of Sherlock's, now famous, dear-stalker hat.

The Boscombe Valley is in Herefordshire. The largest landowner in the area was John Turner, who made his money in Australia. He gave one of his farms rent-free to Charles McCarthy, who had also come from Australian. Both men were widowers, and each had one child. McCarty had James, an eighteen-year-old son, and Turner had Alice, a daughter of the same age. The two men's history went back to their days in Australia. McCarthy was a wagon-driver on a gold shipment that Turner held up. Turner spared McCarthy's life, fled to England with his ill-gotten gains, and bought his Herefordshire estate.

REGENT STREET—W1: [Latitude / Longitude: 51.511142,-0.138904]. Years later, in London, McCarthy saw Turner on Regent Street. McCarthy blackmailed Turner, and threatened to expose his criminal past. The threat resulted in McCarthy acquiring Hatherley Farm, rent-free. **Underground Station: Piccadilly Circus**

Later, when McCarthy insisted that his son be allowed to marry Turner's daughter, Turner snapped, and struck McCarthy with a rock, killing him. They arrested McCarthy's son James for his father's murder, but James was acquitted through Holmes' efforts. A short time later, Turner died a natural death, and the young couple never discovered the dark cloud that covered their family histories.

MAN WITH THE TWISTED LIP - 1889

One evening, in June 1889, Watson and his wife had a late night visitor. It was Kate Whitney. Her husband, Isa, was addicted to opium, and had not come home for two days. She was sure that he was in an East End opium den. A lady could not go into that part of London by herself, so she asked Watson to recover her poor husband.

SWAN "UPPER SWANDAM" LANE—EC4: [Latitude / Longitude: 51.509057,-0.088621]. Kate said that her husband was probably at the Bar of Gold in Upper Swandam Lane, "A vile alley lurking behind the high wharves which line the north side of the river…east of London Bridge". **Underground Station: Monument**

Author's note: I join those who like Swan Lane as the location of "Upper Swandam Lane", even though it is west of London Bridge, and not east. As we all know, Watson did make a few mistakes in his narratives. For example, in this adventure he specified June 19, 1889 as a Friday, when it was in fact a Wednesday. Perhaps he meant July 19.

In addition to finding Isa Whitney in the Bar of Gold, Watson found Holmes. Holmes, disguised as an old man, whispered for Watson to send Isa home in the waiting cab, and wait for him outside. Holmes said that he had to be careful because, the Lascar who ran the Bar of Gold, had sworn vengeance. Watson sent a note to his understanding wife, saying he had "thrown in his lot" with Holmes, who was on a case.

WATERMANS WALK "PAUL'S WHARF"—EC4: [Latitude / Longitude: 51.509076,-0.088642]. Holmes said, "There is a trap-door at the back of that building, near the corner of Paul's Wharf, which could tell some strange tales of what has passed through it upon the moonless nights". **Underground Station: Monument**

Author's note: Watermans Walk fits the location; Today's Paul's Walk is too upstream.

LEE, Lewisham—SE13: [Latitude / Longitude: 51.459907,0.009892]. Holmes was trying to find Neville St. Clair. He and Watson went to The Cedars, St. Clair's house near Lee in Kent. Holmes was staying there while he investigated the disappearance. St. Clair had moved to Kent in May 1884. He appeared to have plenty of money, and took a large country villa. In 1887, he married the daughter of the local brewer, and had two children. **Rail Station: Blackheath**

CANNON STREET RAILWAY STATION—EC4: [Latitude / Longitude: 51.511417,-0.090877]. St. Clair worked in London, and was a man of regular habits, returning home every evening on the 5:14 from Cannon Street Station. "He had no occupation, but was interested in several companies". **Underground Station: Cannon Street**

MARTIN LANE—EC4: [Latitude / Longitude: 51.510616,-0.087873]. The previous Monday, Mrs. St. Clair received word that a package she was expecting, was waiting for her at the Aberdeen Shipping Company. Their offices were on a street that branches out of Upper Swandam (Swan) Lane. Martin Lane matches the location. **Underground Station: Monument**

Having found herself in a very bad part of town, Mrs. St. Clair walked down Upper Swandam (Swan) Lane trying to find a cab. To her surprise, she saw her husband in a second-floor window of the Bar of Gold. After rushing into ground floor, she returned with several constables. The only occupant on the upper floor was Hugh Boone, a crippled wretch who lived there. However, they did find a box of building blocks that Neville had promised to bring home to the children. A further search turned up St. Clair's clothes, with the exception of the coat. There was also blood on the windowsill. The prime suspect was the Lascar manager, but he was on the ground floor when Mrs. St. Clair rushed into the building.

THREADNEEDLE STREET—EC2: [Latitude / Longitude: 51.514159,-0.085874]. Hugh Boone, the crippled lodger, could not explain the presence of St. Clair's clothes. Boone was a professional beggar, and a familiar sight to those who work in the City. He spent his days in Threadneedle Street, selling wax vestas. **Underground Station: Bank**

Boone was taken to the police station, and at low tide, the police found Neville St. Clair's coat in the mud-bank. Every pocket was filled with pennies and halfpennies. Holmes thought that, "It seemed likely enough that the weighted coat had remained when the stripped body had been sucked into the river". However, this would not explain why the rest of the clothes were found in the room.

When Holmes and Watson arrived at The Cedars, they were shocked to hear that Mrs. St. Clair had received a note from her husband. It had a Gravesend postmark, and had been posted the day after St. Clair disappeared. It meant he might still be alive. After Holmes and Watson retired to their rooms, Watson went to sleep, but Holmes spent the night smoking and thinking. In the morning, "The room was full of a dense tobacco haze". Holmes had solved the mystery, and they rushed into London.

WELLINGTON STREET—WC2: [Latitude / Longitude: 51.512289,-0.120765]. From Waterloo Road, Holmes and Watson traveled up Wellington Street, on their way to the old Bow Street Police Court. **Underground Station: Covent Garden**

BOW STREET POLICE COURT—WC2: [Latitude / Longitude: 51.513394,-0.122235]. Inspector Bradstreet was on duty at the Bow Street Police Court when Holmes and Watson arrived. They asked to see Hugh Boone. Holmes had brought a large bath-sponge with him, and proceeded to unmask Boone, who was, in fact, Neville St. Clair, in disguise. **Underground Station: Covent Garden**

Author's note: Founded in 1740, this famous police court was the home of the pre-Scotland Yard London policemen. They were called the Bow Street Runners and were paid by the capture, much as bounty hunters are paid today. The police station closed in 1992, and the adjacent Magistrates' Court closed in 2006.

As a young reporter, St. Clair had gone undercover to write a story on begging. He was amazed at how much money he collected. Later, after co-signing on a friend's loan, he was held responsible. He remembered his skill at begging, and used it to pay off the debt. When he found that he could earn as much in day of begging, as he did in week as a reporter, the choice was obvious. With his "Gentleman's income," he bought a house in the country, married, and raised a family. He rented the upper room in The Bar of Gold, to change from gentleman to beggar, and back again.

THE NAVAL TREATY – 1889?

One July morning, Watson returned to Baker Street to seek Holmes's help. Watson had received a letter from his old public school chum, Percy Phelps. Percy was convalescing in Woking, about 25 miles southwest of London, and asked Watson to bring Holmes on a matter of great importance.

FOREIGN OFFICE, WHITEHALL—SW1: [Latitude / Longitude: 51.502104,-0.126139]. Watson remembered Percy Phelps as a brilliant student, who had won a scholarship to Cambridge. After graduation, he went to work in the Foreign Office at Whitehall. His uncle, Lord Holdhurst, was the Foreign Minister. **Underground Station: Westminster**

WATERLOO RAILWAY STATION—SE1: [Latitude / Longitude: 51.503943,-0.11391]. Holmes and Watson caught an early train from Waterloo Station. Briarbrae, Percy's home, was a large detached house; just a few minutes walk from Woking Station. Later that day, when Holmes and Watson returned to London, they ate at the Waterloo Station's buffet. **Underground Station: Waterloo**

Joseph Harrison, the brother of Percy's fiancée, greeted Holmes and Watson when they arrived at Briarbrae. Percy convalesced in Joseph's old bedchamber, which had been converted into a sickroom. For nearly ten weeks, Annie and a hired nurse cared for Percy night and day. Percy said that his uncle, Lord Holdhurst, had given him an important assignment. He was to remain behind at his desk when everyone had left, and make a copy of a secret Naval Treaty. Charles Gorot shared Percy's office, and he had to wait until Gorot left before beginning his task. Percy hoped he could finish in time to take the eleven-o'clock train to Woking with his future brother-in-law.

At nine, Percy rang for the Tangey, the commissionaire. His charwoman wife answered the bell. Percy asked for a cup of coffee. After some delay, Percy walked down to commissionaire's lodge, and found Mr. Tangey asleep. When he woke him, there was a signal from the call bell in his "empty" office. Percy rushed back, found the treaty missing, and called Scotland Yard. Because Mrs. Tangey had left the building, Percy and Scotland Yard Detective Forbes rushed to the Tangey residence to see if she had stolen it. A search of the house, and a search of Mrs. Tangy by a female policewoman, failed to produce the missing document.

As the full impact of the loss bore on Percy, he became more distraught. A police official drove him to Waterloo Station, and it was only through the help of Dr. Ferrier, a neighbor, that he managed to reach Briarbrae and his quickly created sickroom.

KING CHARLES (CHARLES) STREET—SW1: [Latitude / Longitude: 51.502104,-0.126139]. Percy said that after he discovered the Naval Treaty was missing, he ran to the Charles Street side-door. The door was unlocked, and he thought that whoever stole the naval treaty had entered and left through that door. **Underground Station: Westminster**

"BIG BEN" CLOCK—SW1: [Latitude / Longitude: 51.500946,-0.124115]. When Percy ran to the Foreign Office's Charles Street side-door, he heard three chimes from a neighboring clock. It was a quarter to ten. This had to have come from the nearby Westminster Clock, commonly called "Big Ben". Big Ben refers to the clock's large bell that only chimes on the hour. The quarter chimes come from the "Westminster Quarters" bells. **Underground Station: Westminster**

Author's note: In the British text, it says Percy heard three chimes from "a neighboring church". Percy may have thought it came from a church clock, but the chime had to be from the "Big Ben" clock. Its quarter chimes would overwhelm any nearby church.

CLAPHAM JUNCTION—SW11: [Latitude / Longitude: 51.4655,-0.170749]. After their first visit to Woking, Joseph Harrison drove Holmes and Watson back to the train station. There, they caught the Portsmouth train to London. As they passed Clapham Junction, Holmes remarked, "It's a very cheering thing to come into London by any of these lines which run high and allow you to look down on houses like this". Watson thought he was joking. **Rail Station: Clapham Junction**

From the Woking Station, Holmes sent a telegram to every evening paper in London. Each ad read: ***"10 reward. The number of the cab which dropped a fare at or about the door of the Foreign Office in Charles Street at quarter to ten in the evening of May 23d. Apply 221B Baker Street"***. After eating at Waterloo Station, Holmes and Watson went to meet Detective Forbes and Lord Holdhurst. After getting what information they could, Holmes formed a theory, and asked Watson to accompany him back to Woking the next day.

DOWNING STREET—SW1: [Latitude / Longitude: 51.50317,-0.126196]. Lord Holdhurst, had chambers in Downing Street. It was up to Holmes to find the missing Naval Treaty, and rescue poor Percy's honor. **Underground Station: Westminster**

There were no replies to the newspaper advertisements before Holmes and Watson returned to Woking. In Woking, Percy told them of a strange happening the night before. Percy said he dismissed the night nurse, and was awaked when someone tried to enter his room through the window. The intruder had a cloak wrapped around his face, and a long knife in his hand. Holmes secretly asked Miss Harrison to remain in the sickroom all day, and lock the door when she went to her room. Holmes announced to everyone, that he, Watson, and Percy were going back to London. When they reached the Woking Station, Holmes told Watson to take Percy to Baker Street, while he remained in Woking.

At eight the next morning, Holmes returned at Baker Street with a bandaged hand. He would not tell Percy and Watson about the previous night's adventure until they all had breakfast. When Mrs. Hudson brought in covered dishes, Holmes arranged for the missing treaty to be on Percy's plate. Percy seized Holmes's hand, kissed it, and cried, "You have saved my honour". The day before, Holmes had returned to Briarbrae at dusk, and waited near the sickroom window. At two in the morning, he caught Joseph Harrison breaking into the room. On the day of the theft, Joseph had gone to Percy's office, found the treaty, recognized its value, and took it. When he returned to Woking, he hid the treaty under the floor in his room. When Percy returned home in distress, they converted Joseph's room into a sickroom. Because Percy was attended night and day, Joseph could not retrieve the document. Holmes set up a situation where the room would be vacant, but only accessible through the window.

ADVENTURE OF THE DYING DETECTIVE - 1889?

No. 31 "221B" BAKER STREET—W1: [Latitude / Longitude: 51.517932,-0.155587]. In the second year of his marriage, Watson received a frantic visit from Mrs. Hudson, Holmes's "long-suffering" landlady. She said Holmes was dying, and that Watson must come to Baker Street at once. When he arrived, Holmes told him to stand back, because he had contracted a coolie disease while working a case in Rotherhithe. When Watson started to go for expert medical help, Holmes jumped up, locked the door, and forced Watson to wait until six o'clock. Holmes asked Watson to seek help from Culverton Smith, a well-known expert on oriental diseases. **Underground Station: Marble Arch**

ROTHERHITHE—SE16: [Latitude / Longitude: 51.498849,-0.033048]. In Victorian times, Rotherhithe, the dockside area across the Thames from Wapping, was a very rough place. Holmes said he had picked up a coolie disease there, and returned to Baker Street to die. **Underground Station: Canada Water**

LADBROKE GROVE "LOWER BURKE STREET"—W11: [Latitude / Longitude: 51.512789,-0.20668]. Although Conan Doyle changed the name, Ladbroke Grove fits the location where Culverton Smith rented a house "In the vague borderland between Notting Hill and Kensington". Smith was a well-known planter from Sumatra and an expert on oriental diseases. He had a grudge against Holmes, because Holmes suspected him in the death of his nephew, Victor Savage. **Underground Station: Holland Park**

Holmes asked Watson to plead with Smith to come to Baker Street, but not to return with him. When Watson went outside to hail a cab, he met Inspector Morton of Scotland Yard, who inquired about Holmes. Watson thought he saw a strange look on Morton's face.

Upon arriving at Lower Burke Street, Watson had to force his way in to see Culverton Smith. Although Watson suspected Smith was pleased to hear of Holmes's illness, Smith agreed to come to Baker Street. Following Holmes's instructions, Watson said he had another appointment, and would meet Smith at Baker Street in half an hour. Watson then quickly returned to Baker Street to tell Holmes that Smith was coming. Holmes told Watson to hide behind the bed's headboard.

Smith arrived, and thinking they were alone, admitted he had killed his nephew, and had sent an ivory box to Holmes. The box had a sharp spring inside, with the poisonous disease on its tip. Smith said that after he retrieved the box, there would be no evidence of how he killed Holmes. At that point, Holmes stopped play-acting, and admitted that he had feigned illness to get Smith to admit his guilt. Inspector Morton, who knew of the plan, entered the room and arrested Smith. Smith said it was his word against Holmes's, not realizing that Watson could confirm the confession.

SIMPSON'S IN THE STRAND, No. 100 The Strand—WC2: [**Latitude / Longitude:** <u>51.510906,-0.120463</u>]. After his three day fast to feign illness, Holmes told Watson, "Something nutritious at Simpson's would not be out of place". **Underground Station: Charing Cross**

Author's note: Simpson's, arguably the best-known English restaurant in London, has not changed much since Holmes and Watson dined there. If you order the tableside carved roast beef, remember to give a separate cash tip to the carver.

ADVENTURE OF THE CARDBOARD BOX - 1889?

CROSS ROAD, "CROSS STREET", CROYDON—CR9: [Latitude / Longitude: 51.379499,-0.090684]. One hot August day, Holmes and Watson read that Miss Susan Cushing, of Cross Street, Croydon, had received a cardboard box from Belfast, containing two human ears, packed in coarse rock salt. **Rail Station: East Croydon**

WATERLOO RAILWAY STATION—SE1: [Latitude / Longitude: 51.503943,-0.11391]. Scotland Yard assigned Inspector Lestrade to the case. He sent a note from Croydon, asking for Holmes help. Holmes and Watson left for Croydon from Waterloo Station. **Underground Station: Waterloo**

EAST CROYDON RAILROAD STATION—CR9: [Latitude / Longitude: 51.375722,-0.092229]. When Holmes and Watson arrived at the East Croydon Railroad Station, Lestrade was waiting for them. A five-minute walk brought them to Susan Cushing's house in Cross Street. There, after examining the ears, the package, and talking to Susan, Holmes told Lestrade that this was no practical joke. **Rail Station: East Croydon**

WEST CROYDON RAILROAD STATION—CR0: [Latitude / Longitude: 51.379155,-0.101881]. Holmes learned from Susan, that her sister Sarah had recently moved from Croydon to "New Street" in Wallington. To get there Holmes and Watson had to catch the train from the West Croydon Station. **Rail Station: West Croydon**

WALLINGTON—SM6: [Latitude / Longitude: 51.365846,-0.152683]. On their way to see Sarah, Holmes sent a telegram to his friend Algar, of the Liverpool police force. After arriving in Wallington, they found Sarah Cushing ill. Since they could not talk to her, and had to wait for a reply to the telegram, Holmes suggested they "Have a pleasant little meal at a decent hotel". **Rail Station: Wallington**

TOTTENHAM COURT ROAD—W1: [Latitude / Longitude: 51.518107,-0.131818]. During their meal in Wallington, Holmes talked of nothing but violins. He bragged how he had purchased his Stradivarius from a Jewish pawnbroker in Tottenham Court Road. It was worth at least five hundred guineas, but he had only paid fifty-five shillings. This led to a long discussion of Paganini, and the consumption of a bottle of claret. **Underground Station: Tottenham Court Road**

When they returned to the Croydon police station, Lestrade had a telegram for Holmes. To Lestrade's amazement, Holmes said that the information from Algar confirmed his theory, and that he had solved the case. Holmes also asked that his name be kept out of it, because; "I choose to be only associated with those crimes which present some difficulty in their solution".

KING GEORGE V (ALBERT) DOCK—Liverpool L3: [Latitude / Longitude: 53.400581,-2.991006]. Jim Browner, the steward of a Liverpool boat, sent the ears to Miss S. Cushing, meaning Miss Sarah Cushing. He was aboard the *May Day*, sailing from Belfast to London. Lestrade met the boat at Albert Dock, now called King George V Dock, and arrested Browner. In his letter to Holmes, Lestrade wrote, *"In accordance with the scheme which we had formed in order to test our theories, I went down to Albert Dock".* Holmes thought the use of the word "we" was rather fine. **Dockland Light Rail Station: King George V**

Jim Browner had married Mary Cushing, Susan and Sarah's younger sister. Sarah came for an extended visit, and fell in love with Jim. When he spurned her advances, her passion turned to hate, and she began poisoning Mary's mind against him. Sarah introduced Mary to Alec Fairbairn, with whom she fell in love. When Jim realized what was happening, and who was behind it, he told Sarah, "If Fairbairn shows his face here again; I'll send you one of his ears for a keepsake". Later, Browner found Mary and Alec together. In a blind rage, he killed them, cut off one of their ears, and sent them to Sarah. The package was addressed to "S. Cushing, Croydon", but was delivered to Susan.

116

HOUND OF THE BASKERVILLES - 1889

CHARING CROSS HOSPITAL (site)—**WC2:** **[Latitude / Longitude: 51.50944,-0.123956].** One morning in the autumn of 1889, while Holmes was out, he had a visitor who could not wait. The visitor left his walking stick, and as usual, it revealed more to Holmes than it did to Watson. The stick belonged to Dr. James Mortimer. His colleagues at the Charing Cross Hospital had presented it in 1884, when Dr. Mortimer left to go into private country practice. **Underground Station: Charing Cross**

No. 31 "221B" BAKER STREET—W1: [Latitude / Longitude: 51.517932,-0.155587]. In 1889, Dr. Mortimer was in London to meet Sir Henry Baskerville. Sir Henry's ship from Canada had just arrived at Southampton. Sir Henry was the heir of the late Sir Charles Baskerville. Mortimer came to Baker Street to ask Sherlock's advice. He showed Holmes an old manuscript about the Hound of the Baskervilles. At first, Holmes was skeptical, but became more interested when Dr. Mortimer said, on the night of Sir Charles's death; he had seen footprints of a gigantic hound near the body. **Underground Station: Marble Arch**

WATERLOO RAILWAY STATION—SE1: [Latitude / Longitude: 51.503943,-0.11391]. Dr. Mortimer did not know what to tell Sir Henry when he arrived at Waterloo Station. Sir Henry was the last of the Baskervilles, and Dr. Mortimer felt hesitant about taking the young baronet to his Devonshire estate. Holmes said he needed twenty-four hours to think about the problem, and advised Mortimer to say nothing of the curse until then. Later in the adventure, Waterloo Station is where cabbie John Clayton dropped off his fare after they followed Sir Henry and Dr. Mortimer. **Underground Station: Waterloo**

OXFORD STREET—W1: [Latitude / Longitude: 51.514115,-0.152178]. After Dr. Mortimer left, Holmes sent Watson on errands to keep him out all day. Holmes needed solitude "in those hours of intense mental concentration". Holmes asked Watson to have Bradley's, the Oxford Street tobacconist, send up a pound of their strongest shag. It was almost nine when Watson returned. The room was so thick with smoke that Watson thought there had been a fire. **Underground Station: Bond Street**

STANFORD'S "STAMFORD'S", No. 12-14 Long Acre—WC2: [Latitude / Longitude: 51.512215,-0.126235]. While Watson was out, Holmes sent to Stamford's for a large-scale Ordnance map of that portion of the moor containing Baskerville Hall. **Underground Station: Covent Garden**

Author's note: Although Conan Doyle changed the name slightly, Stanford's famous old map shop, founded in 1852, is still in business.

"NORTHUMBERLAND HOTEL" (site), Northumberland Avenue, between Great Scotland Yard and Whitehall Place— WC2: [Latitude / Longitude: 51.506873,-0.124315]. On the west side of Northumberland Avenue, from Great Scotland Yard south to Whitehall Place, is a building that was the Hotel Metropole. This is my candidate for being the Northumberland Hotel, where Sir Henry Baskerville and Doctor Mortimer stayed. While at the hotel, Sir Henry had one of his new tan boots stolen. He had placed them outside his door to be polished. In the morning, only one boot was there. Later, the new tan boot was returned, and an old black one taken. **Underground Station: Embankment**

Author's note: In Holmes's day, there were three "grand" hotels on Northumberland. The Grand Hotel, No. 8 Northumberland is the only one still open for business. An appropriate substitute is the Royal Horseguards Hotel **[Latitude / Longitude: 51.506071,-0.124415],** at the foot of Northumberland, next to Victoria Embankment Gardens. The hotel fronts on Horseguards Avenue. Because of its location, the Royal Horseguards is one of my favorite London hotels, and an excellent hotel choice for Sherlock Holmes fans.

SHERLOCK HOLMES PUB, 10 Northumberland Street—WC2: [Latitude / Longitude: 51.507237,-0.125332]. The Sherlock Holmes Pub has made a claim for being Baskerville's Northumberland Hotel. By the time of this adventure, the pub had changed its name from The Northumberland Hotel, to The Northumberland Arms. The new name more correctly reflects its character as a modest pub/hostelry. As such, I do not think this could have been the "Northumberland Hotel", at which the wealthy Sir Henry Baskerville stayed. **Underground Station: Embankment**

Authors note: Today, the pub is a Mecca for Sherlock Holmes fans. In addition to traditional pub grub and drinks, they have a decent upstairs restaurant. Be sure to see the glassed-in replica of the 221B Baker Street sitting room, moved here from the 1951 Festival of Britain site.

THE STRAND—WC2: [Latitude / Longitude: 51.509577,-0.123639]. Sir Henry, who had just arrived from Canada, bought a new pair of tan boots in The Strand. He said he paid six dollars for them, but I wonder if he meant pounds. One shoe was stolen at the Northumberland Hotel before he had them on his feet. **Underground Station: Charing Cross**

CHARING CROSS POST OFFICE (site), South Africa House, Trafalgar Square—WC2: [Latitude / Longitude: 51.507808,-0.126823]. Sir Henry received a note at the Northumberland Hotel with a Charing Cross postmark. The note was made of words cut from the previous day's *Times*, and read, **"As you value your life or your reason, keep away from the moor".** To know that he was staying at the Northumberland Hotel, Holmes suspected that someone was following Sir Henry. **Underground Station: Charing Cross**

OXFORD CIRCUS—W1: [Latitude / Longitude: 51.515315,-0.142061]. Having honored Holmes request for 24 hours of silence, Dr. Mortimer brought Sir Henry to Baker Street. After hearing of the Baskerville curse, Sir Henry asked Holmes and Watson to meet them that afternoon at the hotel. As Sir Henry and Mortimer walked back, Holmes and Watson secretly trailed behind, trying to see who was following them. At Oxford Circus, they turned south on Regent Street. **Underground Station: Oxford Circus**

REGENT STREET—W1: [Latitude / Longitude: 51.512112,-0.139732]. As Holmes and Watson walked along Regent Street, they noticed a hansom cab following Sir Henry. They tried to get a good look at the passenger, but the cab sped away, Holmes now knew that Baskerville had been closely shadowed since he arrived in London. Holmes remarked that using a cab had a disadvantage. He had seen the cab's number, "2704". Holmes and Watson went into the Regent Street office of the District Messenger Service. Holmes had previously helped the manager, and asked for the loan of young Cartwright. **Underground Station: Piccadilly Circus**

Holmes sent young Cartwright to each of the twenty-three hotels in the Charing Cross area, and gave him twenty-three shillings, one for each of the hotel outside porters. Cartwright asked to see yesterday's waste paper, and looked for a *Times* with holes cut out of a particular page.

BOND STREET—W1: [Latitude / Longitude: 51.511532,-0.143664]. To kill time before their two o'clock appointment, Holmes and Watson walked to Bond Street, and spent the afternoon in the art galleries. The works of the modern Belgian masters particularly interested Holmes. **Underground Station: Oxford Circus**

PADDINGTON RAILWAY STATION—W2: [Latitude / Longitude: <u>51.515637,-0.175678</u>]. After Holmes and Watson met Sir Henry and Dr. Mortimer at the Northumberland Hotel, they agreed that Watson would accompany Sir Henry to Baskerville Hall, on Saturday's ten-thirty train from Paddington. Because of the press of other business, Holmes said he could not go at that time. **Underground Station: Paddington**

SOUTHWARK, Near Waterloo Station—SE1: [Latitude / Longitude: <u>51.50013,-0.110657</u>]. Although young Cartwright failed to find the hotel from which the note was sent, Holmes did locate the driver of the hansom cab. His name was John Clayton, who lived at the fictional Turpey Street in the Borough of Southwark. Clayton said that his fare was a detective. When Holmes asked the name he had given, Clayton replied, "Mr. Sherlock Holmes," Holmes burst into a hearty laugh, and told Watson, "This time we have…a foeman who is worthy of our steel". Conan Doyle gave 3 Turpey Street as John Clayton's fictitious street address. Since Clayton kept his horse and cab at Shipley's Yard, near Waterloo Station, we can assume he lived nearby. **Underground Station: Waterloo**

TRAFALGAR SQUARE—WC2: [Latitude / Longitude <u>51.508195,-0.127201</u>]. John Clayton said he picked up his fare at Trafalgar Square. First, they drove to the Northumberland Hotel and followed Sir Henry and Dr. Mortimer to Baker Street. Then they followed them as they walked back to the hotel. Clayton said that when they were three-quarters down Regent Street, his fare "threw up the trap, and cried that I should drive to Waterloo Station as hard as I could". **Underground Station: Charing Cross**

ROYAL COLLEGE OF SURGEONS, No. 35 Lincoln's Inn Fields—WC2: [Latitude / Longitude: <u>51.515527,-0.116334</u>]. On Saturday, when they all met at Paddington Station, Dr. Mortimer said that he and Sir Henry had stayed together the whole time in London, except for Friday afternoon, when he went alone to the Museum of the College of Surgeons. **Underground Station: Holborn**

ST. JAMES'S PARK—SW1: [Latitude / Longitude: 51.502813,-0.129575]. Sir Henry said he spent his afternoon walking in the park. He did not say which park, but it was probably St. James's, the nearest park to the Northumberland Hotel. **Underground Station: St. James's Park**

NOTTING HILL—W11: [Latitude / Longitude: 51.519899,-0.200779]. On Saturday, Sir Henry, Mortimer, and Watson left London. Sir Henry had never been to Baskerville Hall, and looked forward to seeing the old family seat. When they arrived, they noticed soldiers patrolling the roads. Selden, the Notting Hill murderer had escaped from Princetown Prison. **Underground Station: Westbourne Park**

Barrymore and his wife greeted the trio when they arrived at Baskerville Hall. The Barrymore's, in addition to the scullery-maid and Perkins the groom, were the Hall's only servants. The wagonette drove on to take Dr. Mortimer home. After dinner, Sir Henry and Watson retired, but were awakened by what they thought was the sound of a woman crying. Watson reported this and all subsequent events to Holmes in London.

The next morning, Watson went into the village of Grimpen to talk to the postmaster. There he met Stapleton, the naturalist of Merripit House. Stapleton followed Holmes's exploits, and knew Watson was Sherlock's companion. Stapleton and his sister Beryl were relative newcomers, having only lived at Merripit House for two years. Stapleton pointed out the great Grimpen Mire, and told Watson, "A false step yonder means death to man or beast". Stapleton knew safe paths through the Mire, and re-discovered the location of Neolithic dwellings. One day, as they explored the moor, Baskerville and Watson stopped for lunch at Merripit House. Sir Henry was immediately attracted to Miss Stapleton, and was puzzled by Stapleton's objection to his attention.

One night, at Baskerville Hall, Watson and Sir Henry caught Barrymore signaling from the upstairs window. After spirited questioning, they found that Selden, the escaped prisoner, was Mrs. Barrymore's younger brother. The Barrymore's had been sending him food, and some of Baskerville's cast-off clothes. Sir Henry and Watson went out to capture Selden. They caught sight of him, but he was too fast and escaped.

Watson caught sight of another tall thin man on the tor. Barrymore said that he had also seen him, and that he was living in "The stone huts, where the old folks used to live". After seeing a boy delivering food, Watson knew where the stranger was staying. When he went to confront him, he found that the stranger was Holmes, who had secretly followed Watson to Devonshire. Watson's reports to Baker Street were being rerouted to Holmes. Holmes also revealed that the lady that everyone thought was Stapleton's sister was in fact, his wife. He was the one who tracked Sir Henry in London.

CRAVEN STREET—WC2: [Latitude / Longitude: 51.507736.-0.125393]. When Sir Henry first arrived in London, Stapleton brought his wife to London and lodged at the "Mexborough Private Hotel" in Craven Street. This may refer to the Craven Hotel at No. 45 Craven Street. Because she did not agree with his plan, he kept her imprisoned in the room while he followed Dr. Mortimer to and from Baker Street. **Underground Station: Charing Cross**

BRITISH MUSEUM, Great Russell Street—WC1: [Latitude / Longitude: 51.518406,-0.12584]. Holmes told Watson, that Stapleton had been a schoolmaster in the North of England, and had used the name Vandeleur. When the school failed, the couple changed their names to Stapleton and moved south. The British Museum considered Stapleton a recognized authority of entomology. **Underground Station: Tottenham Court Road**

As Holmes brought Watson up to date, they heard a terrible scream. Rushing out, they found a man, savaged and killed by a giant hound. At first, they thought the victim was Sir Henry, but it was Selden, the escaped convict, dressed in Baskerville's cast-off clothes. When Holmes and Watson returned to the Hall, Holmes was very interested in the Baskerville family portraits. He could see a family resemblance in Stapleton. He was a Baskerville, and the motive for his plan to kill off the other heirs became clear. Holmes decided to set a trap. After dinner at Merripit House, Baskerville was to say he was walking back to the Hall alone. Stapleton could not let this opportunity go by. Holmes also sent a telegram to Inspector Lestrade, who wrote back, *"Wire received. Coming down with unsigned warrant. Arrive five-forty".*

As Sir Henry left Merripit House, to walk back to Baskerville Hall, Stapleton released the hound. Holmes, Watson and Lestrade waited outside, and managed to wound the beast as it ran by. Just as it pounced on Sir Henry, Holmes emptied five shots into the creature, killing it. Sir Henry, Holmes, Watson and Lestrade went back to Merripit House to arrest Stapleton. He had fled, but left his beaten wife in one of the bedchambers. It was useless to track Stapleton at night, so they waited until morning. In the Grimpen Mire, they followed Stapleton's tracks and found Baskervilles lost black boot. It had been used to give Baskerville's scent to the hound. Stapleton was not found, and Watson hoped he was down in the foul slime.

FULHAM ROAD—SW6: [Latitude / Longitude: 51.480227,-0.198333]. Stapleton bought the hound from Ross & Mangles, dog dealers in Fulham Road. **Underground Station: Fulham Broadway**

ROYAL OPERA HOUSE, Covent Garden—WC2: [Latitude / Longitude: 51.513445,-0.122362]. After the successful conclusion of the case, Holmes reserved a box at the Royal Opera House for "Les Huguenots". Holmes suggested that he and Watson stop at Marcini's for a little dinner on the way. **Underground Station: Covent Garden**

CASE OF IDENTITY - 1889?

No. 31 "221B" BAKER STREET—W1: [Latitude / Longitude: 51.517932,-0.155587]. On the advice of Mrs. Etherege, Mary Sutherland came to seek Sherlock's help. After being shown in by the page, she told Holmes that her fiancé had vanished on their wedding day. **Underground Station: Marble Arch**

CAMBERWELL—SE5: [Latitude / Longitude: 51.473769,-0.091954]. Mary lived with her mother and stepfather at the fictional No. 31 Lyon Place in Camberwell. She was engaged to Hosner Angel, but did not know where he lived. Mary worked as a typist, but also had an income of one hundred pounds a year from inherited stock. Since she lived at home, and did not want to be a burden, she gave the stock income to her mother and stepfather. **Rail Station: Denmark Hill**

TOTTENHAM COURT ROAD—W1: [Latitude / Longitude: 51.518107,-0.131818]. Mary Sutherland's father had been a plumber in the Tottenham Court Road. When he died, her mother carried on the business. When she remarried, her new husband, James Windibank, insisted that she sell the business. Windibank thought a plumbing business was beneath his position as a salesman of French wines. **Tottenham Court Road**

FENCHURCH STREET—EC3: [Latitude / Longitude: 51.511981,-0.08063]. Mary Sutherland's stepfather, James Windibank, worked for Westhouse and Marbank, the great claret importers of Fenchurch Street. Because her father had been a plumber, Mary received an invitation to the Gasfitters Ball. Her stepfather did not want her to go, but she insisted and there, met Hosner Angel. **Underground Station: Aldgate**

LEADENHALL STREET—EC3: [Latitude / Longitude: 51.513313,-0.079342]. Mary Sutherland said Hosner Angel, was a cashier in an office in Leadenhall Street. She did not know which office. When she wrote him, she addressed her letters to general delivery at the Leadenhall Street Post Office. **Underground Station: Aldgate**

James Windibank had to go to France regularly on business. Because he and Mary's mother wanted to keep receiving Mary's stock income, they came up with the scheme to have Windibank disguise himself as Hosner Angel, and romance Mary. They wanted Mary to become so committed to Hosner that when he disappeared, she would not be interested in other men, always hoping that Hosner would return.

ST. SAVIOUR'S CHURCH (site), northwest corner of Whitfield and Maple Streets—W1: [Latitude / Longitude: 51.522632,-0.137565]. Mary and Hosner made plans to marry at St. Saviour's, Church near King's Cross. On the way to the church, Hosner put Mary and her mother in a hansom, and followed in a four-wheeler. When they arrived, the four-wheeler was empty—Hosner Angel had vanished. **Underground Station: Warren Street**

ST. PANCRAS HOTEL, Euston Road—WC1: [Latitude / Longitude: 51.529469,-0.125635]. Mary Sutherland and Hosner Angel planned their wedding breakfast at the St. Pancras Hotel. Built in 1868, this ornate Victorian hotel has reopened as the Renaissance St. Pancras. **Underground Station: King's Cross/St. Pancras**

Holmes exposed Windibank as the scoundrel who deceived his stepdaughter by wooing her in the guise of Hosner Angel. However, since no law was broken, Holmes could not have him arrested. Holmes did not even tell Mary of the plot, because he knew she would not believe him.

ADVENTURE OF THE BLUE CARBUNCLE - 1889?

KILBURN—NW6: [Latitude / Longitude: 51.54403,-0.203215].
Scotland Yard's Inspector Bradstreet suspected John Horner, a plumber,
of stealing the Countess of Morcar's blue carbuncle from her suite at the
Hotel Cosmopolitan. James Ryder, upper-attendant at the hotel, said
that he had shown Horner up to the Countess's dressing room on the
day of the robbery. What the police did not know was that Ryder had
heard from his friend, Maudsley, how thieves could dispose of stolen
property. Maudsley lived in Kilburn. **Underground Station: Kilburn**

PENTONVILLE PRISON, Caledonian Road—N7: [Latitude /
Longitude: 51.544898,-0.117803]. James Ryder's friend Maudsley
served time in Pentonville Prison. **Underground Station: Caledonian
Road & Barnsbury**

Author's note: Construction of this "model" prison was
completed in 1842. It was designed in the panopticon plan, with a
central hall, and five radiating wings. At the time, Pentonville
introduced conditions that were vastly better than those at
Newgate, and other older prisons.

No. 117 BRIXTON ROAD—SW9: [Latitude / Longitude:
51.477162,-0.11235]. After hearing about the blue carbuncle from
Catherine Cusack, the Countess of Morcar's maid, James Ryder stole the
precious gem, and took it to his sister's house. The sister, Maggie Oakshott,
lived at No. 117 Brixton Road. Without telling her, Ryder forced the
gem into the crop of the Christmas goose she was fattening for him.
After John Horner's arrest, Ryder returned to claim his goose. He
took the bird to Kilburn, where he and Maudsley attempted to recover
the gem. To their dismay, Ryder had selected the wrong goose.
Underground Station: Oval

GOODGE STREET and TOTTENHAM COURT ROAD—W1:

[**Latitude / Longitude: 51.520108,-0.133919**]. On his way home with the Christmas goose, Henry Baker was assaulted at the corner of Goodge Street and Tottenham Court Road, by a "knot of roughs". One of the roughs knocked off Henry's hat, and when he raised his walking stick to defend himself, he smashed a shop window. At that point, Peterson, the commissionaire, who was also walking home, saw the fracas, and rushed to help. The roughs and Henry Baker saw him as an official looking person in uniform, and ran away. Peterson, "was left in possession of the field of battle, and also…the spoils of victory," including the battered hat, and the goose. Peterson brought the hat and goose to Holmes. Because there were signs it should be eaten immediately, Holmes gave the goose back to Peterson, and kept the hat. **Underground Station: Goodge Street**

No. 31 "221B" BAKER STREET—W1: [Latitude / Longitude: 51.517932,-0.155587]. Holmes examined Henry Baker's hat as an intellectual exercise. Watson was amazed at what Holmes deduced. At that point, the door flew open and in rushed Peterson, the commissionaire. He had discovered the gem. Holmes placed an advertisement in all of the evening papers, asking for Mr. Henry Baker, whose name had been on the goose tag, to come to 221B Street, to claim his hat and (replacement) goose. When Henry Baker arrived at Baker Street, Holmes learned of the Alpha Inn's goose club. He was convinced that Baker had no knowledge of the gem. **Underground Station: Marble Arch**

Author's note: Holmes and Watson left Baker Street to walk to the Alpha Inn. Watson said, "Our footfalls rang out crisply and loudly as we swung through the doctors' quarter, Wimpole Street, Harley Street, and through Wigmore Street into Oxford Street. In a quarter of an hour, we were in Bloomsbury at the Alpha Inn". We can follow their path on modern streets, some of which have had their names changed since 1889. Because of modern traffic and crossing rules, this 1.6-mile journey will take twice as long today.

BLANDFORD STREET—W1: [Latitude / Longitude: 51.518455,-0.153058]. **From 221B Baker Street,** Blandford Street was the nearest street heading east. On their walk to the Alpha Inn, Holmes and Watson probably took Blandford Street to Marylebone Lane. **Underground Station: Bond Street**

MARYLEBONE LANE—W1: [Latitude / Longitude: 51.517258,-0.150772]. From Blandford Street, Holmes and Watson followed Marylebone Lane as it headed south. **Underground Station: Bond Street**

WIGMORE STREET—W1: [Latitude / Longitude: 51.516445,-0.148251]. Where Marylebone Lane met Wigmore Street, Holmes and Watson turned left and headed east on Wigmore Street. **Underground Station: Bond Street**

WIMPOLE STREET—W1: [Latitude / Longitude: 51.51663,-0.147554]. As Holmes and Watson continued east on Wigmore Street, they crossed Wimpole Street. **Underground Station: Bond Street**

HARLEY STREET—W1: [Latitude / Longitude: 51.516853,-0.145999]. As Holmes and Watson continued east on Wigmore Street, they crossed Harley Street. Cavendish Square was on their right as the street's name changed to Cavendish Place. **Underground Station: Oxford Circus**

CAVENDISH PLACE—W1: [Latitude / Longitude: 51.51736,-0.143684]. As Holmes and Watson continued east on Wigmore Street, they crossed Harley Street as Wigmore Street changed to Cavendish Place. **Underground Station: Oxford Circus**

MORTIMER STREET—W1: [Latitude / Longitude: 51.518056,-0.139215]. Holmes and Watson continued east on Cavendish Place as the street's name changed to Mortimer Street. **Underground Station: Oxford Circus**

WELLS STREET—W1: [Latitude / Longitude: 51.516276,-0.137088]. Holmes and Watson continued east on Mortimer Street until they reached Wells Street. There they turned south toward Oxford Street. **Underground Station: Oxford Circus**

OXFORD STREET—W1: [Latitude / Longitude: 51.516029,-0.135067]. Then, as today, Oxford Street is very busy. Holmes and Watson continued east on Oxford Street. **Underground Station: Oxford Circus**

SOHO STREET—W1: [Latitude / Longitude: 51.516284,-0.132909]. When Holmes and Watson passed Soho Street, they could see Soho Square in the distance. **Underground Station: Tottenham Court Road**

HANWAY PLACE—W1: [Latitude / Longitude: 51.516523,-0.132598]. As they continued on their journey to the Alpha Inn, Holmes and Watson crossed Soho Street before turning north on the narrow Hanway Place. **Underground Station: Tottenham Court Road**

HANWAY STREET—W1: [Latitude / Longitude: 51.517064,-0.130915]. From Hanway Place, Holmes and Watson bore right on Hanway Street toward Tottenham Court Road. Across the road lay Great Russell Street. **Underground Station: Tottenham Court Road**

GREAT RUSSELL STREET—WC1: [Latitude / Longitude: 51.517696,-0.128126]. As Holmes and Watson walked east on Great Russell Street, up ahead, the British Museum was on the left, and the Alpha Inn was on the right. **Underground Station: Tottenham Court Road**

MUSEUM TAVERN, "ALPHA INN", 49 Great Russell Street—WC1: [Latitude / Longitude: 51.518308,-0.126046]. The "Alpha Inn" was near the British Museum, "At the corner of one of the streets which run down into Holborn". Some of the inn's regulars, including Henry Baker, formed a goose club. By contributing a few pence each week, they each received a Christmas, goose. It was Henry Baker's luck to receive the goose with the blue carbuncle. **Underground Station: Holborn**

THE PLOUGH, "ALPHA INN", Little Russell Street—WC1: [Latitude / Longitude: 51.517752,-0.125604]. The Plough, at the corner of Little Russell and Museum Streets is the pub favored by Bernard Davies as being the "Alpha Inn". Like the Museum Tavern, it is "at the corner of one of the streets which run down into Holborn". **Underground Station: Holborn**

Holmes and Watson found that Windigate, the Alpha Inn's proprietor, had bought two dozen geese from Breckinridge's stand in Covent Garden. In spite of the bitter cold, Holmes realized that their trek was not over, as he said, "Faces to the south then, and quick march". This would add .6 of a mile to their walk from Baker Street.

MUSEUM STREET—WC1: [Latitude / Longitude: 51.516509,-0.124615]. Holmes and Watson started their walk from the Alpha Inn to Covent Garden by heading south on Museum Street. ". They crossed New Oxford Street and High Holborn, as they continued on to Drury Lane. **Underground Station: Holborn**

DRURY LANE—WC2: [Latitude / Longitude: 51.515753,-0.123722]. As Museum Street ends at High Holborn, Holmes and Watson continued south on Dury Lane until they reached Shorts Gardens. **Underground Station: Holborn**

SHORTS GARDENS—WC2: [Latitude / Longitude: 51.515295,-0.124252]. From Drury Lane, Holmes and Watson turned southwest on Shorts Gardens, or as Watson put it, "through a zigzag of slums". **Underground Station: Covent Garden**

ENDELL STREET—WC2: [Latitude / Longitude: 51.514091,-0.123931]. From Shorts Garden, Holmes and Watson turned south on Endell Street. When they reached Long Acre, they could see the end of Bow Street to their left. **Underground Station: Covent Garden**

LONG ACRE—WC2: [Latitude / Longitude: 51.513617,-0.123621]. Holmes and Watson zigzagged southwest on Long Acre until they reached James Street, the path to Covent Garden. **Underground Station: Covent Garden**

JAMES STREET—WC2: [Latitude / Longitude: 51.513009,-0.123983]. Holmes and Watson were almost to Covent Garden as they walked down James Street from Long Acre. **Underground Station: Covent Garden**

COVENT GARDEN—WC2: [Latitude / Longitude: 51.51148,-0.12287]. Breckinridge had a goose stand in Covent Garden. The goose with the blue carbuncle was among the two dozen sold to the Alpha Inn. Holmes used trickery to get Breckinridge to tell where he had purchased the geese. As they left, Holmes and Watson saw James Ryder, who was also pestering Breckinridge for information. **Underground Station: Covent Garden**

They took Ryder back to Baker Street, where Holmes said he knew all. The pitiful Ryder collapsed, and begged for mercy. Holmes let him flee the country, and without his testimony, the case against John Horner collapsed.

COPPER BEECHES - 1890?

No. 31 "221B" BAKER STREET—W1: [Latitude / Longitude: 51.517932,-0.155587]. One foggy spring morning, after breakfast, Holmes and Watson discussed how Watson chronicled Sherlock's cases. Holmes wanted the emphasis to be on the logic involved. He told Watson, "You have degraded what should have been a course of lectures into a series of tales", (A fact for which Sherlock Holmes fans are grateful.). As he used tongs to pick up a glowing cinder to light his long cherry-wood pipe, Holmes remarked, "The days of great cases are past". Holmes used a cherry-wood pipe to replace his clay, "when he was in a disputatious rather than a meditative mood". To prove the point, Holmes showed Watson a letter he had received from Violet Hunter. **Underground Station: Marble Arch**

MONTAGUE PLACE—WC1: [Latitude / Longitude: 51.520907,-0.127119]. Violet Hunter's letter came from Montague Place. It read, ***"Dear Mr. Holmes: I am very anxious to consult you as to whether I should or should not accept a situation, which has been offered to me as governess. I shall call at half-past ten tomorrow if I do not inconvenience you. Yours faithfully, Violet Hunter".*** **Underground Station: Russell Square**

Just as Holmes remarked that, he did not know the young lady, the doorbell ring. Miss Hunter "was plainly, but neatly, dressed, with a bright quick face, freckled like a plover's egg". She said, "I have been a governess for five years…in the family of Colonel Spence Murro, but two months ago the colonel received an appointment in Halifax…so I found myself without a situation". She used Westaway's, a well-known agency, to help her find a new governess position. Miss Stoner managed the agency.

One day, when she checked at Westaway's, Miss Stoner was not alone. Mr. Jephro Rucastle was looking for a governess for his six-year-old son. Mr. Rucastle and his wife lived in The Copper Beeches, five miles from Winchester, in Hampshire. Rucastle offered Violet a salary of £100 per year, even though she said she had only received £4 a month from Colonel Munro. However, there were conditions. Violet must wear any dress the Rucastle's might give her, and cut her hair quite short before she arrived. Violet did not feel comfortable with the conditions, and turned down the position.

Violet received a letter from the gentleman himself. She showed it to Holmes. Rucastle increased his offer to £120 per year, explained that his wife was partial to electric blue, and wanted Violet to wear a dress of that color. He said that Violet need not buy the dress, because they had one that belonged to their daughter, who now lived in Philadelphia. The strange offer, and its conditions, worried Violet, and she wanted Holmes's advice. Holmes said, "I confess that it is not the situation which I should like a sister of mine to apply for". If Violet did accept the position, Holmes said, "Any time, day or night, a telegram (from you) would bring me down to your help". The expected telegram came late one night. It read, *"Please be at the Black Swan Hotel at Winchester at midday to-morrow. Do come! I am at my wits end. Hunter"*

WATERLOO RAILWAY STATION—SE1: [Latitude / Longitude: 51.503943,-0.11391]. In the 1890's, as now, trains from London to Winchester leave from Waterloo Station. Holmes and Watson's train left at half-past nine, and arrived in Winchester at 11:30. They were curious about Violet Hunter's predicament, since she had the freedom to meet them in Winchester. **Underground Station: Waterloo**

The Black Swan was in the High Street, and Violet was there to meet them. She explained that although she had not been physically mistreated, she was still uncomfortable with her situation at The Copper Beeches. She said the house was unattractive, but well situated. The grounds in front belong to the house, but the woods on three sides were part of Lord Southerton's preserves. Violet said her employers had been married about seven years. He had been a widower, with a daughter who had gone to Philadelphia. Mrs. Rucastle seemed to have some secret sorrow, and several times Violet caught her crying. Their son, Edward, was spoiled, and enjoyed inflicting pain on small creatures. The house has two servants, an unpleasant couple named Toller.

On the third day after her arrival, Mr. Rucastle had requested Violet put on the blue dress, and sit in a chair with her back to the window. Rucastle then began telling stories that were so funny that Violet became weak from laughter. After an hour or so, Rucastle said the Violet could take off the blue dress, and go mind little Edward in the nursery. Two days later, this performance occurred again, in the same sequence. However, this time, Rucastle asked Violet to read from a yellow-backed novel. Violet noticed that she was always placed with her back to the window. She managed to hide a small piece of broken minor in her handkerchief. Through it, she noticed a man standing in the Southampton Road. Mrs. Rucastle noticed the ruse and said, "Jephro...there is an impertinent fellow upon the road there who stares up at Miss Hunter". Mr. Rucastle asked Violet to turn around and motion him to go away.

Violet was also shown Rucastle's giant mastiff, which prowled the grounds at night to discourage visitors. Rucastle said that Toller was the only person who could handle the dog. Violet thought that someone was being held prisoner in the old wing of the house. Holmes surmised that the prisoner was Alice Rucastle, and that the man in the road was her friend, or fiancé. Violet's height, figure, and hair color, matched Alice Rucastle, and Violet had been brought to The Copper Beeches to indicate to the man that Alice no longer desired his attention.

Holmes and Watson went to the house to free Alice. When they opened the locked room, she was gone. Rucastle burst into the room, and seeing his daughter gone, ran down the steps to release the mastiff. The dog had not been fed for two days, and attacked Rucastle. Watson ran up and shot the dog in the head. They carried Rucastle into the house, and learned from Mrs. Toller that she had helped Mr. Fowler, Alice's fiancé, rescue Alice. Alice was being held prisoner because she would not assign her income to her father. Rucastle survived, a broken man, kept alive by his wife. Mr. Fowler and Alice Rucastle were married, and he received a government appointment in Mauritius.

PADDINGTON RAILWAY STATION—W2: [Latitude / Longitude: 51.515637,-0.175678]. One Thursday morning, Holmes asked Watson to accompany him to the King's Pyland training stable in Dartmoor. Silver Blaze, the horse favored to win the Wessex Cup, was missing, and his trainer murdered. Holmes and Watson were just in time to catch the Dartmoor train from Paddington. On the trip, Holmes wore his ear-flapped traveling cap, (A reference to his famous deerstalker). As an amusement, he calculated the train's speed by observing and timing the passing telegraph poles. **Underground Station: Paddington**

Colonel Ross owned King's Pyland. John Straker, the murdered man, had been his jockey for five years, and a trainer for seven. Mapleton, another training facility owned by Lord Backwater, was nearby. Silas Brown managed Mapleton. The surrounding moor was a complete wilderness, inhabited only by a few roaming gypsies. Holmes assumed that a horse as well known as Silver Blaze would be quickly found, but it was not.

Three stable boys guarded the horses at King's Pyland. At least one was on duty at all times. The night Silver Blaze disappeared; Fitzroy Simpson, a racing tout, tried to get information from the stable boy on duty. The next morning, Silver Blaze was missing, and they found the stable boy drugged. The drug had been put in the boy's curry mutton dinner. John Straker was also missing. They found him, a quarter of a mile from the stables, dead from a blow to the head. In his hands, he had a small knife, and Fitzroy Simpson's cravat.

When Holmes and Watson arrived in Dartmoor, Inspector Gregory and Colonel Ross greeted them. Gregory had arrested Fitzroy Simpson, whose story was that he had just come down to get some advance information on the two favorites, Silver Blaze, and Desborough. He could not explain how his cravat came to be in Straker's hand. In Straker's pocket, they found, a box of vestas, a tallow candle, a brier-root pipe, a tobacco pouch, a sliver watch with a gold chain, five sovereigns in gold, an aluminum pencil case, and a few papers.

The ivory handled knife in his hand had a delicate blade. One of the papers was a milliner's account for thirty-seven pounds fifteen, made out to William Derbyshire. Mrs. Straker said that Derbyshire was a friend of her late husband, and occasionally had his letters addressed to King's Pyland.

After examining the scene of Straker's death, Holmes and Watson walked across the moor toward Mapleton stables. On the way, they found Silver Blaze's tracks, along with the tracks of a man. When they arrived at Mapleton, a belligerent Silas Brown met them, but after Holmes whispered in his ear, he became docile. Brown had found Silver Blaze, and disguised the horse by covering his white markings; Holmes gave him instructions on how to make the matter right, or face dismissal and the law. As they walked back to King's Pyland, Holmes mentioned that Colonel Ross had been a trifle cavalier, and he wanted to knock him down a peg or two. Holmes told the Colonel that he and Watson were returning to London. The Colonel was upset because he thought Holmes was giving up, but Holmes said he had every hope that Silver Blaze would run in next Tuesday's race. As Inspector Gregory and the Colonel escorted them to the train station, Holmes called the Inspectors attention to the lame sheep, and, "To the curious incident of the dog in the night-time". The Inspector said, "The dog did nothing in the night-time". To which Holmes replied, "That was the curious incident".

BOND STREET—W1: [Latitude / Longitude: <u>51.511532,-0.143664</u>]. In London, Holmes learned that William Derbyshire was Straker's other persona. He had purchased an expensive women's outfit from Madame Lesurier, a milliner in Bond Street. **Underground Station: Green Park**

Four days later, Holmes and Watson were in Winchester, for the Wessex Cup Race. Colonel Ross was still in the dark, when a solid black horse, ridden by his jockey, won the race. In the weighing enclosure, Holmes said, "You only have to wash his face and his leg in spirits of wine, and you will find that he is the same old Silver Blaze as ever". Holmes explained that Straker was not a loyal employee. He was living a double life as William Derbyshire. He planned to lame Silver Blaze, and had practiced the procedure on the sheep. After drugging the stable boy, Straker took the horse into the moor to perform the delicate operation. The horse, sensing that something was wrong, struck out, killing Straker.

CLAPHAM JUNCTION—SW11: [Latitude / Longitude: 51.4655,-0.170749]. On their way back to London, Colonel Ross, Holmes and Watson passed through Clapham Junction. Colonel Ross said that Holmes still had not indicated where the horse had been kept. Holmes said he had been looked after by one of the Colonel's neighbors, and that, "We must have a little amnesty in that direction". **Rail Station: Clapham Junction**

VICTORIA RAILWAY STATION—SW1: [Latitude / Longitude: 51.496697,-0.144058]. When Holmes, Watson, and Colonel Ross arrived at Victoria Station, Holmes invited Colonel Ross to Baker Street for a cigar, and offered to answer all of his questions. **Underground Station: Victoria**

SECOND STAIN - 1890?

No. 10 DOWNING STREET—SW1: [Latitude / Longitude: 51.503177,-0.126196]. No. 10 Downing Street is the traditional home of the British Prime Minister. It was from there that Lord Bellinger drove to Baker Street to seek Sherlock's help. The Right Honorable Trelawney Hope, Secretary for European Affairs, came with him. They said they could not involve Scotland Yard for fear of the matter being made public. **Underground Station: Westminster**

No. 31 "221B" BAKER STREET—W1: [Latitude / Longitude: 51.517932,-0.155587]. Trelawney Hope explained that he brought home a very important document, and locked it in his dispatch box. He had seen the document the night before, but this morning, it was gone. At first, the Prime Minister refused to tell Holmes what was in the letter, but when Holmes refused the commission without more information, the Prime Minister relented. He said, "It was from a certain foreign potentate who has been ruffled by some recent Colonial developments". Holmes wrote a name on a piece of paper. The Prime Minister agreed that he was the sender. **Underground Station: Marble Arch**

RICHMOND TERRACE—SW1: [Latitude / Longitude: 51.503171,-0.126096]. In my opinion, Richmond Terrace was the site of the Trelawney Hope's Whitehall Terrace townhouse. In 1890, Richmond Terrace was called Whitehall Terrace. For the Prime Minister to come for lunch, the townhouse had to be near Downing Street. **Underground Station: Westminster**

Because the dispatch box was in Trelawney Hope's third floor bedroom, Holmes thought that a member of the household must have taken the document. If so, it was probably in the hands of one of London's international spies. Trelawney Hope said this was impossible because the maid and his valet were old and trusted servants. After the Prime Minister and Trelawney Hope left, Holmes lit his pipe and thought about the problem. Watson read the morning paper. When Holmes mused, "There are only…three (spies) capable of playing so bold a game…Oberstein, La Rothière, and Eduardo Lucas. I will see each of them". Watson asked, "Is that the Eduardo Lucas of Godolphin Street"? Watson had just read about Lucas's murder. Holmes thought the odds of this being a coincidence were enormous.

GAYFERE "GODOLPHIN" STREET—SW1: [Latitude / Longitude: 51.496715,-0.127716]. Eduardo Lucas lived in the fictitious Godolphin Street. In my opinion, Gayfere Street's location makes it a good candidate for being Godolphin Street. **Underground Station: Westminster**

At that point, Holmes and Watson received an unannounced visit from Lady Hilda, Trelawney Hope's wife. She was a well-known beauty, and the youngest daughter of the Duke of Belminster. She asked Holmes to tell her about the missing paper. He refused, saying, "If your husband thinks fit to keep you in the dark…is it for me…to tell what he has withheld". Lady Hilda left, but begged Holmes not to tell her husband about her visit.

For the next several days, Holmes followed leads, and tried to determine the ties between Eduardo Lucas and the missing document. Watson followed the case in the papers, and read about the arrest of John Mitton, Lucas's valet, and his subsequent release.

HAMMERSMITH—W6: [Latitude / Longitude: 51.493859,-0.221186]. John Mitton, Eduardo Lucas's valet, was out the night of the murder, and had an ironclad alibi. He was visiting a friend in Hammersmith. **Underground Station: Hammersmith**

The newspapers reported that Mme. Fournaye had come to London from Paris to see her husband, and there was evidence she had committed the murder. A comparison of photographs proved that M. Henri Fournaye and Eduardo Lucas was the same person.

CHARING CROSS RAILROAD STATION, The Strand—WC2: [Latitude / Longitude: 51.508497,-0.125551]. When Mme. Fournaye returned to Paris, her wild behavior at the Charing Cross Station attracted attention. **Underground Station: Charing Cross**

Holmes received a note from Lestrade, about a queer matter at Godolphin Street. When Holmes and Watson arrived, Lestrade showed them the "queer trifle" he had found. There was a blood spot on the rug that did not have a corresponding stain on the floor beneath. Lestrade showed Holmes the explanation. There was a bloodstain on the floor, but beneath a different corner of the rug. Lestrade wanted to know who had moved the carpet, and why. Holmes suggested that Lestrade question the constable posted at the front of the house. While Lestrade went outside, Holmes and Watson hurriedly removed the rug, and searched the floor. Holmes found a hidden compartment, but it was empty. They just had time to replace the rug before Lestrade returned. Constable MacPherson admitted he had allowed a young woman to see the crime scene. When she fainted, MacPherson went to the nearby Ivy Plant Pub for some brandy. When he returned, she was gone. As Holmes and Watson left the house, Holmes showed a picture of Lady Hilda to MacPherson, who shouted, "Good Lord, sir!"

MARQUIS OF GRANBY "IVY PLANT PUB", No. 41 Romney Street—SW1: [Latitude / Longitude: 51.495305,-0.127278]. Today, the closest public house to Godolphin (Gayfere) Street is the Marquis of Granby, which was established in 1873. Is this the Ivy Plant Pub mentioned in the story? It makes sense that MacPherson would go to the nearest pub to get brandy. **Underground Station: Westminster**

Lady Hilda was upset when Holmes and Watson came to Whitehall Terrace to see her. She wanted to keep her visit to Baker Street a secret. Holmes said that he had no alternative. "I have been commissioned to recover this immensely important paper. I must therefore ask you…to be kind enough to place it in my hands". After some persuasion, Lady Hilda admitted she had been blackmailed by Lucas, and had given him the document in exchange for an indiscrete letter she had written as a young girl. When she delivered the document to Lucas, Lady Hilda saw where Lucas hid it. The next day, when the papers reported his murder, she went to retrieve the document, and misaligned the rug.

Lady Hilda gave the letter to Holmes. When Trelawney Hope and the Prime Minister came for lunch, Holmes said the he was convinced that the document was still in the dispatch box. When the box was brought down from the bedroom, Holmes managed to slip the document in amongst the other papers, where it was found. The amazed Prime Minister said there was more to this than meets the eye. When he pressed Holmes for more details, Holmes said, "We also have our diplomatic secrets".

RED-HEADED LEAGUE - 1890

No. 31 "221B" BAKER STREET—W1: [Latitude / Longitude: 51.517932,-0.155587]. One October day in 1890, Watson dropped by Baker Street, and found Holmes with Jabez Wilson, a gentleman with fiery red hair. He told a bizarre tale. **Underground Station: Marble Arch**

No. 7 POPPINS "POPE'S" COURT—EC4: [Latitude / Longitude: 51.514358,-0.105175]. Duncan Ross advertised for all redheaded men in London to apply at the offices of the Red-headed League at No. 7 Pope's Court, just off Fleet Street. The ad said that a League vacancy had opened. The position paid £4 a week for nominal services. The described location indicates that "Poppins Court" is Pope's Court. **Underground Station: Blackfriars**

Jabez Wilson had a small pawnbroker's business at Coburg Square, near the City. Vincent Spaulding, his new assistant, urged Jabez to seek the job at the Red-headed League. Spaulding had become Jabez's assistant when he agreed to work for half wages. Jabez said that Spaulding was a good worker, but not without fault. He was addicted to photography, and was always taking pictures and then diving down to the cellar to develop the prints. Spaulding went with Wilson to answer the ad, and managed to get him to the head of the line. After being interviewed by Duncan Ross, who was also redheaded, Jabez was hired. He was told that American millionaire Ezekiah Hopkins had founded the League. Jabez's hours were to be from ten to two, at the League's office, and that he must not leave the building for any reason. His job was to copy the Encyclopedia, provide his own ink, pen, foolscap, and blotting paper.

KING EDWARD STREET—EC1: [Latitude / Longitude: 51.516371,-0.098568]. After working for eight weeks, Jabez Wilson went to the Red-headed League office for his daily task, and found the door locked. The sign on the door said that the League was dissolved. The landlord told him that Duncan Ross was really William Morris, a solicitor, who had moved to new offices at No. 17 King Edward Street, near St. Paul's. When Wilson went to that address, he found it was the manufacturer of artificial kneecaps, and no one there had every heard of Duncan Ross or William Morris. Perplexed, Jabez went to Baker Street to seek Holmes' advice. **Underground Station: St. Paul's**

After Jabez Wilson left Baker Street, Holmes asked Watson not to speak for fifty minutes, because this was a three-pipe problem. Just when Watson thought Holmes had fallen asleep, he jumped up and announced they were going to the City.

BARBICAN (ALDERSGATE) UNDERGROUND STATION—EC1: [Latitude / Longitude: 51.5202,-0.097442]. On their way to Jabez Wilson's pawnshop, Holmes and Watson got off the underground at Aldersgate, (now Barbican) Station. Holmes got a look at Vincent Spaulding by asking for directions to The Strand. He noticed that the knees of Spaulding's trousers were dirty. Holmes took pride in having an exact knowledge of London, and identified one of the nearby businesses as the Coburg Branch of the City and Suburban Bank. **Underground Station: Barbican**

ST. JAMES'S HALL (site) No. 21 Piccadilly—W1: [Latitude / Longitude: 51.509328,-0.13609]. Considering the evidence, Holmes knew the reason for the Red-headed League ruse. Jabez Wilson had to be kept out of his shop, so that a tunnel could be dug from his cellar to the nearby bank. Holmes said the theft would take place on Saturday night when the bank was closed, and discovery of the theft would not take place until Monday morning. With the detective work done, Holmes and Watson had time for play. After a sandwich and cup of coffee, they were off to violin-land at St. James's Hall, where Sarasate was playing. **Underground Station: Piccadilly Circus**

Author's note: The Hall was located where a hotel sits today. In Holmes's day, St. James's Hall was London's leading concert venue.

KENSINGTON CHURCH STREET—W8: [Latitude / Longitude: 51.505477,-0.194109]. After they left St. James's Hall, Watson went to his house on Church Street in Kensington. He agreed to meet Holmes again at ten that night. **Underground Station: High Street Kensington**

HYDE PARK—W2: [Latitude / Longitude: 51.512669,-0.159048]. It was a quarter-past nine when Watson started to walk from Kensington, across Hyde Park, through Oxford Street, to Baker Street. **Underground Station: Marble Arch**

No. 31 "221B" BAKER STREET—W1: [Latitude / Longitude: 51.517932,-0.155587]. When Watson reached Baker Street, there were two hansoms at the door. Two men were with Holmes. One was Peter Jones of Scotland Yard. The other was Mr. Merryweather, a director of the City and Suburban Bank. Merryweather was upset because he was going to miss his regular Saturday night rubber of whist. **Underground Station: Marble Arch**

FARRINGDON "FARRINGTON" STREET—EC1: [Latitude / Longitude: 51.517776,-0.105186]. As the two hansoms made their way to the bank, Holmes explained that one of the criminals involved was John Clay. Clay's grandfather had been a royal duke, and Clay had been to Eton and Oxford. Holmes, Watson, Jones, and Merryweather, "Rattled through an endless labyrinth of gas-lit streets" until they reached Farrington Street. **Underground Station: Farringdon**

After entering the bank, they passed through corridors and iron gates, until they reached the massive cellar vault. It was filled with crates and boxes. As they waited, Merryweather revealed that the vault contained the bank's French gold. The bank had recently borrowed 30,000 gold Napoleons from the Bank of France. They put screens over their lanterns, and sat in the dark. As they waited, Jones said that when the thieves discovered their plan had failed, they would have only one avenue of escape. He had an inspector and two officers waiting for them at the pawnshop end of the tunnel.

John Clay broke through the floor, where Holmes grabbed him. His redheaded partner fled back through the tunnel into the arms of the waiting policemen. When Watson complemented Holmes on the way he had solved the case, Holmes said, "My life is spent in one lone effort to escape from the commonplaces of existence. These little problems help me do so".

ADVENTURE OF THE BERYL CORONET – 1891?

FROM THE BAKER STREET STATION—NW1: [Latitude / Longitude: <u>51.518451,-0.155786</u>]. One bright February morning, Watson noticed Alexander Holder walking toward 221B from the direction of the Metropolitan Station. The Baker Street Underground Station was on the Metropolitan Line, and Watson referred to it as the "Metropolitan Station". Holder had come to ask for Sherlock's help. **Underground Station: Baker Street**

THREADNEEDLE STREET—EC2: [Latitude / Longitude: <u>51.514159,-0.085874</u>]. Alexander Holder was the senior partner in the Threadneedle Street firm of Holder & Stevenson, the second largest private banking house in the City. Based on his appearance, and his plea for help, Watson wondered, "What could have happened.. to bring one of the foremost citizens of London to this most pitiable pass"? **Underground Station: Bank**

STREATHAM—SW16: [Latitude / Longitude: <u>51.436614,-0.125431</u>]. A gentleman from one of noblest families in England asked Alexander Holder for an advance of £50,000. He offered the Beryl Coronet, "one of the most precious public possessions of the empire", as collateral. For safekeeping, Holder took the coronet to Fairbank, his home in Streatham, and locked it in his dressing room bureau. During the night, he caught his son, Arthur, holding the coronet, with a small portion torn off, and three of the thirty-six gems missing. **Rail Station: Streatham**

Holmes and Watson went to Streatham with Holder, and interviewed Mary Holder, Alexander Holder's niece. She said that on the night in qestion, her maid had slipped out to see her sweetheart, Francis Prosper. After examining the downstairs window, Holmes went upstairs to look at the scene of the robbery. He pointed out that breaking the coronet required great strength. Holmes then examined the snow-covered grounds. Before retuning to Baker Street, he asked Mr. Holder to come see him the next morning, between nine and ten.

After returning to Baker Street, Holmes went out on his own, dressed as a "common loafer". He returned once, saying he had been to Streatham again, but did not call at the house. Holmes took off his disguise, and went to "the other side of the West End". Watson waited up until midnight, but finally went to bed. In the morning, he found Holmes in the sitting room with a cup of coffee in one hand, and a newspaper in the other. It was just after nine, when Alexander Holder arrived as requested. He was in a terrible state, and said his niece had deserted him. His spirits perked up when Holmes produced the missing coronet piece. Holmes said that Arthur was innocent, but that Mary had run off with Sir George Burnwell, a dangerous villain. The night of the robbery, Mary had talked to Sir George through the window. When he heard about the coronet, he wanted to steal it. Mary was putty in his hands, and handed the coronet to Sir George.

Sir George tried to get away, but Arthur caught him. They struggled over the coronet, and Sir George fled with the small broken piece. Arthur was trying to return the damaged coronet to his father's room, when his father woke. Angered by his father's accusation, and out of chivalry for Mary, Arthur offered no explanation. After determining the nature of the crime, Holmes went to see Sir George, and with the help of a pistol, got the name of the person to whom he had sold the jewels. Holmes negotiated their return for £1,000 apiece. He then called on Arthur and told him all was well. As for Mary, her life with Sir George was punishment enough.

ADVENTURE OF WISTERIA LODGE - 1891?

No. 31 "221B" BAKER STREET—W1: [Latitude / Longitude: <u>51.517932,-0.155587</u>]. One gloomy March morning in 1892 [sic], Holmes received a telegram from Scott Eccles. After reading it, Holmes asked Watson, "How do you define the word 'grotesque'"? The telegram read, *"Have just had the most incredible and grotesque experience. May I consult you"?* **Underground Station: Marble Arch**

Author's note: We must assume that the "1892" date is an error. Sherlock's struggle at the Reichenbach Falls occurred in 1891, and he did not return to London until 1894. I think the Wisteria Lodge adventure occurred in March 1891.

CHARING CROSS POST OFFICE (site), South Africa House, Trafalgar Square—WC2: [Latitude / Longitude: <u>51.507808,-0.126823</u>]. Scott Eccles sent his telegram to Holmes from the Charing Cross Post Office, but left before the police arrived. **Underground Station: Charing Cross**

A measured step outside their Baker Street door brought in Scott Eccles. He was a stout, tall, gray whiskered man, with a pompous manner. He said, "I have just had the most singular and unpleasant experience". At this point, Mrs. Hudson ushered in Inspector Gregson of Scotland Yard, and Inspector Baynes of the Surrey Constabulary. They had picked up Eccles trail at the post office.

LEE, Lewisham—SE13: [Latitude / Longitude: <u>51.448692, 0.014933</u>]. The inspectors asked, "Are you Mr. John Scott Eccles of Poham House, Lee? We wish a statement…as to the events which led up to the death last night of Mr. Aloysius Garcia, of Wisteria Lodge, near Esher". **Dockland Light Rail Station: Lee**

KENSINGTON—W8: [Latitude / Longitude: 51.502398,-0.194632]. After drinking the brandy and soda Watson provided, Eccles told his story. He was a bachelor, and cultivated a large number of friends. Among them was a retired brewer called Melville, who lived at Albemarle Mansion in Kensington. It was there that Eccles met Garcia, who supposedly held a position at the Spanish Embassy. **Underground Station: Kensington High Street**

WISTERIA LODGE "COPSEHAM", Esher—KT10: [Latitude / Longitude: 51.360266,-0.363128]. As their friendship developed, Eccles agreed to spend a few days at Garcia's Wisteria Lodge, between Esher and Oxshott. The household included a Spanish servant, and a half-breed cook. The house itself was an old tumbledown building. The dinner was so poorly cooked and served, that Eccles wished he could invent some excuse to leave. At one point, Garcia received a note, and became distraught. **Rail Station: Esher**

Eccles went to bed at eleven, and except for Garcia waking him at one o'clock, slept until nine. In the morning, he rang for the servant, but no one responded. He searched the house, and found everyone missing. Eccles was furious, and thought he was the victim of some practical joke. He packed his bag and set off for Esher. There, he called in at Allen Brothers', the land agents, who said Garcia's rent had been paid in advance.

SPANISH EMBASSY (site), No. 1 Grosvenor Gardens—SW1: [Latitude / Longitude: 51.497249,-0.146551]. Back in London, Eccles stopped by the Spanish Embassy. They had never heard of Garcia. Eccles then went to see Melville, who, although he had introduced them, admitted he knew very little about Garcia. **Underground Station: Victoria**

Author's note: In 1891, the Spanish Embassy was located at No. 1 Grosvenor Gardens.

OXSHOTT WARREN "COMMON" Esher—KT10: [Latitude / Longitude: 51.357579,-0.36272]. Inspectors Gregson and Baynes said Garcia's body had been found on Oxshott Common. Blows from a sandbag sap had smashed his head. They placed his death before one o'clock, because it rained at that time, and it was dry beneath the body. This confused Scott Eccles who said Garcia had knocked on his bedroom door at one o'clock. Inspector Baynes found the note Garcia had received at dinner. It read, *"Our one colours, green and white, green open, white shut. Main stair, first corridor, seventh right, green baize. Godspeed, D".* **Rail Station: Esher**

After Scott Eccles went to Scotland Yard to make a written statement, Holmes sent off a reply-paid telegram. The reply came back with the following list of names and addresses. Holmes reasoned that the note received by Garcia referred to the seventh door in a corridor. This meant that it was a large house. The fact that Garcia was on foot, indicated the house was nearby. Holmes asked for a list of the large houses in the Oxshott area, and received the following: *Lord Harringby, The Dingle; Sir George Ffolliott, Oxshott Towers; Mr. Hynes, J.P., Purdey Place; Mr. James Baker Williams, Forton Old Hall; Mr. Henderson, High Gable; and Rev. Joshua Stone, Nether Walsling.*

THE ESHER RAILROAD STATION, Esher—KT10: [Latitude / Longitude: 51.379683,-0.353463]. Later that day, Inspector Baynes returned to Baker Street. Holmes and Watson accompanied him back to Esher. **Rail Station: Esher**

THE BEAR "BULL" INN, No. 71 High Street, Esher—KT10: [Latitude / Longitude: 51.369235,-0.365428]. Holmes and Watson found rooms at the Bull Inn. It was a cold March evening when Holmes, Watson, and Inspector Baynes, walked from the Bull to Wisteria Lodge. Constable Walters was on guard, but his nerves were frayed. Two hours earlier, he had seen a giant face looking through the window. **Rail Station: Esher**

HOLBORN—WC1: [Latitude / Longitude: 51.517503,-0.121209]. When Inspector Baynes and Holmes inspected Wisteria Lodge, they found the place empty. However, there was a great deal of clothing bearing the label of Marx and Co., Holborn. **Underground Station: Holborn**

In the kitchen, they found a wrinkled and shrunken object that looked like a dwarfish human figure. Double bands of white shells were hung around it. The also found the remains of a white cock, and evidence that some animal had been killed and burned. Holmes and Watson remained at the Bull while Baynes attempted to solve the mystery. Holmes spent his time in long solitary walks, or in chatting with the village gossips.

BRITISH MUSEUM, Great Russell Street—WC1: [Latitude / Longitude: 51.518406,-0.12584]. During his investigation, Holmes went to the British Museum. There, he read up on Eckermann's "Voodooism and the Negroid Religions". **Underground Station: Tottenham Court Road**

ESHER POLICE STATION (site), No. 113 High Street, Esher—KT10: [Latitude / Longitude: 51.368342,-0.367204]. One morning at the Bull, Watson opened his morning newspaper and found headlines declaring the Oxshott Mystery solved. The mulatto cook had been charged with the murder. Holmes rushed to see Inspector Baynes, and advised him not to commit himself too far unless he was sure. **Rail Station: Esher**

Holmes's theory was that Garcia had invited Eccles to Wisteria Lodge to provide an alibi from a respectable Englishman. He even went so far as to change the clocks and knock on Eccles's door to show he was home at one o'clock. The note Garcia received, gave directions inside a nearby large house. Obviously, the note came from someone inside that house. Holmes also thought Garcia's servants were in fact his confederates, who fled when Garcia's criminal plan failed. Holmes said 'criminal', because only a criminal would need an alibi.

During his time in the village, Holmes made a reconnaissance of the large houses in the area, and the family history of their occupants. Only one riveted his attention. It was High Gable, and its occupant, Mr. Henderson. Henderson and his secretary, Lucas, were foreigners. The household also included Henderson's two children—girls of eleven and thirteen, and Miss Burnet, their governess. Miss Burnet was English, and a candidate for the inside person who sent the note to Garcia. To support this theory, Miss Burnet has not been seen since Garcia's murder.

Holmes and Watson planned a night visit to High Gable, to see what they could see. At dusk, before they left the Bull, a rustic rushed into their rooms and shouted, "They've gone, Mr. Holmes. They went by the last train. The lady broke away, and I've got her in a cab downstairs". By the look in Miss Burnet's eyes, Holmes knew that she had been drugged with opium. Holmes summoned Inspector Baynes, who said he was also after Henderson. Baynes had arrested the mulatto to give Henderson a false sense of security. Baynes said that Henderson was Don Murillo, once called the Tiger of San Pedro. His name was a terror throughout Central America. When his government was overthrown, he spirited his treasure out of the country, and fled with his two children and trusted aide. They vanished from public view.

When Miss Burnet had recovered, she said that her real name was Signora Victor Durando. Her husband had been the San Pedro minister in London. Don Murillo considered him a threat, and executed him when he was recalled to San Pedro. Signora Durando swore revenge, and joined Don Murillo's household as the children's governess. Garcia and his two companions planned to assassinate Don Murillo, but needed inside information. Don Murillo slept in a different room each night. The plot went wrong when Lopez, the secretary, discovered Miss Burnet as she finished the note describing where Don Murillo would be sleeping that night. He twisted Miss Burnet's arm until she told them Garcia's address. They sent the note she had written, and while Lopez guarded Miss Burnet, Murillo went to murder Garcia.

CURZON PLACE "SQUARE"—W1: [Latitude / Longitude: 51.506145,-0.15081]. Murillo and Lopez managed to escape their police pursuers by entering a London lodging-house, and leaving by the back gate into Curzon Square. They were never seen again. **Underground Station: Hyde Park Corner**

Six months later, the Marquess of Montalva and Senor Rulli, his secretary, were murdered in their rooms at the Hotel Escurial in Madrid. Inspector Baynes came to visit Holmes and Watson at Baker Street with a description of the victims. There was little doubt that justice had been done.

THE FINAL PROBLEM - 1891

No. 31 "221B" BAKER STREET—W1: [Latitude / Longitude: 51.517932,-0.155587]. Holmes returned to Baker Street after being "of assistance to the royal family of Scandinavia, and...the French Republic". One April morning in 1891, Holmes was surprised to receive a visit from Professor Moriarty, whom Holmes called "the Napoleon of crime". Moriarty said that Holmes had "seriously inconvenienced" him, and must withdraw. Holmes refused, but knew that he had put his life in danger. **Underground Station: Marble Arch**

WELBECK and BENTINCK STREETS—W1: [Latitude / Longitude: 51.517289,-0.149215]. At midday, while walking from Baker Street to Oxford Street, Holmes was nearly killed at the intersection of Welbeck and Bentinck Streets. A furiously driven two-horse van just missed him, as it dashed around to Marylebone Lane. **Underground Station: Bond Street**

MARYLEBONE LANE—W1: [Latitude / Longitude: 51.517029,-0.150719]. After just missing Holmes at the corner of Bentinck and Welbeck, the two-horse van dashed west on Bentinck to Marylebone Lane, and was gone in an instant. **Underground Station: Bond Street**

HENRIETTA PLACE—W1: [Latitude / Longitude: 51.515533,-0.147758]. As Holmes walked down Welbeck Street, on his way to Oxford Street, he jogged left on Henrietta Place to Vere Street. **Underground Station: Bond Street**

VERE STREET—W1: [Latitude / Longitude: 51.515306,-0.147513]. As Holmes continued south toward Oxford Street, a brick fell from a Vere Street building, shattering at Holmes's feet. Since this was just after the near "accident" at Bentinck and Welbeck streets, Holmes was convinced that Professor Moriarty's thugs were trying to kill him. **Underground Station: Bond Street**

PALL MALL—SW1: [Latitude / Longitude: 51.505938,-0.136213]. After the "accidents" in Mayfair, Holmes hailed a cab and went to Brother Mycroft's chambers in Pall Mall. He spent the day there before going to see Watson. On the way, a tough with a bludgeon attacked him. Holmes managed to knock him down, but barked his knuckles on the tough's front teeth. **Underground Station: Piccadilly Circus**

Author's note: Since the Diogenes Club, and therefore Mycroft's chambers, were, "Some little distance from the Carlton Club", I suggest they were at the western end of Pall Mall.

LITTLE TITCHFIELD STREET—W1: [Latitude / Longitude: 51.51821,-0.140687]. Watson was surprised to see Holmes enter his consulting-room. In 1891, Watson was married, in private practice, and lived in a house that backed up to Mortimer Street. This means that it is likely that his surgery fronted on Little Titchfield Street. **Underground Station: Oxford Circus**

Holmes asked if he could close the shutters. He was afraid of air guns. He told Watson of Professor Moriarty visit, and asked Watson to go to the Continent with him. Holmes said that he had been assaulted, and commented that, "Professor Moriarty is not a man who lets grass grow under his feet".

MORTIMER STREET—W1: [Latitude / Longitude: 51.51787,-0.140496]. After Watson agreed to go, Holmes gave him complicated instructions on how they would leave London the next day. Holmes left Watson's surgery by scrambling over the back garden wall into Mortimer Street. **Underground Station: Oxford Circus**

LOWTHER ARCADE (site), The Strand—WC2: [Latitude / Longitude: 51.508836,-0.125259]. Holmes told Watson that he should send his luggage on ahead to Victoria Station by trusted messenger. Then, the next morning, he should flag a hansom cab, but not take the first or second one. He should then go to The Strand end of the Lowther Arcade, dash through the Arcade to the rear exit, where a brougham would be waiting. If he followed the instructions exactly, he would reach Victoria Station just in time to catch the Continental Express. **Underground Station: Charing Cross**

ADELAIDE STREET—WC2: [Latitude / Longitude: 51.509063,-0.125828]. The former Lowther Arcade had its main entrance on The Strand, and its back entrance on Adelaide Street. Holmes instructed Watson to exit the hansom at The Strand End, dash through the Arcade, and enter the waiting brougham on Adelaide Street. Mycroft Holmes was the driver. **Underground Station: Charing Cross**

VICTORIA RAILWAY STATION—SW1: [Latitude / Longitude: 51.496697,-0.144058]. Watson followed Holmes's instructions, and arrived at Victoria Station just in time to catch the Continental Express. Moriarty and his thugs were on his heels, but missed the train. **Underground Station: Victoria**

To throw off Moriarty, Holmes and Watson exited the train at Canterbury, made their way cross-country to Newhaven, and then continued on to Dieppe. While Moriarty was in Paris, watching their luggage, Holmes and Watson acquired a couple of carpetbags, and bought whatever they needed, as they traveled across Europe. They made their way to Brussels, where Holmes sent a telegram to Scotland Yard. He groaned when the reply came back. The police had captured most of Moriarty's gang, but Moriarty had escaped. Holmes knew that he was now a dangerous companion, and asked Watson to return to London without him. Of course, Watson refused. The duo went on to Geneva, and began a trek across Switzerland.

157

VICTORIA (GROSVENOR) HOTEL, Buckingham Palace Road—SW1: [Latitude / Longitude: 51.495639,-0.145592]. Holmes and Watson reached the little Alpine village of Meiringen. They stayed at the Englischer Hof, run by Peter Steiler the elder. Steiler spoke excellent English, having served more than three years as waiter, at the Grosvenor Hotel in London. **Underground Station: Victoria**

The next morning Holmes and Watson, set out for the hamlet of Rosenlaui. On the way, they passed the Reichenbach Falls, and took a short sightseeing detour. As they walked back to the main trail, a Swiss lad came with a letter asking Watson to return to the Englischer Hof. An English lady had arrived and needed medical attention. Holmes said he would stay at the falls a little longer and then proceed on to Rosenlaui, where Watson could join him.

When Watson arrived at the Englischer Hof, he found there was no English lady. He rushed back to the falls and found Holmes's silver cigarette case, and a note. It said that Moriarty had confronted Holmes at the falls, and had given him time to write the note. As his last testament, Holmes gave all of his property to his brother Mycroft and his best wishes to Mrs. Hudson and Watson. Since there was no sign of Holmes or Moriarty, Watson could only assume that, they had both gone over the edge locked in their final great struggle.

ADVENTURE OF THE EMPTY HOUSE - 1894

PARK LANE—W1: [Latitude / Longitude: 51.512223,-0.157764]. On March 30, 1894, the Honorable Ronald Adair, second son of the Earl of Maynooth, was murdered. Adair lived with his mother and sister at No. 427 Park Lane (old numbering). **Underground Station: Marble Arch**

Author's note: We know the location was across from Speakers Corner, near the north end of Park Lane. Since Adair was shot from across the street, the house at the Park Lane, Green Street corner is a good candidate.

Adair was a member of several card clubs, and on Friday evening, had played whist at the Bagatelle Card Club. Among those at his table was Colonel Sebastian Moran. When Adair's mother and sister returned home that evening, they found Adair in his room, shot through the head. The door was locked from the inside, and no weapon was found. Although there was a cabstand within a hundred yards of the house, no shot was heard.

SPEAKERS CORNER, HYDE PARK—W1: [Latitude / Longitude: 51.512001,-0.158529]. Watson thought that Holmes had died at Switzerland's Reichenbach Falls in 1891. Using the methods of his old comrade, Watson tried to come up with a theory that would fit the facts of the Adair murder. To view the Park Lane site, Watson strolled across Hyde Park's Speakers' Corner. There, on Park Lane, he saw a group of loafers looking up at Adair's window. While moving through the crowd, Watson bumped into an elderly, deformed man, knocking several books out of his hand. Watson thought that he must be some poor bibliophile. **Underground Station: Marble Arch**

KENSINGTON CHURCH (CHURCH) STREET—W8: [Latitude / Longitude: 51.502265,-0.190998]. After Watson returned to his Kensington surgery, the maid came in and announced that he had a visitor. It was the old bibliophile. He claimed to be Watson's neighbor, with a little bookstore at the corner of Church Street. Watson fainted when the old man dropped his disguise and Holmes stood before him. **Underground Station: High Street Kensington**

Holmes explained that Moriarty had plunged to his death in Reichenbach Falls, but he had escaped using Baritsu, the Japanese wrestling technique. He also explained that, to escape Moriarty's thugs, he had spent three years traveling to Tibet, Persia, Mecca, and Khartoum, before returning to France. It was the Park Lane Mystery, and the chance to catch Colonel Sebastian Moran that brought Holmes back to London.

FOREIGN OFFICE, King Charles Street—SW1: [Latitude / Longitude: 51.502104,-0.126139]. After returning to London, Holmes went to the Foreign Office to brief them on his visit to the Khalifa of Khartoum. **Underground Station: Westminster**

CONDUIT STREET—W1: [Latitude / Longitude: 51.511952,-0.142289]. We learn from Holmes's index of biographies, that Colonel Sebastian Moran was a friend of Moriarty, and the second most dangerous man in London. "He was once with Her Majesty's Indian Army, and the best heavy-game shot that our Eastern Empire has ever produced". He lived at Conduit Street. **Underground Station: Oxford Circus**

CHARING CROSS RAILROAD STATION, The Strand—WC2: [Latitude / Longitude: 51.508497,-0.125551]. While looking for Colonel Sebastian Moran in the "M" section of his Index of Biographies, Holmes mentioned, "Mathews, who knocked out my left canine in the waiting room at Charing Cross". **Underground Station: Charing Cross**

CAVENDISH SQUARE—W1: [**Latitude / Longitude:** 51.516888,-0.14598]. Reunited with his old comrade, Watson found himself beside Holmes, "In a hansom, my revolver in my pocket, and the thrill of adventure in my heart". Watson thought they were bound directly for their old Baker Street quarters, but to insure that they were not being followed, Holmes took a wandering route through mews and stables. He stopped the cab at the northeast corner of Cavendish Square, stepped out, and searched to the right and left, as he did at every subsequent corner. **Underground Station: Oxford Circus**

Author's note: Based on the clues given in the adventure, Bernard Davies suggests the following route from Cavendish Square to *The Empty House*. For a more complete explanation of this subject, see Bernard Davies, *The Mews of Marylebone*. Mr. Davies suggests that Holmes and Watson dismissed the hansom at Cavendish Square, and walked the route. I disagree. The whole purpose of the journey was to remain unobserved, and arrive early. Using a hansom cab makes more sense.

HARLEY STREET—W1: [**Latitude / Longitude:** 51.518845,-0.146953]. From Cavendish Square, Holmes and Watson's hansom drove north on Harley Street toward New Cavendish Street, then called Great Marylebone Street. **Underground Station: Regent's Park**

NEW CAVENDISH STREET—W1: [**Latitude / Longitude:** 51.519226,-0.147882]. Holmes and Watson turned west on Great Marylebone Street, now called New Cavendish Street, before taking a quick right on Wimpole Mews and continuing north. **Underground Station: Regent's Park**

WIMPOLE MEWS—W1: [**Latitude / Longitude:** 51.519766,-0.148154]. The north end of Wimpole Mews ends at Weymouth Street. Here, Holmes and Watson turned left and continued west toward Beaumont Mews. **Underground Station: Regent's Park**

WEYMOUTH STREET—W1: [**Latitude / Longitude:** 51.5203,-0.149463]. Holmes and Watson continued west on Weymouth Street toward Beaumont Mews. **Underground Station: Baker Street**

BEAUMONT MEWS—W1: [Latitude / Longitude: 51.5203,-0.149463]. Holmes and Watson drove north on Beaumont Mews, as it curved west and exited into Marylebone High Street. **Underground Station: Baker Street**

MARYLEBONE HIGH STREET—W1: [Latitude / Longitude: 51.520722,-0.151695]. It was just a quick jog to the north on Marylebone High Street, and then west on Paddington Street. **Underground Station: Baker Street**

PADDINGTON STREET—W1: [Latitude / Longitude: 51.520796,-0.15265]. After a short westward journey, Bernard Davies suggests that Holmes and Watson turned south through the three feet wide Grotto Passage. Its Paddington Street entrance is no longer there, but it had to be near The Church of the Holy Shepherd. **Underground Station: Baker Street**

Author's note: At this point, I must vary from Bernard Davies suggested route. Since I think they were traveling in a hansom cab, I think Holmes and Watson continued west on Paddington Street to Ashland Place.

ASHLAND PLACE—W1: [Latitude / Longitude: 51.520649,-0.153585]. I think Holmes and Watson turned south on Ashland Place until they reached Osslington Buildings on the left. **Underground Station: Baker Street**

OSSLINGTON BUILDINGS—W1: [Latitude / Longitude: 51.519733,-0.153117]. Holmes and Watson continued east on Osslington Buildings, and followed it as it turned south to Paradise Street, now called Moxon Street. **Underground Station: Baker Street**

MOXON STREET—W1: [Latitude / Longitude: 51.519733,-0.153117]. From Osslington Buildings, Holmes and Watson took a short jog on Moxon Street, then called Paradise Street, and continued south on Aybrook Street, then called North Street. **Underground Station: Baker Street**

AYBROOK STREET—W1: [Latitude / Longitude: 51.518475,-0.152881]. Holmes and Watson were getting close to their destination when they continued south on Aybrook Street then called North Street. **Underground Station: Baker Street**

BLANDFORD (SOUTH) STREET—W1: [Latitude / Longitude: 51.518425,-0.152902]. After exiting Aybrook Street, Holmes and Watson turned west cn the Part of Blandford Street that was then called South Street. **Underground Station: Marble Arch**

BLANDFORD STREET—W1: [Latitude / Longitude: 51.518251,-0.155069]. Past Manchester Street, the name of South Street changed to Blandford Street. There, Holmes and Watson approached Kendall's Mews, now called Kendall Place. **Underground Station: Marble Arch**

KENDALL PLACE "KENDALL'S MEWS"—W1: [Latitude / Longitude: 51.518251,-0.155069]. As Holmes and Watson turned south into Kendall's Mews, they stopped behind the empty Camden House, located at No. 34 Baker Street. Their roundabout journey (in a hansom cab) has insured that they had been unobserved, and that no one had followed them. **Underground Station: Marble Arch**

Author's note: The timing of their arrival was critical. Holmes and Watson had to arrive before Colonel Moran. A wax bust of Holmes had been placed in their 221B window, and Mrs. Hudson crawled into the room from time to time to move it. Inspector Lestrade, two uniformed Policemen, and a plain-clothes detective hid in Baker Street. The trap was set.

No. 34 BAKER STREET, (CAMDEN HOUSE)—W1: [Latitude / Longitude: 51.518067,-0.155632]. During the three years of Holmes's exile, his brother, Mycroft, had preserved his Baker Street rooms and papers. Holmes knew that Professor Moriorty's gang would try to kill him, and that the shot would likely come from across Baker Street. With the Camden House being empty, it was the likely the shot would come from there. Holmes and Watson lay in wait for Colonel Sebastian Moran. **Underground Station: Marble Arch**

No. 31 BAKER STREET)—W1: [Latitude / Longitude: 51.517954,-0.155616]. This rather precise description of the location of the Camden House, and the fact that it was across Baker Street from 221B, and that 221B had a back yard big enough for a plane tree, tells us that Mrs. Hudson's house was located where the modern building at No. 31 Baker Street stands today. **Underground Station: Marble Arch**

To Holmes's surprise, Colonel Moran came to the very room in which he and Watson lay-in-wait. Moran made one shot before Holmes and Watson subdued him. A blast from Holmes's police whistle brought Inspector Lestrade, two uniformed policemen, and a plain-clothes detective from the street below. With the air gun they confiscated, the police were able to arrest Moran for the murder of Ronald Adair. Holmes's theory was that Adair had caught Moran cheating at the Bagatelle Club, and to keep from being exposed, Moran killed him.

NORMAN SHAW BUILDINGS, (1894's NEW SCOTLAND YARD)—SW1: [Latitude / Longitude: 51.501677,-0.124102]. The Norman Shaw Buildings, between Whitehall and Victoria Embankment, near Westminster Bridge and Big Ben, is the Scotland Yard Sherlock knew. The building complex is distinctive, being constructed of alternate bands of red brick and white Portland stone. **Underground Station: Westminster**

Author's note: Scotland Yard has moved again. In 1967, "new" New Scotland Yard moved to nearby No. 8-10 Broadway, **[Latitude / Longitude: 51.498511,-0.133853],** an existing office block acquired under a long-term lease. There have been newspaper articles indicating they may open their Black Museum to the public. Will Colonel Sebastian Moran's air rifle be on display?

ADVENTURE OF THE GOLDEN PINCE-NEZ - 1894

It was a cold and rainy November night in 1894, when Holmes and Watson had a midnight visitor. Watson looked out the window, and saw a lone cab coming from Oxford Street. He rushed down to admit their guest, before he woke the whole house. Their visitor was Stanley Hopkins, a promising young detective.

CHARING CROSS RAILROAD STATION, The Strand—WC2: [Latitude / Longitude: 51.508497,-0.125551]. Hopkins had just come from Charing Cross Railway Station. He had come from Yoxley Old Place in Kent, and asked Holmes and Watson to accompany him back there the next morning. **Underground Station: Charing Cross**

Professor Coram, an elderly invalid, was writing a learned book. He had rented Yoxley Old Place, and hired Willoughby Smith as his private secretary. Smith had been murdered, and Hopkins needed Holmes's help. There did not seem to be a motive, or a suspect. At the scene of the murder, Hopkins found a gold pince-nez, with two broken ends of black silk cord attached. It did not belong to anyone in the household, so it must have been snatched from the face of the murderer. He showed the evidence to Holmes, who used his skills to describe the woman who wore them. Hopkins was amazed.

After a few hours sleep, Holmes and Watson met Hopkins at Charing Cross Station and caught the six o'clock train to Chatham. There, Holmes talked to Professor Coram, who was bedridden. Mrs. Marker, the housekeeper, said that in spite of being a heavy smoker, Professor Coram had developed a hearty appetite. After lunch, Holmes, Watson, and Hopkins went back into Professor Coram's bedchamber, where Holmes announced he had solved the case, and that the murderer was hiding in that very room. At that, a lady came out from her hiding spot behind the bookcase. She introduced herself as Anna, the Professor's wife. She said they were Russian, and had both been revolutionaries. Years ago, to save himself, the Professor had betrayed his companions, and fled to England where he lived in fear of retribution.

The Professor had kept some papers that would free Alexis; an innocent man currently imprisoned in a Siberian salt mine. Anna had come to Oxley Old Place to get the documents and free Alexis. Willoughby Smith had caught her, and in an attempt to escape, she struck at him with a letter opener. Having lost her pince-nez in the struggle, and not being able to see well, she fled down the wrong corridor, and ended in the Professor's bedchamber. He recognized her, and hid her behind the bookcase.

CHESHAM HOUSE, BELGRAVE SQUARE, Russian Embassy (site)—SW1: [Latitude / Longitude: 51.498124,-0.153579]. Before coming out of her hiding place, Anna had taken a fatal dose of poison. She gave Holmes the papers that would free Alexis, and asked him to take them to the Russian Embassy. **Underground Station: Hyde Park Corner**
Author's note: In 1894, the Russian Embassy was in Chesham House, Belgrave Square, with their Consulate at 17 Great Winchester Street in The City: **[Latitude / Longitude: 51.516054,-0.084726].**

ADVENTURE OF THE NORWOOD BUILDER - 1895?

No. 31 "221B" BAKER STREET—W1: [Latitude / Longitude: 51.517932,-0.155587]. After the death of Professor Moriarty, Watson sold his small practice in Kensington to Dr. Verner, and moved back to Baker Street. Years later, Watson learned that Verner was a relative of Holmes, and Holmes had provided the money for the purchase. **Underground Station: Marble Arch**

While Holmes complained that, without Moriarty, the state of crime in London was very poor, a knock on the door brought in John Hector McFarlane. At a glance, Holmes commented that McFarlane was, "A bachelor, a solicitor, a Freemason, and an asthmatic". Naturally, McFarlane was amazed, but added that he was also the most unfortunate man in London. He said he had just arrived in London, and was about to be arrested for the murder of Mr. Jonas Oldacre, of Lower Norwood.

ANERLEY ARMS INN, No. 2 Ridsdale Road—SE20: [Latitude / Longitude: 51.411841,-0.0666]. After a late business meeting with Oldacre, McFarlane spent the night at the Anerley Arms Inn, about a mile and a half from Oldacre's Deep Dene House. **Rail Station: Anerley**

ANERLEY RAILWAY STATION—SE20: [Latitude / Longitude: 51.411654,-0.066372]. McFarlane read about Oldacre's disappearance on the morning train from the Anerley Railway Station to London. **Rail Station: Anerley**

LONDON BRIDGE RAILWAY STATION—SW1: [Latitude / Longitude: 51.505848,-0.086521]. After John Hector McFarlane arrived at the London Bridge Station, he came directly to Baker Street. Inspector Lestrade followed, waiting for a warrant before making an arrest. **Underground Station: London Bridge**

GRESHAM HOUSE (BUILDINGS), No. 24 Holborn Viaduct—EC1: [Latitude / Longitude: 51.517012,-0.1047]. McFarlane told Holmes that he was a junior partner in the law firm of Graham & McFarlane, at 426 Gresham Buildings. **Underground Station: Farringdon**

When the police entered Baker Street, Holmes prevailed on Lestrade to let McFarlane tell his story. McFarlane said Oldacre came to the Graham & McFarlane offices the day before, and wanted to have his will written. He wanted to make McFarlane his heir, although the two had never met. McFarlane said his parents had known Oldacre years ago, but knew of no reason for this sudden act of generosity. Oldacre said he was childless, and had always heard that McFarlane was a deserving young man. He swore McFarlane to secrecy, and made him promise that he would not tell his parents. Oldacre said that he had other legal documents at his home in Norwood and asked McFarlane to visit him that evening.

LOWER NORWOOD—SE26: [Latitude / Longitude: 51.42693,-0.056847]. Jonas Oldacre was a well-known builder in Lower Norwood. The fifty-two year old bachelor lived in Deep Dene House at the end of Sydenham Road. **Rail Station: Sydenham**

That evening, after McFarlane left Deep Dene House, fire engines responded to a blaze in the back yard. Oldacre had disappeared, and John Hector McFarlane's bloody walking stick was found in the house. McFarlane did not know of these events until he read the morning newspaper on his way to London.

BLACKHEATH—SE3: [Latitude / Longitude: 51.459907, 0.009892]. John Hector McFarlane lived with his parents at Torrington Lodge, Blackheath. After Lestrade arrested McFarlane, Holmes and Watson went to Blackheath to talk to McFarlane's mother. She said that Oldacre was an old suitor, whom she had rejected when she discovered his cruel character. **Rail Station: Blackheath**

SYDENHAM RAILWAY STATION—E26: [Latitude / Longitude: 51.426631,-0.054836]. With this information, Holmes and Watson took the train to Norwood's Sydenham Railway Station. At Oldacre's Deep Dene House, the police had found several trouser buttons, and some bones, in the backyard fire ashes. One button was marked with the name of Oldacre's tailor. An examination of the house and safe seemed to indicate that some papers were missing. Mrs. Lexington, the housekeeper, was close mouthed, but Holmes felt she knew more than she was saying. **Rail Station: Sydenham**

The next morning, Holmes received a telegram from Lestrade. It read, '*Important fresh evidence to hand. McFarlane's guilt definitely established. Advise you to abandon case*". Holmes and Watson returned to Norwood, where Lestrade showed them McFarlane's bloody fingerprint. This convinced Holmes that McFarlane was innocent. He knew that the print had not been there the day before.

As Lestrade wrote his report in the sitting room at Deep Dene, Holmes and Watson toured the house, inside and out. Holmes then told Lestrade that he should interview one more witness before finishing his report. When Lestrade asked if Holmes could produce the witness, Holmes said yes, but he would need the help of three constables. He asked the constables to get some straw, two buckets of water, and bring them into the house. Watson lit the straw, and Holmes had the three constables yell "fire". With that, a door opened where there had been a solid wall, and out stepped Jonas Oldacre. He claimed that it was all a practical joke, but Holmes knew it was an act of malice, and that Oldacre also wanted to defraud his creditors. As far as the "remains" in the fire, Holmes suggested that Watson "Make rabbits serve your turn" when he recorded the adventure.

ADVENTURE OF THE SOLITARY CYCLIST - 1895

No. 31 "221B" BAKER STREET—W1: [Latitude / Longitude: 51.517932,-0.155587]. Late one Tuesday evening, Miss Violet Smith came to Baker Street. The date was April 23, 1895. Miss Smith told Holmes that she taught music at Chiltern Grange near Farnham, and was engaged to Cyril Morton, a young electrical engineer. **Underground Station: Marble Arch**

IMPERIAL THEATRE (site), Tothill Street—SW1: [Latitude / Longitude: 51.499692,-0.130106]. Violet said her late father had conducted the orchestra at the old Imperial Theatre. **Underground Station: St. James's Park**

Author's note: The Imperial Theatre was part of an amusement complex known as the Royal Aquarium. It covered the site now occupied by the Wesleyan Central Hall, on the north side of Tothill Street.

After her father's death, Violet and her mother were very poor. Her late father's brother, Ralph, had moved to South Africa, but had not kept in touch. In December 1894, an ad appeared in the *Times* asking for the whereabouts of Violet and her mother. Bob Carruthers and Jack Woodley, former associates of Violet's uncle in South Africa, had placed the ad. They said that Violet's uncle had died, and they wanted to make sure that Violet and her mother were provided for. Mr. Carruthers, a widower, asked Violet to come to Chiltern Grange to teach music to his ten-year-old daughter. When Violet said she would miss her mother, Carruthers said she could go home on the weekends, leaving on Saturday, and returning on Monday. The work was pleasant and the pay was above the going rate, but Violet did not like Carruthers' friend, Jack Woodley. When Woodley visited Chiltern Grange, he made advances, and one time, even tried to kiss her. Carruthers came to her rescue, and Woodley had not returned.

Violet needed Holmes's help, because every Saturday morning, when she rode her bicycle to the train station, a bearded man followed on his bicycle. When she returned from London on Mondays, the same man followed her from the train station to Chiltern Grange. He never approached her, and when she stopped, he stopped. Because of other demands, Holmes asked Watson to go, and observe Violet when she returned to Chiltern Grange Monday morning. Holmes also wanted Watson to find out who occupied Charlington Hall, the large house located near the road that ran between the train station and Chiltern Grange.

WATERLOO RAILWAY STATION—SE1: [Latitude / Longitude: 51.503943,-0.11391].

On Monday, Watson caught the 9:13 from Waterloo Station. He wanted to be in place, when Violet Smith arrived in Farnham on the 9:50. From his hiding place, Watson saw the bearded cyclist following her. Watson went to a local estate agent, to ask about Charlington Hall. They referred him to an estate agent in London. **Underground Station: Waterloo**

PALL MALL—SW1: [Latitude / Longitude: 51.508128,-0.129951].

After returning to London, Watson stopped by the estate agent firm at Pall Mall. They said he was too late to get Charlington Hall for the summer. It had been let a month before by a Mr. Williamson. The agent said he was a respectable elderly gentleman, but would say no more. **Underground Station: Piccadilly Circus**

Holmes received a new note from Violet, saying that Mr. Carruthers had proposed, With that, Holmes decided that he had to go down to Farnham for the day. He knew that the place to get local information was in the pub. There, Holmes found that Williamson was a white-bearded man, who is, or had been, a clergyman. Holmes was getting information on Woodley, when he entered the pub and overheard the conversation. A fistfight ensued, and Holmes came home with a cut lip. Woodley went home in a cart.

Violet wrote Holmes, saying she was leaving Mr. Carruthers employment, and returning to London. Holmes and Watson decided to go to Farnham, to insure that she would come to no harm. They were almost too late, because she left Chiltern Grange early, and Woodley waylaid her on the way to the train station. He took her into the grounds of Charlington Hall. Holmes and Watson rushed to rescue her, followed by the bearded cyclist, who was Carruthers in disguise. As they rushed into the grounds, they heard Violet's scream, and found a "wedding group". Woodley cried, "You're too late. She's my wife". Carruthers pulled out a pistol, fired, and cried, "No, she's your widow". Holmes took charge, and sent a boy to get the local police. Watson examined Woodley and said he would live. Of course, the wedding was illegal.

Violet's uncle had been a wealthy man who could not read or write. Since he had no will, all of his property would go to Violet, his only living blood relative. Carruthers and Woodley knew this, and came to England to find her, and have her marry Woodley. They even found a defrocked minister to perform the ceremony. The plan fell apart when Carruthers fell in love with Violet, and could not go through with the scheme. The case ended well, with Violet inheriting a large fortune, and marrying Cyril Morton. Because of the circumstances, Carruthers only served a few months in prison for shooting Woodley.

THREE STUDENTS - 1895

Author's note: This 1895 adventure took place in either Cambridge or Oxford. Watson took pains to disguise its true location. I suggest we think of it as Camford, the composite name used in *The Creeping Man*.

Holmes and Watson were residing in furnished lodgings, while Holmes used the university library to research early English charters. They received a visit from an agitated Hilton Soames, tutor and lecturer at the College of St. Luke's. He begged for Holmes's help in a delicate matter that involved the reputation of St. Luke's, and its students. The next day, examinations for the Fortescue Scholarship would start. Soames had left a critical exam question in his locked room. When he returned, he found the outer door had a key in the lock. His own key was on his person, and the only duplicate was the one belonging to Bannister, his servant of ten years. Bannister had carelessly left his key in the lock.

When Soames entered his room, he found that someone had rummaged through the exam papers. Of the three pages, the first was on the floor, the second was on a table near the window, and the third remained on the desk. Soames also found several shreds from a pencil that had been sharpened on the table. In addition, there was a cut in the leather top of his new writing table, and a small ball of black dough or clay. Soames said he must find the culprit, or the examination would have to be postponed. This would, "throw a cloud not only on the college, but the university". Holmes agreed to look into the matter, and asked if anyone had visited Soames's room after he received the papers. Soames said that Daulat Ras, a young Indian student, had visited him, but the proofs were rolled up, and not visible. Ras was one of the candidates for the Fortescue Scholarship.

Holmes and Watson went to Soames room. They found that someone had been in the adjoining room. There, they found additional small pieces of the black putty-like material. Holmes observed that Soames had ground floor accommodations, while three students were in rooms above. All three students were candidates for the Fortescue Scholarship. When asked about the character of the three students, Soames said, "the lower of the three is Gilchrist, a fine scholar and athlete...the second floor is inhabited by Daulat Ras, the Indian...the top floor belongs to Miles McLaren...a brilliant fellow when he chooses to work". When questioning the servant, Holmes learned that Bannister he had not mentioned the incident to the three students.

Outside at dusk, Holmes could see from the interior lights that all three students were in their rooms. When Holmes asked if he could see their rooms, Soames said it would be no problem. Many visitors were shown through the ancient building. Holmes requested that the students not be told his name. In the first two rooms, Holmes sketched things of architectural interest, broke his pencil, borrowed one, and asked for a penknife to sharpen his own. On the third floor, McLaren refused to open the door, saying he had an exam the next day.

Holmes wished the desponded Soames good night, but said he would be back the next morning, possibly with a suggested course of action. He told Soames, "You can be easy in your mind. We shall certainly find some way out of your difficulty". Holmes took the pencil cuttings, and the two black clay pellets with him. Before breakfast the next morning, Holmes told Watson he has solved the case, and they should put Soames out of misery as soon as possible. Holmes also showed Watson a third little pellet of black doughy clay. He had found their source.

Holmes advised Soames to proceed with the examination, and through an informal court-martial, the culprit would not compete. They rang the bell and Bannister entered the room. Holmes accused Bannister of helping the culprit. When Bannister denied it, Holmes asked him to remain in the room while they brought in Gilchrist. Holmes confronted Gilchrist, who cast a look of reproach at Bannister, who said, "I never said a word—never one word!" With this, Gilchrist admitted that he was guilty, and that after athletic practice, had entered the room, discovered the exam question, and began copying it. When he heard Soames approaching the room, he grabbed his spiked track shoes, tearing the tabletop. Mud from his shoe spikes formed the black pellets. When Gilchrist fled into the adjoining room, he left his gloves on the chair. When Bannister was summoned to the room, he saw the gloves, and hid them. When Soames left to consult Holmes, Bannister helped Gilchrist escape, but convinced him to forgo the exam and leave college. Gilchrist had his resignation letter in his pocket, and told Soames and Holmes that he was accepting a commission with the Rhodesian Police.

Bannister said he had been butler to old Sir Jabez Gilchrist, the young gentleman's father. At the college, Bannister watched out for the son, for old time's sake. When he saw the gloves, he knew what had happened, and hid the truth from Soames. He also convinced Gilchrist that he should not profit from such a deed. Holmes told Gilchrist, "I trust a bright future awaits you in Rhodesia...Let us see, in the future, how high you can rise".

ADVENTURE OF BLACK PETER - 1895

In July of 1895, Holmes was at the top of his game. Among the cases that caught his interest that year was, "The very obscure circumstances which surrounded the death of Captain Peter Carey". Captain Carey retired in 1884, and after a few years, bought Woodman's Lee, near Forrest Grove in Sussex. Carey was a very volatile man, and had earned the nickname "Black Peter". They found Captain Carey murdered, with a steel harpoon driven through his chest, into the wooden wall. Inspector Stanley Hopkins, who Scotland Yard assigned to the case, said, "He was pinned like a beetle on a card."

One morning, when Watson set down for breakfast, Holmes strode into the room with a huge spear under his arm. He had been to the butcher shop to see how much force it would take to drive a harpoon through a pig's body. Holmes found that it would take an extraordinary man to do it in one thrust. During the investigation, Holmes and Inspector Hopkins found John Hopley Neligan, breaking in Captain Carey's hut. Neligan, a frail young man, was trying to find Captain Carey's logbooks. Neligan suspected Captain Carey was involved in his father's disappearance. Hopkins arrested Neligan for Captain Carey's murder, but Holmes knew it would have taken a different sort of man.

THE HIGHWAY "RATCLIFF HIGHWAY"—E1: [Latitude / Longitude: 51.509666,-0.054955]. Holmes asked Watson to send two telegrams. One went to Summer, the Shipping Agent at Ratcliff Highway. It read, *"Send three men on to arrive ten tomorrow morning.—Basil"*. Holmes said that Captain Basil was his name in those parts. The second telegram went to Inspector Hopkins, asking him to come to Baker Street for breakfast at nine-thirty. **Dockland Light Rail Station: Shadwell**

No. 31 "221B" BAKER STREET—W1: [Latitude / Longitude: 51.517932,-0.155587]. The next morning, three sailors showed up at Baker Street. Only one had the strength and skill to drive a harpoon through Captain Carey. He was Patrick Cairns, a harpooner of remarkable appearance. "His fierce bull-dog face was framed in a tangle of hair and beard, and two bold, dark eyes gleamed behind the cover of thick, tufted, overhung eyebrows," After a brief struggle, Holmes, Hopkins, and the armed Watson, managed to subdue him.
Station: Marble Arch

Cairns said he was the spare harpooner on Captain Carey's ship, the *Sea Unicorn*, when they rescued John Neligan's father from his small yacht. Cairns saw Carey throw Mr. Neligan's body overboard, and blackmailed the Captain. When Cairns went to Woodsman's Lee to get more money, Carey attached him with a knife, and Cairns took at harpoon at hand, and killed the Captain. Now Cairns was without money and stranded in London. In his investigation, Holmes found three sailors who had served on the *Sea Unicorn* when the elder Mr. Neligan disappeared. They were in London looking for new billets, and thought they had found one with "Captain Basil".

ADVENTURE OF THE BRUCE-PARTINGTON PLANS - 1895

No. 31 "221B" BAKER STREET—W1: [Latitude / Longitude: 51.517932,-0.155587]. In November 1895, a dense yellow fog settled down on London. Although he attempted to busy himself, Holmes was looking for something to occupy his mind. He received a telegram from his brother Mycroft, which read, *"Must see you over Cadogan West. Coming at once".* Holmes told Watson that the visit must be of some importance, because, "A planet might as well leave its orbit", for Mycroft to change his routine. **Underground Station: Marble Arch**

WOOLWICH ARSENAL, Brookhill Road, Etham—SE18: [Latitude / Longitude: 51.487921, 0.066975]. Mycroft Holmes arrived, with Inspector Lestrade at his heels. Arthur Cadogan West, a clerk at the Woolwich Arsenal, had been found dead outside the Aldgate Underground Station. In his pockets were partial plans of the secret Bruce-Partington submarine. Of the ten papers stolen from the Woolwich Arsenal, only seven were in West's pockets. Mycroft said, "The three most essential (pages) are gone—stolen—vanished". Rail **Station: Woolwich Arsenal**

ALDGATE UNDERGROUND STATION—EC3: [Latitude / Longitude: 51.514524,-0.075896].Arthur Cadogan West's body was found outside Aldgate Station, near the aboveground section of the tracks, just south of Aldgate High Street. Scotland Yard thought he had been thrown from inside the train, but there was no ticket in his pockets. His purse contained two pounds fifteen, so there was no robbery. He also had a checkbook, and two dress-circle tickets for the Woolwich Theatre, dated for that very evening. Holmes had a different theory. He thought Cadogan West's body had been placed on the roof of the train, from where it fell at the sharp bend in the tracks. **Underground Station: Aldgate**

Author's note: Today, the trip from Earl's Court to Aldgate takes about 25 minutes. In 1895 it took 40 minutes. The slower pace may explain why the body stayed on the top of the car so long.

BARNARD'S THEATRE, Beresford Street—SE18: [Latitude / Longitude: 51.49254,0.067331]. Barnard's was the only theater in Woolwich in 1895. **Rail Station: Woolwich Arsenal**

ADMIRALTY HOUSE, Whitehall—SW1: [Latitude / Longitude: 51.505557,-0.126826]. With the death of Arthur Cadogan West, and the missing Bruce-Partington plans, the Admiralty was buzzing like an overturned beehive. Mycroft said, "He had never seen the Prime Minister so upset". **Underground Station: Charing Cross**

LONDON BRIDGE RAILWAY STATION—SW1: [Latitude / Longitude: 51.505848,-0.086521]. Holmes and Watson took their investigation to the Woolwich Arsenal. On their way, Holmes sent Mycroft a telegram from London Bridge Station. It read, *"See some light in the darkness, but it may possibly flicker out. Meanwhile, please send...a complete list of all foreign spies...in England".* **Underground Station: London Bridge**

WOOLWICH ARSENAL RAILWAY STATION—SE18: [Latitude / Longitude: 51.49017,0.069783]. Arthur Cadogan West worked at the Woolwich Arsenal. On Monday night, he suddenly left work. His fiancée, Miss Violet Woolwich, saw him about 7:30 PM. The clerk at the Woollwich Arsenal Railroad Station's ticket office was able to say, with confidence, that he saw Cadogan West Monday night, as he left for London Bridge on the 8:15 train. **Rail Station: Woolwich Arsenal**

While in Woolwich, Holmes and Watson went to see Sir James Walter, the official custodian of the Bruce-Partington Plans. Colonel Valentine Walter, Sir James's brother, told them that Sir James had just died. Sir James and Mr. Sidney Johnson, the senior clerk at the Arsenal, were the only people who had keys to the safe containing the plans. On the night of the theft, Sir James spent the evening with Admiral Sinclair at his Barclay Square home. Sir James had said that his key was with him. Mr. Johnson insisted that his key had never left his possession.

BERKELEY "BARCLAY" SQUARE—W1: [Latitude / Longitude: 51.50919,-0.145993]. Admiral Sinclair lived on Berkeley Square. Watson spelled it B-a-r-c-l-a-y, the way it is pronounced. Holmes confirmed that Sir James spent the evening with Admiral Sinclair. **Underground Station: Green Park**

Mycroft Holmes sent Sherlock the following list of the major international spies in London.

NOTTING HILL—W11: [Latitude / Longitude: 51.509637,-0.201595]. Louis La Rothière of Campden Mansions, Notting Hill was one of the international spies reported by Mycroft. **Underground Station: Notting Hill Gate**

No. 13 GREAT GEORGE STREET—SW1: [Latitude / Longitude: 51.501217,-0.128649]. Adolph Meyer of No. 13 Great George Street, across Parliament Square from Westminster Bridge, was another international spy reported by Mycroft. **Underground Station: Westminster**

No. 28 HOGARTH ROAD, "CAULFIELD GARDENS"— SW5: [Latitude / Longitude: 51.493292,-0.192286]. The name and address that caught Holmes attention was Hugo Oberstein, who lived at "Caulfield Gardens". Oberstein's rear windows overlooked the Circle Line tracks. Many have incorrectly identified "Caulfield Gardens" as Courtfield Gardens or Courtfield Road, but they have no houses there from which a body could be placed on the top of the train. The only houses from which this is physically possible are on the south side of Hogarth Road, particularly No. 28. **Underground Station: Earl's Court**

GLOUCESTER ROAD UNDERGROUND STATION—SW7: [Latitude / Longitude: 51.494485,-0.182567]. Then, as now, the District Line tracks are clear of tunnels between the Gloucester Road and Earl's Court Stations. Herr Oberstein's rear windows at Hogarth Road "Caulfield Gardens" overlooked the tracks. **Underground Station: Gloucester Road**

EARL'S COURT UNDERGROUND STATION—SW5: [Latitude / Longitude: 51.492234,-0.193056]. Then, as now, the District Line tracks are clear of tunnels between the Gloucester Road and Earl's Court Stations. Herr Oberstein's rear windows at Hogarth Road "Caulfield Gardens" overlooked the tracks. **Underground Station: Earl's Court**

GLOUCESTER ROAD—SW7: [Latitude / Longitude: 51.492831,-0.181484]. Holmes asked Watson to come to Goldini's Restaurant in Gloucester Road, and bring, "A jimmy, a dark lantern, a chisel, and a revolver". After dinner, they burgled Oberstein's townhouse, and found a series of personal ads from the *Daily Telegraph,* all were signed, "Pierrot". **Underground Station: Gloucester Road**

No. 135 FLEET STREET, Daily Telegraph (site)—EC4: [Latitude / Longitude: 51.514223,-0.106731]. Holmes and Watson went to the Fleet Street district to place an ad for tomorrows *Daily Telegraph.* The ad read, ***"To-night. Same hour. Same place. Two taps. Most vitally important. Your safety at stake. Pierrot".*** **Underground Station: Blackfriars**

The next night, Sherlock, Watson, Mycroft and Lestrade waited in Oberstein's vacant townhouse. There they caught Colonel Valentine Walter, Sir James's younger brother. Colonel Walter had run up a Stock Exchange debt, stolen the Bruce-Partington plans, and sold them to Oberstein. Cadogan West had seen the theft, followed Walter, and was murdered when he confronted Walter and Oberstein,

CHARING CROSS HOTEL, The Strand—WC2: [Latitude / Longitude: 51.50872,-0.125144]. A message from Colonel Walter to Oberstein (in reality dictated by Holmes), persuaded Oberstein to return to London. The note named the Charing Cross Hotel as their meeting place. Oberstein fell for the ruse. After his capture, they found the missing pages of the Bruce-Partington plans in his luggage. He had planned to auction them to the European navel powers. **Underground Station: Charing Cross**

Author's note: The famous old Charing Cross hotel is located at the center of Sherlock's London. It is near many Sherlock Holmes sites; including the Sherlock Holmes Pub, Simpson's Restaurant, and Northumberland Avenue. The hotel is an excellent choice for Sherlock Holmes fans visiting London.

ADVENTURE OF THE VEILED LODGER - 1896

No. 31 "221B" BAKER STREET—W1: [Latitude / Longitude: 51.517932,-0.155587]. One morning, in late 1896, Holmes sent Watson a note, asking him to come to Baker Street. **Underground Station: Marble Arch**

SOUTH BRIXTON—SW2: [Latitude / Longitude: 51.458045,-0.118757].When Watson arrived, he found Holmes with "an elderly... woman of the buxom landlady type". She was Mrs. Merrilow of South Brixton. At the time, South Brixton was a popular middle-class suburb. **Underground Station: Brixton**

Eugenia Ronder, whose face was terribly mutilated, had been Mrs. Merrilow's lodger for seven years. Mrs. Merrilow came to Holmes because Mrs. Ronder seemed to be wasting away, and during the night, would cry out 'Murder', and 'you cruel beast'! When Mrs. Merrilow suggested Mrs. Ronder get help, she asked Holmes to visit her. If he did not want to come, Mrs. Merrilow was to say she was the wife of Ronder's Wild Beast Show, and mention the name Abbas Parva. That peaked Sherlock's interest, and he said he would be at South Brixton about three o'clock.

To refresh his memory, Holmes referred to his extensive files and reference books. When Watson said, he had no recollection of the Abbas Parva tragedy, Holmes told him that, years ago, the Ronder Wild Beast Show had camped overnight at Abbas Parva, a small village in Berkshire. As was their habit, Ronder and his wife went to feed Sahara King, their North African lion. The whole camp was roused with the roar of the animal, and the screams of Mrs. Ronder. The lion was out of the cage, and Mr. Rudner's skull crushed. Mrs. Ronder was screaming, with her face horribly mutilated. When they drove the lion back into its cage, and carried Mrs. Ronder to her van, she kept screaming, 'Coward'!

The verdict at the inquest was straight forward, but there were some points that bothered Edmunds of the Berkshire Constabulary. For example, why would Mrs. Ronder think that her husband had failed to come to her aid, when he was dead? In addition, although Ronder was killed instantly, there was testimony that the shouting of another man was heard.

When Holmes and Watson arrived at South Brixton, Mrs. Ronder told them that she had lied to Edmunds, when he was investigating the case. There was someone else involved. Even though he was a worthless human being, she had not wanted to have another person's destruction on her conscience. Now, she said, "The person I allude to is dead". Mrs. Ronder had grown up in the circus world. As a young girl, she married Ronder, a ruffian, bully, and drunk. Leonardo, the strong man, tried to help her, and finally their friendship turned to love. Ronder suspected, but did nothing because he was afraid of Leonardo. In frustration, Ronder tortured his wife. The lovers decided that Ronder was not fit to live, and planned his death.

On the night of the lion's attack, Leonardo struck Ronder with a club, and shattered his skull. In the excitement, Mrs. Ronder inadvertently opened the lion cage door. When the lion leaped on Mrs. Ronder, Leonardo lost his nerve, and did not come to her aid. Mrs. Ronder read that Leonardo had recently drowned while bathing near Margate, and she wanted to tell her story. She could not go to the police, because of her involvement in the murder. As Holmes left the room, he sensed that Mrs. Ronder was planning suicide. He said, "Your life is not your own, keep your hands off it". Two days later Holmes received a small blue bottle filled with poisonous Prussic acid. It arrived with a note that said, "**I send you my temptation, I will follow your advice**".

ADVENTURE OF THE SUSSEX VAMPIRE - 1896?

No. 46 OLD JEWRY—EC2: [Latitude / Longitude: <u>51.514698,-0.090584</u>]. On November 19, Holmes received a note from the firm of Morrison, Morrison, and Dodd, at No. 46 Old Jewry. They remembered Holmes's success in the *Matilda Briggs* case, and referred Robert Ferguson on a matter concerning vampires. **Underground Station: Bank**

Author's note: The *Matilda Briggs* was the ship associated with the giant rat of Sumatra. "A story for which the world is not yet prepared".

MINCING LANE—EC3: [Latitude / Longitude: <u>51.510913,-0.081518</u>]. Robert Ferguson was a partner in Ferguson and Muirhead, tea brokers of Mincing Lane. **Underground Station: Aldgate**

HAMMERSMITH—W6: [Latitude / Longitude: <u>51.492446,-0.223675</u>]. Watson handed Holmes his great index volume. Under V, he found "Vampirism in Hungary", and "Vampires in Transylvania". He also found Victor Lynch, the forger, Vittoria, the circus belle, and Vigor, the Hammersmith wonder. Holmes then read the letter he received from Robert Ferguson. **Underground Station: Hammersmith**

RICHMOND RUGBY CLUB—TW9: [Latitude / Longitude: <u>51.465023,-0.30383</u>]. Ferguson's letter said that in his younger days, he played Rugby for Richmond. He remembered Watson as a fellow Rugby player. **Underground Station: Richmond**

OLD DEER PARK—TW9: [Latitude / Longitude: <u>51.469989,-0.293723</u>]. Ferguson recalled the day he threw Watson into the crowd at the Old Deer Park. **Underground Station: Richmond**

BLACKHEATH RUGBY CLUB—SE3: [Latitude / Longitude: <u>51.477995, 0.026863</u>]. Watson said that he also played Rugby on the Blackheath team. **Rail Station: Westcombe Park**

Years ago, Ferguson had married a Peruvian lady. Lately, "The lady began to show some curious traits, quite alien from her ordinarily sweet and gentle disposition". Twice, she was caught in the act of assaulting Ferguson's fifteen-year-old crippled son from his first marriage. Ferguson said, "This was a small matter…compared with her conduct to her own child, a dear boy just under one year of age". About a month ago, the baby's nurse found, "the lady, leaning over the baby…apparently biting his neck. There was a small wound…from which a stream of blood had escaped". Mrs. Ferguson bribed the nurse to hide the incident from her husband, but later, the nurse told him. At first, Ferguson did not believe the nurse, but then they heard the baby cry and rushed to the nursery. There, they found Mrs. Ferguson kneeling over the baby's bed with blood on her lips, and a wound on the baby's neck.

No. 31 "221B" BAKER STREET—W1: [Latitude / Longitude: 51.517932,-0.155587]. Watson wired Ferguson, asking him to come to Baker Street at ten o'clock the next morning. When he arrived, he said his wife would not explain her actions, and had rushed to her room and locked the door. **Underground Station: Marble Arch**

VICTORIA RAILWAY STATION—SW1: [Latitude / Longitude: 51.496697,-0.144058]. Robert Ferguson was relieved when Holmes and Watson agreed to take the 2 o'clock train from Victoria to Lamberley in Sussex. **Underground Station: Victoria**

Holmes and Watson dropped their bags at the Chequers Inn before going to Cheeseman's, Ferguson's home. Holmes noticed: Ferguson's collection of South American weapons, and that the dog had suddenly become lame. He also noticed the slavish devotion Ferguson's oldest son Jack had toward his father. All observations supported Holmes's theory. Holmes thought that Jack had tried to kill the baby with one of the poisoned South American arrows, after first trying it out on the dog. His stepmother saw the wound on the baby's neck, and sucked out the poison. She could not bring herself to tell her husband, because she knew how much he loved Jack. Holmes said, "A year at sea would be my prescription for Master Jacky".

ADVENTURE OF THE MISSING THREE-QUARTER - 1897?

CHARING CROSS TELEGRAPH OFFICE (site), **447 The Strand—WC2:** [Latitude / Longitude: 51.509337,-0.12395]. One gloomy February morning, Holmes received a telegram sent by Cyril Overton from Charing Cross. It read, *"Please await me. Terrible misfortune. Right wing three quarter missing, indispensable to-morrow"*. Later in the adventure, through a bit if trickery, Holmes learned that, Staunton had sent his telegram to Dr. Armstrong in Cambridge. **Underground Station: Charing Cross**

Neither Holmes nor Watson knew Overton, and could not make much sense of his telegram. When Overton arrived, he said that he was the captain of the Cambridge Rugby team, who had come to London for a game. Godfrey Staunton, one of his star players, was missing. Inspector Stanley Hopkins of Scotland Yard had referred Overton to Holmes.

BLACKHEATH RUGBY CLUB—SE3: [Latitude / Longitude: 51.477995, 0.026863]. Staunton, who played three-quarter for Cambridge, had also played for the Blackheath team. Overton was amazed that Holmes had never heard of him. **Rail Station: Westcombe Park**

THE STRAND—WC2: [Latitude / Longitude: 51.509577,-0.123639]. Overton, and the rest of the Cambridge team, were staying at Bentley's Private Hotel, near The Strand. The night before, Godfrey Staunton was seen with a rough looking man, running toward The Strand. Holmes became more interested, when he learned that Staunton was Lord Mount-James's heir. Mount-James was one of the richest men in England. **Underground Station: Charing Cross**

The Bentley's hotel porter said that Staunton had received a telegram about 6 o'clock the night before, and had sent a reply. After examining the ink blotter in Staunton's room, Holmes found, that the reply ended with the words, *"Stand by us for Gods sake"*. The word "us" meant that another person was involved. Holmes also found a medical bill from Dr. Leslie Armstrong in Cambridge.

BAYSWATER—W2: **[Latitude / Longitude:** <u>51.512662,-0.166438</u>**].** Overton notified Lord Mount-James, who came to Bentley's Hotel as quickly as the Bayswater Bus could bring him. Mount-James further lived up to his reputation of being a miser, by offering Holmes ten pounds toward expenses. **Underground Station: Marble Arch**

GRAY'S INN ROAD—WC1: [Latitude / Longitude: <u>51.525647,-0.117116</u>**].** Holmes felt Cambridge was the logical starting point for their investigation. He and Watson caught a cab and rattled up Gray's Inn Road on their way to King's Cross Station. **Underground Station: King's Cross/St. Pancras**

KING'S CROSS RAILWAY STATION—WC2: [Latitude / Longitude: <u>51.530887,-0.122534</u>**].** In trying to locate the missing Godfrey Staunton, Holmes and Watson took the Cambridge train from King's Cross Station. **Underground Station: King's Cross/St. Pancras**

Although it was dark when Holmes and Watson arrived in Cambridge, they immediately went to Dr. Leslie Armstrong's home. He was a famous doctor, and one of the heads of the University's Medical School. At first, Dr. Armstrong denied knowing anything about the disappearance of Godfrey Staunton, but when Holmes produced Armstrong's bill for medical services and mentioned the telegram that Staunton had sent, Armstrong told them to leave his home. Fortunately, there was a little inn across the street, where Watson reserved a room overlooking Dr. Armstrong's house. Holmes noticed that Armstrong took one or two carriage rides each day. They lasted three hours, indicating a radius of ten or twelve miles. Holmes attempted to follow on a rented bicycle, but was unsuccessful.

Holmes sent a query to Overton, and the next evening, and received this reply, ***"Ask for Pompey from Jeremy Dixon, Trinity College"***. Pompey was a squat, flop-eared, white and tan hound. After dousing the coach's rear wheel with aniseed, Holmes used Pompey to track Dr. Armstrong. At the end of the trail, Holmes and Watson found Godfrey Staunton in a country cottage. He was at the bedside of his young wife, who had just died. With the help of Dr. Armstrong, Godfrey had kept the marriage a secret, to keep Lord Mount-James from disinheriting him. Holmes vowed to keep his secret.

ADVENTURE OF THE DEVIL'S FOOT - 1897

This adventure takes place in 1897, and was inaccurately reported in the London newspapers. Thirteen years later, Holmes sent Watson a telegram saying, *"Why not tell them of the Cornish Horror—Strangest case I have handled".* The following is a summary of Watson's story:

HARLEY STREET—W1: [Latitude / Longitude: 51.517596,-0.146384]. In March 1897, Holmes's iron constitution showed signs of wear. Doctor Moore Agar of Harley Street advised Holmes to take a complete rest. Following the Doctor's advice, Holmes and Watson went to Cornwall, rented a small cottage near Poldhu, and found the "The Cornish Horror". **Underground Station: Oxford Circus**

One morning, Roundhay, the local Cornish vicar, told Holmes, "The most extraordinary and tragic affair has occurred during the night". Mr. Mortimer Tregennis, the vicar's lodger, had spent the previous evening with his two brothers, Owen and George, and his sister Brenda. They played whist at the dining-room table. Shortly after ten o'clock, Mortimer left his siblings in good health. The next morning he heard about the tragedy that had occurred. His brothers and sister were found at the dining-room table. His sister was dead, and the two brothers were alive, but demented. They all had a look of horror on their faces. Mortimer Tregennis told Holmes that he had previously fallen out with his brothers and sister over the family inheritance, but now, all was forgiven and forgotten.

To ponder the mystery, Holmes suggested that he and Watson take a walk along the Cornish cliffs. There, they met Dr. Leon Sterndale, the noted African lion-hunter and explorer. He had been on his way to Africa, and had gotten as far as Plymouth when he returned after receiving a telegram about the tragedy. Because he loved Brenda, the news hit him particularly hard.

The next morning, the vicar rushed to Holmes's cottage to tell him that Mortimer Tregennis had died in exactly the same manner as his brothers and sister. Holmes summoned Dr. Sterndale and accused him of killing Mortimer Tregennis. Sterndale admitted the crime, but said he did it to avenge Brenda.

He showed Holmes a packet of reddish-brown powder. The packet read, *Radix pedis diaboli*, "Devil's-foot root". Dr. Sterndale had brought a sample of this little known African poison back to England, and had shown it to Mortimer. Sterndale thought no more about it until he heard about Brenda's death, and knew that Mortimer was the culprit. Holmes understood Sterndale's motivation, and let him return to Africa.

ADVENTURE OF ABBEY GRANGE - 1897

CHARING CROSS RAILROAD STATION, The Strand—WC2: [Latitude / Longitude: 51.508497,-0.125551]. One cold winter morning in 1897, Holmes and Watson left London by train for Abbey Grange, in Marsham, Kent. They were responding to a letter from Inspector Stanley Hopkins. It was not until they had consumed some hot tea in Charing Cross Station, and taken their places on the Kentish train, that they were sufficiently thawed to talk about the Inspector's reason for summoning them. **Underground Station: Charing Cross**

CHARING CROSS TELEGRAPH OFFICE (site), No. 447 The Strand—WC2: [Latitude / Longitude: 51.509337,-0.12395]. After examining the scene of Sir Eustace Brackenstall's murder, and interviewing Lady Brackenstall, Holmes and Watson returned to London. There, they drove to Scotland Yard, but instead of entering, returned to the Charing Cross telegraph office to send a telegram to Inspector Hopkins. Holmes advised Hopkins to drag the Abbey Grange pond. When Hopkins did so, and found the silver, he thought Holmes was a wizard. **Underground Station: Charing Cross**

PALL MALL AND COCKSPUR STREET—SW1: [Latitude / Longitude: 51.507734,-0.13087]. Holmes and Watson went to the shipping office of the Adelaide-Southampton steamship line. It was located at the Cockspur Street end of Pall Mall. At the shipping office, Holmes learned of Captain Jack Crocker's character, and guessed his role in the death of Sir Eustace. **Underground Station: Piccadilly Circus**

No. 31 "221B" BAKER STREET—W1: [Latitude / Longitude: 51.517932,-0.155587]. That evening, at Baker Street, Holmes and Watson received a visit from Captain Crocker. Holmes told him, "Be frank with me and we may do some good. Play tricks with me, and I'll crush you". Crocker told Holmes of Sir Eustace's brutish nature and the events that led to his death. After hearing the "evidence", Holmes appointed Watson as a "British jury", and asked for his verdict. "Not guilty, my lord," said Watson. Holmes told Captain Crocker, "So long as the law does not find some other victim you are safe from me". **Underground Station: Marble Arch**

ADVENTURE OF THE DANCING MEN - 1897

RUSSELL SQUARE—WC1: [Latitude / Longitude: 51.521388,-0.127248]. Hilton Cubitt came from an old Norfolk family. In June 1887, he came to London for Queen Victoria's Diamond Jubilee, and stayed at a boardinghouse in Russell Square. There, he met Elsie Patrick, an American girl with whom he fell in Love. After their marriage, they returned to Riding Thorpe Manor, the Cubitt estate in Norfolk. Their ten years of happy married life changed when Elsie began receiving "dancing men" notes. **Underground Station: Russell Square**

Cubitt came to London to consult Holmes and said, "It is frightening her to death". Previously, Cubitt had sent Holmes some of the mysterious notes. Watson said the figures looked like a child had drawn them. Holmes asked Cubitt to return home, and forward exact copies of any future messages Elsie received.

LIVERPOOL RAILWAY STATION—EC2: [Latitude / Longitude: 51.517503,-0.082659]. Hilton Cubitt sent a telegram to Holmes saying he was returning to London, and would reach Liverpool Street Station at one-twenty. When Cubitt arrived, he brought additional copies of dancing figures notes. **Underground Station: Liverpool Street**

Cubitt said he must return to Norfolk that day, to be with his frightened wife. Holmes said he would join him in a day or two. During this period, Holmes broke the dancing men code. When Holmes and Watson arrived in North Walsham, they found Hilton Cubitt dead, and his wife gravely wounded. Inspector Martin, of the Norfolk Constabulary, was in charge of the murder investigation. After asking questions about nearby farms, Holmes asked the stable boy to take a note to Elrige's farm. Holmes addressed the envelope to Abe Slaney, and enclosed a message in the dancing men code. Thinking the note was from Elsie; Abe came to Riding Thorpe Manor, and was arrested.

Abe and Elsie's father were members of a Chicago criminal gang that used the dancing men code to send secret messages. Elsie's father promised Elsie's hand in marriage to Abe. When she fled to England, Abe followed in an attempt to get her back. When Elsie told Abe that she loved her husband, Abe shot Cubitt. In despair, Elsie tried to kill herself.

ADVENTURE OF THE RETIRED COLOURMAN - 1898?

Holmes was in a melancholy mood when he described a referral by Scotland Yard. He told Watson, that Scotland Yard sent Josiah Amberley, "Just as medical men occasionally send their incurables to a quack".

"THE HAVEN", PARK LODGE, LEE GREEN—SE3: [Latitude / Longitude: 51.457459, 0.011049]. Josiah Amberley had been the junior partner of Brickfall and Amberley, manufacturers of artistic materials. He retired at sixty-one, bought a house in Lee, and a year later, married a younger woman. His house, identified by Bernard Davies as Park Lodge, was located just north of the junction of Lee Road and Lee High Road. **Rail Station: Blackheath**

Author's note: At the time of this adventure, Lee and Lewisham were separate boroughs. Throughout the adventure, Watson insists on using Lewisham as the location, when at this time, it was in fact Lee.

Amberley had one hobby—playing chess. Dr. Ray Ernest, a neighbor, also liked to play, and in his frequent visits, became good friends with Mrs. Amberley. Josiah said the two of them ran off, and took his deed-box. He said it contained most of his life savings.
BLACKHEATH RAILWAY STATION—SE3: [Latitude / Longitude: 51.465888, 0.008989]. Holmes was busy with another case, so Watson agreed to go to Lee. He took the train to Blackheath. Watson said he did not dream that, "Within a week, the affair in which I was engaging would be the…debate of all England". **Rail Station: Blackheath**

In relaying his Lee visit to Holmes, Watson mentioned he saw the same man in Lee, at Blackheath Station, and at London Bridge. Holmes filled in the description with, "A tall, dark, heavily mustached man…with grey tinted sun-glasses…and a Masonic tie-pin". As usual, Watson was amazed. Watson told Holmes that the Haven, Amberley's house, was ill kept, and surrounded by a high brick wall. Inside, it was no better, although Amberley was trying to remedy it, "For a great pot of green paint stood in the centre of the hall, and Amberley was carrying a thick paint brush in his left hand.

THEATRE ROYAL, HAYMARKET, Haymarket Street—SW1: [Latitude / Longitude: 51.508482,-0.131758]. Amberley told Watson how he pampered his wife, and how badly she treated him. Amberley said he had bought two upper circle seats at the Haymarket Theater the night she left. He said his wife complained of a headache, and could not go. Amberley showed the unused ticket to Watson. Watson noted that it was for seat B-31. Later, Holmes found that seat numbers B-30 and B-32 had not been sold that night. Amberley lied when he said he had purchased two tickets. **Underground Station: Piccadilly Circus**

ROYAL ALBERT HALL—SW7: [Latitude / Longitude: 51.501572,-0.177339]. Holmes suggested that he and Watson escape from the weary workaday world, by having an evening of music at Albert Hall. They dressed for dinner, and dined, before the performance. **Underground Station: South Kensington**

The next day, Holmes left early, and did not return until three. Amberley arrived a few minutes later with a telegram he had received. It read, *"Come at once without fail. Can give you information as to your recent loss. Elman, the Vicarage".* The telegram had been sent from Little Purlington, in Essex. Holmes looked in Crockford's Clerical Directory, and found that J. C. Elman was the vicar in Little Purlington.

LIVERPOOL RAILWAY STATION—EC2: [Latitude / Longitude: 51.51755,-0.082924]. There was a 5:20 train from Liverpool Station. Holmes asked Watson to accompany Josiah Amberley to Little Purlington, and make sure he went. "Should he break away or return, get to the nearest telephone exchange and send the single word 'Bolted' I will arrange here that it shall reach me wherever I am". **Underground Station: Liverpool Street**

When Watson and Amberley arrived at Little Purlington, the Vicar said he had sent no telegram. There were no trains returning to London that day, so they had to spend the night. The next day, Watson and Amberley returned to London, and stopped by Baker Street to report to Holmes. They found a note saying that Holmes was in Lewisham, and they should join him there. When they arrived, they found not only Holmes, but also a tall dark man with tinted sunglasses, and a large Masonic tiepin. Holmes introduced him as Mr. Barker. Barker was a private investigator hired by Dr. Ernest's family. Holmes said that he and Barker had the same question, "What did you do with the bodies"? Amberley had thrown them into an unused well, and was using the pot of paint to disguise the odor.

LEE POLICE STATION, No. 410 Lee High Road—SE12: [Latitude / Longitude: 51.456585, 0.01061]. When Amberley tried to take a poison pill, Holmes stopped him, and said, "No short cuts". Holmes and Barker took Amberley to the police station and returned with Inspector MacKinnon. Holmes outlined the clues, and explained to MacKinnon how he solved the case. Naturally, MacKinnon took full credit in the press, and it was left to Watson to tell the true story. **Rail Station: Blackheath**

ADVENTURE OF CHARLES AUGUSTUS MILVERTON - 1899?

REGENT'S PARK ZOO—NW1: [Latitude / Longitude: 51.535795,-0.155906]. Holmes told Watson that Charles Augustus Milverton was, "The worst man in London". Holmes said, "He reminded him of the serpents in the Regent's Park Zoo". **Underground Station: Camden Town**

HAMPSTEAD—NW3: [Latitude / Longitude: 51.556035,-0.181446]. Milverton lived in Appledore Towers, Hampstead. He had his blackmailing claws in Lady Eva Blackwell. Holmes, acting as Lady Eva's agent, failed to reach an agreement with Milverton, and had chosen another course of action. **Underground Station: Hampstead**

Disguised as a plumber, Holmes gained access to Milverton's house, and even became "engaged" to Agatha, Milverton's housemaid. Holmes told Watson he knew "Milverton's house as I know the palm of my hand". One splendid night, Holmes and Watson went to burgle Appledore Towers.

CHURCH ROW, HAMPSTEAD—NW3: [Latitude / Longitude: 51.555515,-0.179926]. At eleven, Holmes and Watson took a cab from Oxford Street to Church Row in Hampstead. From there it was a fifteen-minute walk to Milverton's house. They planned to steal the embarrassing papers, and return to Baker Street by two o'clock. **Underground Station: Hampstead**

Milverton had not gone to bed, and Holmes and Watson hid behind the study room curtains. Milverton was expecting a visit from another lady he was blackmailing. When she arrived, she refused to pay, and in despair, she pulled out a revolver and killed Milverton. After she fled, Holmes locked the study door, scooped out the content of the safe, and threw the papers into the fire. Holmes and Watson then made a hasty retreat over the garden wall.

The next morning, Lestrade came to Baker Street to ask for Holmes' assistance in solving Milverton's murder. Holmes said he could not help, because, "There are certain crimes which the law cannot touch, and which therefore, to some extent, justify private revenge".

OXFORD STREET—W1: [Latitude / Longitude: 51.514956,-0.143691]. Later that day, Holmes and Watson walked along Oxford Street, toward Regent (Oxford) Circus. There, in a shop window, they saw photographs of the celebrities and beauties of the day. Among them, was a picture of their "avenging angel". Watson looked at Holmes, who put a finger to his lips. **Underground Station: Oxford Circus**

ADVENTURE OF THE SIX NAPOLEONS - 1900?

No. 31 "221B" BAKER STREET—W1: [Latitude / Longitude: 51.517932,-0.155587]. It was not uncommon for Inspector Lestrade to stop by Baker Street, and discuss his cases. Lestrade knew that his latest case had some queer elements that would interest Holmes. Lestrade could not understand why anyone would steal and smash plaster busts of Napoleon. **Underground Station: Marble Arch**

No. 310-312 KENNINGTON ROAD—SE11: [Latitude / Longitude: 51.487492,-0.111371]. Lestrade said that the first incident happened four days ago at the shop of Morse Hudson in No. 310-312 Kennington Road. The smashed bust of Napoleon was only worth a few shillings; so it looked like a random case of hooliganism. **Underground Station: Kennington**

Author's note: Bernard Davies identified No. 310-312 Kennington Road as Morse Hudson's shop.

KENNINGTON ROAD—SE11: [Latitude / Longitude: 51.488173,-0.111217]. The second incident was at Dr. Barnicot's, who lived at Kennington Road, and had a branch surgery at Lower Brixton Road. Dr. Barnicot was an admirer of Napoleon, and had purchased two duplicate plaster casts from Morse Hudson. One bust was for his house, and the other for his surgery. When he woke one morning, he found that his house had been burgled, and the bust of Napoleon stolen. It was smashed outside his house. **Underground Station: Kennington**

LOWER BRIXTON ROAD—SW2: [Latitude / Longitude: 51.453044,-0.120857]. When Dr. Barnicot went to his branch surgery in Lower Brixton Road, he was surprised to find that it too had been burgled, and the second plaster cast of Napoleon smashed. **Underground Station: Brixton**

OLD CHURCH ROAD "CHURCH STREET"—E1: [Latitude / Longitude: 51.514518,-0.045245]. Gelder and Co. made the busts of Napoleon. They were located at "Church Street" in Stepney, and were a well-known house in the trade. They sold six to two London area retailers, three to Morse Hudson, and three to Harding Brothers. **Dockland Light Rail Station: Limehouse**

No. 131 PITT STREET—W8: [Latitude / Longitude: 51.50358,-0.194301]. The next morning, Holmes received a telegram from Lestrade, asking Holmes to come to No. 131 Pitt Street. This Kensington address was the residence of Mr. Horace Harker, of the Central Press Association. His house had been burgled the night before, and his plaster bust of Napoleon stolen. This time, a murder was involved. When Harker opened the front door, he found a murdered man on his front steps. The dead man had a photograph in his pocket. It was a picture of Beppo, an Italian piecework man, who had worked for Morse Hudson. **Underground Station: High Street Kensington**

BRIDGE STREET—SW1: [Latitude / Longitude: 51.500982,-0.125166]. Horace Harker worked for the Central Press Association at Bridge Street, just across from the Big Ben Clock Tower. **Underground Station: Westminster**

CAMPDEN GROVE "CAMPDEN HOUSE ROAD"—W8: [Latitude / Longitude: 51.504355,-0.193967]. The bust of Napoleon taken from the house in Pitt Street was found smashed in the front garden of a nearby empty house in Campden House Road. Holmes called to Lestrade's attention that the front garden was beneath a street light. **Underground Station: High Street Kensington**

KENSINGTON HIGH STREET—W8: [Latitude / Longitude: 51.501163,-0.192853]. Harker said he had purchased his bust of Napoleon from Harding Brothers, a shop in the Kensington High Street, just two doors from the underground station. Harding Brothers bought three plaster busts from Gelder and Co., and sold one to Harker, one to Mr. Josiah Brown of Laburnum Lodge, Laburnum Vale, Chiswick, and one to Mr. Sandeford of Lower Grove Road, Reading. **Underground Station: High Street Kensington**

Holmes went to Gelder & Company in Stepney. The manager identified a picture of Beppo as a former employee. A year ago, he had run into the plant with the police on his heels. He was captured and sent to prison, but was out now.

SAFFRON HILL—EC1: [Latitude / Longitude: 51.52044,-0.106872]. Lestrade told Holmes that they had an inspector, who made a specialty of the Saffron Hill Italian Quarter. The inspector recognized the murdered man as Pietro Venucci, who is connected to the Mafia. Lestrade wanted Holmes to come to Saffron Hill with the police, and search for Beppo. **Underground Station: Farringdon**

HAMMERSMITH BRIDGE—W6: [Latitude / Longitude: 51.489914,-0.228986]. Holmes said, "If you come with me to Chiswick tonight…I promise to go to the Italian Quarter with you tomorrow". That night, a four-wheeler dropped them near Hammersmith Bridge. **Underground Station: Hammersmith**

CHISWICK, Hounslow—W4: [Latitude / Longitude: 51.492044,-0.246763]. Holmes, Watson, Lestrade, and the other policemen waited outside Laburnum Villa in Chiswick. There, with the help of the owner, Mr. Josiah Brown, they captured Beppo. He had broken into the house, stolen another Napoleon bust, and smashed it. **Underground Station: Stamford Brook**

After their successful evening in Chiswick, Holmes sent a letter to Mr. Sandeford, in Reading. offering to pay him ten pounds for his Napoleon bust. Sandeford came to Baker Street, and happily took the ten pounds. As Watson and Lestrade watched, Holmes smashed the bust. In the pieces, he found a round, dark object, and cried, "Gentleman…let me introduce you to the famous black pearl of the Borgias". The pearl had been stolen from the Prince and Princess of Colonna. Pietro Venucci's sister, Lucretia, was the Princess's maid. Beppo had the pearl in his possession the day he was chased him into Gelder & Co. He hid the pearl in one of the six Napoleon busts in the drying room. When he got out of prison, he started looking for the pearl. When Holmes finished explaining the crime, Lestrade said, "I've seen you handle a good many cases…but I don't know that I ever knew a more workmanlike one…We're not jealous of you at Scotland Yard. No, sir, we are proud of you, and if you come down to-morrow, there's not a man, from the oldest inspector to the youngest constable, who wouldn't be glad to shake you by the hand".

COX & COMPANY (site), Craig's Court—SW1: [Latitude / Longitude: 51.506672,-0.12729]. Watson revealed that, "somewhere in the vaults of…Cox and Co., at Charing Cross, there is a travel worn and battered tin dispatch box with my name…painted upon the lid". The box is crammed with records of Sherlock's unrecorded cases. **Underground Station: Charing Cross**

Author's note: During the subsequent period of bank consolidations, the office closed, and the dispatch box was undoubtedly moved.

COX AND KINGS BANK (site), No. 6 Waterloo Place—SW1: [Latitude / Longitude: 51.507524,-0.132675]. Cox and King's Bank relocated to the northeast corner of Pall Mall and Waterloo Place. Was this the intermediate resting place of Watson's old tin dispatch box? **Underground Station: Piccadilly Circus**

After breakfast, one windy October morning, Holmes asked Watson if he had heard of J. Neil Gibson, the Gold King. Gibson had been a U.S. Senator, and made a fortune in gold. Five years earlier, he bought Thor Place, a considerable estate in Hampshire. Recently, his wife Maria had been shot, and Grace Dunbar, the children's governess, arrested for the murder. Mrs. Gibson's body was found on Thor Bridge, a half mile from the house. She had been shot in the head. No weapon was found near the body, but a revolver with one shot fired was found on the floor of Miss Dunbar's wardrobe. It was common knowledge that Neil Gibson was very fond of Miss Dunbar, and Miss Dunbar had been seen at Thor Bridge, about the time Mrs. Gibson was shot.

CLARIDGE'S (HOTEL), No. 49 Brook Street—W1: [Latitude / Longitude: 51.512846,-0.148169]. J. Neil Gibson wrote Holmes from Claridge's. He pleaded with Holmes to help prove that Miss Dunbar was innocent. Gibson said he would come to Baker Street at eleven. Before Gibson arrived, Billy announced Marlow Bates, Gibson's estate manager. Bates said he was leaving Gibson's employment, but wanted to tell Holmes that Gibson was cunning, and should not be taken at face value. **Underground Station: Bond Street**

When Gibson arrived at eleven, Holmes forced him to admit his romantic feelings for Miss Dunbar. Gibson even admitted that he had tried to seduce her, and she had stayed only when he agreed not to molest her again. Gibson said that his wife knew of the influence that the girl had over him, and had been bitterly jealous. Gibson's actions disgusted Holmes, but he agreed to take the case for the sake of the young girl.

The next day, Holmes and Watson went to Thor Place, where they met Sergeant Coventry of the local police. He said he would rather have Holmes helping him than Scotland Yard. Coventry mentioned that the revolver they found in Miss Dunbar's room, belonged to Neil Gibson, and was one of a pair. When Holmes asked what happened to the other pistol, Coventry said they could not find it. When they arrived at the bridge, Sergeant Coventry said that Mrs. Gibson was found on her back, and there was no sign of a struggle. She had been shot near the right temple, from very close range. In her hand, she clutched a note from Grace Dunbar, saying, "I will be at Thor Bridge at nine o'clock". When Holmes examined the bridge's railing, he noted a chip on the lower edge of the parapet.

The next morning, Holmes, Watson, and Mr. Joyce Cummings, Miss Dunbar's barrister, went to Winchester Prison to see her. She told Holmes that Mrs. Gibson hated her, and had sent a note asking that the two meet. Miss Dunbar sent a reply, saying she would meet Mrs. Gibson at Thor Bridge. It was this note that Mrs. Gibson had in her clenched hand.

Holmes and Watson went to Sergeant Coventry's cottage, which served as the local police station. Holmes wanted Coventry with him when he tried an experiment with Watson's revolver. Holmes asked Coventry to provide ten yards of stout twine. They went to Thor Bridge where Holmes found a large stone. He tied one end of the twine to the revolver, and the other end to the stone. Holmes hung the stone over the parapet, and stood where Mrs. Gibson had been found. He then released the revolver. It flew toward the parapet, chipping the lower edge, before being dropping into the water. Holmes asked Coventry to get a grappling hook and recover both Watson's revolver, and the revolver that Mrs. Gibson had used to shoot herself. Mrs. Gibson had committed suicide, and attempted to frame Grace Dunbar. When Miss Dunbar was released from prison, Holmes said, "Well Watson, we have helped a remarkable woman, and also a formidable man".

ADVENTURE OF SHOSCOMBE OLD PLACE - 1901?

No. 31 "221B" BAKER STREET—W1: [Latitude / Longitude: 51.517932,-0.155587]. Holmes was using his microscope to help Merivale of Scotland Yard on the St. Pancras case when he asked Watson, "Do you know something of racing"? Watson replied, "I ought to, I pay for it with about half of my wound pension". Holmes had a new client who was part of the horseracing world, and wanted to use Watson's "rich vein" of racing knowledge. **Underground Station: Marble Arch**

CURZON STREET—W1: [Latitude / Longitude: 51.506766,-0.147666]. Holmes questions centered on the Shoscombe Stud and Horse Training Facility, and Sir Robert Norberton. Sir Robert had the reputation of being a dangerous man. He had horsewhipped Sam Brewer, a well-known Curzon Street moneylender on Newmarket Heath, and almost killed him. **Underground Station: Green Park**

Earlier, Billy had shown in John Mason, Holmes's new client. Mason was the chief trainer at the Shoscombe facility. He thought that Sir Robert had gone mad. In fact, the whole household was acting strangely. Lady Beatrice, Sir Robert's sister, had changed her habits and the black Shoscombe spaniel she loved, had been given away to the owner of the Green Dragon Inn. In addition to his quick temper, Sir Robert was in financial difficulty, and Mason was afraid to question him directly. Mason said Sir Robert hoped his horse, Shoscombe Prince, would win the Derby, and solve his financial problems. Sir Robert lived with his sister, the widowed Lady Beatrice Falder. The estate had belonged to her late husband, and he had left her a life interest. At her death, the estate would revert to her dead husband's brother.

PADDINGTON RAILWAY STATION—W2: **[Latitude / Longitude: 51.515637,-0.175678].** In addition to the other strange happenings at Shoscombe Old Place, Mason said that Sir Robert had started going down to the old church crypt at night, and meeting a stranger there. When Holmes asked Mason about the fishing in that part of Berkshire, Mason thought the craziness might be catching. Holmes said that he and Watson would take the train from Paddington Station, and come down posing as a pair of London anglers. They would stay at the Green Dragon, and look into the situation. **Underground Station: Paddington**

Holmes found that Lady Beatrice had died a natural death. Sir Robert kept her death a secret, so his creditors would not claim her assets, including the Shoscombe Prince. Lady Beatrice's maid helped with the deception, and her husband, Mr. Norlett, played the part of the veiled Lady Beatrice during carriage rides. They fooled most people, but not the dog. Sir Robert and Norlett took Lady Beatrice's body to the old family crypt, and put her in one of the old coffins. They disposed of the old bones by burning them in the furnace. Holmes said he would refer the matter to the police, but it was not up to him to express an opinion on Sir Robert's morality or decency.

Watson wrote, "This singular episode ended upon a happier note than Sir Robert deserved. Shoscombe Prince did win the Derby," and Sir Robert, "did net eighty thousand pounds". The police and the coroner were lenient, only giving Sir Robert a mild censure for delaying his sister's death registration.

ADVENTURE OF THREE GABLES - 1902?

HARROW WEALD—HA3: [Latitude / Longitude: 51.601234,-0.338532]. Mrs. Mary Maberley sent an evening letter to Holmes asking him to visit her at Three Gables, her house at Harrow Weald. She had received a very strange offer to buy her house and contents, and wanted Holmes's advice. **Underground Station: Harrow & Wealdstone**

No. 31 "221B" BAKER STREET—W1: [Latitude / Longitude: 51.517932,-0.155587]. At eleven the next morning, Holmes received a visitor, who Watson compared to a "mad bull". Steve Dixie, the Negro bruiser, burst into the room and told Holmes to keep away from Harrow Weald, and other people's business. Holmes knew Barney Stockdale had sent Dixie. Both Dixie and Stockdale were members of the Spencer John Gang. **Underground Station: Marble Arch**

HOLBORN BAR—WC1: [Latitude / Longitude: 51.51817,-0.111129]. Steve Dixie's attitude changed when Holmes mentioned the killing of young Perkins outside the Holborn Bar. The Negro's face turned leaden, and he beat a hurried retreat. **Underground Station: Chancery Lane**

Author's note: The Holborn Bar is near the junction of High Holborn and Grays Inn Road. There, two stone obelisks mark the boundary of the City of London. In my opinion, "outside the Holborn Bar" means outside the City, near the Holborn Bar.

MARYLEBONE RAILWAY STATION—W1: [Latitude / Longitude: 51.522287,-0.163082]. Bernard Davies suggests that Holmes and Watson left London on the Great Central Railway from the new Marylebone terminus. The 12:05 PM to Leicester would have deposited them at Harrow-on-the-Hill in only 16 minutes. This may be the "short railroad journey" to which Watson referred. **Underground Station: Marylebone**

HARROW & WEALDSTONE RAILWAY STATION—HA1: [Latitude / Longitude: 51.591824,-0.334575]. Later that day, a short railroad journey, and a shorter carriage drive, brought Holmes and Watson to Three Gables. **Underground Station: Harrow & Wealdstone**

Author's note: The name "Weald Stone" comes from an ancient sarsen stone, which was later embedded in the wall of the old "Red Lion Inn" at the corner of the High Road and College Road. The ancient tavern is now called the Weald Stone Inn, [**Latitude / Longitude: 51.6045,-0.3396**].

RISINGHOLME, "Three Gables", No. 224 High Road, Harrow—HA3: [Latitude / Longitude: 51.601234,-0.338532]. The elderly lady who summoned them bore every mark of refinement and culture. Holmes remembered her late husband, and knew of her son, Douglas Maberley. Mrs. Maberley said her son had been an attaché in Rome, but died of pneumonia a month ago. . **Underground Station: Harrow & Wealdstone**

Author's note: Bernard Davies identified Risingholme as "Three Gables". The old house has fallen on hard times. It is hemmed in by other buildings, and its garden is overgrown. It is not the villa to which the refined Mrs. Maberley returned from her round-the-world tour.

Mrs. Maberley said she had received a strange offer to buy her home. Because she wanted to travel around the world, she named a high price. The estate agent agreed to the price, and said his client also wanted the furnishings. After they agreed on the value of the house and furnishings, the estate agent returned with a written sales agreement. Thinking she needed some legal advice, Mrs. Maberley consulted Lawyer Sutro, who said it was a very strange agreement. Mrs. Maberley was required to leave everything. Even if she took her personal possessions, such as clothes and jewels, they would have to be checked. The estate agent said his client wanted everything or nothing. Mrs. Maberley said, "Then it must be nothing".

210

As Mrs. Maberley told her story to Holmes and Watson, Holmes heard Susan, the new housemaid, listening at the door. She was the one who posted Mrs. Maberley's letter to Holmes, and alerted Barney Stockdale. Holmes managed to wheedle out of Susan that a rich woman was behind the scheme. Later, Holmes discovered that Susan was Barney Stockdale's wife. Since Mrs. Maberley had been in the house for nearly two years, and had received no earlier offers, Holmes surmised that something of value had arrived recently. Mrs. Maberley said she had made no recent purchases, but on the way out, Holmes noticed several unpacked trunks and boxes. After his death, Douglas's things had been shipped from Italy. Holmes asked Mrs. Maberley to have his things taken to her bedroom, and examined as soon as possible.

BOODLE'S, No. 28 St. James's Street—SW1: [Latitude / Longitude: 51.506719,-0.139496]. On their way to Baker Street, Holmes told Watson, "This is a case for Langdale Pike". Pike spent his waking hours in the bow window of a St. James's gentleman's club, gathering London gossip. **Underground Station: Green Park**

Author's note: The bow window obviously refers to Boodle's, a club formed in 1762. Then, as now, Boodle's famous bow window faces St. James's Street.

The next morning, Holmes received a telegram from Lawyer Sutro. It said, *"Please come at once. Client's house burgled in the night. Police in possession".* When Holmes and Watson arrived, they found that Mrs. Maberley had been chloroformed, but did manage to grasp one sheet of paper from the burglars. It was in her son's handwriting, and seemed to be the two hundred and forty-fifth page of a novel.

GROSVENOR SQUARE—W1: [Latitude / Longitude: <u>51.511954,-0.152671</u>]. Holmes asked Watson to accompany him to Grosvenor Square, "for it is safer to have a witness when you are dealing with such a lady as Isadora Klein. Holmes learned, presumably from Langdale Pike, that she was the lady behind the mischief. Isadora Klein was a celebrated Spanish beauty and the widow of the sugar king. She lived in one of the finest corner-houses on Grosvenor Square. **Underground Station: Bond Street**

When Holmes threatened to go to the police, Isadora Klein admitted that she was behind the burglary. Douglas Maberley had fallen in love with her, and wanted to marry. To her, marriage with a penniless diplomat was unthinkable. Isadora hired Barney Stockdale and his boys to "convince" Douglas that marriage was out of the question, and admitted they were "a little rough in doing so". Because of the way he was treated, Douglas's love turned to hate, and he wrote a book about their affair. He sent one manuscript to Isadora, and kept another copy to send to the publisher. When Douglas died, Isadora knew the manuscript was in his personal effects. She had to get it, or all of London would know what she had done. Holmes asked Isadora, "How much does it cost to go round the world in first-class style? Could it be done on five thousand pounds"? When Isadora said that was about right, Holmes asked for a check in that amount. He gave it to Mrs. Maberley, who deserved a change of air.

ADVENTURE OF THE RED CIRCLE - 1902?

No. 13 GREAT ORMOND "Orme" STREET—WC1: [Latitude / Longitude: 51.521488,-0.121654]. The Warrens lived in a "High, thin, yellow-brick edifice" at Great Orme Street, northeast of the British Museum. Mrs. Warren consulted Holmes about her new lodger. The lodger offered a generous five pounds a week, but insisted on the following terms: He must have his own key, and he must not be disturbed. **Underground Station: Russell Square**

Mrs. Warren became concerned when, except for the first night, her lodger never left his room. If he needed something, he slipped printed notes under the door. His food was brought up on a tray and placed on a chair by the door. He only went out the first day, and then returned very late. Holmes suspected that there might have been a lodger substitution.

No. 9 GREAT ORMOND STREET—WC1: [Latitude / Longitude: 51.522545,-0.117914]. At one point, the lodger slipped a note under the door, asking that Mrs. Warren start delivering the *Daily Gazette*. Holmes thought that the newspaper's agony columns might be the way in which the lodger received messages. In the columns since the lodger arrived, Holmes found several cryptic messages, all signed by the letter G. The latest message read, ***"High red house with white stone facings, third floor, second window left, after dusk, G"***. **Underground Station: Russell Square**

Author's note: North American readers should remember that what the British call the third floor is your fourth floor.

Before Holmes and Watson could make a reconnaissance of Mrs. Warren's neighborhood, she burst into Baker Street, and said, "They had knocked my old man about".

TOTTENHAM COURT ROAD—W1: [Latitude / Longitude: 51.520942,-0.134678]. Mr. Warren was a timekeeper at Morton and Waylight's in Tottenham Court Road. He was on his way to work at seven, when two men came up behind him, threw a coat over his head, and shoved him into a waiting cab. **Underground Station: Goodge Street**

HAMPSTEAD HEATH—NW3: [Latitude / Longitude: 51.567334,-0.181239]. The men drove Mr. Warren around for about an hour, before depositing him on Hampstead Heath. He took the bus home. Mrs. Warren wanted to evict her lodger right then, but thought she had better get Holmes's advice first. **Underground Station: Hampstead Heath**

Holmes advised Mrs. Warren to do nothing. It was clear that some danger was threatening her lodger, and Holmes wanted to see him. Holmes asked when the lodger had lunch. Mrs. Warren said at one o'clock. Holmes and Watson went to Mrs. Warren's house at half-past twelve. Before entering the Warren's house, they saw a nearby, unoccupied "High red house with stone facings". At the Warren's, they arranged a hiding place, from which they could see the lodger retrieve the lunch tray. The lodger was a woman! When Holmes and Watson returned that night, they saw a Morse code signal from the red house. It was in Italian. When the signal suddenly stopped, Holmes and Watson rushed to the red house. Outside they found Detective Gregson of Scotland Yard. With him was Leverton, an American Pinkerton Agent. They were on the trail of the Red Circle's Giuseppe Gorgiano.

After Holmes explained what he knew, they all rushed up to the room from which the signals had been sent. There they found Gorgiano, stabbed to death. Holmes went to the window and signaled 'Vieni' to the lady at Mrs. Warrens. When she rushed to join them, they learned she was Emilia Lucca, Gennaro Lucca's wife. Her husband had killed Gorgiano in self-defense, and fled.

In Italy, as a young man, Gennaro had joined the Neapolitan Red Circle. When Gennaro and his new bride fled to America, they thought they had left the old associations behind. In New York, they met Gorgiano, the Red Circle member who had initiated Gennaro in Naples. Gorgiano started a new Red Circle mob in New York, and ordered Gennaro to honor his oath. One evening, Gorgiano tried to force himself on Emilia. When Gennaro came to her defense, Gorgiano became his mortal enemy. Emilia said that she and Gennaro fled to London, but Gorgiano followed. Both Scotland Yard and Pinkerton's thought Gennaro would get a vote of thanks, and not an arrest, for killing Gorgiano.

ROYAL OPERA HOUSE, Covent Garden—WC2: [Latitude / Longitude: 51.513445,-0.122362]. With the case safely in the hands of the police, Holmes said to Watson, "it is not eight o'clock and a Wagner night at Covent Garden! If we hurry, we might be in time for the second act". **Underground Station: Covent Garden**

In June 1902, the month Holmes refused a knighthood; he asked Watson, "Have you ever heard the name…Garrideb?" Watson looked in the telephone directory and found one, 'N. Garrideb'. Holmes said that Nathan Garrideb had written, asking for advice. At that point, Mrs. Hudson brought up a business card. Their visitor was "John Garrideb, Counsellor at Law, Moorville, Kansas, U.S.A.". He explained that a wealthy American, Alexander Hamilton Garrideb had died and left his fortune to any three Garridebs, but only if three could be found. The name was so unusual, that John said he found none in the United States. He had recently come to London and found Nathan Garrideb, giving him hope that there might be a third Garrideb to share the inheritance. The problem was that John and Nathan were both bachelors, with no male Garrideb relatives. John seemed upset that Nathan had brought Holmes into the affair.

No. 31 "221B" BAKER STREET—W1: [Latitude / Longitude: 51.517932,-0.155587]. After John Garrideb left Baker Street, Holmes said, "What on earth could be the object of this man telling us such rigmarole of lies?" Holmes noticed that his clothes and boots were English, but at least a year's wear. In addition, his American accent had been worn smooth by years in London. Finally, there had been no advertisement for Garridebs in the agony columns. To get more information, Holmes telephoned Nathan Garrideb, and made an appointment to visit him at six. **Underground Station: Marble Arch**

Author's note: In 1902, London's telephone exchange only had a capacity for 14,000 line users. This reference to using telephones in June 1902 meant that Sherlock (and Nathan Garrideb) were in a very select group.

CONNAUGHT PLACE "Little Ryder Street"—W2: [Latitude / Longitude: 51.513603,-0.161988]. For the past five years, Nathan Garrideb had lived in "an abode of Bohemian bachelors" at 136 Little Ryder Street, "one of the smaller offshoots from the Edgware Road, within a stone-cast of old Tyburn Tree of evil memory". Although Conan Doyle disguised the street name, the location described fits Connaught Place. **Underground Station: Marble Arch**

TYBURN TREE (site)—W1: [Latitude / Longitude: 51.512662,-0.158819]. The Tyburn Tree was the old gallows where London executed its criminals. The first recorded hanging was in 1196, and the last in 1783. The Tree is gone, but its site is marked by a stone plaque on the traffic island at the junction of Edgware Road and Oxford Street. As Watson indicated, it is "within a stone-cast" of Connaught Place. **Underground Station: Marble Arch**

CHRISTIE'S AUCTION HOUSE, No. 8 King Street—SW1: [Latitude / Longitude: 51.506285,-0.137994]. Nathan Garrideb rarely left his quarters, except to go to Christie's or Sotheby's to bid on additions to his natural history collection. Christie's Auction House was founded in 1766. In 1902, it was located at Number 8 King Street. **Underground Station: Green Park**

SOTHEBY'S, No. 3 Wellington Street—WC2: [Latitude / Longitude: 51.511654,-0.119519]. When Nathan Garrideb left his quarters to go to Sotheby's, it was to bid on additions to his natural history collection. In 1902, Sotheby's auction house was located at 3 Wellington Street. **Underground Station: Covent Garden**

As Holmes talked with Nathan Garrideb, John Garrideb arrived with an ad from a Birmingham newspaper. It indicated that Howard Garrideb, a contractor in Aston, sold hand plows and buckboards. Holmes and Watson noticed that the ad used the American spelling for ploughs. It was a typical American advertisement, purporting to be from an English firm.

EUSTON RAILWAY STATION—NW1: [Latitude / Longitude: 51.528401,-0.131943]. The smooth talking John convinced Nathan to take the midday train to Aston, near Birmingham to meet Howard the next day. John said they had found their third Garrideb! After John left, Holmes asked Nathan for permission to examine his natural history collection, while he was away. **Underground Station: Euston**

Author's note: Bernard Davies identified train service to Aston, as a "halt-on-demand" stop. Nathan had to take London & Western's 12:05 train from Euston.

WATERLOO ROAD—SE1: [Latitude / Longitude: 51.503644,-0.111613]. With Inspector Lestrade's help, Holmes identified John Garrideb as James Winter, alias Morecroft, alias Killer Evans, an American criminal with a sinister and murderous reputation. He came to London in 1893, and shot Roger Prescott, a Chicago forger, in a Waterloo Road nightclub. **Underground Station: Waterloo**

EDGWARE ROAD—W2: [Latitude / Longitude: 51.515393,-0.163381]. Holloway and Steele, the house agent firm for Nathan Garrideb, were located in Edgware Road. From them, Holmes found that the previous tenant at No. 136 "Little Ryder Street" fit the description of Roger Prescott, the man killed by 'Killer Evans'. **Underground Station: Edgware Road**

The next day, Holmes and Watson went to Little Ryder Street, and waited in a dark corner. In about an hour, they heard the door open and saw 'Killer Evans' enter the room. He threw back the carpet, and opened a trap door. Holmes and Watson rushed him, but before they subdued him, he fired two shots. One grazed Watson's thigh. Holmes clubbed 'Killer Evans' with his pistol and Watson called Scotland Yard. Under the trap door, they found Roger Prescott's counterfeiting paraphernalia. 'Killer Evans' was sent back to prison for attempted murder.

BRIXTON—SW9: [**Latitude / Longitude:** 51.471159,-0.112578].
Sadly, Nathan Garrideb could not stand the shock of the deception.
The last Holmes heard, London's only Garrideb was in a Brixton
nursing home. As Bernard Davies said, "The kind with bars on the
windows". Nathan had "quite lost his reason". **Underground Station: Stockwell**

DISAPPEARANCE OF LADY FRANCES CARFAX - 1902?

CHARING CROSS TURKISH BATH (site), Craven Street—WC2: [Latitude / Longitude: 51.507006,-0.123854]. Looking at Watson's boots, Holmes said, "But why Turkish?" Holmes was referring to the fact that the boots had been tied by someone other than Watson, which meant he had been to the Charing Cross Turkish Bath. The establishment was located on the upper floor of the wedge shaped building where Craven Street joins Northumberland Avenue. **Underground Station: Embankment**

Author's note: The women's entrance to the Charing Cross Turkish Bath was in Craven Passage, across from the south side of the Sherlock Holmes Pub: [Latitude / Longitude: 51.507237,-0.125332]. In Sherlock's day, Craven Passage was the Northumberland Passage. Look for the Turkish design of the women's entrance.

OXFORD STREET—W1: [Latitude / Longitude: 51.514017,-0.153068]. Before he understood Holmes's meaning, Watson said that his boots were English, and he had bought them at Latimer's in Oxford Street. **Underground Station: Bond Street**

CAMBERWELL—SE5: [Latitude / Longitude: 51.473769,-0.091954]. Sherlock had accepted a commission to find Lady Frances Carfax. She was the sole survivor of the late Earl of Rufton's direct family. Lady Frances was a person of regular habits and for four years had written every second week to her old governess, Miss Susan Dobney. Miss Dobney, who lived in Camberwell, contacted Holmes when Lady Frances failed to write for five weeks. **Railroad Station: Denmark Hill**

Through her bank records, Holmes traced Lady Frances to the Hôtel National, on Lake Geneva. Holmes asked Watson to go there and start the investigation. Watson learned that Lady Frances had moved to Baden, where she stayed at the Englischer Hof for a fortnight. There, she met Dr. Shlessinger and his wife. The three of them left for London, but the manager had not heard from them since.

THE LANGHAM HOTEL, Portland Place—W1: [Latitude / Longitude: 51.518077,-0.143875]. The Englischer Hof manager said that a bearded Englishman was also trying to find Lady Frances. Holmes arrived from England and told Watson that he had learned the identity of the bearded man. He was the Hon. Philip Green, who loved Lady Frances, and was trying to find her. Green, the son of a famous admiral of the same name, used the Langham Hotel as his London address. **Underground Station: Oxford Circus**

Author's note: Today, this exclusive Victorian hotel is restored to its former glory, and is an excellent hotel for those trying to find Sherlock Holmes's London.

Holmes requested additional information from the Englischer Hof manager. He told Holmes that Dr. Shlessinger's left ear was "Jagged or torn". This convinced Holmes, that Dr. Shlessinger was in fact, Henry (Holy) Peters, "One of the most unscrupulous rascals that Australia has ever evolved". His so-called wife was an Englishwoman named Fraser. In an effort to find Lady Frances, Holmes enlisted the aid of Inspector Lestrade. After a week, the pawning of Lady Frances's pendent gave them a flash of hope.

WESTMINSTER BRIDGE ROAD—SE1: [Latitude / Longitude: 51.499386,-0.113416]. Lady Frances's silver-and-brilliant pendant was pawned at Bovington's in Westminster Road. The man who pawned the pendant was a large clean-shaven man of clerical appearance. This obviously referred to Shlessinger. Holmes allowed Philip Green to watch Bovington's Pawnshop to see if Shlessinger returned. Green promised to take no action without Holmes's instruction. **Underground Station: Lambeth North**

STIMSON & CO. UNDERTAKERS (site), No. 345 Kennington Road—SE11: [Latitude / Longitude: 51.4874,-0.111347]. Mrs. Fraser came to pawn another pendant. Green followed her as she walked to Stimson and Co., an undertaker in Kennington Road. Stimson had been commissioned to make an unusually deep casket for Shlessinger. **Underground Station: Kennington**

Author's note: Bernard Davies identified No. 345 Kennington Road as the site of Stimson & Co.

BRIXTON—SW9: [Latitude / Longitude: 51.473214,-0.113758]. From Stimson and Co., Mrs. Fraser hailed a cab and went to the fictional Poultney Square in Brixton. When Green reported what he had seen, Holmes and Watson rushed to the "Poultney Square" house. **Underground Station: Brixton**

HOUSES OF PARLIAMENT—SW1: [Latitude / Longitude: 51.500945,-0.123661]. On their way to "Poultney Square", Holmes and Watson passed the Houses of Parliament. **Underground Station: Westminster**

WESTMINSTER BRIDGE—SW1: [Latitude / Longitude: 51.500857,-0.122808]. On their way to "Poultney Square", Holmes and Watson passed the Houses of Parliament as they crossed Westminster Bridge. **Underground Station: Westminster**

BRIXTON ROAD—SW9: [Latitude / Longitude: 51.476518,-0.112524]. The morning of the funeral, Holmes finally realized how Shlessinger planned to dispose of Lady Frances Carfax. He and Watson rushed along Brixton Road to Poultney Square. **Underground Station: Oval**

BRIXTON WORKHOUSE INFIRMARY (site)—SW9: [Latitude / Longitude: 51.463065,-0.120656]. When Holmes and Watson arrived, they confronted Shlessinger, and attempted to search his house. They found a large casket with the body of ninety-year-old Rose Spender inside. Shlessinger had obtained her body from the Brixton Workhouse Infirmary. The funeral would be at eight the next morning. Without a warrant, the police forced Holmes and Watson to leave, but promised to watch the house overnight. **Underground Station: Brixton**

FIRBANK ROAD (VILLAS)—SE15: [Latitude / Longitude: 51.470624,-0.058504]. Dr. Horsom, of No. 13 Firbank Villas, had certified Rose Spender's death. She was old nurse of Shlessinger's "wife". **Train Station: Queen Road Peckham**

They were just in time to stop the hearse from leaving. Lady Frances was chloroformed and placed in the casket, under the body of the old woman. Holmes and Watson just managed to revive Lady Frances. By the time Lestrade arrived, Shlessinger and his "wife" escaped.

ADVENTURE OF THE ILLUSTRIOUS CLIENT - 1902

CHARING CROSS TURKISH BATH (site), Craven Street—WC2: [Latitude / Longitude: 51.507006,-0.123854]. On September 3, 1902, Holmes and Watson were enjoying a smoke in the Charing Cross Turkish Bath. The establishment was located on the upper floor of the wedge shaped building where Craven Street joins Northumberland Avenue. **Underground Station: Embankment**

Author's note: [Latitude / Longitude: 51.507237,-0.125332]. The women's entrance to the Charing Cross Turkish Bath was in Craven Passage, across from the south side of the Sherlock Holmes Pub. In Sherlock's day, Craven Passage was the Northumberland Passage. Look for the Turkish design of the women's entrance.

CARLTON CLUB (site)—SW1: [Latitude / Longitude: 51.506577,-0.134204]. When Watson asked Holmes "whether anything was stirring", Holmes drew a note from his coat. The note was from Colonel Sir James Damery, asking Holmes to call upon him at the Carlton Club. In 1902, the Carlton Club was located on the south side of Pall Mall, at Carlton Gardens. Sir James wanted to consult Holmes on Violet de Merville's infatuation with Baron Adelbert Gruner. Violet was the daughter of General de Merville of Khyber fame. **Underground Station: Piccadilly Circus**

No. 9 QUEEN ANNE STREET—W1: [Latitude / Longitude: 51.518261,-0.145711]. In 1902, Watson was living at No. 9 Queen Anne Street. **Underground Station: Oxford Circus**

Author's note: Holmes referred to Watson as "His Boswell". I think Conan Doyle placed him in Queen Anne Street, because the original Boswell, James, lived there when he wrote the *Life of Samuel Johnson.*

Holmes and Watson met Sir James at the Carlton Club. He referred to Baron Gruner as one of the most dangerous men in Europe. Holmes knew of Gruner, and was sure he was involved with the "accidental" death of his wife. Now, this scoundrel was in England, and had snared the affections of the young and innocent Violet de Merville. Holmes knew that Sir James was acting as an intermediary, but could not get him to divulge the name of his "illustrious client". We can assume that the client was a person of considerable importance, perhaps even a "royal personage".

KINGSTON-UPON-THAMES—KT2: [Latitude / Longitude: 51.382048,-0.260715]. Sir James told Holmes that Baron Gruner's current residence was Vernon Lodge, near Kingston. **Rail Station: Maden Manor**

HURLINGHAM PARK—SW6: [Latitude / Longitude: 51.470484,-0.202657]. Sir James said that Baron Gruner was a horse fancier, and played polo at Hurlingham Park. He also had expensive tastes, and was a recognized authority on Chinese pottery, having written a book on the subject. **Underground Station: Putney Bridge**

Before Holmes met Watson at Simpson's for dinner, he went to see Baron Gruner to test him. Gruner said he had expected Holmes to get involved "Sooner or later", and advised him "To draw off at once".

SIMPSON'S IN THE STRAND, 100 The Strand—WC2: [Latitude / Longitude: 51.510906,-0.120463]. This old restaurant has not changed much since Watson called it "Our Strand Restaurant". When Watson joined Holmes at the table in Simpson's front window, Holmes said, "Johnson is on the prowl". Holmes was referring to Shinwell Johnson, who before he began assisting Holmes, had been a dangerous villain. Johnson had even served two terms in Parkhurst Prison on the Isle of Wight. With his underworld contacts, Johnson was a valuable asset. **Underground Station: Charing Cross**

No. 31 "221B" BAKER STREET—W1: [Latitude / Longitude: 51.517932,-0.155587]. Shinwell Johnson was waiting for Holmes and Watson when they returned to Baker Street, and introduced them to Kitty Winter. Baron Gruner had treated Kitty badly, and she wanted revenge. She knew Gruner kept a brown leather scrapbook that listed the women he had abused. It had everything about them: photographs, names, and details. Kitty said that the last time she saw the book; it was "In the pigeon-hole of the old bureau in Gruner's inner study". **Underground Station: Marble Arch**

BERKELEY SQUARE—W1: [Latitude / Longitude: 51.50919,-0.145993]. Holmes made an appointment for Kitty to tell her story to Violet de Merville. Violet lived with her father, General de Merville, at No. 104 (old numbering) Berkeley Square. Their house was, "One of those…London castles which would make a church seem frivolous". When they arrived, Violet was unmoved, saying, "You have called to malign my fiancé…it is only by my father's request that I see you at all". **Underground Station: Green Park**

NORTHUMBERLAND AVENUE—SW1: [Latitude / Longitude: 51.50728,-0.126772]. Two days later, Watson was walking north on Northumberland, toward the Charing Cross Station, when he saw a one-legged newsvendor displaying a placard that read, "**MURDEROUS ATTACK UPON SHERLOCK HOLMES**". Watson felt a pang of horror. **Underground Station: Charing Cross**

CAFÉ ROYAL—No. 68 Regent Street (site)—W1: [Latitude / Longitude: 51.509849,-0.135908]. Watson bought a newspaper, and learned that two men, armed with sticks, attacked Holmes in Regent Street, outside the Café Royal. **Underground Station: Piccadilly Circus**

GLASSHOUSE STREET—W1: [Latitude / Longitude: 51.510282,-0.134927]. Holmes escaped by running through the Café Royal, into Glasshouse Street. The article went on to say that, Holmes's injuries were serious, and that he had been carried to Charing Cross Hospital, but insisted on returning to Baker Street. **Underground Station: Piccadilly Circus**

CHARING CROSS HOSPITAL (site), William IV and Agar Streets—WC2: [Latitude / Longitude: <u>51.50944,-0.123956</u>]. **Holmes was taken to t**he old Charing Cross Hospital, located in the triangular site, where William IV and Agar Streets meet The Strand. They treated Holmes for the injuries he received from thugs near the Café Royal. **Underground Station: Charing Cross**

Watson rushed to Baker Street and found Sir Leslie Oakshot, the famous surgeon, with Holmes. Sir Leslie said that Holmes was in no immediate danger. Holmes asked Watson, to exaggerate the extent of his injuries when talking to the press. Holmes also wanted Watson to tell Shinwell Johnson to get Kitty Winter out of the way. Holmes said, "Those beauties will be after her now". "For six days the public was under the impression that Holmes was at the door of death". In fact, he was planning his campaign to bring down Baron Gruner. The plan involved Gruner's love of Chinese pottery, and involved Watson taking a twenty-four hour crash course on the subject.

LONDON LIBRARY, St. James's Square—SW1: [Latitude / Longitude: <u>51.507434,-0.136281</u>]. Watson's friend Lomax, the Sub-librarian at the London Library, helped Watson study books on Chinese pottery. **Underground Station: Piccadilly Circus**

Author's note: Thomas Carlyle built the London Library in 1841, as an alternative to the British Museum's library. Annual and life memberships are still available.

The bait to get Watson into Baron Gruner's villa was the sale of a delicate blue Ming saucer. Holmes said that the sight of it "Would drive a real connoisseur wild". The little treasure was from the illustrious person's private collection.

HALF MOON STREET—W1: [Latitude / Longitude: <u>51.506082,-0.144822</u>]. The ruse required Watson to assume an alias. He became Dr. Hill Barton, who supposedly lived at No. 369 Half Moon Street. As Barton, Watson went to see Baron Gruner about selling the rare blue Ming saucer. **Underground Station: Green Park**

CHRISTIE'S AUCTION HOUSE, No. 8 King Street—SW1: [Latitude / Longitude: 51.506285,-0.137994]. If pressed for a price on the blue Ming saucer, Watson was to suggest that Christie's or Sotheby's value it. **Underground Station: Green Park**

SOTHEBY'S (site), No. 3 Wellington Street—WC2: [Latitude / Longitude: 51.511554,-0.119476]. Watson, posing as Dr. Hill Barton, took the Ming saucer to Baron Gruner. If pressed on its value, Watson was to suggest a valuation at Christie's or Sotheby's. **Underground Station: Covent Garden**

Author's note: In 1902, Sotheby's Auction House was located at No. 3 Wellington Street. In 1917, they moved to their current location at No. 35-35 New Bond Street: **[Latitude / Longitude: 51.511834,-0.143951].**

As Baron Gruner examined the blue Ming saucer, Sherlock slipped into the adjoining study. A noise alerted Gruner, and when he dashed in, Holmes escaped through the open window. When Gruner ran after him, a woman's arm threw vitriol acid into Gruner's face. He cried out, "It was that hell-cat Kitty Winter". As Watson was treating Gruner, a Scotland Yard inspector arrived, and Watson handed him his real card. After Scotland Yard and Gruner's private doctors arrived, Watson returned to Baker Street to join Holmes, who was there with Gruner's brown leather scrapbook.

Holmes used the damming book to stop the wedding. Kitty Winter was arrested on the charge of vitriol throwing, but when the extenuating circumstances became known, she received the lightest possible punishment. Holmes was also threatened with prosecution for burglary, but with the influence of the illustrious client, British law became flexible.

ADVENTURE OF THE BLANCHED SOLDIER - 1903

No. 31 "221B" BAKER STREET—W1: [Latitude / Longitude: 51.517932,-0.155587]. In January 1903, Holmes received a visit from James Dodd. He came to consult Holmes on a mystery concerning his friend, Lance-Corporal Godfrey Emsworth. **Underground Station: Marble Arch**

THROGMORTON STREET—EC2: [Latitude / Longitude: 51.51464,-0.087741]. Dodd had been a soldier in the Boer War, and was now a stockbroker in Throgmorton Street. **Underground Station: Bank**

In an attempt to see his old mate, Dodd went to Tuxbury Old Place, near Bedford. Colonel Emsworth, Godfrey's father, said that Godfrey was on a world cruise, but Dodd saw Godfrey looking through the window, "His face bleached with fish-belly whiteness". When Dodd told Colonel Emsworth what he had seen, the Colonel ordered Dodd to leave.

EUSTON RAILWAY STATION—NW1: [Latitude / Longitude: 51.528401,-0.131943]. Because of the press of other cases, Holmes could not accompany Dodd back to Tuxbury Old Place until the following week. When he and Watson did go, Holmes arranged for Sir James Saunders to meet them at Euston Station. After taking the train to Bedfordshire, the trio took a carriage to Tuxbury Old Place to confront Colonel Emsworth. **Underground Station: Euston**

It was only when Holmes forced Colonel Emsworth to admit he thought his son had leprosy, that the Colonel allowed them to see his son. Sir James, a noted dermatologist, examined Godfrey and said that he did not have leprosy, but rather had a "Well-marked case of pseudo-leprosy, or ichthyosis, which was possibly curable and certainly non-infective".

ADVENTURE OF THE PRIORY SCHOOL - 1903?

No. 31 "221B" BAKER STREET—W1: [Latitude / Longitude: 51.517932,-0.155587]. One May morning, just before noon, a discombobulated visitor arrived at Baker Street. Thorneycroft Huxtable, M.A., Ph.D., etc., burst into the room and collapsed on the bearskin hearthrug. Holmes plucked a return ticket from his pocket, and noted that he had come from Mackleton, in the North of England. **Underground Station: Marble Arch**

EUSTON RAILWAY STATION—NW1: [Latitude / Longitude: 51.528401,-0.131943]. Bernard Davies makes a convincing argument that Dr. Huxtable arrived at London's Euston Station before 11 o'clock on the London & Northwestern line. **Underground Station: Euston**

When Dr. Huxtable recovered, he begged Holmes to accompany him back to Mackleton. Ten-year-old Lord Saltire, the only son of the Duke of Holdernesse, had been abducted from the Priory School, where Dr. Huxtable was founder and headmaster. Heidegger, the German master, and his bicycle were also missing. Lord Saltire did not have a bicycle, and no other bicycles were missing. Huxtable said that the Duke was offering five thousand pounds for the return of his son, and an additional one thousand pounds for the identity of the person who took him.

ADMIRALTY HOUSE, Whitehall—SW1: [Latitude / Longitude: 51.505557,-0.126826]. The Duke of Holdernesse had been Lord of the Admiralty, with offices at Whitehall. **Underground Station: Charing Cross**

CARLTON HOUSE TERRACE—SW1: [Latitude / Longitude: 51.506031,-0.132952]. The Duke of Holdernesse's London residence was at Carlton House Terrace. **Underground Station: Piccadilly Circus**

**ST PANCRAS RAILWAY STATION—NW1: [Latitude /
Longitude:** 51.530887,-0.122534**].** Holmes and Watson
accompanied Dr. Huxtable back to Mackleton on the Western line
from St Pancras Station. **Underground Station: Kings Cross St.
Pancras**

It was dark when Holmes, Watson and Huxtable arrived at the
Priory School. After examining Lord Saltire's and the German master's
rooms, Holmes obtained a large ordnance map of the neighborhood. The
main road, which ran past the school, ran past a constable station on the
east, and the Red Bull Inn on the west. Inquiries indicated that no one had
passed these two points, the night of the disappearance. There were no
side roads for a mile either way. Holmes determined the place to search
was the moor to the north, toward Holdernesse Hall and the Fighting Cock
Inn.

The next morning, Holmes and Watson explored the moor. In
addition to sheep and cow tracks, they found bicycle tracks, but not from
Heidegger's bicycle. Heidegger used Palmer tires, and the tracks were
from Dunlops. In some places, cow tracks obliterated the bicycle tracks.
When they finally found the tracks from Heidegger's bicycle, they also
found his body. His skull had been crushed. Holmes sent a local peat
cutter to notify Dr. Huxtable. Holmes and Watson continued north to
the Chesterfield High Road, and the Fighting Cock Inn. There they
found two horses, newly shod with old shoes, and new nails. When
the landlord, Reuben Hayes found them examining the horses, he
ordered them to leave. Holmes and Watson walked out of view but
continued to observe the Inn. They saw an agitated James Wilder,
the duke's secretary; arrive at the Inn on his bicycle. A minute
later, the landlord fled in the direction of Chesterfield.

Then, another man joined Wilder. Holmes and Watson
crept to the Inn where Holmes saw that Wilder's bicycle had
Dunlop tires. With a boost from Watson, Holmes was able to see in
the upper window. The person who had joined Wilder was the
Duke himself. Before returning to the school, Holmes and Watson
went to Mackleton Station to send telegrams to the police.

The next morning Holmes and Watson went to Holdernesse Hall. The Duke admitted that James Wilder was his illegitimate son, who hated his younger half-brother. Wilder hired Hayes to kidnap Lord Saltire. In the process, Hayes killed the German master, who was trying to rescue the boy. When the news that Heidegger's body had been found reached Holdernesse Hall, Wilder panicked and told the Duke everything. Wilder then went to the Fighting Cock Inn to tell Hayes to flee. In an attempt to save his older son, the Duke joined Wilder at the Inn and asked Mrs. Hayes to keep the boy for three more days. Their story would then be that Reuben Hayes had kidnapped the boy for ransom, but fled before he could be arrested. Holmes said that this story might not hold up, because Hayes was already in police custody, and that the boy should be retrieved at once. Holmes said that the only way for the Duke to avoid a public scandal, was for Hayes not to implicate Wilder. Holmes also reminded the Duke of the reward he had promised. The Duke wrote a check for twelve thousand pounds, twice the amount promised.

The Duke also explained the mystery of the cattle tracks. He said that some of his ancestors had used horseshoes made in the impression of cattle hoofs. They were in the family museum, and Wilder and Hayes had used them. Holmes said that they were, "The second most interesting object that I have seen in the North". When Watson asked, what the first, he patted the pocket that contained the check.

CAPITAL AND COUNTIES BANK (site), No. 123 Oxford Street— W1: [Latitude / Longitude: <u>51.515967,-0.135999</u>]. Was this the bank where Holmes deposited the Duke of Holdernesse's check? **Underground Station: Tottenham Court Road**

ADVENTURE OF THE CREEPING MAN - 1903?

Author's Note: This adventure takes place primarily in a hypothetical university town, a combination of Cambridge and Oxford, or "Camford" as Watson called it.

No. 31 "221B" BAKER STREET—W1: [Latitude / Longitude: 51.517932,-0.155587]. Trevor Bennett came to London to ask for Sherlock's help. Bennett was Professor Presbury's professional assistant, and lived in the Professor's house. Bennett was engaged to Professor Presbury's daughter. The 61-year-old Professor was also engaged, to a much younger woman. **Underground Station: Marble Arch**

Bennett became concerned when Professor Presbury's character changed after a secret visit to Prague. A colleague there was experimenting with a "Strength-giving serum, tabooed because he refused to reveal its source". Late one night, following the trip to Prague, Bennett observed the Professor crawling on all fours. Holmes and Watson went to Camford to solve the mystery.

COMMERCIAL STREET (ROAD)—E1: [Latitude / Longitude: 51.521762,-0.07608]. Professor Presbury was receiving strange correspondence and packages from a store on London's Commercial Road. Holmes sent a telegram to Mercer, his general utility man, to check on the source of the packages. Mercer's reply read, *"Have visited the Commercial Road and seen Dorak. Suave Person, Bohemian, elderly. Keeps large general store".* **Underground Station: Shoreditch High Street**

After the Professor received another package from Dorak, Holmes and Watson went to Presbury's house in Camford. There, they observed the strange behavior of the Professor and his wolfhound, Roy. Roy reacted to Presbury as if he were a wild animal. Holmes discovered that, in an attempt to regain his youth and vigor, Professor Presbury was experimenting with a dangerous serum extracted from, we can assume, the testicles of a Langur, a Himalayan monkey. Holmes said, "When one tries to rise above Nature, one is liable to fall below it".

ADVENTURE OF THE MAZARIN STONE - 1903?

No. 10 DOWNING STREET—SW1: [Latitude / Longitude: 51.503177,-0.126196]. No. 10 Downing Street is the traditional home of the British Head of Government. When the Prime Minister and the Home Secretary came to visit Holmes, they must have come from No. 10. They asked Holmes to find the missing Crown Jewel. **Underground Station: Westminster**

Author's note: Today, the entrance to Downing Street is guarded by an iron gate at Parliament Street, an extension of Whitehall.

No. 31 "221B" BAKER STREET—W1: [Latitude / Longitude: 51.517932,-0.155587]. Once he was on the case, Holmes hardly stopped to eat. When Watson dropped by Baker Street one evening, Billy, the young page, said that Mr. Holmes was asleep. He had been out at all hours in various disguises. Billy said the Prime Minister and the Home Secretary had been to Baker Street, as had Lord Cantlemere, who was against bringing Holmes into the case. Hearing Watson and Billy talking, Holmes came out of his bedroom. He told Watson that he expected to be murdered that evening by Count Negretto Sylvius. Upon hearing this shocking statement, Watson offered to drop everything and help. **Underground Station: Marble Arch**

MINORIES—EC3: [Latitude / Longitude: 51.513176,-0.075681]. Holmes had followed Count Sylvius to Old Straubenzee's workshop in the Minories. Straubenzee made an air gun that Holmes thought was pointed at him from the other side of Baker Street. Holmes had a new wax likeness of himself made, and expected it to be shot in the head at any moment. **Underground Station: Aldgate**

Author's note: We learned in *The Empty House*, that the empty building across the street from 221B was the Camden House, located at No. 34 Baker Street: **[Latitude / Longitude: 51.518067,-0.155632].**

At that point, Billy came in with the card of a caller. It was Count Sylvius himself. Holmes asked Watson to slip out through the adjoining bedchamber, and bring back Inspector Youghal of Scotland Yard's Criminal Investigation Division. Holmes told Sylvius that he knew all about his past activities—activities that would send him to prison for twenty years. Nevertheless, Holmes said he would keep the information to himself, if Sylvius would give up the great yellow diamond, and behave himself in the future. Holmes then asked Billy to go into the street and ask Sam Merton, Count Sylvius's partner-in-crime, to come up. Holmes said he would go into his bedchamber, and play his violin for five minutes, leaving Sylvius and Merton to consider his offer.

LIME STREET—EC3: [**Latitude / Longitude:** <u>51.512589,-0.082226</u>]. With Holmes playing his violin, Sylvius and Merton thought they were alone. Count Sylvius revealed that he had the diamond on him. He told Merton to take the jewel to Van Seddar in Lime Street. Sylvius said he would stay and stall Holmes to allow Van Seddar to spirit the diamond to Amsterdam. **Underground Station: Monument**

Author's note: Lime Street is named for the lime sellers who once congregated there.

At that point, Holmes sprang out of the chair where he had taken the place of the wax likeness. In a single movement, he grabbed the jewel with one hand, and held a pistol to Sylvius' head with the other. Holmes had constructed a third door out of his bedchamber. It opened behind the sitting room curtains. From this secret doorway, he had assumed the position of the dummy. The violin they heard playing was Holmes's new Gramophone.

Author's note: Gramophone is the British version of the American Phonograph. Rival manufacturers used the two names.

When Watson arrived with Inspector Youghal, and his C.I.D. squad, they arrested the two thieves, and led them away. As Holmes and Watson congratulated themselves, Billie came in with Lord Cantlemere's card. To have some fun with the old Lord, who thought Holmes was in over his head, Holmes slipped the stone into Cantlemere's coat pocket.

When Holmes got Lord Cantlemere to concede that the person who possessed the jewel should be arrested, Holmes asked him to reach into his right hand overcoat pocket. Even after being the brunt of a joke, Cantlemere said he had to, "Withdraw any reflection I have made upon your amazing professional powers".

THE LION'S MANE - 1907

Author's note: This adventure occurs near Sherlock's retirement home in Sussex. After leaving London, he saw little of Watson, except for an occasional weekend visit. In this adventure, Holmes acted as his own chronicler.

Holmes's villa commanded a view of the English Channel. The path to the water was long and dangerous, and ended on a pebble beach. The beach extended for several miles in both directions, broken only by a cove and the little village of Fulworth. Holmes's cottage was isolated, except for The Gables, Harold Stackhurst's well-known coaching establishment. Stackhurst was an all-round scholar who had been a varsity rower. He and Holmes became good friends.

In July of 1907, a gale washed the beach clean, and formed new swimming pools. The next morning, Holmes walked the cliff path, where he met Stackhurst. Stackhurst was going to the beach for a swim. There, he expected to see Fitzroy McPherson, who had gone to the beach earlier. McPherson was a science master whose life had been marred by a weak heart, but he was a natural athlete, and often swam in the beach pools. As Holmes and Stackhurst reached the beach path, they saw McPherson staggering in great agony. He managed to say, "The Lion's Mane" before dying. His Burberry overcoat was thrown over his shoulders, and when Stackhurst and Holmes removed it, they found his body covered with dark red welts.

As they examined the body, Ian Murdoch, a mathematical coach at The Gables, joined them. Normally, several students would have accompanied McPherson on his morning swim, but Murdoch had held them back for academic work. Murdoch was a strange young man, with a ferocious temper. There was no great sympathy between McPherson and Murdoch, but he seemed genuinely shocked at the sight before him. Murdoch said he had come straight from The Gables. Holmes sent him to Fulworth to report the matter to the police. As Holmes examined the beach path, he saw the no one else had gone down to the beach that morning. At the beach, he found McPherson's dry towel, indicating he either had not gone into the water, or had not dried himself if he did.

When Holmes returned to the body, Murdoch had arrived with Anderson, the village constable. Holmes advised him to send for his superior, and a doctor. The body was moved to The Gables, where the inquest would be held. Some letters were found in McPherson's desk that showed his romantic interest in Maud Bellamy. Maud was the daughter of Tom Bellamy, the owner of Fulworth Boats and Bathing-Cots. The letters indicated that the couple had made an appointment to meet that evening.

When Holmes walked to Fulworth to talk to Tom Bellamy and his daughter, they saw Murdoch coming out of The Haven, Bellamy's house. He refused to say why he was there. Holmes found that Tom Bellamy, and his son William, had been angry at McPherson's attention to Maud. However, her strong character prompted her to tell Holmes, "Bring them to justice…you have my sympathy and my help, whoever they may be". Maud said that she and Fitzroy McPherson were engaged, and planned to meet at the beach that evening. She also said that Ian Murdoch had once been a suitor, but that had changed when he understood her relationship with Fitzroy.

The inquest threw no light on the matter, and after a week, Holmes was still in the dark. Then, there was the incident of the dog. McPherson's dog had eaten nothing for a week, and had been found dead at the very spot where his master died. When Holmes examined the dog's body, he found it had died in great pain.

Holmes received a call from Inspector Bardle of the Sussex Constabulary, asking for Holmes's opinion on whether he should arrest Murdoch or not? Holmes said he was forming a theory, but it still had some loose ends. Then, the outer door swung open, and Ian Murdoch staggered in, followed by Stackhurst. Murdoch was in great pain, which was somewhat soothed by brandy and an application of salad oil to his wounds. They were the same wounds found on McPherson. Leaving Murdoch in the care of the housekeeper, Holmes, Stackhurst, and Inspector Bardle went down to the beach to confront the murderer. It was *Cyanea capillata, a* deadly jellyfish with the appearance of a tangled mass torn from a lion's mane. The gale had washed it into the swimming pool.

HIS LAST BOW - 1914

Prior to August 1914, and the start of World War I, Von Bork was the ideal German secret agent in Great Britain. From his country house near Harwich in Essex, he competed with the British aristocracy in sailing, hunting, and polo.

OLYMPIA—W14: [Latitude / Longitude: 51.495612,-0.210264]. Von Bork even matched his English friends by taking a prize in The Horse of the Year competition at Olympia. Baron Von Herling, the chief secretary of the German legation, told Von Bork that he would receive a warm welcome when he returned to Berlin. **Underground Station: Olympia**

ADMIRALTY HOUSE, Whitehall—SW1: [Latitude / Longitude: 51.505557,-0.126826]. Von Bork complained to Von Herling, that The Admiralty had received an alarm on the Naval Signals he had been accumulating, and changed every code. Nevertheless, thanks to his checkbook, and his agent Altamont, he would soon get the new signals. Von Bork told Von Herling that he paid Altamont five hundred pounds for the revised codes, and explained that Altamont was an Irish-American who hated the British. **Underground Station: Charing Cross**

GERMAN EMBASSY (SITE), No. 7 CARLTON HOUSE TERRACE—SW1: [Latitude / Longitude: 51.506188,-0.132544]. Baron Von Herling wanted Von Bork to bring the new Naval Signals to London. Von Herling said, "When you get the signal book through the little door...you can put a finis to your record in England". **Underground Station: Piccadilly Circus**

Author's note: Today, the former embassy is the home of The Royal Society. Albert Speer magnificently redesigned the interior of the building in the 1930's on orders from Adolf Hitler. The building was transferred to The Royal Society after World War II.

THE LITTLE DOOR—SW1: [Latitude / Longitude: 51.505818,-0.130926]. There are two small doors on the Carlton House Terrace steps. One is near the former German Embassy. Von Bork had to put the new Naval Signals through the little west door. **Underground Station: Piccadilly Circus**

After Von Herling left, Altamont arrived at Von Bork's country house, and delivered bad news. Five of Von Bork's best agents had been arrested. After delivering his package, Altamont wanted to be paid. Von Bork wrote him a check, and examined the package. To his surprise, he found a book titled: *Practical Handbook of Bee Culture* instead of the new naval signals. In that instant, Watson, who had come as Altamont's chauffeur, held a chloroformed sponge to Von Bork's face. Altamont, of course, was Holmes. They took Von Bork to Scotland Yard. It had taken two years for Holmes to set up his Altamont cover story, including extended stays in Chicago, and Buffalo.

CLARIDGE'S (HOTEL), No. 49 Brook Street—W1: [Latitude / Longitude: 51.512846,-0.148169]. After capturing Von Bork, Holmes returned to Claridge's, shaved off his goatee, and reappeared as himself. **Underground Station: Bond Street**

Author's note: In 1914, Holmes had given up his Baker Street rooms. In my opinion, Altamont (Holmes) stayed at Claridge's, courtesy of the German money he received from Von Bork. Of the six deluxe London hotels mentioned in the Sherlock Holmes adventures, Claridge's is the only one in which Sherlock was a guest. It is a wonderful place for Sherlock Holmes fans to stay while in London, if they have the wherewithal.

UNDERGROUND STATIONS

ALDGATE (Zone 1)

LLOYD'S REGISTER OF SHIPPING, No. 71 Fenchurch Street—EC3: [Latitude / Longitude: <u>51.512593,-0.078943</u>]. After John Openshaw's murder, Holmes spent the day at Lloyd's, going over ship files. When he returned to Baker Street, he placed five orange pips in an envelope, with "S. H. for J. O." written under the flap. He addressed the envelope to, "Captain James Calhoun, Bark *Lone Star*, Savannah, Georgia". Holmes told Watson that the *Lone Star* was the only ship of American registry, that matched the dates and places of the case. **1885 – Five Orange Pips**

FENCHURCH STREET—EC3: [Latitude / Longitude: <u>51.511981,-0.08063</u>]. Mary Sutherland's stepfather, James Windibank, worked for Westhouse and Marbank, the great claret importers of Fenchurch Street. Because her father had been a plumber, Mary received an invitation to the Gasfitters Ball. Her stepfather did not want her to go, but she insisted and there, met Hosner Angel. **1889? – Case of Identity**

LEADENHALL STREET—EC3: [Latitude / Longitude: <u>51.513313,-0.079342</u>]. Mary Sutherland said Hosner Angel, was a cashier in an office in Leadenhall Street. She did not know which office. When she wrote him, she addressed her letters to general delivery at the Leadenhall Street Post Office. **1889? – Case of Identity**

ALDGATE UNDERGROUND STATION—EC3: [Latitude / Longitude: <u>51.514524,-0.075896</u>].Arthur Cadogan West's body was found outside Aldgate Station, near the aboveground section of the tracks, just south of Aldgate High Street. Scotland Yard thought he had been thrown from inside the train, but there was no ticket in his pockets. His purse contained two pounds fifteen, so there was no robbery. He also had a checkbook, and two dress-circle tickets for the Woolwich Theatre, dated for that very evening. Holmes had a different theory. He thought Cadogan West's body had been placed on the roof of the train, from where it fell at the sharp bend in the tracks. **1895 – The Bruce-Partington Plans**

Author's note: Today, the trip from Earl's Court to Aldgate takes about 25 minutes. In 1895, the trip took 40 minutes. The slower pace may explain why the body stayed on the top of the car so long.

MINORIES—EC3: [Latitude / Longitude: 51.513176,-0.075681]. Holmes had followed Count Sylvius to Old Straubenzee's workshop in the Minories. Straubenzee made an air gun that Holmes thought was pointed at him from the other side of Baker Street. Holmes had a new wax likeness of himself made, and expected it to be shot in the head at any moment. **1903? – The Mazarin Stone**

Author's note: We learned in *The Empty House*, that the empty building across the street from 221B was the Camden House, located at No. 34 Baker Street: **[Latitude / Longitude: 51.518067,-0.155632].**

ALDGATE EAST (Zone 1)

No. 13 CAMPERDOWN "DUNCAN" STREET—E1: [Latitude / Longitude: 51.514275,-0.071154]. A few minutes after eight, a woman arrived in response to the ad. The woman said her name was Mrs. Sawyer, and that she lived on Duncan Street near Houndsditch. She said the ring belonged to her daughter Sally. Later, when Holmes went to the Duncan Street address, he found it belonged to a respectable paperhanger named Keswick, who had never heard of Mrs. Sawyer. Holmes surmised that "Mrs. Sawyer" must be an active man, and an incomparable actor. Duncan Street is now Camperdown Street. **1881? – Study in Scarlet**

MINCING LANE—EC3: [Latitude / Longitude: 51.510913,-0.081518]. Robert Ferguson was a partner in Ferguson and Muirhead, tea brokers of Mincing Lane. **1896? – The Sussex Vampire**

BAKER STREET (Zone 1

ABBEY HOUSE (site), 221 Baker Street—NW1: [Latitude / Longitude: 51.523504,-0.1578668]. With the expansion and modern numbering of Baker Street, the Abbey Building Society building had the luck (good or bad) of containing the 221 Baker Street address. People from all over the world wrote Sherlock and the Royal Mail delivered the letters to the Abbey Building Society. They had to hire a full-time, "Secretary to Mr. Holmes", to handle the correspondence. I think they enjoyed the notoriety. because in the 1951 Festival of Britain, they hosted the display of Sherlock Holmes material. The main attraction was a replica of the famous 221B sitting room, which drew 54,000 paid attendance during four months of the London exhibition. The replica room now resides behind glass at the Sherlock Holmes Pub on Northumberland Street.

SHERLOCK HOLMES MUSEUM, 239 Baker Street—NW1: [Latitude / Longitude: 51.523795,-0.158374]. The blue plaque on the Sherlock Holmes Museum says 221B, but that is the name under which the business is recorded, and not the official postal address. In 2002, when the Abbey National Building Society vacated their headquarters, the museum took on the task of receiving and answering the mail addressed to Sherlock Holmes at 221B Baker Street. The ground floor of the museum has a memorabilia gift shop, and the upper floors are furnished as Conan Doyle described Holmes and Watson's lodgings. This is an excellent place for you to start your search for Sherlock's London.

SHERLOCK HOLMES STATUE, Baker Street & Marylebone Road, NW1: [Latitude / Longitude: 51.522496,-0.156147]. G. K. Chesterton, noting the astonishing popularity of Sherlock Holmes, proposed that Baker Street needed a statue of Holmes. The idea was finally realized in September 1999, when a nine-foot bronze statue by the English sculptor John Doubleday was unveiled outside of the Marylebone exit of the Baker Street Underground Station.

MARYLEBONE ROAD BRANCH LIBRARY, 109-117 Marylebone Road—NW1: [Latitude / Longitude: 51.521595,-0.160235]. This branch of the Westminster City Libraries contains the Sherlock Holmes Collection. It includes stories, information about his creator Conan Doyle, photographs, cuttings and journals. The Collection is accessible by appointment only, telephone (020) 7641 1206.

SHERLOCK HOLMES WALKING TOUR—London Walks, Telephone (020) 7624 3978: [Latitude / Longitude: 51.522483,-0.157671]. Join this guided walking tour of the Sherlock Holmes sites near Baker Street. No reservations are needed. Just join the group at 1:30 PM every Tuesday, at the Baker Street exit of the Baker Street Underground Station. Call to re-confirm dates and time.

FROM THE "METROPOLITAN" STATION—NW1: [Latitude / Longitude: 51.518451,-0.155786]. One bright February morning, Watson noticed Alexander Holder walking toward 221B from the direction of the Metropolitan Station. The Baker Street Underground Station was on the Metropolitan Line, and Watson referred to it as the "Metropolitan Station". Holder had come to ask for Sherlock's help. **1891? – The Beryl Coronet**

WEYMOUTH STREET—W1: [Latitude / Longitude: 51.5203,-0.149463]. Holmes and Watson continued west on Weymouth Street toward Beaumont Mews. **1894 – The Empty House**

BEAUMONT MEWS—W1: [Latitude / Longitude: 51.5203,-0.149463]. Holmes and Watson drove north on Beaumont Mews, as it curved west into Marylebone High Street. **1894 – The Empty House**

MARYLEBONE HIGH STREET—W1: [Latitude / Longitude: 51.520722,-0.151695]. It was just a quick jog to the north on Marylebone High Street, and then west on Paddington Street. **1894 – The Empty House**

PADDINGTON STREET—W1: [Latitude / Longitude: 51.520796,-0.15265]. After a short westward journey, Bernard Davies suggests that Holmes and Watson turned south through the three feet wide Grotto Passage. Its Paddington Street entrance is no longer there, but it had to be near The Church of the Holy Shepherd. **1894 – The Empty House**

ASHLAND PLACE—W1: [Latitude / Longitude: 51.520649,-0.153585]. I think Holmes and Watson turned south on Ashland Place until they reached Osslington Buildings on the left. **1894 – The Empty House**

OSSLINGTON BUILDINGS—W1: [Latitude / Longitude: 51.519733,-0.153117]. Holmes and Watson continued east on Osslington Buildings, and followed it as it turned south to Paradise Street, now called Moxon Street. **1894 – The Empty House**

MOXON STREET—W1: [Latitude / Longitude: 51.519733,-0.153117]. From Osslington Buildings, Holmes and Watson took a short jog on Moxon Street, then called Paradise Street, and continued south on Aybrook Street, then called North Street. **Underground Station: Baker Street**

AYBROOK STREET—W1: [Latitude / Longitude: 51.518475,-0.152881]. Holmes and Watson were getting close to their destination when they continued south on Aybrook Street then called North Street. **1894 – The Empty House**

BANK (Zone 1)

THE CITY—EC2: [Latitude / Longitude: 51.512589,-0.087011].
Outside, a cabby was waiting to take them to the train station. Inside was
Hall Pycroft, "A well-built...young fellow, with a frank, honest face and a
slight, crisp yellow moustache". He dressed like a smart young City man,
but could not hide his cockney beginnings. On the train, Pycroft repeated
his story to Watson. **1889? – The Stock-Broker's Clerk**

THREADNEEDLE STREET—EC2: [Latitude / Longitude:
51.514159,-0.085874]. Hugh Boone, the crippled lodger, could not
explain the presence of St. Clair's clothes. Boone was a professional
beggar, and a familiar sight to those who work in the City. He spent
his days in Threadneedle Street, selling wax vestas. **1889 – Man with
the Twisted Lip**

THREADNEEDLE STREET—EC2: [Latitude / Longitude:
51.514159,-0.085874]. Alexander Holder was the senior partner in the
Threadneedle Street firm of Holder & Stevenson, the second largest
private banking house in the City. Based on his appearance, and his
plea for help, Watson wondered, "What could have happened...to
bring one of the foremost citizens of London to this most pitiable
pass"? **1891? – The Beryl Coronet**

No. 46 OLD JEWRY—EC2: [Latitude / Longitude: 51.514698,-
0.090584]. On November 19, Holmes received a note from the firm of
Morrison, Morrison, and Dodd, at No. 46 Old Jewry. They remembered
Holmes's successful action in the case of the *Matilda Briggs*, and
referred Robert Ferguson on a matter concerning vampires. **1896? –
The Sussex Vampire**

THROGMORTON STREET—EC2: [Latitude / Longitude:
51.51464,-0.087741]. Dodd had been a soldier in the Boer War, and
was now a stockbroker in Throgmorton Street. **1903 – The Blanched
Soldier**

BARBICAN (Zone 1)

BARBICAN "ALDERSGATE" UNDERGROUND STATION—EC1: [Latitude / Longitude: 51.5202,-0.097442]. On their way to Jabez Wilson's pawnshop, Holmes and Watson got off the underground at Aldersgate, (now Barbican) Station. Holmes got a look at Vincent Spaulding by asking for directions to The Strand. He noticed that the knees of Spaulding's trousers were dirty. Holmes took pride in having an exact knowledge of London, and identified one of the nearby businesses as the Coburg Branch of the City and Suburban Bank. **1890 – Red-Headed League**

BLACKFRIARS (Zone 1)

POPPINS "POPE'S" COURT—EC4: [Latitude / Longitude: 51.514358,-0.105175]. Duncan Ross advertised for all redheaded men in London to apply at the offices of the Red-headed League at No. 7 Pope's Court, just off Fleet Street. The ad said that a League vacancy had opened. The position paid £4 a week for nominal services. The described location indicates that "Poppins Court" is Pope's Court. **1890 – Red-Headed League**

No. 135 FLEET STREET, Daily Telegraph (site)—EC4: [Latitude / Longitude: 51.514223,-0.106731]. Holmes and Watson went to the Fleet Street district to place an ad for tomorrows *Daily Telegraph*. The ad read, *"To-night. Same hour. Same place. Two taps. Most vitally important. Your safety at stake. Pierrot".* **1895 – The Bruce-Partington Plans**

BOND STREET (Zone 1)

GROSVENOR SQUARE—W1: [Latitude / Longitude: <u>51.511792,-0.150194</u>]. Lord St. Simon's letter to Holmes came from Grosvenor Mansions, Grosvenor Square. St. Simon was the second son of the Duke of Balmoral. **1886 - The Noble Bachelor**

BROOK STREET—W1: [Latitude / Longitude: <u>51.512949,-0.1472</u>]. Their guest introduced himself as Dr. Percy Trevelyan. He lived at 403 Brook Street, in the Cavendish Square quarter. **1886? – The Resident Patient**

OXFORD STREET—W1: [Latitude / Longitude: <u>51.514658,-0.146878</u>]. Holmes and Watson crossed Oxford Street, as Holmes pondered Blessington's attitude. **1886? – The Resident Patient**

BOND STREET—W1: [Latitude / Longitude: <u>51.514418,-0.146685</u>]. On their way from Baker Street to the Diogenes Club, Holmes and Watson probably walked south on Bond Street. **1887? – The Greek Interpreter**

OXFORD STREET—W1: [Latitude / Longitude: <u>51.514115,-0.152178</u>]. After Dr. Mortimer left, Holmes sent Watson on errands to keep him out all day. Holmes needed solitude "in those hours of intense mental concentration". Holmes asked Watson to have Bradley's, the Oxford Street tobacconist, send up a pound of their strongest shag. It was almost nine when Watson returned. The room was so thick with smoke that Watson thought there had been a fire. **1889 – Hound of the Baskervilles**

BLANDFORD STREET—W1: [Latitude / Longitude: <u>51.518455,-0.153058</u>]. **From 221B Baker Street,** Blandford Street was the nearest street heading east. On their walk to the Alpha Inn, Holmes and Watson probably took Blandford Street to Marylebone Lane. **1889? - The Blue Carbuncle**

MARYLEBONE LANE—W1: [Latitude / Longitude: <u>51.517258,-0.150772</u>]. From Blandford Street, Holmes and Watson followed Marylebone Lane as it headed south. **1889? - The Blue Carbuncle**

WIGMORE STREET—W1: [Latitude / Longitude: 51.516445,-0.148251]. Where Marylebone Lane met Wigmore Street, Holmes and Watson turned left and headed east on Wigmore Street. **1889? - The Blue Carbuncle**

WIMPOLE STREET—W1: [Latitude / Longitude: 51.51663,-0.147554]. As Holmes and Watson continued east on Wigmore Street, they crossed Wimpole Street. **1889? - The Blue Carbuncle**

WELBECK and BENTINCK STREETS—W1: [Latitude / Longitude: 51.517289,-0.149215]. At midday, while walking from Baker Street to Oxford Street, Holmes was nearly killed at the intersection of Welbeck and Bentinck Streets. A furiously driven two-horse van just missed him, as it dashed around to Marylebone Lane. **1891 – The Final Problem**

MARYLEBONE LANE—W1: [Latitude / Longitude: 51.517029,-0.150719]. After just missing Holmes at the corner of Bentinck and Welbeck, the two-horse van dashed west on Bentinck to Marylebone Lane, and was gone in an instant. **1891 – The Final Problem**

HENRIETTA PLACE—W1: [Latitude / Longitude: 51.515533,-0.147758]. As Holmes walked down Welbeck Street, on his way to Oxford Street, he jogged left on Henrietta Place to Vere Street. **1891 – The Final Problem**

VERE STREET—W1: [Latitude / Longitude: 51.515306,-0.147513]. As Holmes continued south toward Oxford Street, a brick fell from a Vere Street building, shattering at Holmes's feet. Since this was just after the near "accident" at Bentinck and Welbeck streets, Holmes was convinced that Professor Moriarty's thugs were trying to kill him. **1891 – The Final Problem**

CLARIDGE'S (HOTEL), 49 Brook Street—W1: [Latitude / Longitude: 51.512846,-0.148169]. J. Neil Gibson wrote Holmes from Claridge's. He pleaded with Holmes to help prove that Miss Dunbar was innocent. Gibson said he would come to Baker Street at eleven. Before Gibson arrived, Billy announced Marlow Bates, Gibson's estate manager. Bates said he was leaving Gibson's employment, but wanted to tell Holmes that Gibson was cunning. **1900? – Thor Bridge**

GROSVENOR SQUARE—W1: [Latitude / Longitude: 51.511954,-0.152671]. Holmes asked Watson to accompany him to Grosvenor Square, "for it is safer to have a witness when you are dealing with such a lady as Isadora Klein. Holmes learned, presumably from Langdale Pike, that she was the lady behind the mischief. Isadora Klein was a celebrated Spanish beauty and the widow of the sugar king. She lived in one of the finest corner-houses on Grosvenor Square. **1902? – Three Gables**

OXFORD STREET—W1: [Latitude / Longitude: 51.514017,-0.153068]. Before he understood Holmes's meaning, Watson said that his boots were English, and he had bought them at Latimer's in Oxford Street. **1902? – Lady Frances Carfax**

CLARIDGE'S (HOTEL), 49 Brook Street—W1: [Latitude / Longitude: 51.512846,-0.148169]. After capturing Von Bork, Holmes returned to Claridge's, shaved off his goatee, and reappeared as himself. **1914 – His Last Bow**

Author's note: In 1914, Holmes had given up his Baker Street rooms. In my opinion, Altamont (Holmes) stayed at Claridge's, courtesy of the German money he received from Von Bork. Of the five Central London hotels mentioned in the Sherlock Holmes adventures, Claridge's is the only one in which Sherlock was a guest. It is a wonderful place for Sherlock Holmes fans to stay while in London, if they have the wherewithal.

BRIXTON (Zone 2)

LAURISTON GARDENS (site), Brixton Road—SW9: [Latitude / Longitude: 51.466777,-0.11309]. On the way to Lauriston Gardens, Holmes and Watson traveled along Brixton Road. When they arrived, Inspector Gregson asked Holmes to examine the murder site. **1881? – Study in Scarlet**

Author's note: Bernard Davies identified Lauriston Gardens as a group of four detached, double-fronted houses on the East side of Brixton Road, between Villa Road and St John's Crescent. Today, Max Roach Park occupies the site.

BRIXTON ROAD POLICE STATION, corner of Brixton & Cresham Roads—SW9: [Latitude / Longitude 51.464754,-0.114193]. Holmes asked Gregson if he and Lestrade had taken a cab to Lauriston Gardens. He already knew they had not, but he wanted to confirm his observations. This meant that the two Scotland Yard men had walked from the Brixton Road Police Station, just a quarter of a mile away. **1881? – Study in Scarlet**

WHITE HART TAVERN, Lilford & Loughborough Roads— SW5: [Latitude / Longitude: 51.470575,-0.106884]. Holmes placed an ad in the evening paper. It read, *"In Brixton Road, this morning. A plain gold wedding ring, found in the roadway between the White Hart Tavern and Holland Grove. Apply Dr. Watson, 221B Baker Street, between eight and nine this evening."* Holmes apologized to Watson for using his name. **1881? – Study in Scarlet**

BRIXTON HILL—SW2: [Latitude / Longitude: 51.452972,-0.121064]. Toby, Holmes and Watson continued north as Streatham Hill's name changed to Brixton Hill. **1887 – Sign of Four**

BRIXTON ROAD—SW9: [Latitude / Longitude: 51.462635,-0.115077]. Near Brixton Station, Toby, Holmes and Watson continued northward on Brixton Road. **1887 – Sign of Four**

SOUTH BRIXTON—SW2: [Latitude / Longitude: 51.458045,-0.118757].When Watson arrived, he found Holmes with "an elderly... woman of the buxom landlady type". She was Mrs. Merrilow of South Brixton. At the time, South Brixton was a popular middle-class suburb. **1896 – The Veiled Lodger**

LOWER BRIXTON ROAD—SW2: [Latitude / Longitude: 51.453044,-0.120857]. When Dr. Barnicot went to his branch surgery in Lower Brixton Road, he was surprised to find that it too had been burgled, and the second plaster cast of Napoleon smashed. **1900? – The Six Napoleons**

BRIXTON—SW9: [Latitude / Longitude: 51.473214,-0.113758]. From Stimson and Co., Mrs. Fraser hailed a cab and went to the fictional Poultney Square in Brixton. When Green reported what he had seen, Holmes and Watson rushed to the "Poultney Square" house. **1902? – Lady Frances Carfax**

BRIXTON WORKHOUSE INFIRMARY (site)—SW9: [Latitude / Longitude: 51.463065,-0.120656]. When Holmes and Watson arrived, they confronted Shlessinger, and attempted to search his house. They found a large casket with the body of ninety-year-old Rose Spender inside. Shlessinger had obtained her body from the Brixton Workhouse Infirmary. The funeral would be at eight the next morning. Without a warrant, the police forced Holmes and Watson to leave, but promised to watch the house overnight. **1902? – Lady Frances Carfax**

CALEDONIAN ROAD & BARNSBURY (Zone 2)

PENTONVILLE PRISON, Caledonian Road—N7: [Latitude / Longitude: 51.544898,-0.117803]. James Ryder's friend Maudsley served time in Pentonville Prison. **1889? - The Blue Carbuncle**

CAMDEN TOWN (Zone 2)

REGENT'S PARK ZOO—NW1: [Latitude / Longitude: 51.535795,-0.155906]. Holmes told Watson that Charles Augustus Milverton was, "The worst man in London". Holmes said, "He reminded him of the serpents in the Regent's Park Zoo". **1899? – Charles Augustus Milverton**

CANADA WATER (Zone 2)

ROTHERHITHE—SE16: [Latitude / Longitude: 51.498849,-0.033048]. In Victorian times, Rotherhithe, the dockside area across the Thames from Wapping, was a very rough place. Holmes said he had picked up a coolie disease there, and returned to Baker Street to die. **1889 – The Dying Detective**

CANNON STREET (Zone 1)

CANNON STREET RAILWAY STATION—EC4: [Latitude / Longitude: 51.511417,-0.090877]. St. Clair worked in London, and was a man of regular habits, returning home every evening on the 5:14 from Cannon Street Station. "He had no occupation, but was interested in several companies". **1889 – Man with the Twisted Lip**

CHANCERY LANE (Zone 1)

HOLBORN BAR—WC1: [Latitude / Longitude: 51.51817,-0.111129]. Steve Dixie's attitude changed when Holmes mentioned the killing of young Perkins outside the Holborn Bar. The Negro's face turned leaden, and he beat a hurried retreat. **1902? – Three Gables**

Author's note: The Holborn Bar is near the junction of High Holborn and Grays Inn Road. There, two stone obelisks mark the boundary of the City of London. In my opinion, "outside the Holborn Bar" means outside the City, near the Holborn Bar.

CHARING CROSS (Zone 1)

ADMIRALTY HOUSE, Whitehall—SW1: [Latitude / Longitude: 51.505557,-0.126826]. The Old Admiralty Offices in Whitehall are where it was set down that the convict ship *Gloria Scott* was lost at sea. No word ever leaked out as to her true fate. **1874 - The "Gloria Scott"**

THE STRAND—WC2: [Latitude / Longitude: 51.509577,-0.123639]. Having neither "kith nor kin" in England, Watson moved to London, "That great cesspool into which all the loungers and idlers of the Empire are irresistibly drawn." At first, he stayed at a small private hotel in The Strand. Watson soon found that his "wound pension" of eleven shillings and sixpence a day could not support his London life style. He made up his mind to leave the hotel, and take up less expensive quarters. **Underground Station: 1881? – Study in Scarlet**

AMERICAN EXCHANGE, The Strand—WC2: [Latitude / Longitude: 51.508624,-0.125379]. The two letters were addressed to the American Exchange, The Strand. The letters were from the Guion Steamship Company, and referred to the sailing of their boats from Liverpool to New York. In the 1880's, the American Exchange was located at 449 The Strand, with a kiosk style booth on the south side of the street, between the two exit gates of the Charing Cross Railroad Station. **1881? – Study in Scarlet**

TRAFALGAR SQUARE FOUNTAIN—WC2: [Latitude / Longitude: 51.508061,-0.127214]. When Inspector Lestrade told Holmes about dragging the Serpentine, Holmes laughed and asked if he was also dragging the Trafalgar Square Fountain, "Because you have just as good a chance of finding this lady in the one as in the other". **1886 - The Noble Bachelor**

THE GRAND HOTEL—WC2: [Latitude / Longitude: 51.50738,-0.127255]. One of the three luxury Northumberland hotels was The Grand Hotel, located in the curved front building on the east side of Northumberland, across from Trafalgar Square. **1887? – The Greek Interpreter**

CHARING CROSS—WC2: [Latitude / Longitude: 51.507347,-0.128016]. One night, a Mr. Latimer called on Paul Melas and said he needed a Greek interpreter. He asked Melas to accompany him to Kensington. They left in a four-wheeled carriage, and set off from Pall Mall, through Charing Cross. Melas was alarmed to see that Latimer carried a lead weighted bludgeon. **1887? – The Greek Interpreter**

THE STRAND—WC2: [Latitude / Longitude: 51.509577,-0.123639]. Mary Morstan arrived at Baker Street in a four-wheeler. She, Holmes, and Watson, drove down The Strand toward the Lyceum. It was a damp, foggy, September evening, and "the lamps were but misty splotches of diffused light". **1887 – Sign of Four**

SIMPSON'S IN THE STRAND, No. 100 The Strand—WC2: [Latitude / Longitude: 51.510906,-0.120463]. After his three day fast to feign illness, Holmes told Watson, "Something nutritious at Simpson's would not be out of place". **1889 – The Dying Detective**

Author's note: Simpson's, arguably the best-known English restaurant in London, has not changed much since Holmes and Watson dined there. If you order the tableside carved roast beef, remember to give a separate cash tip to the carver.

CHARING CROSS HOSPITAL (site)—WC2: [Latitude / Longitude: 51.50944,-0.123956]. One morning in the autumn of 1889, while Holmes was out, he had a visitor who could not wait. The visitor left his walking stick, and as usual, it revealed more to Holmes than it did to Watson. The stick belonged to Dr. James Mortimer. His colleagues at the Charing Cross Hospital had presented it in 1884, when Dr. Mortimer left to go into private country practice. **1889 – Hound of the Baskervilles**

THE STRAND—WC2: [Latitude / Longitude: 51.509577,-0.123639]. Sir Henry, who had just arrived from Canada, bought a new pair of tan boots in The Strand. He said he paid six dollars for them, but I wonder if he meant pounds. One shoe was stolen at the Northumberland Hotel before he had them on his feet. **1889 – Hound of the Baskervilles**

CHARING CROSS POST OFFICE (site), South Africa House, Trafalgar Square—WC2: [Latitude / Longitude: 51.507808,-0.126823]. Sir Henry received a note at the Northumberland Hotel with a Charing Cross postmark. The note was made of words cut from the previous day's *Times*, and read, **"As you value your life or your reason, keep away from the moor"**. To know that he was staying at the Northumberland Hotel, Holmes suspected that someone was following Sir Henry. **1889 – Hound of the Baskervilles**

TRAFALGAR SQUARE—WC2: [Latitude / Longitude: 51.508195,-0.127201]. John Clayton said he picked up his fare at Trafalgar Square. First, they drove to the Northumberland Hotel and followed Sir Henry and Dr. Mortimer to Baker Street. Then they followed them as they walked back to the hotel. Clayton said that when they were three-quarters down Regent Street, his fare "threw up the trap, and cried that I should drive to Waterloo Station as hard as I could". **1889 – Hound of the Baskervilles**

CRAVEN STREET—WC2: [Latitude / Longitude: 51.507736,-0.125393]. When Sir Henry first arrived in London, Stapleton brought his wife to London and lodged at the "Mexborough Private Hotel" in Craven Street. This may refer to the Craven Hotel at No. 45 Craven Street. Because she did not agree with his plan, he kept her imprisoned in the room while he followed Dr. Mortimer to and from Baker Street. **1889 – Hound of the Baskervilles**

CHARING CROSS RAILROAD STATION, The Strand—WC2: [Latitude / Longitude: 51.508497,-0.125551]. When Mme. Fournaye returned to Paris, her wild behavior at the Charing Cross Station attracted attention. **1890? – Second Stain**

LOWTHER ARCADE (site), The Strand—WC2: [Latitude / Longitude: 51.508836,-0.125259]. Holmes told Watson that he should send his luggage on ahead to Victoria Station by trusted messenger. Then, the next morning, he should flag a hansom cab, but not take the first or second one. He should then go to The Strand end of the Lowther Arcade, dash through the Arcade to the rear exit, where a brougham would be waiting. If he followed the instructions exactly, he would reach Victoria Station just in time to catch the Continental Express. **1891 – The Final Problem**

ADELAIDE STREET—WC2: [Latitude / Longitude: 51.509063,-0.125828]. The former Lowther Arcade had its main entrance on The Strand, and its back entrance on Adelaide Street. Holmes instructed Watson to exit the hansom at The Strand End, dash through the Arcade, and enter the waiting brougham on Adelaide Street. Mycroft Holmes was the driver. **1891 – The Final Problem**

CHARING CROSS POST OFFICE (site), South Africa House, Trafalgar Square—WC2: [Latitude / Longitude: 51.507808,-0.126823]. Scott Eccles sent his telegram to Holmes from the Charing Cross Post Office, but left before the police arrived. **1891? – Wisteria Lodge**

CHARING CROSS RAILROAD STATION, The Strand—WC2: [Latitude / Longitude: 51.508497,-0.125551]. While looking for Colonel Sebastian Moran in the "M" section of his Index of Biographies, Holmes mentioned, "Mathews, who knocked out my left canine in the waiting room at Charing Cross". **1894 – The Empty House**

CHARING CROSS RAILROAD STATION, The Strand—WC2: [Latitude / Longitude: 51.508497,-0.125551]. Hopkins had just come from Charing Cross Railway Station. He had come from Yoxley Old Place in Kent, and asked Holmes and Watson to accompany him back there the next morning. **U1894 – The Golden Pince-Nez**

ADMIRALTY HOUSE, Whitehall—SW1: [Latitude / Longitude: 51.505557,-0.126826]. With the death of Arthur Cadogan West, and the missing Bruce-Partington plans, the Admiralty was buzzing like an overturned beehive. Mycroft said, "He had never seen the Prime Minister so upset". **1895 – The Bruce-Partington Plans**

CHARING CROSS HOTEL, The Strand—WC2: [Latitude / Longitude: 51.50872,-0.125144]. A message from Colonel Walter to Oberstein (in reality dictated by Holmes), persuaded Oberstein to return to London. The note named the Charing Cross Hotel as their meeting place. Oberstein fell for the ruse. After his capture, they found the missing pages of the Bruce-Partington plans in his luggage. He had planned to auction them to the European navel powers. **1895 – The Bruce-Partington Plans**

Author's note: The famous old Charing Cross hotel is located at the center of Sherlock's London. It is near many Sherlock Holmes sites; including the Sherlock Holmes Pub, Simpson's Restaurant, and Northumberland Avenue. The hotel is an excellent choice for Sherlock Holmes fans visiting London.

CHARING CROSS TELEGRAPH OFFICE (site), 447 The Strand—WC2: [Latitude / Longitude: 51.509337,-0.12395]. One gloomy February morning, Holmes received a telegram sent by Cyril Overton from Charing Cross. It read, *"Please await me. Terrible misfortune. Right wing three quarter missing, indispensable to-morrow"*. Later in the adventure, through a bit if trickery, Holmes learned that, Staunton had sent his telegram to Dr. Armstrong in Cambridge. **1897? – The Missing Three-Quarter**

THE STRAND—WC2: [Latitude / Longitude: 51.509577,-0.123639]. Overton, and the rest of the Cambridge team, were staying at Bentley's Private Hotel, near The Strand. The night before, Godfrey Staunton was seen with a rough looking man, running toward The Strand. Holmes became more interested, when he learned that Staunton was Lord Mount-James's heir. Mount-James was one of the richest men in England. **1897? – The Missing Three-Quarter**

CHARING CROSS RAILROAD STATION, The Strand—WC2: [Latitude / Longitude: 51.508497,-0.125551]. One cold winter morning in 1897, Holmes and Watson left London by train for Abbey Grange, in Marsham, Kent. They were responding to a letter from Inspector Stanley Hopkins. It was not until they had consumed some hot tea in Charing Cross Station, and taken their places on the Kentish train, that they were sufficiently thawed to talk about the Inspector's reason for summoning them. **1897 – Abbey Grange**

CHARING CROSS TELEGRAPH OFFICE (site), 447 The Strand—WC2: [Latitude / Longitude: 51.509337,-0.12395]. After examining the scene of Sir Eustace Brackenstall's murder, and interviewing Lady Brackenstall, Holmes and Watson returned to London. There, they drove to Scotland Yard, but instead of entering, returned to the Charing Cross telegraph office to send a telegram to Inspector Hopkins. Holmes advised Hopkins to drag the Abbey Grange pond. When Hopkins did so, and found the silver, he thought Holmes was a wizard. **1897 – Abbey Grange**

COX & COMPANY (site), Craig's Court—SW1: [Latitude / Longitude: 51.506672,-0.12729]. Watson revealed that, "somewhere in the vaults of…Cox and Co., at Charing Cross, there is a travel worn and battered tin dispatch box with my name…painted upon the lid". The box is crammed with records of Sherlock's unrecorded cases. **1900? – Thor Bridge**

Author's note: During the subsequent period of bank consolidations, the office closed, and the dispatch box was undoubtedly moved.

SIMPSON'S IN THE STRAND, No. 100 The Strand—WC2: [Latitude / Longitude: 51.510906,-0.120463]. This old restaurant has not changed much since Watson called it "Our Strand Restaurant". When Watson joined Holmes at the table in Simpson's front window, Holmes said, "Johnson is on the prowl". Holmes was referring to Shinwell Johnson, who before he began assisting Holmes, had been a dangerous villain. Johnson had even served two terms in Parkhurst Prison on the Isle of Wight. With his underworld contacts, Johnson was a valuable asset. **1902 – The Illustrious Client**

NORTHUMBERLAND AVENUE—SW1: [Latitude / Longitude: 51.50728,-0.126772]. Two days later, Watson was walking north on Northumberland, toward the Charing Cross Station, when he saw a one-legged newsvendor displaying a placard that read, **"MURDEROUS ATTACK UPON SHERLOCK HOLMES".** Watson felt a pang of horror. **1902 – The Illustrious Client**

ADMIRALTY HOUSE, Whitehall—SW1: [Latitude / Longitude: 51.505557,-0.126826]. The Duke of Holdernesse had been Lord of the Admiralty, with offices at Whitehall. **1903? – The Priory School**

ADMIRALTY HOUSE, Whitehall—SW1: [Latitude / Longitude: 51.505557,-0.126826]. Von Bork complained to Von Herling, that The Admiralty had received an alarm on the Naval Signals he had been accumulating, and changed every code. Nevertheless, thanks to his checkbook, and his agent Altamont, he would soon get the new signals. Von Bork told Von Herling that he paid Altamont five hundred pounds for the revised codes, and explained that Altamont was an Irish-American who hated the British. **1914 – His Last Bow**

COVENT GARDEN (Zone 1)

THE STRAND MAGAZINE (site), 12 Burleigh Street—WC2: [Latitude / Longitude: 51.51116,-0.120335]. This site is where most of the Sherlock Holmes adventures were published. The new Strand Magazine was launched in January 1891.

ODEON, COVENT GARDEN, 135 Shaftesbury Avenue— WC2: [Latitude / Longitude: 51.514231,-0.128081]. This movie house was originally the Seville Theatre. It opened in 1931 and presented plays and musicals. From 1965 to 1970, under Brian Epstein's ownership, it was famous for rock concerts. On the side of the building is a frieze by Gilbert Bayes, which contains London's oldest sculpture of Sherlock Holmes, and perhaps Moriarty.

LYCEUM THEATER, 21 Wellington Street—WC2: [Latitude / Longitude: 51.511641,-0.11952].The morning of her visit to Baker Street, Mary Morstan received a strange letter. It instructed her to be, *"At the third pillar from the left outside the Lyceum Theatre tonight at seven o'clock"*. Holmes compared the handwriting on the letter, to the handwriting on the boxes that contained the pearls. They were from the same person. **1887 – Sign of Four**

Author's note: The Lyceum Theater is a London landmark. After several fires in the 19th Century, it reopened in 1904. Originally known for Victorian melodramas and lavish Shakespearean productions, the Lyceum became a dance hall after World War II, and converted to a legitimate theater in 1996.

WELLINGTON STREET—WC2: [Latitude / Longitude: 51.512289,-0.120765]. From Waterloo Road, Holmes and Watson traveled up Wellington Street. on their way to the old Bow Street Police Court. **1889 – Man with the Twisted Lip**

BOW STREET POLICE COURT—WC2: [Latitude / Longitude: 51.513394,-0.122235]. Inspector Bradstreet was on duty at the Bow Street Police Court when Holmes and Watson arrived. They asked to see Hugh Boone. Holmes had brought a large bath-sponge with him, and proceeded to unmask Boone, who was, in fact, Neville St. Clair, in disguise. **1889 – Man with the Twisted Lip**

Author's note: Founded in 1740, this famous police court was the home of the pre-Scotland Yard London policemen. They were called the Bow Street Runners and were paid by the capture, much as bounty hunters are paid today. The police station closed in 1992, and the adjacent Magistrates' Court closed in 2006.

STANFORD'S "STAMFORD'S", 12-14 Long Acre—WC2: [Latitude / Longitude: 51.512215,-0.126235]. While Watson was out, Holmes sent to Stamford's for a large-scale Ordnance map of that portion of the moor containing Baskerville Hall. **1889 – Hound of the Baskervilles**

Author's note: Although Conan Doyle changed the name slightly, Stanford's famous old map shop, founded in 1852, is still in business.

ROYAL OPERA HOUSE, Covent Garden—WC2: [Latitude / Longitude: 51.513445,-0.122362]. After the successful conclusion of the case, Holmes reserved a box at the Royal Opera House for "Les Huguenots". Holmes suggested that he and Watson stop at Marcini's for a little dinner on the way. **1889 – Hound of the Baskervilles**

SHORTS GARDENS—WC2: [Latitude / Longitude: 51.515295,-0.124252]. From Drury Lane, Holmes and Watson turned southwest on Shorts Gardens, or as Watson put it, "through a zigzag of slums". **1889? - The Blue Carbuncle**

ENDELL STREET—WC2: [Latitude / Longitude: 51.514091,-0.123931]. From Shorts Garden, Holmes and Watson turned south on Endell Street. When they reached Long Acre, they could see the end of Bow Street to their left. **1889? - The Blue Carbuncle**

LONG ACRE—WC2: [Latitude / Longitude: 51.513617,-0.123621]. Holmes and Watson zigzagged southwest on Long Acre until they reached James Street, the path to Covent Garden. **1889? - The Blue Carbuncle**

JAMES STREET—WC2: [Latitude / Longitude: 51.513009,-0.123983]. Holmes and Watson were almost to Covent Garden as they walked down James Street from Long Acre. **1889? - The Blue Carbuncle**

COVENT GARDEN—WC2: [Latitude / Longitude: 51.51148,-0.12287]. Breckinridge had a goose stand in Covent Garden. The goose with the blue carbuncle was among the two dozen sold to the Alpha Inn. Holmes used trickery to get Breckinridge to tell where he had purchased the geese. As they left, Holmes and Watson saw James Ryder, who was also pestering Breckinridge for information. **1889? - The Blue Carbuncle**

ROYAL OPERA HOUSE, Covent Garden—WC2: [Latitude / Longitude: 51.513445,-0.122362]. With the case safely in the hands of the police, Holmes said to Watson, "it is not eight o'clock and a Wagner night at Covent Garden! If we hurry, we might be in time for the second act". **1902? – The Red Circle**

SOTHEBY'S, No. 3 Wellington Street—WC2: [Latitude / Longitude: 51.511654,-0.119519]. When Nathan Garrideb left his quarters to go to Sotheby's, it was to bid on additions to his natural history collection. In 1902, Sotheby's auction house was located at 3 Wellington Street. **1902 – The Three Garridebs**

SOTHEBY'S, No. 3 Wellington Street—WC2: [Latitude / Longitude: 51.511654,-0.119519]. Watson, posing as Dr. Hill Barton, took the Ming saucer to Baron Gruner. If pressed on its value, Watson was to suggest a valuation at Christie's or Sotheby's. In 1902, Sotheby's Auction House was located at 3 Wellington Street. In 1917, they moved to their current location at 35-35 New Bond Street. **1902 – The Illustrious Client**

CUTTY SARK (Dockland Light Railway) (Zone 2)

GREENWICH—SE10: [Latitude / Longitude: 51.484491,-0.004463]. At Greenwich, the police launch was about three hundred paces behind the *Aurora*. **1887 – Sign of Four**

GREENWICH—SE10: [Latitude / Longitude: 51.478097,-0.016748]. For seven years, Victor Hatherley had apprenticed with Venner & Matheson, the well-known engineering firm in Greenwich. In 1887, he went into practice for himself, but the business had not done well. **1889 – The Engineer's Thumb**

EARL'S COURT (Zone 1)

No. 28 HOGARTH ROAD, "CAULFIELD GARDENS"—SW5: [**Latitude / Longitude: 51.493292,-0.192286**]. The name and address that caught Holmes attention was Hugo Oberstein, who lived at "Caulfield Gardens". Oberstein's rear windows overlooked the Circle Line tracks. Many have incorrectly identified "Caulfield Gardens" as Courtfield Gardens or Courtfield Road, but they have no houses there from which a body could be placed on the top of the train. The only houses from which this is physically possible are on the south side of Hogarth Road, particularly No. 28. **1895 – The Bruce-Partington Plans**

EARL'S COURT UNDERGROUND STATION—SW5: [**Latitude / Longitude: 51.492234,-0.193056**]. Then, as now, the District Line tracks are clear of tunnels between the Gloucester Road and Earl's Court Stations. Herr Oberstein's rear windows at Hogarth Road "Caulfield Gardens" overlooked the tracks. **1895 – The Bruce-Partington Plans**

EDGWARE ROAD (Zone 1)

CHURCH OF ST. MARK "CHURCH OF ST. MONICA", Old Marylebone Road—NW1: [**Latitude / Longitude: 51.518481,-0.167137**]. Godfrey Norton and Irene Adler were married in The Church of St. Monica, Edgware Road. The most likely candidate is the Church of St. Mark, located on Old Marylebone Lane, near Edgware Road. **1888 – Scandal in Bohemia**

EDGWARE ROAD—W2: [**Latitude / Longitude: 51.515393,-0.163381**]. Holloway and Steele, the house agent firm for Nathan Garrideb, were located in Edgware Road. From them, Holmes found that the previous tenant at No. 136 "Little Ryder Street" fit the description of Roger Prescott, the man killed by 'Killer Evans'. **1902 – The Three Garridebs**

EMBANKMENT (Zone 1)

METROPOLE HOTEL (site), Northumberland Avenue, between Great Scotland Yard and Whitehall Place—WC2: [Latitude / Longitude: 51.506873,-0.124315**].** On the West side of Northumberland Avenue, south from Great Scotland Yard to Whitehall Place, was the site of The Metropole Hotel. The Metropole is a likely candidate for being "The...select London hotel," where Francis Hay Moulton stayed. "Eight shillings for a bed" gave Holmes a clue. Holmes said, "There are not many (hotels) in London which charge at that rate". **1886 - The Noble Bachelor**

GREAT SCOTLAND YARD—SW1: [Latitude / Longitude: 51.506386,-0.125586**].** During the Regency period, in addition to a street called Great Scotland Yard, there were two small alleys, know as Little and Middle Scotland Yard. These alleys were merged into a broad street now called Whitehall Place. In 1829, the headquarters of the police force's new Metropolitan Division was established at No. 4 Whitehall Place, with a rear entrance on Great Scotland Yard. With the disappearance of Little and Middle Scotland Yards, the word "Great" became superfluous, and the police headquarters became known as Scotland Yard. They took the name with them on subsequent moves. The Great Scotland Yard street still curves between Northumberland Avenue and Whitehall.

SHERLOCK HOLMES WALKING TOUR—London Walks, Telephone (020) 7624 3978: [Latitude / Longitude: 51.507316,-0.122604**].** There is a guided walking tour of the Sherlock Holmes sites near Charing Cross. No reservations are needed. Just join the group at 2:30 PM every Thursday, at the north entrance of the Embankment Underground Station. Call to re-confirm date and time.

VICTORIA EMBANKMENT—WC2: [Latitude / Longitude: 51.509637,-0.118543]. Holmes wondered how members of the Klan decoyed John Openshaw from Waterloo Bridge to the Victoria Embankment. **1885 – Five Orange Pips**

NORTHUMBERLAND AVENUE—WC2: [Latitude / Longitude: 51.50697,-0.124991]. Mycroft told Sherlock and Watson that Mr. Melas often acted as a guide to the wealthy Orientals who stayed at the Northumberland Avenue hotels. The three luxury Northumberland Avenue hotels were The Metropole Hotel, The Hotel Victoria, and The Grand Hotel. All were new in 1887. **Underground Station: Embankment**

METROPOLE HOTEL (site), Northumberland Avenue, between Great Scotland Yard and Whitehall Place—WC2: [Latitude / Longitude: 51.506873,-0.124315]. One of the three luxury Northumberland hotels was The Metropole, located on the west side of Northumberland Avenue, between Great Scotland Yard and Whitehall Place. **Underground Station: Embankment**

HOTEL VICTORIA—WC2: [Latitude / Longitude: 51.506939,-0.124715]. One of the three luxury Northumberland hotels was The Hotel Victoria, located at 8 Northumberland Avenue. It is now confusingly called The Grand Hotel. **Underground Station: Embankment**

SHERLOCK HOLMES PUB, No. 10 Northumberland Street—WC2: [Latitude / Longitude: 51.50723,-0.125334]. The Sherlock Holmes Pub has made a claim for being Baskerville's Northumberland Hotel. By the time of this adventure, the pub had changed its name from The Northumberland Hotel, to The Northumberland Arms. The new name more correctly reflects its character as a modest pub/hostelry. As such, I do not think this could have been the "Northumberland Hotel", at which the wealthy Sir Henry Baskerville stayed. **1889 – Hound of the Baskervilles**

Authors note: Today, the pub is a Mecca for Sherlock Holmes fans. In addition to traditional pub grub and drinks, they have a decent upstairs restaurant. Be sure to see the glassed-in replica of the 221B Baker Street sitting room, moved here from the 1951 Festival of Britain site.

CHARING CROSS TURKISH BATH (site), Craven Street—WC2: [Latitude / Longitude: 51.507006,-0.123854]. Looking at Watson's boots, Holmes said, "But why Turkish?" Holmes was referring to the fact that the boots had been tied by someone other than Watson, which meant he had been to the Charing Cross Turkish Bath. The establishment was located on the upper floor of the wedge shaped building where Craven Street joins Northumberland Avenue. **1902? – Lady Frances Carfax**

Author's note: [Latitude / Longitude: 51.507237,-0.125332]. The women's entrance to the Charing Cross Turkish Bath was in Craven Passage, across from the south side of the Sherlock Holmes Pub. In Sherlock's day, Craven Passage was the Northumberland Passage. Look for the Turkish design of the women's entrance.

CHARING CROSS TURKISH BATH (site), Craven Street—WC2: [Latitude / Longitude: 51.507237,-0.125332]. On September 3, 1902, Holmes and Watson were enjoying a smoke in the Charing Cross Turkish Bath. The establishment was located on the upper floor of the wedge shaped building where Craven Street joins Northumberland Avenue. **1902 – The Illustrious Client**

EUSTON (Zone 1)

EUSTON RAILWAY STATION—NW1: [Latitude / Longitude: 51.528401,-0.131943]. At about half-past eight on Tuesday, Enoch Drebber and Joseph Stangerson had been seen on a Euston Station platform, where they were waiting for the 9:15 Liverpool Express. **1881? – Study in Scarlet**

LITTLE GEORGE STREET (site)—NW1: [Latitude / Longitude: 51.527987,-0.13656]. Halliday's Private Hotel was located in Little George Street. The word *RACHE*, written in blood, was above Joseph Stangerson's body. A milk delivery boy had seen someone using a ladder to enter, or exit, the room's open window. The boy said the man was tall, had a reddish face, and was dressed in a long brown coat. **1881? – Study in Scarlet**

Author's note: Little George Street no longer exists. In 1881, it ran east west between Hampstead Road, and Cardington Road, on the south side of St James Gardens. The nearby Exmouth Arms Pub was open for business in 1881. As for its location of Halliday's Hotel, there were no hotels, private or otherwise, in Little George Street. Bernard Davies has identified the one hotel in the neighborhood that matches the Canon's description --- Emms' Private Hotel at No. 56 Drummond Street, near the corner of Cardington Street, along the side of Euston Station.

EMMS' PRIVATE HOTEL, No. 56 Drummond Street (site)—NW1: [Latitude / Longitude: 51.527731,-0.135227]. Emms' was the only private hotel in the neighborhood that fits Watson's description. Emms' no longer exists, and was located where the modern Hotel Ibis sits today. **1881? – Study in Scarlet**

EUSTON RAILWAY STATION—NW1: [Latitude / Longitude: 51.528401,-0.131943]. In the 1880's, as it does today, trains to Birmingham leave from London's Euston Station. **1889? – The Stock-Broker's Clerk**

EUSTON RAILWAY STATION—NW1: [Latitude / Longitude: 51.528401,-0.131943]. The smooth talking John convinced Nathan to take the midday train to Aston, near Birmingham to meet Howard the next day. John said they had found their third Garrideb! After John left, Holmes asked Nathan for permission to examine his natural history collection, while he was away. **1902 – The Three Garridebs**

Author's note: Bernard Davies identified train service to Aston, as a "halt-on-demand" stop. Nathan had to take London & Western's 12:05 train from Euston.

EUSTON RAILWAY STATION—NW1: [Latitude / Longitude: 51.528401,-0.131943]. Because of the press of other cases, Holmes could not accompany Dodd back to Tuxbury Old Place until the following week. When he and Watson did go, Holmes arranged for Sir James Saunders to meet them at Euston Station. After taking the train to Bedfordshire, the trio took a carriage to Tuxbury Old Place to confront Colonel Emsworth. **1903 – The Blanched Soldier**

EUSTON RAILWAY STATION—NW1: [Latitude / Longitude: 51.528401,-0.131943]. Bernard Davies makes a convincing argument that Dr. Huxtable arrived at London's Euston Station before 11 o'clock on the London & Northwestern line. **1903? – The Priory School**

EUSTON SQUARE (Zone 1)

UNIVERSITY COLLEGE, LONDON (Former University of London), Gower Street—WC1: [Latitude / Longitude: 51.524369,-0.1345]. In 1878, Watson received his medical degree from the University of London. The primary buildings for medical studies were on Gower Street. **1881? – Study in Scarlet**

UNIVERSITY COLLEGE HOSPITAL (site), Gower Street—WC1: [Latitude / Longitude: 51.524369,-0.1345]. In addition to St. Bartholomew's Hospital (St. Bart's), Watson could have learned his surgical skills at the old University College Hospital. The new hospital, built between 1897 and 1906, is on the same spot. **1881? – Study in Scarlet**

GORDON SQUARE—WC1: [Latitude / Longitude: 51.52473,-0.130552]. Holmes went to Moulton's hotel, and found he had left, but was having his mail forwarded to 226 Gordon Square. There, he found the young couple. He offered them a chance to come to Baker Street, dine with St. Simon, and explain the situation. **1886 - The Noble Bachelor**

UNIVERSITY COLLEGE, LONDON (Former University of London), Gower Street—WC1: [Latitude / Longitude: 51.524369,-0.1345]. When Trevelyan received his medical degree from the University of London, the primary buildings for medical classes were on Gower Street. **1886? – The Resident Patient**

UNIVERSITY COLLEGE HOSPITAL (site), Gower Street—WC1: [Latitude / Longitude: 51.524369,-0.1345]. Trevelyan would have learned some of his surgical skills at the old University College Hospital. The 'new' hospital, built between 1897 and 1906, is on the same site. **1886? – The Resident Patient**

FARRINGDON (Zone 1)

ST. BARTHOLOMEW'S (ST. BART'S) HOSPITAL—EC1: [Latitude / Longitude: 51.518033,-0.10098]. Stamford introduced Watson and Holmes in St. Bart's chemical laboratory. Holmes told Watson, "You have been in Afghanistan, I perceive." This was the first time Holmes astonished Watson with his special abilities. **1881? – Study in Scarlet**

Author's note: St. Bart's has an excellent small museum, just inside the Henry VIII Gate. Among the items displayed, is the plaque commemorating the first meeting of Holmes and Watson.

FARRINGDON "FARRINGTON" STREET—EC1: [Latitude / Longitude: 51.517776,-0.105186]. As the two hansoms made their way to the bank, Holmes explained that one of the criminals involved was John Clay. Clay's grandfather had been a royal duke, and Clay had been to Eton and Oxford. Holmes, Watson, Jones, and Merryweather, "Rattled through an endless labyrinth of gas-lit streets" until they reached Farrington Street. **1890 – Red-Headed League**

GRESHAM HOUSE (BUILDINGS), No. 24 Holborn Viaduct—EC1: [Latitude / Longitude: 51.517012,-0.1047]. McFarlane told Holmes that he was a junior partner in the law firm of Graham & McFarlane, at No. 426 Gresham Buildings. **1895? – The Norwood Builder**

SAFFRON HILL—EC1: [Latitude / Longitude: 51.52044,-0.106872]. Lestrade told Holmes that they had an inspector, who made a specialty of the Saffron Hill Italian Quarter. The inspector recognized the murdered man as Pietro Venucci, who is connected to the Mafia. Lestrade wanted Holmes to come to Saffron Hill with the police, and search for Beppo. **1900? – The Six Napoleons**

FULHAM BROADWAY (Zone 2)

FULHAM ROAD—SW6: [Latitude / Longitude: 51.480227,-0.198333]. Stapleton bought the hound from Ross & Mangles, dog dealers in Fulham Road. **1889 – Hound of the Baskervilles**

GLOUCESTER ROAD (Zone 1)

GLOUCESTER ROAD UNDERGROUND STATION—SW7: [Latitude / Longitude: 51.494485,-0.182567]. Then, as now, the District Line tracks are clear of tunnels between the Gloucester Road and Earl's Court Stations. Herr Oberstein's rear windows at Hogarth Road "Caulfield Gardens" overlooked the tracks. **1895 – The Bruce-Partington Plans**

GLOUCESTER ROAD—SW7: [**Latitude / Longitude:** <u>51.492831,-0.181484</u>]. Holmes asked Watson to come to Goldini's Restaurant in Gloucester Road, and bring, "A jimmy, a dark lantern, a chisel, and a revolver". After dinner, they burgled Oberstein's townhouse, and found a series of personal ads from the *Daily Telegraph,* all were signed, "Pierrot". **1895 – The Bruce-Partington Plans**

GOODGE STREET (Zone 1)

GOODGE STREET and TOTTENHAM COURT ROAD—W1: [**Latitude / Longitude:** <u>51.520108,-0.133919</u>]. On his way home with the Christmas goose, Henry Baker was assaulted at the corner of Goodge Street and Tottenham Court Road, by a "knot of roughs". One of the roughs knocked off Henry's hat, and when he raised his walking stick to defend himself, he smashed a shop window. At that point, Peterson, the commissionaire, who was also walking home, saw the fracas, and rushed to help. The roughs and Henry Baker saw him as an official looking person in uniform, and ran away. Peterson, "was left in possession of the field of battle, and also…the spoils of victory," including the battered hat, and the goose. Peterson brought the hat and goose to Holmes. Because there were signs it should be eaten immediately, Holmes gave the goose back to Peterson, and kept the hat. **1889? - The Blue Carbuncle**

TOTTENHAM COURT ROAD—W1: [**Latitude / Longitude:** <u>51.520942,-0.134678</u>]. Mr. Warren was a timekeeper at Morton and Waylight's in Tottenham Court Road. He was on his way to work at seven, when two men came up behind him, threw a coat over his head, and shoved him into a waiting cab. **1902? – The Red Circle**

MUSEUM OF MANKIND (Former University of London offices), **Burlington Gardens—W1:** [Latitude / Longitude: 51.509889.-0.140459]. When Watson was studying for his medical degree, the University of London used Burlington Gardens for administrative offices. **1881? – Study in Scarlet**

MUSEUM OF MANKIND (Former University of London offices), **Burlington Gardens—W1:** [Latitude / Longitude: 51.509889,-0.140459]. In the 1880's, the University of London used the Burlington Gardens for administrative offices. **1886? – The Resident Patient**

PICCADILLY—W1: [Latitude / Longitude: 51.508052,-0.140183]. Holmes and Watson crossed Piccadilly, between Bond Street and St. James's Street, on their way south to Pall Mall and the Diogenes Club. **1887? – The Greek Interpreter**

ST. JAMES'S STREET—SW1: [Latitude / Longitude: 51.506383,-0.139174]. On their way to Mycroft's club in Pall Mall, Holmes and Watson walked south from Piccadilly on St. James's Street. **1887? – The Greek Interpreter**

Author's note: As Holmes and Watson reached the south end of St. James's Street, they passed the old St. James's Palace **[Latitude / Longitude: 51.505293,-0.137727]**. Built between 1531 and 1536, the palace was the official residence of English Sovereigns for over 300 years. Foreign ambassadors are still accredited to the Court of St. James's.

BOND STREET—W1: [Latitude / Longitude: 51.511532,-0.143664]. In London, Holmes learned that William Derbyshire was Straker's other persona. He had purchased an expensive women's outfit from Madame Lesurier, a milliner in Bond Street. **1890? – Silver Blaze**

BERKELEY "BARCLAY" SQUARE—W1: [Latitude / Longitude: 51.50919,-0.145993]. Admiral Sinclair lived on Berkeley Square. Watson spelled it B-a-r-c-l-a-y, the way it is pronounced. Holmes confirmed that Sir James spent the evening with Admiral Sinclair. **1895 – The Bruce-Partington Plans**

CURZON STREET—W1: [Latitude / Longitude: 51.506766,-0.147666]. Holmes questions centered on the Shoscombe Stud and Horse Training Facility, and Sir Robert Norberton. Sir Robert had the reputation of being a dangerous man. He had horsewhipped Sam Brewer, a well-known Curzon Street moneylender on Newmarket Heath, and almost killed him. **1901? – Shoscombe Old Place**

BOODLE'S, 28 St. James's Street—SW1: [Latitude / Longitude: 51.506719,-0.139496]. On their way back to Baker Street, Holmes told Watson, "This is a case for Langdale Pike". Pike spent his waking hours in the bow window of a St. James's gentleman's club, gathering London gossip. **1902? – Three Gables**

CHRISTIE'S AUCTION HOUSE, No. 8 King Street—SW1: [Latitude / Longitude: 51.506285,-0.137994]. Nathan Garrideb rarely left his quarters, except to go to Christie's or Sotheby's to bid on additions to his natural history collection. Christie's Auction House was founded in 1766. In 1902, it was located at Number 8 King Street. **1902 – The Three Garridebs**

BERKELEY SQUARE—W1: [Latitude / Longitude: 51.50919,-0.145993]. Holmes made an appointment for Kitty to tell her story to Violet de Merville. Violet lived with her father, General de Merville, at 104 Berkeley Square. Their house was, "One of those…London castles which would make a church seem frivolous". When they arrived, Violet was unmoved, saying, "You have called to malign my fiancé…it is only by my father's request that I see you at all". **1902 – The Illustrious Client**

HALF MOON STREET—W1: [Latitude / Longitude: 51.506082,-0.144822]. The ruse required Watson to assume an alias. He became Dr. Hill Barton, who supposedly lived at No. 369 Half Moon Street. As Barton, Watson went to see Baron Gruner about selling the rare blue Ming saucer. **1902 – The Illustrious Client**

CHRISTIE'S AUCTION HOUSE, No. 8 King Street—SW1: [Latitude / Longitude: 51.506285,-0.137994]. If pressed for a price on the blue Ming saucer, Watson was to suggest that Christie's or Sotheby's value it. **1902 – The Illustrious Client**

HAMMERSMITH (Zone 2)

HAMMERSMITH—W6: [Latitude / Longitude: 51.493859,-0.221186]. John Mitton, Eduardo Lucas's valet, was out the night of the murder, and had an ironclad alibi. He was visiting a friend in Hammersmith. **1890? – Second Stain**

HAMMERSMITH—W6: [Latitude / Longitude: 51.492446,-0.223675]. Watson handed Holmes his great index volume. Under V, he found "Vampirism in Hungary", and "Vampires in Transylvania". He also found Victor Lynch, the forger, Vittoria, the circus belle, and Vigor, the Hammersmith wonder. Holmes then read the letter he received from Robert Ferguson. **1896? – The Sussex Vampire**

HAMMERSMITH BRIDGE—W6: [Latitude / Longitude: 51.489914,-0.228986]. Holmes said, "If you come with me to Chiswick tonight…I promise to go to the Italian Quarter with you tomorrow". That night, a four-wheeler dropped them near Hammersmith Bridge. **1900? – The Six Napoleons**

HAMPSTEAD HEATH (Zone 2)

HAMPSTEAD—NW3: [Latitude / Longitude: 51.558825,-0.172446]. Cecil James Barker, of Hales Lodge Hampstead, was a frequent visitor to Birlstone Manor. Although Barker was English, he had known Douglas in America. Ames, the butler, described Barker as, "An easy-going…gentleman…But, my word! I had rather not be the man that crossed him". **1887? - Valley of Fear**

LOMBARD STREET—EC3: [Latitude / Longitude: 51.512589,-0.087011]. Hall Pycroft lived in Hampstead, at the fictitious Potter's Terrace. Before reporting to his new position at Mawson & Williams's, he received a visit from Arthur Pinner, whose card said he was a "Financial Agent" for a Birmingham hardware company. **1889? – The Stock-Broker's Clerk**

HAMPSTEAD—NW3: [Latitude / Longitude: 51.556035,-0.181446]. Milverton lived in Appledore Towers, Hampstead. He had his blackmailing claws in Lady Eva Blackwell. Holmes, acting as Lady Eva's agent, failed to reach an agreement with Milverton, and had chosen another course of action. **1899? – Charles Augustus Milverton**

CHURCH ROW, HAMPSTEAD—NW3: [Latitude / Longitude: 51.555515,-0.179926]. At eleven, Holmes and Watson took a cab from Oxford Street to Church Row in Hampstead. From there it was a fifteen-minute walk to Milverton's house. They planned to steal the embarrassing papers, and return to Baker Street by two o'clock. **1899? – Charles Augustus Milverton**

HAMPSTEAD HEATH—NW3: [Latitude / Longitude: 51.567334,-0.181239]. The men drove Mr. Warren around for about an hour, before depositing him on Hampstead Heath. He took the bus home. Mrs. Warren wanted to evict her lodger right then, but thought she had better get Holmes's advice first. **1902? – The Red Circle**

HARROW & WEALDSTONE (Zone 5)

HARROW WEALD—HA3: [**Latitude / Longitude:** 51.601234,-0.338532]. Mrs. Mary Maberley sent an evening letter to Holmes asking him to visit her at Three Gables, her house at Harrow Weald. She had received a very strange offer to buy her house and contents, and wanted Holmes's advice. **1902? – Three Gables**

HARROW & WEALDSTONE RAILWAY STATION—HA1: [**Latitude / Longitude:** 51.591824,-0.334575]. Later that day, a short railroad journey, and a shorter carriage drive, brought Holmes and Watson to Three Gables. **1902? – Three Gables**

Author's note: The name "Weald Stone" comes from an ancient sarsen stone, which was later embedded in the wall of the old "Red Lion Inn" at the corner of the High Road and College Road. The ancient tavern is now called the Weald Stone Inn, [**Latitude / Longitude:** 51.6045,-0.3396].

RISINGHOLME, "Three Gables", No. 224 High Road, Harrow—**HA3:** [**Latitude / Longitude:** 51.601234,-0.338532]. The elderly lady who summoned them bore every mark of refinement and culture. Holmes remembered her late husband, and knew of her son, Douglas Maberley. Mrs. Maberley said her son had been an attaché in Rome, but died of pneumonia a month ago. **1902? – Three Gables**

Author's note: Bernard Davies identified Risingholme as "Three Gables". The old house has fallen on hard times. It is hemmed in by other buildings, and what remains of its garden is overgrown. It is not the villa to which the refined Mrs. Maberley returned from her round-the-world tour.

KENSINGTON CHURCH STREET—W8: [Latitude / Longitude: 51.505477,-0.194109]. After they left St. James's Hall, Watson went to his house on Church Street in Kensington. He agreed to meet Holmes again at ten that night. **1890 – Red-Headed League**

KENSINGTON—W8: [Latitude / Longitude: 51.502398,-0.194632]. After drinking the brandy and soda Watson provided, Eccles told his story. He was a bachelor, and cultivated a large number of friends. Among them was a retired brewer called Melville, who lived at Albemarle Mansion in Kensington. It was there that Eccles met Garcia, who supposedly held a position at the Spanish Embassy. **1891? – Wisteria Lodge**

KENSINGTON CHURCH (CHURCH) STREET—W8: [Latitude / Longitude: 51.502265,-0.190998]. After Watson returned to his Kensington surgery, the maid came in and announced that he had a visitor. It was the old bibliophile. He claimed to be Watson's neighbor, with a little bookstore at the corner of Church Street. Watson fainted when the old man dropped his disguise and Holmes stood before him. **1894 – The Empty House**

No. 131 PITT STREET—W8: [Latitude / Longitude: 51.50358,-0.194301]. The next morning, Holmes received a telegram from Lestrade, asking Holmes to come to No. 131 Pitt Street. This Kensington address was the residence of Mr. Horace Harker, of the Central Press Association. His house had been burgled the night before, and his plaster bust of Napoleon stolen. This time, a murder was involved. When Harker opened the front door, he found a murdered man on his front steps. The dead man had a photograph in his pocket. It was a picture of Beppo, an Italian piecework man, who had worked for Morse Hudson. **1900? – The Six Napoleons**

CAMPDEN GROVE "CAMPDEN HOUSE ROAD"—W8: [Latitude / Longitude: <u>51.504355,-0.193967</u>]. **The** bust of Napoleon taken from the house in Pitt Street was found smashed in the front garden of a nearby empty house in Campden House Road. Holmes called to Lestrade's attention that the front garden was beneath a street light. **1900?** **– The Six Napoleons**

KENSINGTON HIGH STREET—W8: [Latitude / Longitude: <u>51.501163,-0.192853</u>]. Harker said he had purchased his bust of Napoleon from Harding Brothers, a shop in the Kensington High Street. The shop was two doors from the underground station. Harding Brothers bought three plaster busts from Gelder and Co., and sold one to Harker, one to Mr. Josiah Brown of Laburnum Lodge, Laburnum Vale, Chiswick, and one to Mr. Sandeford of Lower Grove Road, Reading. **1900? – The Six Napoleons**

HOLBORN (Zone 1)

HOLBORN RESTAURANT (site), Holborn—WC2: [Latitude / Longitude: <u>51.517467,-0.120574</u>]. The Holborn Restaurant was located on the southwest corner of today's Holborn and Kingsway. During lunch, Watson mentioned that he was looking for "comfortable rooms at a reasonable price." Stamford said that was strange because, "You are the second man today who has used that expression to me." The other person was Sherlock Holmes. **1881? – Study in Scarlet**

Author's note: Kingsway was constructed in 1905.

ROYAL COLLEGE OF SURGEONS, 35 Lincoln's Inn Fields— WC2: [Latitude / Longitude: <u>51.515527,-0.116334</u>]. On Saturday, when they all met at Paddington Station, Dr. Mortimer said that he and Sir Henry had stayed together the whole time in London, except for Friday afternoon, when he went alone to the Museum of the College of Surgeons. **1889 – Hound of the Baskervilles**

MUSEUM TAVERN, "ALPHA INN", 49 Great Russell Street—WC1: [Latitude / Longitude: 51.518308,-0.126046]. The "Alpha Inn" was near the British Museum, "At the corner of one of the streets which run down into Holborn". Some of the inn's regulars, including Henry Baker, formed a goose club. By contributing a few pence each week, they each received a Christmas, goose. It was Henry Baker's luck to receive the goose with the blue carbuncle. **1889? - The Blue Carbuncle**

THE PLOUGH, "ALPHA INN", Little Russell Street—WC1: [Latitude / Longitude: 51.517752,-0.125604]. The Plough, at the corner of Little Russell and Museum Streets is the pub favored by Bernard Davies as being the "Alpha Inn". Like the Museum Tavern, it is "at the corner of one of the streets which run down into Holborn". **1889? - The Blue Carbuncle**

MUSEUM STREET—WC1: [Latitude / Longitude: 51.516837,-0.124787]. Holmes and Watson started their walk from the Alpha Inn to Covent Garden by heading south on Museum Street. ". They crossed New Oxford Street and High Holborn, as they continued on to Drury Lane. **1889? - The Blue Carbuncle**

DRURY LANE—WC2: [Latitude / Longitude: 51.515996,-0.124049]. As Museum Street ends at High Holborn, Holmes and Watson continued south on Dury Lane until they reached Shorts Gardens. **1889? - The Blue Carbuncle**

HOLBORN—WC1: [Latitude / Longitude: 51.517503,-0.121209]. When Inspector Baynes and Holmes inspected Wisteria Lodge, they found the place empty. However, there was a great deal of clothing bearing the label of Marx and Co., Holborn. **1891? – Wisteria Lodge**

HOLLAND PARK (Zone 1)

LADBROKE GROVE "LOWER BURKE STREET"—W11: [**Latitude / Longitude:** 51.512789,-0.20668]. Although Conan Doyle changed the name, Ladbroke Grove fits the location where Culverton Smith rented a house "In the vague borderland between Notting Hill and Kensington". Smith was a well-known planter from Sumatra and an expert on oriental diseases. He had a grudge against Holmes, because Holmes suspected him in the death of his nephew, Victor Savage. **1889 – The Dying Detective**

HYDE PARK CORNER (Zone 1)

CURZON PLACE "SQUARE"—W1: [**Latitude / Longitude:** 51.506145,-0.15081]. Murillo and Lopez managed to escape their police pursuers by entering a London lodging-house, and leaving by the back gate into Curzon Square. They were never seen again. **1891? – Wisteria Lodge**

CHESHAM HOUSE, BELGRAVE SQUARE, Russian Embassy (site)—SW1: [**Latitude / Longitude:** 51.498124,-0.153579]. Before coming out of her hiding place, Anna had taken a fatal dose of poison. She gave Holmes the papers that would free Alexis, and asked him to take them to the Russian Embassy. **1894 – The Golden Pince-Nez**

Author's note: In 1894, the Russian Embassy was in Chesham House, Belgrave Square, with their Consulate at 17 Great Winchester Street in The City: [**Latitude / Longitude:** 51.516054,-0.084726].

ISLAND GARDENS (Dockland Light Railway) (Zone 2)

ISLE OF DOGS—E14: [Latitude / Longitude: 51.488125,-0.022495]. In their attempt to catch the *Aurora*, supposedly "The fastest boat on the river", the police steam launch sped past the Isle of Dogs. **1887 – Sign of Four**

KENNINGTON (Zone 2)

AU AULTON PLACE, "Audley Court"—SE11: [Latitude / Longitude: 51.486117,-0.109459]. Holmes and Watson then went to see the constable, who found Drebber's body. His name was John Rance, who lived at No. 46 Audley Court, Kennington Park Gate. Bernard Davies identified the address as Aulton Place, a narrow alley off Stannary Street. **1881? – Study in Scarlet**

No. 129 CAMBERWELL ROAD—SE5: [Latitude / Longitude: 51.48108,-0.094332]. Enoch Drebber bought a hat from Underwood, a haberdasher at No. 129 Camberwell Road. Drebber gave Mrs. Charpentier's boarding house as his London address. **1881? – Study in Scarlet**

No. 310-312 KENNINGTON ROAD—SE11: [Latitude / Longitude: 51.487492,-0.111371]. Lestrade said that the first incident happened four days ago at the shop of Morse Hudson at No. 310-312 Kennington Road. The smashed bust of Napoleon was only worth a few shillings; so it looked like a random case of hooliganism. **1900? – The Six Napoleons**

Author's note: Bernard Davies identified No. 310-312 Kennington Road as Morse Hudson's shop.

KENNINGTON ROAD—SE11: [Latitude / Longitude: 51.488173,-0.111217]. The second incident was at Dr. Barnicot's, who lived at Kennington Road, and had a branch surgery at Lower Brixton Road. Dr. Barnicot was an admirer of Napoleon, and had purchased two duplicate plaster casts from Morse Hudson. One bust was for his house, and the other for his surgery. When he woke one morning, he found that his house had been burgled, and the bust of Napoleon stolen. It was smashed outside his house. **1900? – The Six Napoleons**

STIMSON & CO. UNDERTAKERS (site), No. 345 Kennington Road—SE11: [Latitude / Longitude: 51.4874,-0.111347]. Mrs. Fraser came to pawn another pendant. Green followed her as she walked to Stimson and Co., an undertaker in Kennington Road. Stimson had been commissioned to make an unusually deep casket for Shlessinger. **1902? – Lady Frances Carfax**

Author's note: Bernard Davies identified No. 345 Kennington Road as the site of Stimson & Co. Undertakers.

KENSINGTON (OLYMPIA) (Zone 2)

OLYMPIA—W14: [Latitude / Longitude: 51.495612,-0.210264]. Von Bork even matched his English friends by taking a prize in The Horse of the Year competition at Olympia. Baron Von Herling, the chief secretary of the German legation, told Von Bork that he would receive a warm welcome when he returned to Berlin. **1914 – His Last Bow**

KILBURN PARK (Zone 2)

KILBURN—NW6: [Latitude / Longitude: 51.54403,-0.203215].
Scotland Yard's Inspector Bradstreet suspected John Horner, a plumber,
of stealing the Countess of Morcar's blue carbuncle from her suite at the
Hotel Cosmopolitan. James Ryder, upper-attendant at the hotel, said
that he had shown Horner up to the Countess's dressing room on the
day of the robbery. What the police did not know was that Ryder had
heard from his friend, Maudsley, how thieves could dispose of stolen
property. Maudsley lived in Kilburn. **1889? - The Blue Carbuncle**

KINGS CROSS / ST PANCRAS (Zone 1)

ST. PANCRAS HOTEL, Euston Road—WC1: [Latitude /
Longitude: 51.529469,-0.125635]. Mary Sutherland and Hosner
Angel planned their wedding breakfast at the St. Pancras Hotel. Built
in 1868, this ornate Victorian hotel has reopened as the Renaissance
St. Pancras. **1889? – Case of Identity**

GRAY'S INN ROAD—WC1: [Latitude / Longitude: 51.525647,-
0.117116]. Holmes felt Cambridge was the logical starting point for their
investigation. He and Watson caught a cab and rattled up Gray's Inn Road
on their way to King's Cross Station. **1897? – The Missing Three-
Quarter**

KING'S CROSS RAILWAY STATION—WC2: [Latitude /
Longitude: 51.530887,-0.122534]. In trying to locate the missing
Godfrey Staunton, Holmes and Watson took the Cambridge train from
King's Cross Station. **1897? – The Missing Three-Quarter**

ST PANCRAS RAILWAY STATION—NW1: [Latitude /
Longitude: 51.530887,-0.122534]. Holmes and Watson
accompanied Dr. Huxtable back to Mackleton on the Western line
from St Pancras Station. **1903? – The Priory School**

LAMBETH NORTH (Zone 1)

WESTMINSTER BRIDGE ROAD—SE1: [Latitude / Longitude: 51.499386,-0.113416]. Lady Frances's silver-and-brilliant pendant was pawned at Bovington's in Westminster Road. The man who pawned the pendant was a large clean-shaven man of clerical appearance. This obviously referred to Shlessinger. Holmes allowed Philip Green to watch Bovington's Pawnshop to see if Shlessinger returned. Green promised to take no action without Holmes's instruction. **1902? – Lady Frances Carfax**

LANCASTER GATE (Zone 1)

LANCASTER GATE—W2: [Latitude / Longitude: 51.513667,-0.175915]. Hatty disappeared from her Lancaster Gate wedding breakfast, and St. Simon and the bride's father went to the police. Their first line of inquiry was to find Flora Millar. She had tried to force her way into the wedding breakfast, indicating she had some claim on Lord St. Simon. **1886 - The Noble Bachelor**

HYDE PARK—W2: [Latitude / Longitude: 51.512036,-0.172305]. After bolting from her wedding breakfast, Hatty Doran was seen walking in Hyde Park with Flora Millar. Flora had been on "very friendly footing" with Lord St. Simon, and had created a disturbance outside the Lancaster Gate house. **1886 - The Noble Bachelor**

THE SERPENTINE (LAKE), Hyde Park—W2: [Latitude / Longitude: 51.511582,-0.175781]. In a futile effort to find Hatty, Inspector Lestrade began dragging The Serpentine, in Hyde Park. **1886 - The Noble Bachelor**

Author's note: This Hyde Park boating lake dates from 1730 when Queen Caroline, wife of George II, ordered the damming of the River Westbourne.

LIMEHOUSE (Dockland Light Railway) (Zone 2)

WEST INDIA DOCKS—E14: [Latitude / Longitude: 51.503098,-0.025744]. When the police launch raced after the *Aurora*, they sped through the Pool of London, and past the West India Docks. To keep up, it took every bit of speed they had. **1887 – Sign of Four**

OLD CHURCH ROAD "CHURCH STREET"—E1: [Latitude / Longitude: 51.514518,-0.045245]. Gelder and Co. made the busts of Napoleon. They were located at "Church Street" in Stepney, and were a well-known house in the trade. They sold six to two London area retailers, three to Morse Hudson, and three to Harding Brothers. **1900? – The Six Napoleons**

LIVERPOOL STREET (Zone 1)

LIVERPOOL RAILWAY STATION—EC2: [Latitude / Longitude: 51.517503,-0.082659]. Hilton Cubitt sent a telegram to Holmes saying he was returning to London, and would reach Liverpool Street Station at one-twenty. When Cubitt arrived, he brought additional copies of dancing figures notes. **1897 – The Dancing Men**

LIVERPOOL RAILWAY STATION—EC2: [Latitude / Longitude: 51.517503,-0.082659]. There was a 5:20 train from Liverpool Station. Holmes asked Watson to accompany Josiah Amberley to Little Purlington, and make sure he went. "Should he break away or return, get to the nearest telephone exchange and send the single word 'Bolted' I will arrange here that it shall reach me wherever I am". **1898? – The Retired Colourman**

LONDON BRIDGE (Zone 1)

LONDON BRIDGE RAILWAY STATION—SW1: [Latitude / Longitude: 51.505848,-0.086521]. When Holmes left London to visit Hurlstone, in western Sussex, he took the train from the London Bridge Station. **1879 – The Musgrave Ritual**

**LONDON BRIDGE RAILWAY STATION—SW1: [Latitude /
Longitude: 51.505848,-0.086521].** In the 1880's, the train service from the
City to Norbury would have used the London Bridge Railway Station. **1887? –
The Yellow Face**

**LONDON BRIDGE RAILWAY STATION—SW1: [Latitude /
Longitude: 51.505848,-0.086521].** It took an hour for Inspector
Gregson to get a warrant to enter the house in Beckenham, and an
additional forty minute train ride from London Bridge Station. **1887?
– The Greek Interpreter**

**JACOBSON'S BOAT YARD (site)—SE1: [Latitude / Longitude:
51.50553,-0.075306].** Holmes told the police launch to go downstream
to the Tower of London, and stand off opposite Jacobson's boat yard, on
the Surrey (south) side of the river. **1887 – Sign of Four**

**LONDON BRIDGE RAILWAY STATION—SW1: [Latitude /
Longitude: 51.505848,-0.086521].** After John Hector McFarlane
arrived at the London Bridge Station, he came directly to Baker Street.
Inspector Lestrade followed, waiting for a warrant before making an
arrest. **1895? – The Norwood Builder**

**LONDON BRIDGE RAILWAY STATION—SW1: [Latitude /
Longitude: 51.505848,-0.086521].** Holmes and Watson took their
investigation to the Woolwich Arsenal. On their way, Holmes sent
Mycroft a telegram from London Bridge Station. It read, *"See some
light in the darkness, but it may possibly flicker out. Meanwhile,
please send…a complete list of all foreign spies…in England"*. **1895
– The Bruce-Partington Plans**

MANSION HOUSE (Zone 1)

DOCTORS' COMMONS (site), Godliman Street—EC4: [Latitude / Longitude: 51.512072,-0.099838]. On the Faraday Building, at the north side of Queen Victoria Street, on the corner of Godliman Street, there is a blue plaque saying that this was the site of the Doctors' Commons, demolished in 1867. The Doctors' Commons was the old ecclesiastical court that had jurisdiction over marriage licenses; divorce documents, and wills, etc. They ceased to operate in 1858-59, when wills and divorces passed to the civil authorities, and the records moved to Somerset House. In 1883, the term "Doctors' Commons" remained in common usage. **1883 – The Speckled Band**

MARBLE ARCH (Zone 1)

No. 31 "221B" BAKER STREET—W1: [Latitude / Longitude: 51.517932,-0.155587]. The *Gloria Scott* was Sherlock's first published adventure, and occurred before he met Watson. Watson learned of the case one winter evening at Baker Street, when Holmes handed him some papers and said, "These are the documents in the extraordinary case of the *Gloria Scott*, and the message which struck Justice of the Peace Trevor dead with horror." The note read, *"The supply of game for London is going steadily up. Head-keeper Hudson we believe has been now told to receive all order for fly-paper and for preservation of your hen-pheasant's life."* Watson said the note made no sense. **1874 - THE "GLORIA SCOTT"**

No. 31 "221B" BAKER STREET—W1: [Latitude / Longitude: 51.517932,-0.155587]. Watson learned of the Musgrave Ritual when he commented on Holmes untidy habits. Holmes kept "his cigars in a coal-shuttle, his tobacco in the toe end of a Persian slipper, and his unanswered correspondence transfixed by a jack-knife into the very center of his wooden mantelpiece." When Watson suggested they needed to tidy up, Holmes went into his bedroom and pulled out a large tin box. In it were items and papers from his early cases. One item was a small wooden box. Inside was "a crumpled piece of paper, an old-fashioned brass key, a peg of wood with a ball of string ..., and three rusty old discs of metal." Holmes said, "These are all I have...to remind me of the adventure of the Musgrave Ritual". **1879 - THE MUSGRAVE RITUAL**

No. 31 "221B" BAKER STREET—W1: [Latitude / Longitude: 51.517932,-0.155587]. The day after they met, Holmes and Watson went to inspect the rooms at Mrs. Hudson's 221B Baker Street. They consisted of "A couple of comfortable bedrooms and a single large airy sitting room, cheerfully furnished, and illuminated by two broad windows." In later adventures, we learn that Watson's bedroom was on the floor above, and Sherlock's bedroom eventually had three doors: one leading to the sitting room, a second exiting into the hall-way, and a third hidden door, added later, which opened behind the sitting room curtains. **1881? – Study in Scarlet**

Author's note: In the late nineteenth century, the name "Baker Street" applied only that section of the modern street, south of Paddington Street. The portion of the street north of Paddington was known as York Place. In addition, the highest house number, on nineteenth century Baker Street, was 85. This means that Conan Doyle hid the true location of 221B, until he revealed it as today's No. 31 Baker Street in *The Adventure of the Empty House.*

No. 31 "221B" BAKER STREET—W1: [Latitude / Longitude: 51.517932,-0.155587]. One April morning, in 1883, Holmes woke Watson, saying, "Mrs. Hudson has been knocked up, she retorted upon me, and I on you." An excited young lady had arrived at Baker Street, and insisted on seeing Holmes. Her name was Helen Stoner, and she lived with her stepfather, the last survivor of the Roylotts of Stoke Moran. **1883 – The Speckled Band**

No. 31 "221B" BAKER STREET—W1: [Latitude / Longitude: 51.517932,-0.155587]. On a blustery and rainy September night in 1885, Holmes and Watson were enjoying a quiet evening. Although Watson was now married, his wife was visiting her mother, and he was spending the night at Baker Street. There was a knock at the door and a young John Openshaw entered. **1885 – Five Orange Pips**

Author's note: As a puzzle for Sherlock Holmes fans, Conan Doyle indicated that Watson was married in 1885, two years before he met Mary Morstan. Was this an earlier marriage, or a typographical error?

No. 31 "221B" BAKER STREET—W1: [Latitude / Longitude: 51.517932,-0.155587]. One rainy October afternoon in 1886, Holmes received a letter from Lord St. Simon, concerning his missing bride. Inspector Lestrade had referred St. Simon to Holmes. **1886 - The Noble Bachelor**

No. 31 "221B" BAKER STREET—W1: [Latitude / Longitude: 51.517932,-0.155587]. To explain the situation, Holmes arranged for a catering firm to lay on a late supper at Baker Street for St. Simon and the young couple. He ordered, "Cold woodcock, a pheasant, a *pâté de foie gras* pie with a group of ancient and cobwebby bottles". **1886 - The Noble Bachelor**

No. 31 "221B" BAKER STREET—W1: [Latitude / Longitude: 51.517932,-0.155587]. Inspector Lanner started the hunt for the missing page, while Holmes and Watson returned to Baker Street. After breakfast, Holmes went out to get answers for a few remaining questions. He asked Lanner and Trevelyan to come to Baker Street at three. When they arrived, Lanner said he had found the page. Holmes said he knew the identity of the three men. They were Biddle, Hayward, and Moffat. The inspector cried, "The Worthingdon bank gang". That meant that Blessington must be Sutton, the man who had turned informer. Biddle, Hayward and Moffat had been sent to prison for fifteen years, and had just been released. **1886? – The Resident Patient**

No. 31 "221B" BAKER STREET—W1: [Latitude / Longitude: 51.517932,-0.155587]. Watson received a telegram from France, saying that Holmes was lying ill in the Hotel Dulong in Lyons. Watson hurried to Lyons and brought Holmes back to Baker Street to recover. Watson was delighted when Colonel Hayter invited them to visit his home near Reigate in Surrey. Watson accepted, knowing that a week of country springtime was what Holmes needed. **1887 – The Reigate Squires**

HYDE PARK—W2: [Latitude / Longitude: 51.51083,-0.157821]. Holmes and Watson took an early spring walk in the Park. Their two-hour stroll could have been in Regent's Park, but I think it was more likely to be in Hyde Park. When they returned at five, they found they had missed a client. The pageboy said the visitor had waited half an hour, and said he would return. **1887? – The Yellow Face**

No. 31 "221B" BAKER STREET—W1: [Latitude / Longitude: 51.517932,-0.155587]. September 1887 was the month that Mary Morstan, Watson's future wife, came to Baker Street. Before she arrived, Holmes amazed Watson by deducing he had been to the Wigmore Street Post Office to send a telegram. **1887 – Sign of Four**

No. 31 "221B" BAKER STREET—W1: [Latitude / Longitude: 51.517932,-0.155587]. At Baker Street, as Watson napped, and dreamed of Mary Morstan, Holmes researched the identity of the strange little man who murdered Bartholomew Sholto. Everything pointed to a small savage, but there were no people like that on the Indian subcontinent. Then Holmes read about the cannibal natives of the Andaman Islands in the Bay of Bengal. They fit the description. All that day, and the next, there was no word on the location of the *Aurora*. Holmes even went out himself to search. After the Irregulars found the *Aurora*, Holmes sent a telegram to Athelney Jones, asking him to come to Baker Street if he wanted to be in at the finish. Jones was there when Holmes returned. **1887 – Sign of Four**

WIGMORE STREET POST OFFICE (supposed site), No. 132 Wigmore Street—W1: [Latitude / Longitude: 51.515784,-0.152761]. Holmes amazed Watson by saying that he had been to the Wigmore Street Post Office to send a telegram. Holmes deduced the Wigmore Street location from the reddish dirt on Watson's shoe. They were taking up the pavement squares across the street from the Post Office, and the reddish color of the earth there was unique in the neighborhood. The fact that Watson had been with Holmes most of the morning, and had not written a letter, indicated that the only reason for his going to the post office was to send a telegram. **1887 – Sign of Four**

Author's note: In 1887, there was no post office on Wigmore Street, and there was a perfectly good post office at No. 66 Baker Street: **[Latitude / Longitude: 51.519292,-0.15619].** Placing an imaginary post office on Wigmore Street creates a quandary. For a complete explanation of this puzzle, read Bernard Davies' paper, *"Dr Watson's Deuteronomy"*.

No. 31 "221B" BAKER STREET—W1: [Latitude / Longitude: 51.517932,-0.155587]. On January 7, at the end of the 1880's, Holmes received a letter from Porlock, the nom-de-plum of an associate of Professor Moriarty. Porlock sent Holmes a coded message. It read, *"534   C2   13   127   36   31   4   17   21   41   Douglas   109   293   5   37   Birlstone 26   Birlstone 9   47   171".* **1887? - Valley of Fear**

No. 31 "221B" BAKER STREET—W1: [Latitude / Longitude: 51.517932,-0.155587]. After Watson's marriage, Holmes remained at their old quarters in Baker Street. One evening—it was March 20, 1888—Watson was passing through Baker Street and decided to stop by and see his old friend. Holmes showed him a note that had come that day in the last post. It said that Holmes would receive a masked visitor at quarter to eight. This visitor wanted to consult him on, "matters which are of an importance which can hardly be exaggerated". The note was written on expensive Bohemian paper. Holmes also noted, because of the sentence construction, that the writer's native language was German. **1888 – Scandal in Bohemia**

No. 31 "221B" BAKER STREET—W1: [Latitude / Longitude: 51.517932,-0.155587]. After hearing how Hatherley lost his thumb, Watson suggested that they go to Baker Street, before going to the police. After giving them a hearty breakfast of streaked rashers and eggs, Holmes invited Hatherley to tell his story. **1889 – The Engineer's Thumb**

No. 31 "221B" BAKER STREET—W1: [Latitude / Longitude: 51.517932,-0.155587]. In the second year of his marriage, Watson received a frantic visit from Mrs. Hudson, Holmes's "long-suffering" landlady. She said Holmes was dying, and that Watson must come to Baker Street at once. When he arrived, Holmes told him to stand back, because he had contracted a coolie disease while working a case in Rotherhithe. When Watson started to go for expert medical help, Holmes jumped up, locked the door, and forced Watson to wait until six o'clock. Holmes asked Watson to seek help from Culverton Smith, a well-known expert on oriental diseases. **1889 – The Dying Detective**

No. 31 "221B" BAKER STREET—W1: [Latitude / Longitude: 51.517932,-0.155587]. In 1889, Dr. Mortimer was in London to meet Sir Henry Baskerville after his ship from Canada. Sir Henry was the heir of the late Sir Charles Baskerville. Mortimer came to Baker Street to ask Sherlock's advice. He showed Holmes an old manuscript about the Hound of the Baskervilles. At first, Holmes was skeptical, but became more interested when Dr. Mortimer said, on the night of Sir Charles's death; he had seen footprints of a gigantic hound near the body. **1889 – Hound of the Baskervilles**

No. 31 "221B" BAKER STREET—W1: [Latitude / Longitude: 51.517932,-0.155587]. On the advice of Mrs. Etherege, Mary Sutherland came to seek Sherlock's help. After being shown in by the page, she told Holmes that her fiancé had vanished on their wedding day. **1889? – Case of Identity**

No. 31 "221B" BAKER STREET—W1: [Latitude / Longitude: 51.517932,-0.155587]. Holmes examined Henry Baker's hat as an intellectual exercise. As usual, Watson was amazed at what Holmes could deduce from an object. At that point, the door flew open and in rushed Peterson, the commissionaire. He had discovered the gem. Holmes placed an advertisement in all of the evening papers, asking for Mr. Henry Baker, whose name had been on the goose tag, to come to 221B Street, to claim his hat and (replacement) goose. When Henry Baker arrived at Baker Street, Holmes learned of the Alpha Inn's goose club. He was convinced that Baker had no knowledge of the gem. **1889? - The Blue Carbuncle**

Author's note: Holmes and Watson left Baker Street to walk to the Alpha Inn. Watson said, "Our footfalls rang out crisply and loudly as we swung through the doctors' quarter, Wimpole Street, Harley Street, and through Wigmore Street into Oxford Street. In a quarter of an hour, we were in Bloomsbury at the Alpha Inn". We can follow their path on modern streets, some of which have had their names changed since 1889. Because of modern traffic and crossing rules, this 1.6-mile journey will take twice as long today.

No. 31 "221B" BAKER STREET—W1: [Latitude / Longitude: 51.517932,-0.155587]. One foggy spring morning, after breakfast, Holmes and Watson discussed how Watson chronicled Sherlock's cases. Holmes wanted the emphasis to be on the logic involved. He told Watson, "You have degraded what should have been a course of lectures into a series of tales", (A fact for which Sherlock Holmes fans are grateful.). As he used tongs to pick up a glowing cinder to light his long cherry-wood pipe, Holmes remarked, "The days of great cases are past". Holmes used a cherry-wood pipe to replace his clay, "when he was in a disputatious rather than a meditative mood". To prove the point, Holmes showed Watson a letter he had received from Violet Hunter. **1890? – Copper Beeches**

No. 31 "221B" BAKER STREET—W1: [Latitude / Longitude: 51.517932,-0.155587]. Trelawney Hope explained that he brought home a very important document, and locked it in his dispatch box. He had seen the document the night before, but this morning, it was gone. At first, the Prime Minister refused to tell Holmes what was in the letter, but when Holmes refused the commission without more information, the Prime Minister relented. He said, "It was from a certain foreign potentate who has been ruffled by some recent Colonial developments". Holmes wrote a name on a piece of paper. The Prime Minister agreed that he was the sender. **1890? – Second Stain**

HYDE PARK—W2: [Latitude / Longitude: 51.512669,-0.159048]. It was a quarter-past nine when Watson started to walk from Kensington, across Hyde Park, through Oxford Street, to Baker Street. **1890 – Red-Headed League**

No. 31 "221B" BAKER STREET—W1: [Latitude / Longitude: 51.517932,-0.155587]. One October day in 1890, Watson dropped by Baker Street, and found Holmes with Jabez Wilson, a gentleman with fiery red hair. He told a bizarre tale. **1890 – Red-Headed League**

No. 31 "221B" BAKER STREET—W1: [Latitude / Longitude: 51.517932,-0.155587]. When Watson reached Baker Street, there were two hansoms at the door. Two men were with Holmes. One was Peter Jones of Scotland Yard. The other was Mr. Merryweather, a director of the City and Suburban Bank. Merryweather was upset because he was going to miss his regular Saturday night rubber of whist. **1890 – Red-Headed League**

No. 31 "221B" BAKER STREET—W1: [Latitude / Longitude: 51.517932,-0.155587]. Holmes returned to Baker Street after being "of assistance to the royal family of Scandinavia, and…the French Republic". One April morning in 1891, Holmes was surprised to receive a visit from Professor Moriarty, whom Holmes called "the Napoleon of crime". Moriarty said that Holmes had "seriously inconvenienced" him, and must withdraw. Holmes refused, but knew that he had put his life in danger. **1891 – The Final Problem**

No. 31 "221B" BAKER STREET—W1: [Latitude / Longitude: 51.517932,-0.155587]. One gloomy March morning in 1892 [sic], Holmes received a telegram from Scott Eccles. After reading it, Holmes asked Watson, "How do you define the word 'grotesque'"? The telegram read, *"Have just had the most incredible and grotesque experience. May I consult you"?* 1891? – **Wisteria Lodge**

Author's note: We must assume that the "1892" date is a typographical error. Sherlock's struggle at the Reichenbach Falls occurred in 1891, and he did not return to London until 1894. I think the Wisteria Lodge adventure occurred in March 1891.

PARK LANE—W1: [Latitude / Longitude: 51.512223,-0.157764]. On March 30, 1894, the Honorable Ronald Adair, second son of the Earl of Maynooth, was murdered. Adair lived with his mother and sister at 427 Park Lane (old numbering). **1894 – The Empty House**

Author's note: We know the location was across from Speakers Corner, near the north end of Park Lane. Since Adair was shot from across the street, the house at the Park Lane, Green Street corner is a good candidate.

SPEAKERS CORNER, HYDE PARK—W1: [Latitude / Longitude: 51.512001,-0.158529]. Watson thought that Holmes had died at Switzerland's Reichenbach Falls in 1891. Using the methods of his old comrade, Watson tried to come up with a theory that would fit the facts of the Adair murder. To view the Park Lane site, Watson strolled across Hyde Park's Speakers' Corner. There, on Park Lane, he saw a group of loafers looking up at Adair's window. While moving through the crowd, Watson bumped into an elderly, deformed man, knocking several books out of his hand. Watson thought that he must be some poor bibliophile. **1894 – The Empty House**

BLANDFORD (SOUTH) STREET—W1: [Latitude / Longitude: 51.518425,-0.152902]. After exiting Aybrook Street, Holmes and Watson turned west on the Part of Blandford Street that was then called South Street. **1894 – The Empty House**

BLANDFORD STREET—W1: [Latitude / Longitude: 51.518251,-0.155069]. Past Manchester Street, the name of South Street changes to Blandford Street. There, Holmes and Watson approached Kendall's Mews, now called Kendall Place. **1894 – The Empty House**

KENDALL PLACE "KENDALL'S MEWS"—W1: [Latitude / Longitude: 51.518251,-0.155069]. As Holmes and Watson turned south into Kendall's Mews, they stopped behind the empty Camden House, located at No. 34 Baker Street. Their roundabout journey (in a hansom cab) has insured that they had been unobserved, and that no one had followed them. **1894 – The Empty House**

Author's note: The timing of their arrival was critical. Holmes and Watson had to arrive before Colonel Moran. A wax bust of Holmes had been placed in their 221B window, and Mrs. Hudson crawled into the room from time to time to move it. Inspector Lestrade, two uniformed Policemen, and a plain-clothes detective hid in Baker Street. The trap was set.

No. 34 BAKER STREET, (CAMDEN HOUSE)—W1: [Latitude / Longitude: 51.518067,-0.155632]. During the three years of Holmes's exile, his brother, Mycroft, had preserved his Baker Street rooms and papers. Holmes knew that Professor Moriorty's gang would try to kill him, and that the shot would likely come from across Baker Street. With the Camden House being empty, it was the likely the shot would come from there. Holmes and Watson lay in wait for Colonel Sebastian Moran. **1894 – The Empty House**

No. 31 BAKER STREET)—W1: [Latitude / Longitude: 51.517932,-0.155587]. This rather precise description of the location of the Camden House, and the fact that it was across Baker Street from 221B, and that 221B had a back yard big enough for a plane tree, tells us that Mrs. Hudson's house was located where the building at No. 31 Baker Street stands today. **1894 – The Empty House**

No. 31 "221B" BAKER STREET—W1: [Latitude / Longitude: 51.517932,-0.155587]. After the death of Professor Moriarty, Watson sold his small practice in Kensington to Dr. Verner, and moved back to Baker Street. Years later, Watson learned that Verner was a relative of Holmes, and Holmes had provided the money for the purchase. **1895? – The Norwood Builder**

No. 31 "221B" BAKER STREET—W1: [Latitude / Longitude: 51.517932,-0.155587]. Late one Tuesday evening, Miss Violet Smith came to Baker Street. The date was April 23, 1895. Miss Smith told Holmes that she taught music at Chiltern Grange near Farnham, and was engaged to Cyril Morton, a young electrical engineer. **1895 – The Solitary Cyclist**

No. 31 "221B" BAKER STREET—W1: [Latitude / Longitude: 51.517932,-0.155587]. The next morning, three sailors showed up at Baker Street. Only one had the strength and skill to drive a harpoon through Captain Carey. He was Patrick Cairns, a harpooner of remarkable appearance. "His fierce bull-dog face was framed in a tangle of hair and beard, and two bold, dark eyes gleamed behind the cover of thick, tufted, overhung eyebrows," After a brief struggle, Holmes, Hopkins, and the armed Watson, managed to subdue him. **1895 – Black Peter**

No. 31 "221B" BAKER STREET—W1: [Latitude / Longitude: 51.517932,-0.155587]. In November 1895, a dense yellow fog settled down on London. Although he attempted to busy himself, Holmes was looking for something to occupy his mind. He received a telegram from his brother Mycroft, which read, *"Must see you over Cadogan West. Coming at once".* Holmes told Watson that the visit must be of some importance, because, "A planet might as well leave its orbit", for Mycroft to change his routine. **1895 – The Bruce-Partington Plans**

No. 31 "221B" BAKER STREET—W1: [Latitude / Longitude: 51.517932,-0.155587]. One morning, in late 1896, Holmes sent Watson a note, asking him to come to Baker Street. **1896 – The Veiled Lodger**

No. 31 "221B" BAKER STREET—W1: [Latitude / Longitude: 51.517932,-0.155587]. Watson wired Ferguson, asking him to come to Baker Street at ten o'clock the next morning. When he arrived, he said his wife would not explain her actions, and had rushed to her room and locked the door. **1896? – The Sussex Vampire**

BAYSWATER—W2: [Latitude / Longitude: 51.512589,-0.166576]. Overton notified Lord Mount-James, who came to Bentley's Hotel as quickly as the Bayswater Bus could bring him. Mount-James further lived up to his reputation of being a miser, by offering Holmes ten pounds toward expenses. **1897? – The Missing Three-Quarter**

No. 31 "221B" BAKER STREET—W1: [Latitude / Longitude: 51.517932,-0.155587]. That evening, at Baker Street, Holmes and Watson received a visit from Captain Crocker. Holmes told him, "Be frank with me and we may do some good. Play tricks with me, and I'll crush you". Crocker told Holmes of Sir Eustace's brutish nature and the events that led to his death. After hearing the "evidence", Holmes appointed Watson as a "British jury", and asked for his verdict. "Not guilty, my lord," said Watson. Holmes told Captain Crocker, "So long as the law does not find some other victim you are safe from me". **1897 – Abbey Grange**

No. 31 "221B" BAKER STREET—W1: [Latitude / Longitude: 51.517932,-0.155587]. It was not uncommon for Inspector Lestrade to stop by Baker Street, and discuss his cases. Lestrade knew that his latest case had some queer elements that would interest Holmes. Lestrade could not understand why anyone would steal and smash plaster busts of Napoleon. **1900? – The Six Napoleons**

No. 31 "221B" BAKER STREET—W1: [Latitude / Longitude: 51.517932,-0.155587]. Holmes was using his microscope to help Merivale of Scotland Yard on the St. Pancras case when he asked Watson, "Do you know something of racing"? Watson replied, "I ought to, I pay for it with about half of my wound pension". Holmes had a new client who was part of the horseracing world, and wanted to use Watson's "rich vein" of racing knowledge. **1901? – Shoscombe Old Place**

No. 31 "221B" BAKER STREET—W1: [Latitude / Longitude: 51.517932,-0.155587]. At eleven the next morning, Holmes received a visitor, who Watson compared to a "mad bull". Steve Dixie, the Negro bruiser, burst into the room and told Holmes to keep away from Harrow Weald, and other people's business. Holmes knew Barney Stockdale had sent Dixie. Both Dixie and Stockdale were members of the Spencer John Gang. **1902? – Three Gables**

No. 31 "221B" BAKER STREET—W1: [Latitude / Longitude: 51.517932,-0.155587]. After John Garrideb left Baker Street, Holmes said, "What on earth could be the object of this man telling us such rigmarole of lies?" Holmes noticed that his clothes and boots were English, and had at least a year's wear. In addition, although he had an American accent, it had been worn smooth by years in London. Finally, there had been no advertisement for Garridebs in the agony columns. To get more information, Holmes telephoned Nathan Garrideb, and made an appointment to visit him at six. **1902 – The Three Garridebs**

Author's note: In 1902, London's telephone exchange only had a capacity for 14,000 line users. This reference to using telephones in June 1902 meant that Sherlock (and Nathan Garrideb) were in a very select group. As mentioned in *The Retired Colourman*, Holmes may have had his telephone installed as early as 1889.

CONNAUGHT PLACE "No. 136 Little Ryder Street"—W2: [Latitude / Longitude: 51.513603,-0.161988]. For the past five years, Nathan Garrideb had lived in "an abode of Bohemian bachelors" at No. 136 Little Ryder Street, "one of the smaller offshoots from the Edgware Road, within a stone-cast of old Tyburn Tree of evil memory". Although Conan Doyle disguised the street name, the location described fits Connaught Place. **1902 – The Three Garridebs**

TYBURN TREE (site)—W1: [Latitude / Longitude: <u>51.512662,-0.158819</u>]. The Tyburn Tree was the old gallows where London executed its criminals. The first recorded hanging was in 1196, and the last in 1783. The site, marked by a stone plaque on the traffic island at the junction of Edgware Road and Oxford Street, is "within a stone-cast" of Connaught Place. **1902 – The Three Garridebs**

No. 31 "221B" BAKER STREET—W1: [Latitude / Longitude: <u>51.517932,-0.155587</u>]. Shinwell Johnson was waiting for Holmes and Watson when they returned to Baker Street, and introduced them to Kitty Winter. Baron Gruner had treated Kitty badly, and she wanted revenge. She knew Gruner kept a brown leather scrapbook that listed the women he had abused. It had everything about them: photographs, names, and details. Kitty said that the last time she saw the book; it was "In the pigeon-hole of the old bureau in Gruner's inner study". **1902 – The Illustrious Client**

No. 31 "221B" BAKER STREET—W1: [Latitude / Longitude: <u>51.517932,-0.155587</u>]. In January 1903, Holmes received a visit from James Dodd. He came to consult Holmes on a mystery concerning his friend, Lance-Corporal Godfrey Emsworth. **1903 – The Blanched Soldier**

No. 31 "221B" BAKER STREET—W1: [Latitude / Longitude: <u>51.517932,-0.155587</u>]. One May morning, just before noon, a discombobulated visitor arrived at Baker Street. Thorneycroft Huxtable, M.A., Ph.D., etc., burst into the room and collapsed on the bearskin hearthrug. Holmes plucked a return ticket from his pocket, and noted that he had come from Mackleton, in the North of England. **1903? – The Priory School**

No. 31 "221B" BAKER STREET—W1: [Latitude / Longitude: <u>51.517932,-0.155587</u>]. Trevor Bennett came to London to ask for Sherlock's help. Bennett was Professor Presbury's professional assistant, and lived in the Professor's house. Bennett was engaged to Professor Presbury's daughter. The 61-year-old Professor was also engaged, to a much younger woman. **Underground Station: Marble Arch**

No. 31 "221B" BAKER STREET—W1: [Latitude / Longitude: 51.517932,-0.155587]. Once he was on the case, Holmes hardly stopped to eat. When Watson dropped by Baker Street one evening, Billy, the young page, said that Mr. Holmes was asleep. He had been out at all hours in various disguises. Billy said the Prime Minister and the Home Secretary had been to Baker Street, as had Lord Cantlemere, who was against bringing Holmes into the case. Hearing Watson and Billy talking, Holmes came out of his bedroom. He told Watson that he expected to be murdered that evening by Count Negretto Sylvius. Upon hearing this shocking statement, Watson offered to drop everything and help. **1903? – The Mazarin Stone**

MARYLEBONE (Zone 1)

MARYLEBONE RAILWAY STATION—W1: [Latitude / Longitude: 51.522287,-0.163082]. Bernard Davies suggests that Holmes and Watson left London on the Great Central Railway from the new Marylebone terminus. The 12:05 PM to Leicester would have deposited them at Harrow-on-the-Hill in only 16 minutes. This may be the "short railroad journey" to which Watson referred. **1902? – Three Gables**

MONUMENT (Zone 1)

LOMBARD STREET—EC3: [Latitude / Longitude: 51.51227,-0.086324]. The advertised position was with Mawson & Williams's, the great stock-broking firm in Lombard Street. The ad specified a response by letter only. After he sent in his application, Pycroft was surprised to receive a reply by return mail. He had the job and was to report the next Monday. **1889? – The Stock-Broker's Clerk**

SWAN "UPPER SWANDAM" LANE—EC4: [Latitude / Longitude: 51.509056,-0.088609]. Kate said that her husband was probably at the Bar of Gold in Upper Swandam Lane, "A vile alley lurking behind the high wharves which line the north side of the river…east of London Bridge". **1889 – Man with the Twisted Lip**

Author's note: I join those who like Swan Lane as the location of "Upper Swandam Lane", even though it is west of London Bridge, and not east. As we all know, Watson did make a few mistakes in his narratives. For example, in this adventure he specified June 19, 1889 as a Friday, when it was in fact a Wednesday. Perhaps he meant July 19.

WATERMANS WALK "PAUL'S WHARF"—EC4: [Latitude / Longitude: 51.509083,-0.089618]. Holmes said, "There is a trap-door at the back of that building, near the corner of Paul's Wharf, which could tell some strange tales of what has passed through it upon the moonless nights". **1889 – Man with the Twisted Lip**

Author's note: Watermans Walk fits the location; Today's Paul's Walk is too upstream.

MARTIN LANE—EC4: [Latitude / Longitude: 51.510616,-0.087873]. The previous Monday, Mrs. St. Clair received word that a package she was expecting, was waiting for her at the Aberdeen Shipping Company. Their offices were on a street that branches out of Upper Swandam (Swan) Lane. Martin Lane matches the location. **1889 – Man with the Twisted Lip**

LIME STREET—EC3: [Latitude / Longitude: 51.512201,-0.083159]. With Holmes playing his violin, Sylvius and Merton thought they were alone. Count Sylvius revealed that he had the diamond on him. He told Merton to take the jewel to Van Seddar in Lime Street. Sylvius said he would stay and stall Holmes to allow Van Seddar to spirit the diamond to Amsterdam. **1903? – The Mazarin Stone**

Author's note: Lime Street is named for the lime sellers who once congregated there.

MOORGATE (Zone 1)

DRAPERS' GARDEN—EC2: [Latitude / Longitude: 51.516189,- 0.087805]. Pycroft said he "used to have a billet at Coxon & Woodhouse's, of Draper Gardens". He and twenty-six other clerks were let go after the Venezuelan loan problem. Although Pycroft wore out his boots trying to find a new position, he was near the end of his tether when he saw a help wanted ad. **1889? – The Stock-Broker's Clerk**

Author's note: Drapers Garden is at the junction of Throgmorton and Copthall Avenues. The land had been used by the Drapers' Company for gardens, but was later used for offices buildings, including Coxon & Woodhouse.

NOTTING HILL GATE (Zone 1)

NOTTING HILL—W11: [Latitude / Longitude: 51.509637,- 0.201595]. Louis La Rothière of Campden Mansions, Notting Hill was one of the international spies reported by Mycroft. **1895 – The Bruce-Partington Plans**

OVAL (Zone 2)

HENRY "HENRIETTA" STREET—SW9: [Latitude / Longitude: 51.477458,-0.108383]. Constable Rance said it began to rain at one o'clock, when he met Constable Harry Murcher, "him who has the Holland Grove beat" at the corner of "Henrietta Street". Henry Street is no longer there, but it entered the north side of Vassall Road, just west of the Holland Grove. **1881? – Study in Scarlet**

CAMBERWELL NEW ROAD—SE11: [Latitude / Longitude: 51.481672,-0.111625]. Holmes, Watson and Toby found themselves east of The Oval, where Brixton Road meets Kennington Park. There, they turned left on Camberwell New Road, continued across Kennington Park Road, as the name changed to Harleyford Street. **1887** – Sign of Four

HARLEYFORD STREET—SE11: [Latitude / Longitude: 51.482187,-0.112621]. Watson remarked that the men they were pursuing had certainly taken a zigzag path. **1887 – Sign of Four**

KENNINGTON OVAL—SE11: [Latitude / Longitude: 51.48283,-0.115038]. Toby led Holmes and Watson around the south side of The Oval on Harleyford Road. **1887 – Sign of Four**

HARLEYFORD ROAD—SE11: [Latitude / Longitude: 51.484768,-0.118579]. In my opinion, it must have been at the junction of Harleyford Road and Durham Street where Toby picked up a false creosote scent. He followed this false trail up Harleyford Road. **1887 – Sign of Four**

117 BRIXTON ROAD—SW9: [Latitude / Longitude: 51.477162,-0.11235]. After hearing about the blue carbuncle from Catherine Cusack, the Countess of Morcar's maid, James Ryder stole the precious gem, and took it to his sister's house. The sister, Maggie Oakshott, lived at 117 Brixton Road. Without telling her, Ryder forced the gem into the crop of the Christmas goose she was fattening for him. After John Horner's arrest, Ryder returned to claim his goose. He took the bird to Kilburn, where he and Maudsley attempted to recover the gem. To their dismay, Ryder had selected the wrong goose. **1889? - The Blue Carbuncle**

BRIXTON ROAD—SW9: [Latitude / Longitude: 51.476518,-0.112524]. The morning of the funeral, Holmes finally realized how Shlessinger planned to dispose of Lady Frances Carfax. He and Watson rushed along Brixton Road to Poultney Square. **1902? – Lady Frances Carfax**

OXFORD CIRCUS (Zone 1)

ST. GEORGE'S, HANOVER SQUARE, No. 2A Mill Street—W1: [Latitude / Longitude: 51.512486,-0.143133]. The society papers said the wedding would take place at St. George's, Hanover Square. After the ceremony, a wedding breakfast was held at Lancaster Gate, where Aloysius Doran, the bride's father, had taken a furnished house. **1886 - The Noble Bachelor**

CAVENDISH SQUARE—W1: [Latitude / Longitude: 51.516888,-0.14598]. Percy Trevelyan said, "A [medical] specialist who aims high is compelled to start in one of a dozen streets in the Cavendish Square quarter". This is still true today. **1886? – The Resident Patient**

HARLEY STREET—W1: [Latitude / Longitude: 51.517653,-0.146323]. When Holmes questioned Blessington, he refused to say why he was afraid. Holmes said he could not help unless he did. When Blessington still refused, Holmes and Watson left. They were halfway down Harley Street before Watson could get a word out of Holmes. **1886? – The Resident Patient**

TOWARD OXFORD "REGENT" CIRCUS—W1: [Latitude / Longitude: 51.514592,-0.147661]. On their way from Baker Street to the Diogenes Club, Holmes and Watson walked east on Oxford Street toward "Regent" (Oxford) Circus. They must have turned south before reaching the Circus, because they entered the west end of Pall Mall from St. James's Street. **1887? – The Greek Interpreter**

THE LANGHAM HOTEL, Portland Place—W1: [Latitude / Longitude: 51.518077,-0.143875]. Mary Morstan said that her father had been a senior captain in an Indian regiment. When Mary's mother died, her father sent Mary to live in Edinburgh. In 1878, Captain Morstan obtained leave, and telegraphed Mary from London's Langham Hotel, saying that he had arrived safely. When Mary went to see her father, he was not there. The hotel said he had gone out the night before and did not return. His luggages, and curiosities from his service on the Andaman Islands, were in his room. Mary contacted the police and advertised in the newspapers, but to no avail. Mary did find a strange note in her father's papers. It had the notation, *"The Sign of the Four—Jonathan Small, Mahomet Singh, Abdullah Khan, Dost Akbar"*. **1887 – Sign of Four**

THE LANGHAM HOTEL, Portland Place—W1: [Latitude / Longitude: 51.518077,-0.143875]. The King said he was staying at the Langham Hotel, under the name Count Von Kramm. **1888 – Scandal in Bohemia**

BOND STREET—W1: [Latitude / Longitude: 51.511532,-0.143664]. To kill time before their two o'clock appointment, Holmes and Watson walked to Bond Street, and spent the afternoon in the art galleries. The works of the modern Belgian masters particularly interested Holmes. **1889 – Hound of the Baskervilles**

HARLEY STREET—W1: [Latitude / Longitude: 51.516853,-0.145999]. As Holmes and Watson continued east on Wigmore Street, they crossed Harley Street. Cavendish Square was on their right as the street's name changed to Cavendish Place. **1889? - The Blue Carbuncle**

CAVENDISH PLACE—W1: [Latitude / Longitude: 51.51736,-0.143684]. As Holmes and Watson continued east on Wigmore Street, they crossed Harley Street as Wigmore Street changed to Cavendish Place. **1889? - The Blue Carbuncle**

MORTIMER STREET—W1: [Latitude / Longitude: 51.51801,-0.139421]. Holmes and Watson continued east on Cavendish Place as the street's name changed to Mortimer Street. **1889? - The Blue Carbuncle**

WELLS STREET—W1: [Latitude / Longitude: 51.516276,-0.137088]. Holmes and Watson continued east on Mortimer Street until they reached Wells Street. There they turned south toward Oxford Street. **1889? - The Blue Carbuncle**

OXFORD STREET—W1: [Latitude / Longitude: 51.516029,-0.135067]. **Then, as today, Oxford Street is very busy.** Holmes and Watson continued east on Oxford Street. **1889? - The Blue Carbuncle**

LITTLE TITCHFIELD STREET—W1: [Latitude / Longitude: 51.51821,-0.140687]. Watson was surprised to see Holmes enter his consulting-room. In 1891, Watson was married, in private practice, and lived in a house that backed up to Mortimer Street. This means that it is likely that his surgery fronted on Little Titchfield Street. **1891 – The Final Problem**

MORTIMER STREET—W1: [Latitude / Longitude: 51.51787,-0.140496]. After Watson agreed to go, Holmes gave him complicated instructions on how they would leave London the next day. Holmes left Watson's surgery by scrambling over the back garden wall into Mortimer Street. **1891 – The Final Problem**

CONDUIT STREET—W1: [Latitude / Longitude: 51.511952,-0.142289]. We learn from Holmes's index of biographies, that Colonel Sebastian Moran was a friend of Moriarty, and the second most dangerous man in London. "He was once with Her Majesty's Indian Army, and the best heavy-game shot that our Eastern Empire has ever produced". He lived at Conduit Street. **1894 – The Empty House**

CAVENDISH SQUARE—W1: [Latitude / Longitude: 51.516888,-0.14598]. Reunited with his old comrade, Watson found himself beside Holmes, "In a hansom, my revolver in my pocket, and the thrill of adventure in my heart". Watson thought they were bound directly for their old Baker Street quarters, but Holmes took a wandering route through mews and stables. He stopped the cab at the northeast corner of Cavendish Square, stepped out, and searched to the right and left, as he did at every subsequent corner. **1894 – The Empty House**

Author's note: Based on the clues given in the adventure, Bernard Davies suggests the following route from Cavendish Square to *The Empty House*. For a more complete explanation of this subject, see Bernard Davies, *The Mews of Marylebone*. Mr. Davies suggests that Holmes and Watson dismissed the hansom at Cavendish Square, and walked the route. I disagree. The whole purpose of the journey was to remain unobserved, and arrive early. Using a hansom cab makes more sense.

HARLEY STREET—W1: [Latitude / Longitude: 51.517643,-0.146341]. In March 1897, Holmes's iron constitution showed signs of wear. Doctor Moore Agar of Harley Street advised Holmes to take a complete rest. Following the Doctor's advice, Holmes and Watson went to Cornwall, rented a small cottage near Poldhu, and found the "The Cornish Horror". **Underground Station: Oxford Circus**

OXFORD STREET—W1: [Latitude / Longitude: 51.514956,-0.143691]. Later that day, Holmes and Watson walked along Oxford Street, toward Regent (Oxford) Circus. There, in a shop window, they saw photographs of the celebrities and beauties of the day. Among them, was a picture of their "avenging angel". Watson looked at Holmes, who put a finger to his lips. **1899? – Charles Augustus Milverton**

THE LANGHAM HOTEL, Portland Place—W1: [Latitude / Longitude: 51.518077,-0.143875]. The Englischer Hof manager said that a bearded Englishman was also trying to find Lady Frances. Holmes arrived from England and told Watson that he had learned the identity of the bearded man. He was the Hon. Philip Green, who loved Lady Frances, and was trying to find her. Green, the son of a famous admiral of the same name, used the Langham Hotel as his London address. **1902? – Lady Frances Carfax**

Author's note: During Holmes's time, the fact that you were a guest at the Langham automatically marked you as a gentleman. Today, this exclusive Victorian hotel is restored to its former glory, and is an excellent hotel for those trying to find Sherlock Holmes's London.

No. 9 QUEEN ANNE STREET—W1: [**Latitude / Longitude: 51.518261,-0.145711**]. In 1902, Watson was living at No. 9 Queen Anne Street. **1902 – The Illustrious Client**

Author's note: Holmes referred to Watson as "His Boswell". I think Conan Doyle placed him in Queen Anne Street, because the original Boswell, James, lived there when he wrote the *Life of Samuel Johnson.*

PADDINGTON (Zone 1)

PADDINGTON—W2: [**Latitude / Longitude: 51.514567,-0.173905**]. Shortly after his marriage, Watson bought a Paddington medical practice from old Mr. Farquhar. For three months he worked hard to increase the number of patients, and saw very little of Holmes. Watson was surprised when Holmes arrived in Paddington early one morning, and asked if Watson could accompany him to Birmingham. **1889? – The Stock-Broker's Clerk**

PADDINGTON RAILWAY STATION—W2: [**Latitude / Longitude: 51.515637,-0.175678**]. In the summer of 1889, shortly after his marriage, Watson set up private practice near the Paddington station. Early one morning, two men came from the Station. One was a station guard, and the other was Victor Hatherley. Hatherley had previously departed from Paddington to meet Colonel Lysander Stark in Eyford, near Reading. When he returned, he had lost his thumb, and needed medical attention. **1889 – The Engineer's Thumb**

PADDINGTON RAILWAY STATION—W2: [**Latitude / Longitude: 51.515637,-0.175678**]. Watson arrived at Paddington Station, and found, "Sherlock Holmes…pacing up and down the platform, his tall gaunt figure made even gaunter and taller by his long grey traveling-cloak and the close-fitting cloth cap" **1889 – Boscombe Valley Mystery**

Author's note: This may be the first mention of Sherlock's, now famous, dear-stalker hat.

PADDINGTON RAILWAY STATION—W2: [**Latitude** / **Longitude:** 51.515637,-0.175678]. After Holmes and Watson met Sir Henry and Dr. Mortimer at the Northumberland Hotel, they agreed that Watson would accompany Sir Henry to Baskerville Hall, on Saturday's ten-thirty train from Paddington. Because of the press of other business, Holmes said he could not go at that time. **1889 – Hound of the Baskervilles**

PADDINGTON RAILWAY STATION—W2: [**Latitude** / **Longitude:** 51.515637,-0.175678]. One Thursday morning, Holmes asked Watson to accompany him to the King's Pyland training stable in Dartmoor. Silver Blaze, the horse favored to win the Wessex Cup, was missing, and his trainer murdered. Holmes and Watson were just in time to catch the Dartmoor train from Paddington. On the trip, Holmes wore his ear-flapped traveling cap, (A reference to his famous deerstalker). As an amusement, he calculated the train's speed by observing and timing the passing telegraph poles. **1890? – Silver Blaze**

PADDINGTON RAILWAY STATION—W2: [**Latitude** / **Longitude:** 51.515637,-0.175678]. In addition to the other strange happenings at Shoscombe Old Place, Mason said that Sir Robert had started going down to the old church crypt at night, and meeting a stranger there. When Holmes asked Mason about the fishing in that part of Berkshire, Mason thought the craziness might be catching. Holmes said that he and Watson would take the train from Paddington Station, and come down posing as a pair of London anglers. They would stay at the Green Dragon, and look into the situation. **1901? – Shoscombe Old Place**

PICCADILLY CIRCUS (Zone 1)

REFORM CLUB, 104 Pall Mall—SW1: [Latitude / Longitude: 51.506819,-0.133629]. Founded in 1836, The Reform Club was one of the three gentlemen's clubs joined by Sir Arthur Conan Doyle. He was a member from June 1892.

THE ATHENAEUM, 107 Pall Mall—SW1: [Latitude / Longitude: 51.507053,-0.132619]. Founded in 1824, The Athenaeum was one of the three gentlemen's clubs joined by Sir Arthur Conan Doyle. He was a member from March 1901.

THE ROYAL AUTOMOBILE CLUB, 89 Pall Mall—SW1: [Latitude / Longitude: 51.506258,-0.135217]. Founded in 1897, The Royal Automobile Club was one of the three gentlemen's clubs joined by Sir Arthur Conan Doyle. He became a member in 1903, shortly after buying his first automobile.

CRITERION GRILL, No. 224 Piccadilly—W1: [Latitude / Longitude: 51.510162,-0.134436]. The day Watson made up his mind to move out of his Strand hotel, he went to The Criterion Bar. There, he met young Stamford. Stamford had been a dresser under Watson at "St. Bart's." Watson asked Stamford to have lunch with him at The Holborn Restaurant. **1881? – Study in Scarlet**

Author's note: The Criterion has reopened. The spacious and ornate dining room is in the Criterion Theatre Building at Piccadilly Circus. Ask if they still have the good-value pre-theater dinner. Also, look for the wall plaque that commemorates the event that resulted in Watson meeting Holmes.

HAYMARKET—WC2: [Latitude / Longitude: 51.50943,-0.132619]. From Charing Cross, Latimer and Melas probably traveled up Haymarket to Shaftesbury Avenue. **1887? – The Greek Interpreter**

SHAFTSBURY AVENUE—WC2: [Latitude / Longitude: 51.51203,-0.131965]. The carriage with Melas and Latimer continued up Shaftsbury Avenue towards Oxford Street. **1887? – The Greek Interpreter**

PALL MALL—SW1: [Latitude / Longitude: 51.505938,-0.136213]. Mycroft Holmes lived in Pall Mall chambers. His Diogenes Club was just opposite. Holmes said that the Diogenes Club was the queerest club in London, and Mycroft was one of its queerest members. He was at his club every day from quarter to five to twenty to eight. **1887? – The Greek Interpreter**

CARLTON CLUB (site)—SW1: [Latitude / Longitude: 51.506577,-0.134204]. Watson said that the Diogenes Club was, "Some little distance from the Carlton". The Carlton Club, formed in 1832, moved to their new Pall Mall building at Carlton Gardens four years later. **1887? – The Greek Interpreter**

Author's note: Today, the Carlton Club is located at No. 69 St. James's Street, SW1.

REGENT STREET—W1: [Latitude / Longitude: 51.511142,-0.138904]. Godfrey Norton rushed into Gross and Hankey's in Regent Street, before going to the Church of St. Monica. Because of the last minute nature of the wedding, we can assume that Gross and Hankey's was the jewelry store, where he bought the wedding ring(s). **1888 – Scandal in Bohemia**

REGENT STREET—W1: [Latitude / Longitude: 51.511142,-0.138904]. Years later, in London, McCarthy saw Turner on Regent Street. McCarthy blackmailed Turner, and threatened to expose his criminal past. The threat resulted in McCarthy acquiring Hatherley Farm, rent-free. **1889 – Boscombe Valley Mystery**

REGENT STREET—W1: [Latitude / Longitude: 51.512112,-0.139732]. As Holmes and Watson walked along Regent Street, they noticed a hansom cab following Sir Henry. They tried to get a good look at the passenger, but the cab sped away, Holmes now knew that Baskerville had been closely shadowed since he arrived in London. Holmes remarked that using a cab had a disadvantage. He had seen the cab's number, "2704". Holmes and Watson went into the Regent Street office of the District Messenger Service. Holmes had previously helped the manager, and asked for the loan of young Cartwright. **1889 – Hound of the Baskervilles**

ST. JAMES'S HALL (site) 21 Piccadilly—W1: [Latitude / Longitude: 51.509328,-0.13609]. Considering the evidence, Holmes knew the reason for the Red-headed League ruse. Jabez Wilson had to be kept out of his shop, so that a tunnel could be dug from his cellar to the nearby bank. Holmes said the theft would take place on Saturday night when the bank was closed, and discovery of the theft would not take place until Monday morning. With the detective work done, Holmes and Watson had time for play. After a sandwich and cup of coffee, they were off to violin-land at St. James's Hall, where Sarasate was playing. The Hall was located where a hotel sits today. In Holmes's day, St. James's Hall was London's leading concert venue. **1890 – Red-Headed League**

PALL MALL—SW1: [Latitude / Longitude: 51.505744,-0.136546]. After the "accidents" in Mayfair, Holmes hailed a cab and went to Brother Mycroft's chambers in Pall Mall. He spent the day there before going to see Watson. On the way, a tough with a bludgeon attacked him. Holmes managed to knock him down, but barked his knuckles on the tough's front teeth. **1891 – The Final Problem**

Author's note: Since the Diogenes Club, and therefore Mycroft's chambers, were, "Some little distance from the Carlton Club", I suggest they were at the western end of Pall Mall.

PALL MALL—SW1: [Latitude / Longitude: 51.507894,-0.130581].
After returning to London, Watson stopped by the estate agent firm at Pall Mall. They said he was too late to get Charlington Hall for the summer. It had been let a month before by a Mr. Williamson. The agent said he was a respectable elderly gentleman, but would say no more. **1895 – The Solitary Cyclist**

PALL MALL AND COCKSPUR STREET—SW1: [Latitude / Longitude: 51.507674,-0.130852]. Holmes and Watson went to the shipping office of the Adelaide-Southampton steamship line. It was located at the Cockspur Street end of Pall Mall. At the shipping office, Holmes learned of Captain Jack Crocker's character, and guessed his role in the death of Sir Eustace. **1897 – Abbey Grange**

THEATRE ROYAL, HAYMARKET, Haymarket Street—SW1: [Latitude / Longitude: 51.508542,-0.131664]. Amberley told Watson how he pampered his wife, and how badly she treated him. Amberley said he had bought two upper circle seats at the Haymarket Theater the night she left. He said his wife complained of a headache, and could not go. Amberley showed the unused ticket to Watson. Watson noted that it was for seat B-31. Later, Holmes found that seat numbers B-30 and B-32 had not been sold that night. Amberley lied when he said he had purchased two tickets. **1898? – The Retired Colourman**

COX AND KINGS BANK (site), No. 6 Waterloo Place—SW1: [Latitude / Longitude: 51.507524,-0.132675]. Cox and King's Bank relocated to the northeast corner of Pall Mall and Waterloo Place. Was this the intermediate resting place of Watson's old tin dispatch box? **1900? – Thor Bridge**

CARLTON CLUB (site)—SW1: [Latitude / Longitude: 51.506577,-0.134204]. When Watson asked Holmes "whether anything was stirring", Holmes drew a note from his coat. The note was from Colonel Sir James Damery, asking Holmes to call upon him at the Carlton Club. In 1902, the Carlton Club was located on the south side of Pall Mall, at Carlton Gardens. Sir James wanted to consult Holmes on Violet de Merville's infatuation with Baron Adelbert Gruner. Violet was the daughter of General de Merville of Khyber fame. **1902 – The Illustrious Client**

CAFÉ ROYAL—No. 68 Regent Street (site)—W1: [Latitude / Longitude: 51.509849,-0.135908]. Watson bought a newspaper, and learned that two men, armed with sticks, attacked Holmes in Regent Street, outside the Café Royal. **1902 – The Illustrious Client**

GLASSHOUSE STREET—W1: [Latitude / Longitude: 51.510282,-0.134927]. Holmes escaped by running through the Café Royal, into Glasshouse Street. The article went on to say that, Holmes's injuries were serious, and that he had been carried to Charing Cross Hospital, but insisted on returning to Baker Street. **1902 – The Illustrious Client**

LONDON LIBRARY, St. James's Square—SW1: [Latitude / Longitude: 51.507434,-0.136281]. Watson's friend Lomax, the Sub-librarian at the London Library, helped Watson study books on Chinese pottery. **1902 – The Illustrious Client**

Author's note: Thomas Carlyle built the London Library in 1841, as an alternative to the British Museum's library. Annual and life memberships are still available. The cost of a life membership varies with your age.

CARLTON HOUSE TERRACE—SW1: [Latitude / Longitude: 51.506031,-0.132952]. The Duke of Holdernesse's London residence was at Carlton House Terrace. **1903? – The Priory School**

GERMAN EMBASSY (SITE), No. 7 CARLTON HOUSE TERRACE—SW1: [Latitude / Longitude: 51.506188,-0.132544]. Baron Von Herling wanted Von Bork to bring the new Naval Signals to London. Von Herling said, "When you get the signal book through the little door…you can put a finis to your record in England". **1914 – His Last Bow**

Author's note: Today, the former embassy is the home of The Royal Society. Albert Speer magnificently redesigned the interior of the building in the 1930's on orders from Adolf Hitler. The building was transferred to The Royal Society after World War II.

THE LITTLE DOOR—SW1: [Latitude / Longitude: 51.505818,-0.130926]. There are two small doors on the Carlton House Terrace steps. One is near the former German Embassy. Von Bork had to put the new Naval Signals through the little west door. **1914 – His Last Bow**

PIMLICO (Zone 1)

ROCHESTER ROW—SW1: [Latitude / Longitude: 51.494218,-0.136794]. As Holmes, Watson, and Mary Morstan continued their journey to Lambeth, Holmes muttered Rochester Row. **1887 – Sign of Four**

VINCENT SQUARE—SW1: [Latitude / Longitude: 51.494218,-0.136794]. On their way down Rochester Row, they passed near Vincent Square. If it had been a sunny day, they could have seen it through Vane Street. **1887 – Sign of Four**

VAUXHALL BRIDGE ROAD—SW1: [Latitude / Longitude: 51.490553,-0.133427]. From Rochester Row, they turned left on Vauxhall Bridge Road, toward the river. **1887 – Sign of Four**

MILLBANK PENITENTIARY (site)—SW1: [Latitude / Longitude: 51.492464,-0.125291]. At the end of their long walk, Holmes and Watson returned Toby and took a wherry to the north side of the river, near Millbank Penitentiary. **1887 – Sign of Four**

Author's note: In 1887, Millbank Penitentiary was the largest prison in London, and contained men only. They could not communicate with each other for the first half of their sentence. The prison closed in 1890 and was demolished in 1903.

MILLBANK at VAUXHALL BRIDGE—SW1: [Latitude / Longitude: 51.48907,-0.128814]. Holmes, Watson and Jones made their way back upstream. They used their searchlight to look for the Islander, but there was no sign of him. The police launch landed at Vauxhall Bridge, and Watson, accompanied by an inspector, took the treasure box to Mary Morstan. **1887 – Sign of Four**

PUTNEY BRIDGE (Zone 2)

HURLINGHAM PARK—SW6: [Latitude / Longitude: 51.470484,-0.202657]. Sir James said that Baron Gruner was a horse fancier, and played polo at Hurlingham Park. He also had expensive tastes, and was a recognized authority on Chinese pottery, having written a book on the subject. **1902 – The Illustrious Client**

REGENTS PARK (Zone 1)

No. 2 UPPER WIMPOLE STREET—W1: [Latitude / Longitude: 51.52054,-0.149369]. For a few months, Sir Arthur Conan Doyle practiced his short-lived ophthalmic practice at number No. 2 Upper Wimpole Street. The scarcity of patients gave him time to write. A plaque erected by the Westminster City Council marks the building.

HARLEY STREET—W1: [Latitude / Longitude: 51.519158,-0.14701]. From Cavendish Square, Holmes and Watson's hansom drove north on Harley Street toward New Cavendish Street, then called Great Marylebone Street. **1894 – The Empty House**

NEW CAVENDISH STREET—W1: [Latitude / Longitude: 51.519226,-0.147882]. Holmes and Watson turned west on Great Marylebone Street, now called New Cavendish Street, before taking a quick right on Wimpole Mews and continuing north. **1894 – The Empty House**

WIMPOLE MEWS—W1: [Latitude / Longitude: 51.519226,-0.147882]. The north end of Wimpole Mews ends at Weymouth Street. Here, Holmes and Watson turned left and continued west toward Beaumont Mews. **1894 – The Empty House**

RICHMOND (Zone 4)

RICHMOND RUGBY CLUB—TW9: [Latitude / Longitude: 51.465023,-0.30383]. Ferguson's letter said that in his younger days, he played Rugby for Richmond. He remembered Watson as a fellow Rugby player. **1896? – The Sussex Vampire**

OLD DEER PARK—TW9: [Latitude / Longitude: 51.469989,-0.293723]. Ferguson recalled the day he threw Watson into the crowd at the Old Deer Park. **1896? – The Sussex Vampire**

RUSSELL SQUARE (Zone 1)

MONTAGUE STREET—WC1: [Latitude / Longitude: 51.519069,-0.12463]. After Holmes's observations, the old man felt uneasy around Holmes. To keep from embarrassing Victor, Holmes returned to his Montague Street rooms in London. There, Holmes received a telegram from Trevor, imploring him to return to Donnithorpe. **1874 – THE "GLORIA SCOTT"**

MONTAGUE STREET—WC1: [Latitude / Longitude: 51.519069,-0.12463]. In his early days in London, Holmes had rooms in Montague Street. He was just out of college, and wanted quarters near the British Museum's Reading Room. One morning, he received a visit from Reginald Musgrave. Musgrave had been at Sherlock's college, and after his father's death, had taken over the family estate. Musgrave said he needed Holmes's help. **1879 – THE MUSGRAVE RITUAL**

Author's note: There is no indication that Holmes's Montague Street rooms were at the same location in 1879, as they were in 1874. In fact, since it is likely that he finished college between these dates, and given the state of his finances, it does not seem logical that he would have retained London quarters.

RUSKIN PRIVATE HOTEL, No. 23/24 Montague Street—WC1: [Latitude / Longitude: 51.519614,-0.125197]. Author's note: On one of my trips to London, I talked to the owner of the private Ruskin Hotel. He claimed his modest Bed & Breakfast was the location of Sherlock's Montague Street rooms. I do not know where he got the idea, but it makes a good story, and is probably good for business. **1879 – THE MUSGRAVE RITUAL**

MONTAGUE PLACE—WC1: [Latitude / Longitude: 51.520907,-0.127119]. Violet Hunter's letter came from Montague Place. It read, *"Dear Mr. Holmes: I am very anxious to consult you as to whether I should or should not accept a situation, which has been offered to me as governess. I shall call at half-past ten tomorrow if I do not inconvenience you. Yours faithfully, Violet Hunter".* **1890? – Copper Beeches**

RUSSELL SQUARE—WC1: [Latitude / Longitude: 51.521388,-0.127248]. Hilton Cubitt came from an old Norfolk family. In June 1887, he came to London for Queen Victoria's Diamond Jubilee, and stayed at a boardinghouse in Russell Square. There, he met Elsie Patrick, an American girl with whom he fell in Love. After their marriage, they returned to Riding Thorpe Manor, the Cubitt estate in Norfolk. Their ten years of happy married life changed when Elsie began receiving "dancing men" notes. **1897 – The Dancing Men**

No. 13 GREAT ORMOND "Orme" STREET—WC1: [Latitude / Longitude: 51.521488,-0.121654]. The Warrens lived in a "High, thin, yellow-brick edifice" at Great Orme Street, northeast of the British Museum. Mrs. Warren consulted Holmes about her new lodger. The

No. 9 GREAT ORMOND STREET—WC1: [Latitude / Longitude: 51.522545,-0.117914]. At one point, the lodger slipped a note under the door, asking that Mrs. Warren start delivering the *Daily Gazette*. Holmes thought that the newspaper's agony columns might be the way in which the lodger received messages. In the columns since the lodger arrived, Holmes found several cryptic messages, all signed by the letter G. The latest message read, *"High red house with white stone facings, third floor, second window left, after dusk, G".* **1902? – The Red Circle**

Author's note: North American readers should remember that what the British call the third floor is your fourth floor.

SHADWELL (Dockland Light Railway) (Zone 2)

THE HIGHWAY "RATCLIFF HIGHWAY"—E1: [Latitude / Longitude: 51.509666,-0.054955]. The papers were full of the Brixton Murder, and the Daily Telegraph compared it to, "The Ratcliff Highway murders." The Ratcliff Highway, in Wapping, had a sinister reputation. Watson began saving the press clippings, putting him on the road to becoming Holmes's "Boswell". **1881? – Study in Scarlet**

THE HIGHWAY "RATCLIFF HIGHWAY"—E1: [Latitude / Longitude: 51.509666,-0.054955]. Holmes asked Watson to send two telegrams. One went to Summer, the Shipping Agent at Ratcliff Highway. It read, "*Send three men on to arrive ten tomorrow morning.—Basil*". Holmes said that Captain Basil was his name in those parts. The second telegram went to Inspector Hopkins, asking him to come to Baker Street for breakfast at nine-thirty. **1895 – Black Peter**

SOUTH KENSINGTON (Zone 1)

ROYAL ALBERT HALL—SW7: [Latitude / Longitude: 51.501572,-0.177339]. Holmes suggested that he and Watson escape from the weary workaday world, by having an evening of music at Albert Hall. They dressed for dinner, and dined, before the performance. **1898? – The Retired Colourman**

STAMFORD BROOK (Zone 2)

CHISWICK, Hounslow—W4: [Latitude / Longitude: 51.492044,-0.246763]. Holmes, Watson, Lestrade, and the other policemen waited outside Laburnum Villa in Chiswick. There, with the help of the owner, Mr. Josiah Brown, they captured Beppo. He had broken into the house, stolen another Napoleon bust, and smashed it. **1900? – The Six Napoleons**

ST JAMES'S PARK (Zone 1)

VICTORIA STREET—SW1: [Latitude / Longitude: 51.497612,-0.135099]. As they traveled down Victoria Street, with the fog, and his limited knowledge of London, Watson lost his way. Holmes, on the other hand, had a map of London in his head, and began muttering names as they rattled through squares and streets. **1887 – Sign of Four**

GREAT PETER STREET POST OFFICE, Great Smith Street—SW1: [Latitude / Longitude: 51.496944,-0.129382]. On their way back to Baker Street, Holmes wired ahead from the Great Peter Street Post Office to mobilize the "Baker Street Irregulars". Holmes instructed Wiggins, their dirty little lieutenant, to search the riverside for the *Aurora,* but to do so without raising suspicion. **1887 – Sign of Four**

Author's note: The Great Peter Post Office was on a corner, and actually fronted on Great Smith Street.

ST. JAMES'S PARK—SW1: [Latitude / Longitude: 51.502813,-0.129575]. Sir Henry said he spent his afternoon walking in the park. He did not say which park, but it was probably St. James's, the nearest park to the Northumberland Hotel. **1889 – Hound of the Baskervilles**

IMPERIAL THEATRE (site), Tothill Street—SW1: [Latitude / Longitude: 51.499692,-0.130106]. Violet said her late father had conducted the orchestra at the old Imperial Theatre. **1895 – The Solitary Cyclist**

Author's note: The Imperial Theatre was part of an amusement complex known as the Royal Aquarium. It covered the site now occupied by the Wesleyan Central Hall, on the north side of Tothill Street.

ST. JOHN'S WOOD (Zone 2)

ST. JOHN'S WOOD—NW8: [Latitude / Longitude: 51.53237,-0.173582]. Irene Adler lived in Briony Lodge, at the fictional Serpentine Avenue, St. John's Wood. Holmes devised a plan to find where she hid the picture. **1888 – Scandal in Bohemia**

STOCKWELL (Zone 2)

SUB-DISTRICT POST, MONEY ORDER AND TELEGRAPH OFFICE, No. 304 Brixton Road—SW9: [Latitude / Longitude: 51.469866,-0.112588]. Having determined that Gregson wired Cleveland, but did not ask the correct questions, Holmes and Watson walked to the nearby telegraph office to dispatch their own wire. The building that contained the telegraph office is marked as the home of The Eagle Printing Works. **1881? – Study in Scarlet**

WHITE HORSE PUB (site), No. 1 Loughborough Road—SW9: [Latitude / Longitude: 51.470491,-0.112181]. **Author's note:** The ad, as written, makes no sense. It says that the ring was "In Brixton Road, but the White Hart Public House is 400 feet away. It is more likely that Watson wrote "White Hart" instead of "White Horse", the latter pub was on the corner of Loughborough & Brixton Roads. The building is still there, but no longer a pub. **1881? – Study in Scarlet**

PRIORY ROAD—SW8: [Latitude / Longitude: 51.475304,-0.1301]. From Wandsworth Road, they turned left on Lansdowne Way. In Sherlock's day, the Western section of Lansdowne Way was called Priory Road. **1887 – Sign of Four**

LANSDOWNE WAY—SW8: [Latitude / Longitude: <u>51.474903,-0.127943</u>]. Williams continued on Priory Road as its name changed to Lansdowne Way. **1887 – Sign of Four**

LARKHALL LANE—SW8: [Latitude / Longitude: <u>51.474689,-0.126774</u>]. As they were driven east on Lansdowne Way, Holmes, Watson and Mary passed Larkhall Lane on the right. Watson called it "Lark Hall" Lane. **1887 – Sign of Four**

BINFIELD ROAD—SW4: [Latitude / Longitude: <u>51.473498,-0.124798</u>]. From Lansdowne Way, the coachman turned right on Binfield Road toward Stockwell Place. **1887 – Sign of Four**

STOCKWELL PLACE (site)—SW8: [Latitude / Longitude: <u>51.472362,-0.122137</u>]. Thanks to Bernard Davies, we now know that Stockwell Place was not a street, but rather a group of Victorian houses on the east side of Clapham Road, just north of the Stockwell Road junction, opposite Binfield Road. At least one of the old houses remains. **1887 – Sign of Four**

STOCKWELL ROAD—SW9: [Latitude / Longitude: <u>51.47019,-0.12042</u>]. After Williams traveled through the Binfield / Clapham Road junction, I think he drove Holmes, Watson and Mary Morstan down Stockwell Road. **1887 – Sign of Four**

STOCKWELL LANE—SW9: [Latitude / Longitude: <u>51.469769,-0.119069</u>]. To get to Robert Street, I think Williams turned right on Stockwell Lane to Sidney Road. **Underground Station: Stockwell**

SIDNEY ROAD—SW9: [Latitude / Longitude: <u>51.47005,-0.117116</u>]. The coach with Holmes, Watson and Mary continued down Sidney Road to Robert Street. **1887 – Sign of Four**

ROBERT STREET—SW9: [Latitude / Longitude: <u>51.470584,-0.115185</u>]. Holmes, Watson and Mary were getting close to their destination as they were driven down Robert Street, now called Robsart Street. **1887 – Sign of Four**

BRIXTON ROAD—SW9: [Latitude / Longitude: 51.470664,-0.11261]. The coachman had to take a short jog to the right on Brixton Road, to continue his journey from Robert Street to Loughborough Road. **1887 – Sign of Four**

BRIXTON—SW9: [Latitude / Longitude: 51.471159,-0.112578]. Sadly, Nathan Garrideb could not stand the shock of the deception. The last Holmes heard, London's only Garrideb was in a Brixton nursing home. As Bernard Davies said, "The kind with bars on the windows". Nathan had "quite lost his reason". **1902 – The Three Garridebs**

ST PAUL'S (Zone 1)

.

KING EDWARD STREET—EC1: [Latitude / Longitude: 51.516371,-0.098568]. After working for eight weeks, Jabez Wilson went to the Red-headed League office for his daily task, and found the door locked. The sign on the door said that the League was dissolved. The landlord told him that Duncan Ross was really William Morris, a solicitor, who had moved to new offices at No. 17 King Edward Street, near St. Paul's. When Wilson went to that address, he found it was the manufacturer of artificial kneecaps, and no one there had every heard of Duncan Ross or William Morris. Perplexed, Jabez went to Baker Street to seek Holmes' advice. **1890 – Red-Headed League**

TEMPLE (Zone 1)

SOMERSET HOUSE, The Strand—WC2: [Latitude / Longitude: 51.511834,-0.117642]. Built on the site of the mansion built for Edward VI's uncle, Somerset House contains the national archives of wills. In 1883, this is where Holmes would have come to examine Mrs. Stoner's will. Sherlock used the vernacular, "Doctors' Commons". **1883 – The Speckled Band**

WATERLOO BRIDGE—WC2: [Latitude / Longitude: 51.509534,-0.117613]. John Openshaw drowned in the Thames, near Waterloo Bridge. Holmes and Watson read about the tragedy in the morning newspaper. Holmes told Watson that K.K.K. were not initials, but an acronym for the Klu Klux Klan. **1885 – Five Orange Pips**

THE STRAND—WC2: [Latitude / Longitude: 51.509577,-0.123639]. At seven o'clock one humid and rainy October evening, Holmes and Watson grew weary of their Baker Street sitting room, and took a three-hour ramble through the West End. On their walk, they watched the ebb and flow of life on The Strand. **1886? – The Resident Patient**

FLEET STREET—EC4: [Latitude / Longitude: 51.51381,-0.111419]. Having walked as far as Fleet Street, if was ten o'clock before Holmes and Watson returned to Baker Street. A brougham was waiting at their door. From the instruments inside, Holmes surmised their visitor was a medical doctor. **1886? – The Resident Patient**

INNER TEMPLE—EC4: [Latitude / Longitude: 51.513806,-0.110968]. Godfrey Norton practiced law in the Inner Temple. At first, Holmes did not know if Irene Adler was Norton's client, friend, or mistress. "If the former, she had probably transferred the photograph to his keeping. If the latter, it was less likely". **1888 – Scandal in Bohemia**

TOTTENHAM COURT ROAD (Zone 1)

ODEON THEATRE, No. 135-149 Shaftesbury Avenue—WC2: [Latitude / Longitude: 51.514171,-0.127965]. This building, once the Saville Theatre, has a magnificent frieze that includes Sherlock Holmes and perhaps Professor Moriarty. The 1931 frieze is the creation of Gilbert Bayes and if you consider a frieze a statue, it becomes the earliest Sherlock Holmes statue in London, predating the one at the Baker Street Underground Station by sixty-eight years.

BRITISH MUSEUM, Great Russell Street—WC1: [Latitude / Longitude: 51.518406,-0.12584]. The Museum's famous Reading Room contains an enormous collection of scientific works. This is where young Sherlock studied those branches of science, which would later make him so efficient in his chosen profession. **1879 – THE MUSGRAVE RITUAL**

OXFORD STREET—W1: [Latitude / Longitude: 51.517022,-0.125903]. When the carriage reached Oxford Street, Mr. Melas commented that this was a roundabout way to Kensington. At that point, Mr. Latimer covered the windows. When they arrived at their destination, the trip had taken an hour and thirty-five minutes. Obviously, they were not in Kensington. **1887? – The Greek Interpreter**

TOTTENHAM COURT ROAD—W1: [Latitude / Longitude: 51.518107,-0.131818]. During their meal in Wallington, Holmes talked of nothing but violins. He bragged how he had purchased his Stradivarius from a Jewish pawnbroker in Tottenham Court Road. It was worth at least five hundred guineas, but he had only paid fifty-five shillings. This led to a long discussion of Paganini, and the consumption of a bottle of claret. **1889? – The Cardboard Box**

BRITISH MUSEUM, Great Russell Street—WC1: [Latitude / Longitude: 51.518406,-0.12584]. Holmes told Watson, that Stapleton had been a schoolmaster in the North of England, and had used the name Vandeleur. When the school failed, the couple changed their names to Stapleton and moved south. The British Museum considered Stapleton a recognized authority of entomology. **Underground Station: 1889 – Hound of the Baskervilles**

TOTTENHAM COURT ROAD—W1: [Latitude / Longitude: 51.518107,-0.131818]. Mary Sutherland's father had been a plumber in the Tottenham Court Road. When he died, her mother carried on the business. When she remarried, her new husband, James Windibank, insisted that she sell the business. Windibank thought a plumbing business was beneath his position as a salesman of French wines. **1889? – Case of Identity**

SOHO STREET—W1: [Latitude / Longitude: 51.516274,-0.132934]. When Holmes and Watson passed Soho Street, they could see Soho Square in the distance. **1889? - The Blue Carbuncle**

HANWAY PLACE—W1: [Latitude / Longitude: 51.516523,-0.132598]. As they continued on their journey to the Alpha Inn, Holmes and Watson crossed Soho Street before turning north on the narrow Hanway Place. **1889? - The Blue Carbuncle**

HANWAY STREET—W1: [Latitude / Longitude: 51.517064,-0.130915]. From Hanway Place, Holmes and Watson bore right on Hanway Street toward Tottenham Court Road. Across the street lay Great Russell Street. **1889? - The Blue Carbuncle**

GREAT RUSSELL STREET—WC1: [Latitude / Longitude: 51.517756,-0.128063]. As Holmes and Watson walked east on Great Russell Street, up ahead, the British Museum was on the left, and the Alpha Inn was on the right. **1889? - The Blue Carbuncle**

BRITISH MUSEUM, Great Russell Street—WC1: [Latitude / Longitude: 51.518406,-0.12584]. During his investigation, Holmes went to the British Museum. There, he read up on Eckermann's "Voodooism and the Negroid Religions". **1891? – Wisteria Lodge**

CAPITAL AND COUNTIES BANK (site), No. 123 Oxford Street—W1: [Latitude / Longitude: 51.515967,-0.135999]. Was this the bank where Holmes deposited the Duke of Holdernesse's check? **1903? – The Priory School**

TOWER HILL (Zone 1)

TOWER OF LONDON—SE1: [Latitude / Longitude: 51.507313,-0.074308]. Holmes told the police launch to go downstream to the Tower of London. **1887 – Sign of Four**

TOWER BRIDGE—E1: [Latitude / Longitude: 51.50553,-0.075306]. As the police launch continued downstream, they passed the construction site of the new Tower Bridge. **1887 – Sign of Four**

POOL OF LONDON—E1: [Latitude / Longitude: 51.50553,-0.075306]. After Holmes saw the signal from one of his "Baker Street Irregulars", the police steam launch started after the *Aurora* as she sped downstream into the Pool of London. **1887 – Sign of Four**

Author's note: The term "Pool of London" generally refers to the stretch of the River Thames between London Bridge and Rotherhithe. This was the farthest point upstream that could accommodate a tall ship.

VAUXHALL (Zone 1)

VAUXHALL BRIDGE—SE8: [Latitude / Longitude: 51.487371,-0.126473]. As they crossed the Thames, Holmes remarked that he could catch glimpses of the river through the fog. **1887 – Sign of Four**

WANDSWORTH ROAD—SW8: [Latitude / Longitude: 51.478425,-0.12922]. On the Lambeth side of the river, Holmes, Watson and Mary were driven south on Wandsworth Road. **1887 – Sign of Four**

Author's note: For some reason, American texts persist in calling this "Wordsworth" Road.

BLACK PRINCE ROAD, "No. 3 Pinchin Lane"—SE1: [Latitude / Longitude: 51.492446,-0.121568]. After escorting Mary Morstan back to Lower Camberwell, Watson stopped at No. 3 Pinchin Lane, an address in the "lower quarter of Lambeth, "down near the water's edge". Black Prince Road then called Princes Road, fits the description. Watson told Sherman, the old bird stuffer, that Holmes needed Toby. **1887 – Sign of Four**

Author's note: The east was gradually getting light as Holmes, Watson and Toby started their trek from Pondicherry Lodge. Bernard Davies suggests the following conjectural "Creosote Trail". Their quarry occasionally used parallel side roads on their six-mile trek.

KENNINGTON LANE—SE11: [Latitude / Longitude: 51.486291,-0.122956]. On the wrong trail, Toby led Holmes and Watson on Kennington Lane toward Vauxhall Bridge. **1887 – Sign of Four**

BONDWAY—SE8: [Latitude / Longitude: 51.483164,-0.12557]. From Kennington Lane, Toby led Holmes and Watson down Bond Street, now called Bondway, to Miles Street. **1887 – Sign of Four**

MILES STREET—SE8: [Latitude / Longitude: 51.483311,-0.126772]. Holmes, Watson and Toby continued west on Miles Street, to Wandsworth Road. **1887 – Sign of Four**

WANDSWORTH ROAD)—SW8: [Latitude / Longitude: 51.483699,-0.127033]. Toby led Holmes and Watson north on Wandsworth Road, pass Knights Place, to Nine Elms Lane. **Underground Station: Vauxhall**

KNIGHT'S PLACE (site)—SW8: [Latitude / Longitude: 51.483365,-0.127183]. Knight's Place was a terrace of houses on the west side of Wandsworth Road between Miles Street and Nine Elms Lane. **1887 – Sign of Four**

NINE ELMS LANE—SW8: [Latitude / Longitude: 51.484794,-0.127995]. Toby had followed the wrong trail along Nine Elms Lane to Broderick and Nelson's timber yard. After reaching a false end, the dog "waddled around in circles…as if to ask for sympathy in his embarrassment". Holmes and Watson had to backtrack to find their quarry. **1887 – Sign of Four**

BELMONT PLACE (site)—SW8: [Latitude / Longitude: 51.484273,-0.126046]. In backtracking to the place they lost the true scent, Holmes, Watson and Toby passed Belmont Place, a terrace of houses located on the east side of Wandsworth Road, across from Knight's Place. **1887 – Sign of Four**

DURHAM STREET—SE11: [Latitude / Longitude: 51.485708,-0.118865]. If Toby had not followed the false scent, he would have led Holmes and Watson up Durham Street to Kennington Lane. **1887 – Sign of Four**

KENNINGTON LANE—SE11: [Latitude / Longitude: 51.486436,-0.119208]. Toby had been misled when the scent trail split. Holmes and Watson may have backtracked to Durham Street, and followed it to where their quarry had crossed Kennington Lane. **1887 – Sign of Four**

TYERS STREET—SE11: [Latitude / Longitude: 51.488258,-0.119294]. Tyers Street is across Kennington Lane from Durham Street. The true trail led Toby, Holmes and Watson north on Tyers Street. **1887 – Sign of Four**

BLACK PRINCE ROAD—SE11: [Latitude / Longitude: 51.491386,-0.117953]. Toby led Holmes and Watson down Tyers Street to Princes Street now called Black Prince Road. **1887 – Sign of Four**

BROAD STREET—SE1: [Latitude / Longitude: 51.490967,-0.116969]. The river end of Black Prince Road was called Broad Street. Today, it is Black Prince Road, West. Toby led Holmes and Watson to Mordecai Smith's boatyard. There, their quarry had hired the *Aurora.* Mrs. Smith said the boat was the fastest steam launch on the river, a claim that would later be tested. **1887 – Sign of Four**

VICTORIA (Zone 1)

VICTORIA RAILWAY STATION—SW1: [Latitude / Longitude: 51.496697,-0.144058]. After his strange experience, Mr. Melas was just able to return to Victoria Station on the last train from Clapham Junction. The next day, he related the story to Mycroft Holmes, who knew that Sherlock would be interested. **1887? – The Greek Interpreter**

ARTILLERY ROW—SW1: [Latitude / Longitude: 51.496864,-0.135625]. To reach Vauxhall Bridge from Victoria Street, Williams probably turned South on Artillery Row. **1887 – Sign of Four**

GREYCOAT PLACE—SW1: [Latitude / Longitude: 51.496416,-0.135303]. From Artillery Row, Williams turned left on Greycoat Place to reach Rochester Row. **1887 – Sign of Four**

VICTORIA RAILWAY STATION—SW1: [Latitude / Longitude: 51.496697,-0.144058]. MacDonald asked Holmes and Watson to join him on the trip to Birlstone Manor. They had to leave Baker Street in five minutes in order to catch the train from Victoria Station. **1887? - Valley of Fear**

No. 16A VICTORIA STREET—SW1: [Latitude / Longitude: 51.49666,-0.144314]. When Watson examined Hatherley's card, he saw that he was a hydraulic engineer, with professional chambers in a third floor walkup at No. 16A Victoria Street. **1889 – The Engineer's Thumb**

VICTORIA RAILWAY STATION—SW1: [Latitude / Longitude: 51.496697,-0.144058]. When Holmes, Watson, and Colonel Ross arrived at Victoria Station, Holmes invited Colonel Ross to Baker Street for a cigar, and offered to answer all of his questions. **1890? – Silver Blaze**

VICTORIA RAILWAY STATION—SW1: [Latitude / Longitude: 51.496697,-0.144058]. Watson followed Holmes's instructions, and arrived at Victoria Station just in time to catch the Continental Express. Moriarty and his thugs were on his heels, but missed the train. **1891 – The Final Problem**

VICTORIA (GROSVENOR) HOTEL, Buckingham Palace Road—SW1: [Latitude / Longitude: 51.495639,-0.145592]. Holmes and Watson reached the little Alpine village of Meiringen. They stayed at the Englischer Hof, run by Peter Steiler the elder. Steiler spoke excellent English, having served more than three years as waiter, at the Grosvenor Hotel in London. **1891 – The Final Problem**

SPANISH EMBASSY (site), No. 1 Grosvenor Gardens—SW1: [Latitude / Longitude: 51.497249,-0.146551]. Back in London, Eccles stopped by the Spanish Embassy. They had never heard of Garcia. Eccles then went to see Melville, who, although he had introduced them, admitted he knew very little about Garcia. **1891? – Wisteria Lodge**

VICTORIA RAILWAY STATION—SW1: [Latitude / Longitude: 51.496697,-0.144058]. Robert Ferguson was relieved when Holmes and Watson agreed to take the 2 o'clock train from Victoria to Lamberley in Sussex. **1896? – The Sussex Vampire**

WARREN STREET (Zone 1)

ST. SAVIOUR'S CHURCH (site), northwest corner of Whitfield and Maple Streets—W1: [Latitude / Longitude: 51.522632,-0.137565]. Mary and Hosner made plans to marry at St. Saviour's, Church near King's Cross. On the way to the church, Hosner put Mary and her mother in a hansom, and followed in a four-wheeler. When they arrived, the four-wheeler was empty—Hosner Angel had vanished. **1889? – Case of Identity**

WATERLOO (Zone 1)

WATERLOO RAILWAY STATION—SE1: [Latitude / Longitude: 51.503943,-0.11391]. Helen Stoner left Leatherhead on the first train to Waterloo Station. She wanted to consult Holmes on the strange events at Stoke Moran. Later in the day, Holmes and Watson left London from Waterloo Station. **1883 – The Speckled Band**

WATERLOO RAILWAY STATION—SE1: [Latitude / Longitude: 51.503943,-0.11391]. John Openshaw had arrived in London at Waterloo Station. After Openshaw visited Holmes, he tried to catch the late train back to Horsham, but on the way to Waterloo Station, he was attacked and killed. **1885 – Five Orange Pips**

WATERLOO RAILWAY STATION—SE1: [Latitude / Longitude: 51.503943,-0.11391]. One summer night, a few months after his marriage, Watson was staying up late. His wife and the rest of the household had gone to bed, when there was a knock at the door. It was Holmes, who had just come from Waterloo Station. He had arrived from Aldershot, and asked Watson to accompany him when he returned the next day. **1888 – The Crooked Man**

WATERLOO RAILWAY STATION—SE1: [Latitude / Longitude: 51.503943,-0.11391]. Holmes and Watson caught an early train from Waterloo Station. Briarbrae, Percy's home, was a large detached house; just a few minutes walk from Woking Station. Later that day, when Holmes and Watson returned to London, they ate at the Waterloo Station's buffet. **1889? – The Naval Treaty**

WATERLOO RAILWAY STATION—SE1: [Latitude / Longitude: 51.503943,-0.11391]. Scotland Yard assigned Inspector Lestrade to the case. He sent a note from Croydon, asking for Holmes help. Holmes and Watson left for Croydon from Waterloo Station. **1889? – The Cardboard Box**

WATERLOO RAILWAY STATION—SE1: [Latitude / Longitude: 51.503943,-0.11391]. Dr. Mortimer did not know what to tell Sir Henry when he arrived at Waterloo Station. Sir Henry was the last of the Baskervilles, and Dr. Mortimer felt hesitant about taking the young baronet to his Devonshire estate. Holmes said he needed twenty-four hours to think about the problem, and advised Mortimer to say nothing of the curse until then. Later in the adventure, Waterloo Station is where cabbie John Clayton dropped off his fare after they followed Sir Henry and Dr. Mortimer. **1889 – Hound of the Baskervilles**

SOUTHWARK, Near Waterloo Station—SE1: [Latitude / Longitude: 51.50013,-0.110657]. Although young Cartwright failed to find the hotel from which the note was sent, Holmes did locate the driver of the hansom cab. His name was John Clayton, who lived at the fictional Turpey Street in the Borough of Southwark. Clayton said that his fare was a detective. When Holmes asked the name he had given, Clayton replied, "Mr. Sherlock Holmes," Holmes burst into a hearty laugh, and told Watson, "This time we have…a foeman who is worthy of our steel". Conan Doyle gave 3 Turpey Street as John Clayton's fictitious street address. Since Clayton kept his horse and cab at Shipley's Yard, near Waterloo Station, we can assume he lived nearby. **1889 – Hound of the Baskervilles**

WATERLOO RAILWAY STATION—SE1: [Latitude / Longitude: 51.503943,-0.11391]. In the 1890's, as now, trains from London to Winchester leave from Waterloo Station. Holmes and Watson's train left at half-past nine, and arrived in Winchester at 11:30. They were curious about Violet Hunter's predicament, since she had the freedom to meet them in Winchester. **1890? – Copper Beeches**

WATERLOO RAILWAY STATION—SE1: [Latitude / Longitude: 51.503943,-0.11391]. On Monday, Watson caught the 9:13 from Waterloo Station. He wanted to be in place, when Violet Smith arrived in Farnham on the 9:50. From his hiding place, Watson saw the bearded cyclist following her. **1895 – The Solitary Cyclist**

WATERLOO ROAD—SE1: [Latitude / Longitude: 51.503644,-0.111613]. With Inspector Lestrade's help, Holmes identified John Garrideb as James Winter, alias Morecroft, alias Killer Evans, an American criminal with a sinister and murderous reputation. He came to London in 1893, and shot Roger Prescott, a Chicago forger, in a Waterloo Road nightclub. **1902 – The Three Garridebs**

WESTBOURNE PARK (Zone 2)

NOTTING HILL—W11: [**Latitude / Longitude:** 51.520529,-0.201715]. On Saturday, Sir Henry, Mortimer, and Watson left London. Sir Henry had never been to Baskerville Hall, and looked forward to seeing the old family seat. When they arrived, they noticed soldiers patrolling the roads. Selden, the Notting Hill murderer had escaped from Princetown Prison. **1889 – Hound of the Baskervilles**

WESTMINSTER (Zone 1)

HOUSES OF PARLIAMENT—SW1: [**Latitude / Longitude:** 51.500945,-0.123661]. After his father's death, Reginald Musgrave began managing the Hurlstone estate, and became a Member of Parliament. **1879 – THE MUSGRAVE RITUAL**

WHITEHALL—SW1: [**Latitude / Longitude:** 51.503534,-0.126218]. *The Greek Interpreter* is the adventure in which Watson first met Mycroft, Sherlock's older brother. Mycroft worked at the government offices in Whitehall. According to Sherlock, Mycroft had a better analytical mind. Sherlock thought their abilities came from their grandmother, who was a sister of Vernet, the French artist. Holmes took Watson to the Diogenes Club, where Mycroft was a founding member. **1887? – The Greek Interpreter**

Author's note: In *The Adventure of the Bruce-Partington Plans*, we learn that Mycroft was one of the most indispensable men in the British government. To paraphrase Holmes: "He has the tidiest and most orderly brain, with the greatest capacity for storing facts. The conclusions of every department are passed to him. All other men are specialists, but his specialism is omniscience. Again and again his word decided the national policy".

WHITEHALL—SW1: [Latitude / Longitude: 51.503534,-0.126218]. From Trafalgar Square, Holmes, Watson and Mary's most likely route was down Whitehall and through its Parliament Street lower end. There may have been too much fog to see Downing Street on the right, but surely, Watson saw the Houses of Parliament and Big Ben. **1887 – Sign of Four**

PARLIAMENT STREET—SW1: [Latitude / Longitude: 51.501425,-0.126205]. As they continued down Whitehall, the street's name changed to Parliament Street. **1887 – Sign of Four**

Author's note: Parliament Street had been a small side road alongside Westminster Palace. When the palace was destroyed, Parliament Street was widened to match Whitehall and became its lower end. The present appearance of the street is largely the result of 19th century redevelopment.

VICTORIA SQUARE—SW1: [Latitude / Longitude: 51.500245,-0.126676]. To continue their journey, Holmes, Watson and Mary Morstan must have traveled around Victoria Square to Victoria Street. **1887 – Sign of Four**

WESTMINSTER PIER (STAIRS)—SW1: [Latitude / Longitude: 51.501036,-0.123811]. Holmes asked Athelney Jones to have a fast police steam launch at the Westminster Stairs at seven o'clock. As it turned out, the police launch was just fast enough. **1887 – Sign of Four**

FOREIGN OFFICE, WHITEHALL—SW1: [Latitude / Longitude: 51.502104,-0.126139]. Watson remembered Percy Phelps as a brilliant student, who had won a scholarship to Cambridge. After graduation, he went to work in the Foreign Office at Whitehall. His uncle, Lord Holdhurst, was the Foreign Minister. **1889? – The Naval Treaty**

KING CHARLES (CHARLES) STREET—SW1: [Latitude / Longitude: 51.502104,-0.126139]. Percy said that after he discovered the Naval Treaty was missing, he ran to the Charles Street side-door. The door was unlocked, and he thought that whoever stole the naval treaty had entered and left through that door. **1889? – The Naval Treaty**

337

"BIG BEN" CLOCK TOWER—SW1: [Latitude / Longitude: 51.500946,-0.124115]. When Percy ran to the Foreign Office's Charles Street side-door, he heard three chimes from a neighboring clock. It was a quarter to ten. This had to have come from the nearby Westminster Clock, commonly called "Big Ben". Big Ben refers to the clock's large bell that only chimes on the hour. The quarter chimes come from the "Westminster Quarters" bells. **1889? – The Naval Treaty**

Author's note: In the British text, it says Percy heard three chimes from "a neighboring church". Percy may have thought it came from a church clock, but the chime had to be from the "Big Ben" clock. Its chimes would overwhelm any nearby church.

DOWNING STREET—SW1: [Latitude / Longitude: 51.503177,-0.126196]. Lord Holdhurst, had chambers in Downing Street. It was up to Holmes to find the missing Naval Treaty, and rescue poor Percy's honor. **1889? – The Naval Treaty**

Author's note: We do not know Lord Holdhurst's Downing Street address, but it was not Number 10 or 11. Number 10 is the traditional home of the Prim Minister, and Number 11 is the traditional home of the Chancellor of the Exchequer.

No. 10 DOWNING STREET—SW1: [Latitude / Longitude: 51.503177,-0.126196]. 10 Downing Street is the traditional home of the British Prime Minister. It was from there that Lord Bellinger drove to Baker Street to seek Sherlock's help. The Right Honorable Trelawney Hope, Secretary for European Affairs, came with him. They said they could not involve Scotland Yard for fear of the matter being made public. **1890? – Second Stain**

RICHMOND TERRACE—SW1: [Latitude / Longitude: 51.503166,-0.124948]. In my opinion, Richmond Terrace was the site of the Trelawney Hope's Whitehall Terrace townhouse. In 1890, Richmond Terrace was called Whitehall Terrace. For the Prime Minister to come for lunch, the townhouse had to be near Downing Street. **1890? – Second Stain**

GAYFERE "GODOLPHIN" STREET—SW1: [Latitude / Longitude: 51.496715,-0.127716]. Eduardo Lucas lived in the fictitious Godolphin Street. In my opinion, Gayfere Street's location makes it a good candidate for being Godolphin Street. **1890? – Second Stain**

MARQUIS OF GRANBY "IVY PLANT PUB", No. 41 Romney Street—SW1: [Latitude / Longitude: 51.495305,-0.127278].Today, the closest public house to Godolphin (Gayfere) Street is the Marquis of Granby, which was established in 1873. Is this the Ivy Plant Pub mentioned in the story? It makes sense that MacPherson would go to the nearest pub to get brandy. **1890? – Second Stain**

FOREIGN OFFICE, King Charles Street—SW1: [Latitude / Longitude: 51.502104,-0.126139]. After returning to London, Holmes went to the Foreign Office to brief them on his visit to the Khalifa of Khartoum. **1894 – The Empty House**

NORMAN SHAW BUILDINGS, (1894's NEW SCOTLAND YARD)—SW1: [Latitude / Longitude: 51.502374,-0.126139]. The Norman Shaw Buildings, between Whitehall and Victoria Embankment, near Westminster Bridge and Big Ben, is the Scotland Yard Sherlock knew. The building complex is distinctive, being constructed of alternate bands of red brick and white Portland stone. **1894 – The Empty House**

Author's note: Scotland Yard has moved again. In 1967, "new" New Scotland Yard moved to nearby No. 8-10 Broadway, **[Latitude / Longitude: 51.498511,-0.133853],** an existing office block acquired under a long-term lease. There have been newspaper articles indicating they may open their Black Museum to the public. Will Colonel Sebastian Moran's air rifle be on display?

13 GREAT GEORGE STREET—SW1: [Latitude / Longitude: 51.501217,-0.128649]. Adolph Meyer of No. 13 Great George Street, across Parliament Square from Westminster Bridge, was another international spy reported by Mycroft. **1895 – The Bruce-Partington Plans**

BRIDGE STREET—SW1: [Latitude / Longitude: 51.500982,-0.125166]. Horace Harker worked for the Central Press Association at Bridge Street, just across from the Big Ben Clock Tower. **1900? – The Six Napoleons**

HOUSES OF PARLIAMENT—SW1: [Latitude / Longitude: 51.500945,-0.123661]. On their way to "Poultney Square", Holmes and Watson passed the Houses of Parliament. **1902? – Lady Frances Carfax**

WESTMINSTER BRIDGE—SW1: [Latitude / Longitude: 51.500857,-0.122808]. On their way to "Poultney Square", Holmes and Watson passed the Houses of Parliament as they crossed Westminster Bridge. **1902? – Lady Frances Carfax**

No. 10 DOWNING STREET—SW1: [Latitude / Longitude: 51.503177,-0.126196]. No. 10 Downing Street is the traditional home of the British Head of Government. When the Prime Minister and the Home Secretary came to visit Holmes, they must have come from No. 10. They asked Holmes to find the missing Crown Jewel. **1903? – The Mazarin Stone**

Author's note: Today, the entrance to Downing Street is guarded by an iron gate at Parliament Street, an extension of Whitehall.

RAIL STATIONS

ANERLEY (Zone 4)

ANERLEY ARMS INN, No. 2 Ridsdale Road—SE20: [Latitude / Longitude: 51.411841,-0.0666]. After a late business meeting with Oldacre, McFarlane spent the night at the Anerley Arms Inn, about a mile and a half from Oldacre's Deep Dene House. **1895? – The Norwood Builder**

ANERLEY RAILWAY STATION—SE20: [Latitude / Longitude: 51.411654,-0.066372]..McFarlane read about Oldacre's disappearance on the morning train from the Anerley Railway Station to London. **1895? – The Norwood Builder**

BECKENHAM HILL (Zone 4)

BECKENHAM—BR3: [Latitude / Longitude: 51.425491,-0.021286]. After hearing Melas's story, Sherlock asked Mycroft if he had taken any action. Mycroft said he had placed an advertisement in all of the London dailies, asking for information on Paul and Sophy Kratides. Sherlock warned Melas to be on his guard, because the ads indicated that he had talked about his experience. J. Davenport, from Lower Brixton, answered the ad. He said he knew Sophy, and that she lived at The Myrtles in Beckenham. **1887? – The Greek Interpreter**

BECKENHAM HILL RAILWAY STATION—BR3: [Latitude / Longitude: 51.425491,-0.021286]. Proceeding from the Beckenham Railway Station, they found The Myrtles dark. Melas and Paul Kratides were upstairs, poisoned from the fumes of a charcoal fire. Kratides was dead but Melas survived. **1887? – The Greek Interpreter**

BLACKHEATH (Zone 3)

LEE, Lewisham—SE13: [Latitude / Longitude: 51.459907,0.009892]. Holmes was trying to find Neville St. Clair. He and Watson went to The Cedars, St. Clair's house near Lee in Kent. Holmes was staying there while he investigated the disappearance. St. Clair had moved to Kent in May 1884. He appeared to have plenty of money, and took a large country villa. In 1887, he married the daughter of the local brewer, and had two children. **1889 – Man with the Twisted Lip**

"THE HAVEN", PARK LODGE, LEE GREEN—SE3: [Latitude / Longitude: 51.457459, 0.011049]. Josiah Amberley had been the junior partner of Brickfall and Amberley, manufacturers of artistic materials. He retired at sixty-one, bought a house in Lee, and a year later, married a younger woman. His house, identified by Bernard Davies as Park Lodge, was located just north of the junction of Lee Road and Lee High Road. **1898? – The Retired Colourman**

Author's note: At the time of this adventure, Lee and Lewisham were separate boroughs. Throughout the adventure, Watson insists on using Lewisham as the location, when at this time, it was in fact Lee.

BLACKHEATH RAILWAY STATION—SE3: [Latitude / Longitude: 51.465888, 0.008989]. Holmes was busy with another case, so Watson agreed to go to Lee. He took the train to Blackheath. Watson said he did not dream that, "Within a week, the affair in which I was engaging would be the…debate of all England". **1898? – The Retired Colourman**

LEE POLICE STATION, No. 410 Lee High Road—SE12: [Latitude / Longitude: 51.456585, 0.01061]. When Amberley tried to take a poison pill, Holmes stopped him. and said, "No short cuts". Holmes and Barker took Amberley to the police station and returned with Inspector MacKinnon. Holmes outlined the clues, and explained to MacKinnon how he solved the case. Naturally, MacKinnon took full credit in the press, and it was left to Watson to tell the true story. **1898? – The Retired Colourman**

BLACKWALL (Zone 2)

BLACKWALL REACH—E14: [Latitude / Longitude: 51.501276,-0.008801]. When they reached Blackwall, the police launch was only two hundred and fifty paces behind the *Aurora*. **1887 – Sign of Four**

CLAPHAM JUNCTION (Zone 2)

CLAPHAM JUNCTION—SW11: [Latitude / Longitude: 51.4655,-0.170749]. After walking across Wandsworth Common to Clapham Junction, Mr. Melas was just in time to catch the last train to Victoria Station. **1887? – The Greek Interpreter**

CLAPHAM JUNCTION—SW11: [Latitude / Longitude: 51.4655,-0.170749]. After their first visit to Woking, Joseph Harrison drove Holmes and Watson back to the train station. There, they caught the Portsmouth train to London. As they passed Clapham Junction, Holmes remarked, "It's a very cheering thing to come into London by any of these lines which run high and allow you to look down on houses like this". Watson thought he was joking. **1889? – The Naval Treaty**

CLAPHAM JUNCTION—SW11: [Latitude / Longitude: 51.4655,-0.170749]. On their way back to London, Colonel Ross, Holmes and Watson passed through Clapham Junction. Colonel Ross said that Holmes still had not indicated where the horse had been kept. Holmes said he had been looked after by one of the Colonel's neighbors, and that, "We must have a little amnesty in that direction". **1890? – Silver Blaze**

CRYSTAL PALACE (Zone 3)

CRYSTAL PALACE—SW20: [Latitude / Longitude: 51.422494,-0.07714]. Disturbed by the actions of his wife, Munro did not go into the City the next day. He walked as far as the Crystal Palace before returning home. **1887? – The Yellow Face**
Author's note: In 1851, the Crystal Palace was built in Hyde Park for the Great Exhibition. After the exhibition, the Crystal Palace moved to Sydenham Hill in South London, and was re-opened by Queen Victoria on June 10, 1854. It was destroyed by fire in 1936

DENMARK HILL (Zone 2)

KING'S COLLEGE HOSPITAL, Denmark Hill—SE5: [Latitude / Longitude: 51.468641,-0.091889]. After graduation, Trevelyan devoted himself to research, and obtained a small position in King's College Hospital. There, he won the Bruce Pinkerton prize, and was thought to have a distinguished career ahead of him. However, a lack of capital prevented him from finding proper quarters. **1886? – The Resident Patient**

CAMBERWELL—SE5: [Latitude / Longitude: 51.470762,-0.086861]. Mary Morstan came to see Holmes on the advice of Mrs. Cecil Forrester of Lower Camberwell. Mrs. Forrester employed Mary as a governess. **1887 – Sign of Four**

CAMBERWELL—SE5: [Latitude / Longitude: 51.475257,-0.092291]. After Holmes explained the exercise they had just gone through, MacDonald wanted to lay his hands on Porlock. MacDonald noticed that Porlock's letters came from Camberwell, and Holmes sent him money there. **1887? - Valley of Fear**

CAMBERWELL—SE5: [Latitude / Longitude: 51.473769,-0.091954]. Mary lived with her mother and stepfather at the fictional No. 31 Lyon Place in Camberwell. She was engaged to Hosner Angel, but did not know where he lived. Mary worked as a typist, but also had an income of one hundred pounds a year from inherited stock. Since she lived at home, and did not want to be a burden, she gave the stock income to her mother and stepfather. **1889? – Case of Identity**

CAMBERWELL—SE5: [Latitude / Longitude: 51.473769,-0.091954]. Sherlock had accepted a commission to find Lady Frances Carfax. She was the sole survivor of the late Earl of Rufton's direct family. Lady Frances was a person of regular habits and for four years had written every second week to her old governess, Miss Susan Dobney. Miss Dobney, who lived in Camberwell, contacted Holmes when Lady Frances failed to write for five weeks. **1902? – Lady Frances Carfax**

DEPTFORD (Zone 2)

DEPTFORD REACH—SE10: [Latitude / Longitude: 51.48275,-0.01884]. The police launch sped through the Pool of London, past the West India Docks, and down the long Deptford Reach. They were gaining on the *Aurora*. **1887 – Sign of Four**

EAST CROYDON (Zone 5)

CROSS ROAD, "CROSS STREET", CROYDON—CR9:
[Latitude / Longitude: 51.379499,-0.090684]. One hot August day,
Holmes and Watson read that Miss Susan Cushing, of Cross Street,
Croydon, had received a cardboard box from Belfast, containing two
human ears, packed in coarse rock salt. **1889? – The Cardboard
Box**

EAST CROYDON RAILROAD STATION—CR9: [Latitude /
Longitude: 51.375722,-0.092229]. Scotland Yard assigned Inspector
Lestrade to the case. He sent a note to Holmes asking for help. When
Holmes and Watson arrived at the East Croydon Railroad Station,
Lestrade was waiting for them. A five-minute walk brought them to
Susan Cushing's house in Cross Street. There, after examining the
ears, the package, and talking to Susan, Holmes told Lestrade that this
was no practical joke. **1889? – The Cardboard Box**

ESHER (Outside of Zone 6)

WISTERIA LODGE "COPSEHAM", Esher—KT10: [Latitude /
Longitude: 51.360266,-0.363128]. As their friendship developed,
Eccles agreed to spend a few days at Garcia's Wisteria Lodge,
between Esher and Oxshott. The household included a Spanish
servant, and a half-breed cook. The house itself was an old
tumbledown building. The dinner was so poorly cooked and served,
that Eccles wished he could invent some excuse to leave. At one point,
Garcia received a note, and became distraught. **1891? – Wisteria
Lodge**

THE ESHER RAILROAD STATION, Esher—KT10: [Latitude /
Longitude: 51.379683,-0.353463]. Later that day, Inspector Baynes
returned to Baker Street. Holmes and Watson accompanied him back
to Esher. **1891? – Wisteria Lodge**

THE BEAR "BULL" INN, No. 71 High Street, Esher—KT10: [Latitude / Longitude: 51.369235,-0.365428]. **Holmes and Watson** found rooms at the Bull Inn. It was a cold March evening when Holmes, Watson, and Inspector Baynes, walked from the Bull to Wisteria Lodge. Constable Walters was on guard, but his nerves were frayed. Two hours earlier, he had seen a giant face looking through the window. **1891? – Wisteria Lodge**

ESHER POLICE STATION, No. 113 High Street, Esher—KT10: [Latitude / Longitude: 51.368342,-0.367204]. One morning at the Bull, Watson opened his morning newspaper and found headlines declaring the Oxshott Mystery solved. The mulatto cook had been charged with the murder. Holmes rushed to see Inspector Baynes, and advised him not to commit himself too far unless he was sure. **1891? – Wisteria Lodge**

HERNE HILL (Zone 2)

MILKWOOD ROAD—SE24: Latitude / Longitude: 51.456966,-0.103405]. After continuing about half a mile on Milkwood Road, Holmes, Watson and Mary turned left on Gubyon Avenue and its line of new terrace houses. They stopped at No. 13. **1887 – Sign of Four**

No. 13 GUBYON AVENUE—SE24: Latitude / Longitude: 51.455184,-0.101516]. Watson said, "At last the cab drew up at the third house in a new terrace". Bernard Davies identifies the house as No. 13 Gubyon Avenue. As they entered the house, a Hindu servant led them to a room outfitted in Oriental splendor. There they met Thaddeus Sholto, the son of the late Major Sholto. Thaddeus told Mary of their fathers' involvement in finding Indian treasure. Thaddeus said that he wanted justice for Mary, and was going to see that she got it, regardless of what his brother Bartholomew thought. Bartholomew was living in Pondicherry Lodge, their father's old house in Upper Norwood. **1887 – Sign of Four**

LEE (Zone 3)

LEE, Lewisham—SE13: [**Latitude / Longitude:** <u>51.448692, 0.014933</u>]. The inspectors asked, "Are you Mr. John Scott Eccles of Poham House, Lee? We wish a statement…as to the events which led up to the death last night of Mr. Aloysius Garcia, of Wisteria Lodge, near Esher". **1891? – Wisteria Lodge**

LIVERPOOL JAMES STREET (Zone 3)

KING GEORGE V (ALBERT) DOCK—Liverpool L3: [**Latitude / Longitude:** <u>53.400581,-2.991006</u>]. After his day at Lloyd's of London, Holmes went to King George V Dock, now called Albert Dock. The *Lone Star* had left London by the early tide, bound for Savannah, Georgia. Holmes determined that the Captain and two mates were the only native-born Americans on the ship, and that the three of them had been away from the boat on the night John Openshaw was murdered. Holmes sent his envelope with the five orange pips, so that it, and the police, would be waiting for Captain Calhoun when he docked in Savannah. **1885 – Five Orange Pips**

LOUGHBOROUGH JUNCTION (Zone 2)

DOVER "TORQUAY" TERRACE, Coldharbour Lane—SE5: [**Latitude / Longitude:** <u>51.467149,-0.099714</u>]. The American gentleman, Edward Drebber, and his private secretary, Joseph Stangerson, stayed at Mrs. Charpentier's boarding house in Torquay Terrace, Coldharbour Lane. Keeping the nautical theme, Watson substituted the word "Torquay" for Dover. Bernard Davies identifies Mrs. Charpentier's house was the first house in Dover Terrace, at the corner of Harbour Road. **1881? – Study in Scarlet**

LOUGHBOROUGH ROAD—SW9: [Latitude / Longitude: 51.469461,-0.106409]. Then, as today, Loughborough Road turns south on its path from Brixton Road to Cold Harbour Lane. **1887 – Sign of Four**

COLDHARBOUR LANE—SW9: [Latitude / Longitude: 51.469461,-0.106409]. From the Lyceum Theatre, Holmes, Watson, and Mary had been driven through a labyrinth of Lambeth streets, to Coldharbour Lane. Watson called it Cold Harbour. Holmes remarked that, "Our quest does not appear to take us to very fashionable regions". **1887 – Sign of Four**

Author's note: Watson noted, "We had reached a questionable and forbidding neighborhood…long lines of dull brick houses". Then came rows of two-storied villas, each with a fronting of miniature garden, and…lines of new…brick buildings". This indicates that Thaddeus Sholto's house was in a brand-new terrace, and could not have been in Coldharbour Lane, which was fully developed in 1887. Williams must have continued on past Coldharbour Lane.

HINTON ROAD—SW9: [Latitude / Longitude: 51.465352,-0.102532]. As Loughborough Road crossed Coldharbour Lane, the name changed to Hinton Road. After 500 feet, they bore right on Milkwood Road, and continued their southward journey. **1887 – Sign of Four**

MADEN MANOR (Zone 4)

KINGSTON-UPON-THAMES—KT2: [Latitude / Longitude: 51.382048,-0.260715]. Sir James told Holmes that Baron Gruner's current residence was Vernon Lodge, near Kingston. **1902 – The Illustrious Client**

NORBURY (Zone 3)

NORBURY—SW16: [Latitude / Longitude: 51.410601,-0.117806].
Grant Munro was a hop merchant in the City. With the addition of Effie's income,
they took a nice eighty-pound-a-year villa at Norbury. Recently, a nearby cottage
was let, and Munro saw a face in the upper window. He could not tell whether the
face belonged to a man or woman, but its color was a chalky yellow. **1887? – The
Yellow Face**
NORBURY RAILWAY STATION—SW16: [Latitude /
Longitude: 51.412056,-0.123618]. The next day Munro went to see
Holmes, who advised him to return to Norbury. If he found the
cottage occupied, he was to notify Holmes, but not enter. Holmes
received a message, that the cottage was occupied and that Munro
would meet him at the train station. **1887? – The Yellow Face**

BEULAH HILL—SE19: [Latitude / Longitude: 51.417011,-
0.09804]. At the junction of Grange Road and Beulah Hill, Toby
led Holmes and Watson northwest on Beulah Hill. **1887 – Sign of
Four**

NORWOOD JUNCTION (Zone 4)

No. 12 TENNISON ROAD—SE25: [Latitude / Longitude:
51.395136,-0.080638]. Conan Doyle's former house at number No.
12 Tennison Road, received a blue historical plaque in 1973.
UPPER NORWOOD—SE25: [Latitude / Longitude: 51.402958,-
0.088041]. When Captain Morstan disappeared, the police
contacted Major Sholto, the Captain's only known London friend.
Sholto and Morstan had served in the same regiment. Sholto had
retired to Upper Norwood, and said he did not know Morstan was
in London. **1887 – Sign of Four**

"PONDICHERRY LODGE", Kilravock House, No. 103-105 Ross Road, Norwood—SE25: [Latitude / Longitude: 51.402958,-0.088041]. When the late Major John Sholto retired from the army, he returned from India with a large fortune. He and his two boys, Thaddeus and Bartholomew, lived in luxury at Pondicherry Lodge in Norwood. Major Sholto lived in constant fear, and hired two prizefighters as porters. Thaddeus said that his father also had a marked aversion to men with wooden legs. **1887 – Sign of Four**

Author's note: The Cannon offers several clues to describe "Pondicherry Lodge", and its location. Bernard Davies describes the Lodge as, "a very large square house of unusual height, with a plain, gentle sloping roof having dormer windows. It was almost certainly built before 1870, and stood in its own spacious grounds on a high road or street, surrounded by a high wall. It must face either north-west of south-west (more or less) and stand on a steep hillside so that its back appears much higher than its front. Mr. Davies suggests the house must be on the extreme southern borders of Upper Norwood and, must not be too far from the railway yet not too close to a police station. After an extensive search, Mr. Davies identified Kilravock House on Ross Road as the true "Pondicherry Lodge". Today, eight flats occupy Kilravock. Its roofline has been modified, the surrounding wall torn down, and the extensive grounds sold off.

SOUTH NORWOOD POLICE STATION, No. 83 High Street—SE25: [Latitude / Longitude: 51.39861,-0.076153]. The police were summoned from the nearby South Norwood Police Station. Before Athelney Jones and his police squad arrived, Holmes spent half an hour examining the crime scene. He determined that a small agile man had gained access to the room through the attic. He had lowered a rope out the window, where a man with a wooden leg hauled himself up. In the attic, Holmes found small naked footprints. A further examination showed that the small, bare-footed man had stepped in creosote. Holmes said he knew, "A dog that would follow this scent to the world's end". **1887 – Sign of Four**

Author's note: The substantial brick station building is still there, but is now a bank.

WHARNCLIFFE ROAD—SE25: [Latitude / Longitude: 51.404738,-0.088041]. From Pondicherry Lodge on Ross Road, Toby led Holmes and Watson up Wharncliffe Road. **1887 – Sign of Four**

GRANGE ROAD—SE19: [Latitude / Longitude: 51.409891,-0.089028]. On their northward journey, Toby led Holmes and Watson into Grange Road. **1887 – Sign of Four**

QUEENS ROAD PECKHAM (Zone 2)

PECKHAM—SE15: [Latitude / Longitude: 51.476218,-0.06404]. "Mrs. Sawyer" said that her daughter Sally Dennis lived in Peckham with her husband Tom. **1881? – Study in Scarlet**

FIRBANK ROAD (VILLAS)—SE15: [Latitude / Longitude: 51.470624,-0.058504]. Dr. Horsom, of 13 Firbank Villas, had certified Rose Spender's death. She was old nurse of Shlessinger's "wife". **1902? – Lady Frances Carfax**

SHOREDITCH HIGH STREET (Zone 2)

BISHOPSGATE TERMINUS (site)—E1: [Latitude / Longitude: 51.523399,-0.077453]. During Holmes's first two years in college, Victor Trevor was his only close friend. Victor invited Holmes to spend a month at Donnithorpe, the elder Trevor's estate in Norfolk. In 1874, Holmes left London on a Great Eastern Line train, from the old Bishopsgate Terminus at the junction of Shoreditch High Street and Bethnal Green Road. **1874 – THE "GLORIA SCOTT"**

COMMERCIAL STREET (ROAD)—E1: [**Latitude / Longitude:** 51.521762,-0.07608]. Professor Presbury was receiving strange correspondence and packages from a store on London's Commercial Road. Holmes sent a telegram to Mercer, his general utility man, to check on the source of the packages. Mercer's reply read, *"Have visited the Commercial Road and seen Dorak. Suave Person, Bohemian, elderly. Keeps large general store"*. Underground 1903? – The Creeping Man

STREATHAM (Zone 3)

CROWN LANE—SW16: [**Latitude / Longitude:** 51.423247,-0.111923]. When they came to Crown Lane, Toby indicated that their quarry had taken a westward jog. **1887 – Sign of Four**

LEIGHAM COURT ROAD—SW16: [**Latitude / Longitude:** 51.426445,-0.114133]. From Crown Lane, Toby followed the creosote scent north on Leigham Court Road. **1887 – Sign of Four**

STREATHAM—SW16: [**Latitude / Longitude:** 51.436614,-0.125431]. A gentleman from one of noblest families in England asked Alexander Holder for an advance of £50,000. He offered the Beryl Coronet, "one of the most precious public possessions of the empire", as collateral. For safekeeping, Holder took the coronet to Fairbank, his home in Streatham, and locked it in his dressing room bureau. During the night, he caught his son, Arthur, holding the coronet, with a small portion torn off, and three of the thirty-six gems missing. **1891? – The Beryl Coronet**

STREATHAM HILL (Zone 3)

STREATHAM HILL—SW2: [Latitude / Longitude: 51.44,-0.125749]. Leigham Court Road ended at the rail station. Toby led Holmes and Watson north on Streatham Hill. 1887 – Sign of Four

SYDENHAM (Zone 4)

LOWER NORWOOD—SE26: [Latitude / Longitude: <u>51.42693,-0.056847</u>]. Jonas Oldacre was a well-known builder in Lower Norwood. The fifty-two year old bachelor lived in Deep Dene House at the end of Sydenham Road. **1895? – The Norwood Builder**

WALLINGTON (Zone 5)

WALLINGTON—SM6: [Latitude / Longitude: <u>51.365846,-0.152683</u>]. Holmes learned from Susan, that her sister Sarah had recently moved from Croydon to "New Street" in Wallington. On their way to see Sarah, Holmes sent a telegram to his friend Algar, of the Liverpool police force. After arriving in Wallington, they found Sarah Cushing ill. Since they could not talk to her, and had to wait for a reply to the telegram, Holmes suggested they "Have a pleasant little meal at a decent hotel". **1889? – The Cardboard Box**

WANDSWORTH COMMON (Zone 3)

WANDSWORTH COMMON—SW17: [Latitude / Longitude: <u>51.455692,-0.168786</u>]. Latimer and Kemp paid Melas five sovereigns for his services, and warned him to tell no one of his experience. They took Melas to Wandsworth Common. **1887? – The Greek Interpreter**

WESTCOMBE PARK (Zone 3)

BLACKHEATH RUGBY CLUB—SE3: [Latitude / Longitude: <u>51.477995, 0.026863</u>]. Watson said that he also played Rugby on the Blackheath team. **1896? – The Sussex Vampire**

BLACKHEATH RUGBY CLUB—SE3: [Latitude / Longitude: 51.477995, 0.026863]. Staunton, who played three-quarter for Cambridge, had also played for the Blackheath team. Overton was amazed that Holmes had never heard of him. **1897? – The Missing Three-Quarter**

WEST CROYDON (Outside Zone 6)

WEST CROYDON RAILROAD STATION—CR0: [Latitude / Longitude: 51.379155.-0.101881]. Holmes learned from Susan, that her sister Sarah had recently moved from Croydon to "New Street" in Wallington. To get there Holmes and Watson had to catch the train from the West Croydon Station, which was slightly less than a mile away. **1889? – The Cardboard Box**

WOOLWICH ARSENAL (Zone 4)

WOOLWICH ARSENAL, Brookhill Road, Etham—SE18: [Latitude / Longitude: 51.487921, 0.066975]. Mycroft Holmes arrived, with Inspector Lestrade at his heels. Arthur Cadogan West, a clerk at the Woolwich Arsenal, had been found dead outside the Aldgate Underground Station. In his pockets were partial plans of the secret Bruce-Partington submarine. Of the ten papers stolen from the Woolwich Arsenal, only seven were in West's pockets. Mycroft said, "The three most essential (pages) are gone—stolen—vanished". **1895 – The Bruce-Partington Plans**

BARNARD'S THEATRE, Beresford Street—SE18: [Latitude / Longitude: 51.49254,0.067331]. Barnard's was the only theater in Woolwich in 1895. **1895 – The Bruce-Partington Plans**

WOOLWICH ARSENAL RAILWAY STATION—SE18: [Latitude / Longitude: <u>51.49017,0.069783</u>]. Arthur Cadogan West worked at the Woolwich Arsenal. On Monday night, he suddenly left work. His fiancée, Miss Violet Woolwich, saw him about 7:30 PM. The clerk at the Woollwich Arsenal Railroad Station's ticket office was able to say, with confidence, that he saw Cadogan West Monday night, as he left for London Bridge on the 8:15 train. **1895 – The Bruce-Partington Plans**

<u>WOOLWICH DOCK (Zone 4)</u>

BARKING LEVEL—RM9: [Latitude / Longitude: <u>51.504495,0.089049</u>]. The two boats were flying at a tremendous pace as they passed "Barking Level upon and the melancholy Plumstead Marshes upon the other". **1887 – Sign of Four**

PLUMSTEAD—SE28: [Latitude / Longitude: <u>51.504495,0.089049</u>]. As the police steam launch continued downstream, Barking Level was on the left and Plumstead Marshes on the right. This area is upstream from today's Thames Flood Barrier. **1887 – Sign of Four**

WALKING TOURS - IN SHERLOCK HOLMES AND WATSON'S FOOTSTEPS

Finding "221B" Baker Street

Walking distance .6 mile — about 15 minutes

Use caution — Cross streets at designated points, look left, and obey instructions

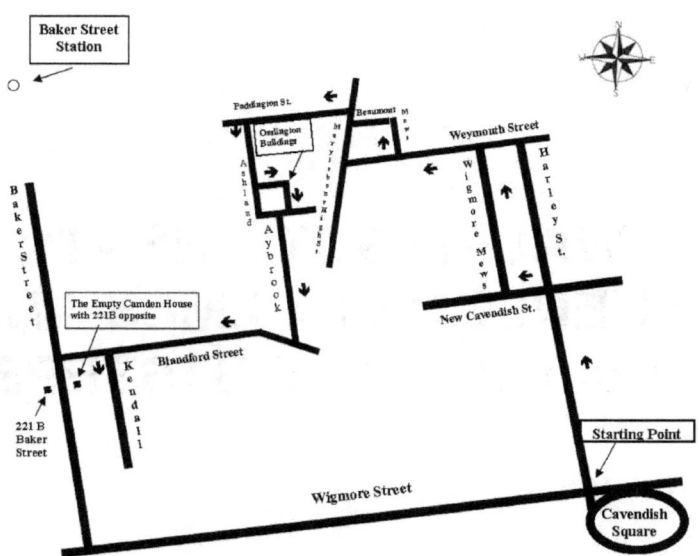

In *The Adventure of the Empty House*, Sherlock Holmes and Doctor Watson took a wandering route through mews and stables from Cavendish Square to Kendall Place. There they entered the back of the empty Camden House, at today's 32-34 Baker Street. Across the street, Watson was surprised to see their old lodgings. This places "221B" at today's No. 31 Baker Street. As they waited, Holmes was surprised when Col. Sebastian Moran entered the same room to make his deadly shot.

© *Thomas Bruce Wheeler, 2011*

358

Toby's False Trail

Walking Distance .6 mile — about 14 minutes, one way

Use caution — Cross streets at designated points, look right, and obey instructions.

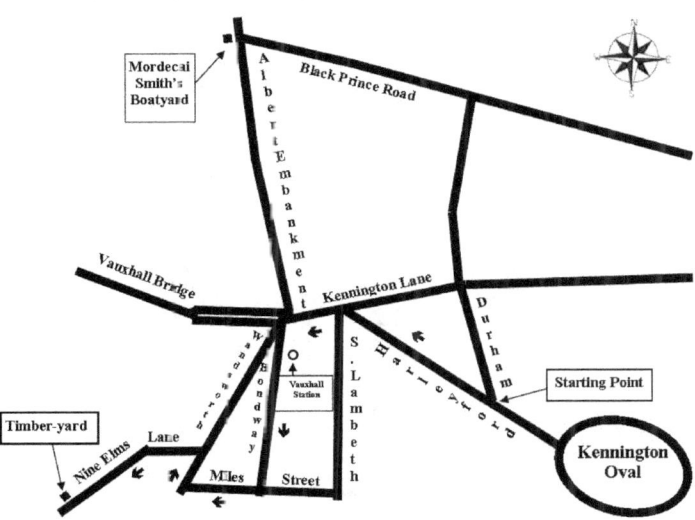

In *The Sign of Four*, Holmes and Watson noticed that the small killer of Bartholomew Sholto had stepped in creosote. Holmes sent Watson to get Toby, "a dog that would follow the scent to the world's end". At Harleyford Road and Durham Street, Toby incorrectly followed a timber-yard wagon that was carrying a cask of creosote. On the false trail, they walked east on **Kennington Lane** to **Vauxhall Bridge Road**, and then continued south on **Bond Street**, now called **Bondway**, to **Miles Street**. Here they turned west to jog across **Wandsworth Road** to **Nine Elms Lane**. When they arrived at the **Nine Elms Lane Timber-yard**, Toby "waddled around in circles...as if to ask for sympathy in his embarrassment."

© *Thomas Bruce Wheeler, 2011*

Toby's True Trail

Walking Distance .7 mile — about 14 minutes, one way

Use caution — Cross streets at designated points, look right, and obey instructions.

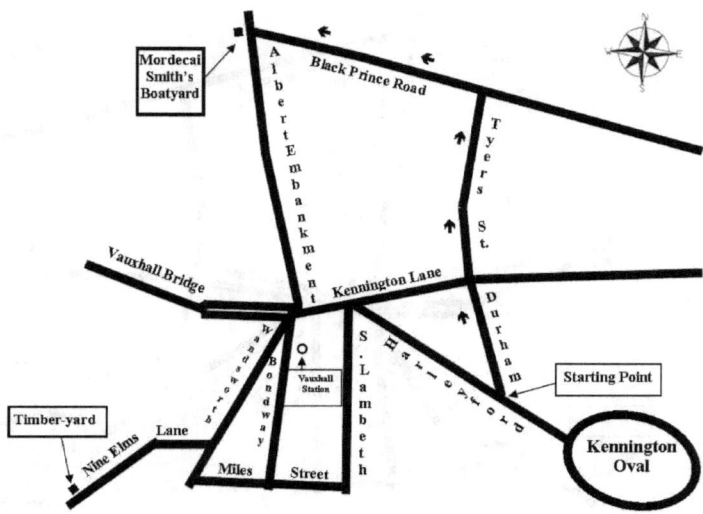

In *The Sign of Four*, after following the false trail to the **Nine Elms Lane Timber-yard**, Holmes, Watson and Toby backtracked to the point where they lost the true trail. I think this point was where **Durham Street** branches north out of **Harleyford Lane**. From here, Toby led them up north on **Durham** and **Tyers Streets**. At **Prince Street**, now called **Black Prince Road**, they turned left and walked west toward the Thames. In Sherlock's day, the riverside part of **Black Prince Road** was called **Broad Street**. Where **Broad Street** met the river, they found that their quarry had hired the fast steam launch *Aurora* from **Mordecai Smith's Boatyard**.

© *Thomas Bruce Wheeler, 2011*

Following Baskerville

Walking Distance 1.1 miles — about 23 minutes

Use caution — Cross streets at designated points, look right, and obey instructions.

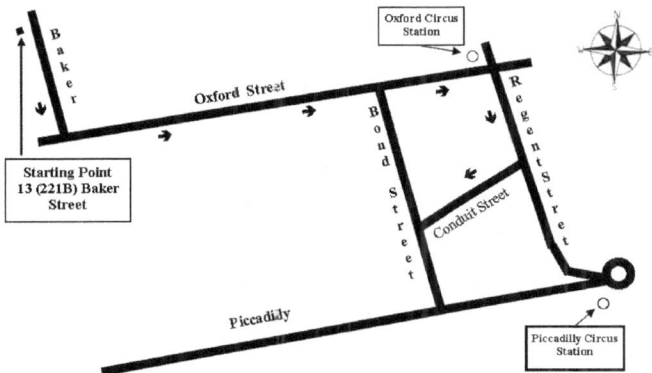

In *The Hound of the Baskervilles*, Holmes and Watson met Sir Henry and Dr. Mortimer at **Baker Street.** They made an appointment to meet again that afternoon at the Northumberland Hotel. As Sir Henry and Dr. Mortimer walked back to their hotel, Holmes and Watson secretly trailed behind to see who was following Sir Henry. At **Oxford Street**, they turned east toward **Oxford Circus**, and then south on **Regent Street**. Three quarters of the way to **Piccadilly Circus**, Holmes noticed a bearded man in a hansom following Baskerville, but he sped away. Holmes now knew that Baskerville had been closely shadowed since he arrived in London. Holmes remarked that using a cab had a disadvantage. He had seen the cab's number, "2704". Holmes and Watson went into the Regent Street office of the District Messenger Service. Holmes had previously helped the manager, and asked for the loan of young Cartwright. To fill the time before their two o'clock appointment at the hotel, Holmes and Watson visited the picture galleries in **Bond Street.**

© *Thomas Bruce Wheeler* 2011

To Mycroft's Diogenes Club

Walking distance 1.5 miles —- about 29 minutes

Use caution — Cross streets at designated points, look left and obey instructions

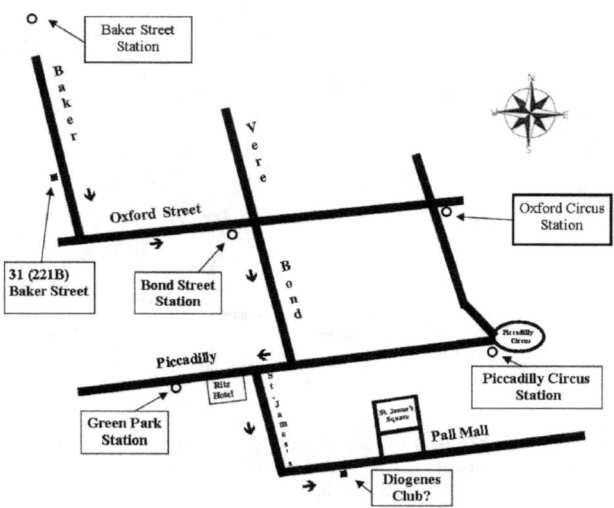

In *The Greek Interpreter*, Mycroft Holmes asked Sherlock Holmes and Dr. Watson to visit him. Mycroft lived in **Pall Mall** quarters, just across the street from his Diogenes Club. Sherlock said, "The Diogenes Club is the queerest club in London, and Mycroft one of the queerest men." On their way from Baker Street to the Diogenes Club, Holmes and Watson walked from Baker Street, then east on Oxford Street toward Regent (Oxford) Circus. Because they entered Pall Mall from its western end, I think they walked south on Bond Street, and continued on St. James's Street to Pall Mall.

© *Thomas Bruce Wheeler, 2011*

The Goose Club Walk

Walking distance .6 mile — about 12 minutes

Use caution — Cross streets at designated points, look right, and obey instructions.

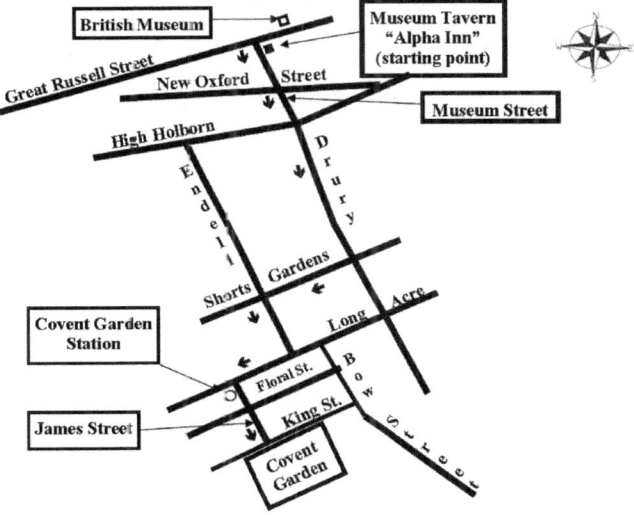

In *The Blue Carbuncle,* Holmes and Watson found that Windigate, the Alpha Inn's proprietor, had bought two dozen geese from Breckinridge's stand in Covent Garden. . In spite of the bitter cold, Holmes realized that their trek was not over, as he said to Watson, "Faces to the south then, and quick march". They walked from the **Alpha Inn** to **Covent Garden** by heading south on **Museum Street.** They crossed **New Oxford Street** and **High Holborn,** and continued south on **Drury Lane**. From **Drury Lane**, Holmes and Watson turned southwest on **Shorts Gardens**, or as Watson put it, "through a zigzag of slums". From **Shorts Garden**, Holmes and Watson turned south on **Endell Street**. When they reached **Long Acre**, they could see the end of **Bow Street** to their left. Holmes and Watson were almost to **Covent Garden** as they turned left on **James Street.** Breckinridge had a goose stand in Covent Garden. The goose with the blue carbuncle was among the two dozen sold to the Alpha Inn. Holmes used trickery to get Breckinridge to tell where he had purchased the geese.

© *Thomas Bruce Wheeler, 2011*

363

NAMED CHARACTERS

Excluding Sherlock, Watson and Mrs. Hudson, there are four hundred and fifty-four named characters in this book. This includes those known by more than one name (AKA). Conan Doyle favored last names starting with M and S (with sixty-three and sixty respectively), followed by B (forty-eight). His favorite given name for men was James and John, with fourteen each. Mary and Violet were his favorite given names for women, with seven and four respectively.

A

Acton, County Magistrate: REIGATE SQUIRES

Adair, the Honorable Ronald: EMPTY HOUSE

Adair, Lady Hilda: EMPTY HOUSE

Adler, Irene, contralto Prima Donna: SCANDAL IN BOHEMIA

Agar, Moore, Doctor: DEVIL'S FOOT

Agatha, the housemaid: CHARLES AUGUSTUS MILVERTON

Akbar, Dost: SIGN OF FOUR

Alexis: GOLDEN PINCE-NEZ

Algar, Police Official: CARDBOARD BOX

Allen, Mrs.: VALLEY OF FEAR

Altamont, AKA Sherlock Holmes: LAST BOW

Amberley, Josiah: RETIRED COLOURMAN

Amberley, Mrs.: RETIRED COLOURMAN

Ames, Mr.: VALLEY OF FEAR

Anderson, Constable: LION'S MANE

Angel, Hosner, AKA James Windibank: CASE OF IDENTITY

Anna, AKA Mrs. Coram: GOLDEN PINCE-NEZ

Armitage, James, AKA Justice of the Peace Trevor: GLORIA SCOTT

Armstrong, Doctor Leslie: MISSING THREE-QUARTER

B

Backwater, Lord: SILVER BLAZE

Baker, Henry: BLUE CARBUNCLE

Balmoral, Duke of: NOBLE BACHELOR

Balmoral, Lord: EMPTY HOUSE

Bannister, Mr.: THREE STUDENTS

Barclay, Colonel James: CROOKED MAN

Barclay, Nancy: CROOKED MAN

Bardle, Police Official: LION'S MANE

Barker, Cecil: VALLEY OF FEAR

Barker, Mr.: RETIRED COLOURMAN

Barnicot, Doctor: SIX NAPOLEONS

Barrymore, Mr.: HOUND OF THE BASKERVILLES

Barrymore, Mrs.: HOUND OF THE BASKERVILLES

Barton, Hill, AKA Doctor John Watson: ILLUSTRIOUS CLIENT

Basil, Captain, AKA Sherlock Holmes: BLACK PETER

Baskerville, Sir Henry: HOUND OF THE BASKERVILLES

Baskerville, Sir Charles: HOUND OF THE BASKERVILLES

Bates, Marlow: THOR BRIDGE

Bathsheba: CROOKED MAN

Baynes, Inspector: WISTERIA LODGE

Becher, Doctor, AKA Mr. Ferguson: ENGINEER'S THUMB

Beddington, Mr., AKA Arthur Pinner: STOCK-BROKERS CLERK

Beddoes, Mr., AKA Evans: GLORIA SCOTT

Bellamy, Maud: LION'S MANE

Bellamy, Tom: LION'S MANE

Bellamy, William: LION'S MANE

Bellinger, Lord: SECOND STAIN

Belminster, Duke of: SECOND STAIN

Bennett, Trevor: CREEPING MAN

Beppo: SIX NAPOLEONS

Biddle, Mr.: RESIDENT PATIENT

Billy, the pageboy: VALLEY OF FEAR, THOR BRIDGE,

MAZARIN STONE, CASE OF IDENTITY, YELLOW FACE, and SHOSCOMBE OLD PLACE

Black Peter, AKA Captain Peter Carey: BLACK PETER

Blackwell, Lady Eva: CHARLES AUGUSTUS MILVERTON

Blessington, Mr., AKA Sutton: RESIDENT PATIENT

Boone, Hugh, AKA Neville St. Clair: TWISTED LIP

Brackenstall, Lady: ABBEY GRANGE

Brackenstall, Sir Eustace: ABBEY GRANGE

Bradstreet, Inspector: BLUE CARBUNCLE, ENGINEER'S THUMB, TWISTED LIP

Breckinridge, Mr.: BLUE CARBUNCLE

Brewer, Sam: SHOSCOMBE OLD PLACE

Brown, Josiah: SIX NAPOLEONS

Brown, Silas: SILVER BLAZE

Browner, Jim: CARDBOARD BOX

Browner, Mary, AKA Mary Cushing: CARDBOARD BOX

Brunton, Richard: MUSGRAVE RITUAL

Burnet, Miss, AKA Signora Durando: WISTERIA LODGE

Burnwell, Sir George: BERYL CORONET

C

Cadogan, Arthur: BRUCE-PARTINGTON PLANS

Cairns, Patrick: BLACK PETER

Calhoun, James, Captain: FIVE ORANGE PIPS

Cantlemere, Lord: MAZARIN STONE

Carey, Captain Peter, AKA Black Peter: BLACK PETER

Carfax, Lady Frances: LADY FRANCES CARFAX

Carruthers, Bob: SOLITARY CYCLIST

Cartwright, young: HOUND OF THE BASKERVILLES

Charpentier, Madam: STUDY IN SCARLET

Charpentier, Alice: STUDY IN SCARLET

Charpentier, Sub-Lieutenant Arthur: STUDY IN SCARLET

Circus Belle, AKA Vittoria: SUSSEX VAMPIRE

Clay, John, AKA Vincent Spaulding: RED-HEADED
LEAGUE

Clayton, John, the cabbie: HOUND OF THE
BASKERVILLES

Colonna, Prince of: SIX NAPOLEONS

Colonna, Princes of: SIX NAPOLEONS

Coram, Mrs., AKA Anna: GOLDEN PINCE-NEZ

Coram, Professor: GOLDEN PINCE-NEZ

Coventry, Police Sergeant: THOR BRIDGE

Crocker, Jack, Captain: ABBEY GRANGE

Cubitt, Hilton: DANCING MEN

Cubitt, Elsie, AKA Elsie Patrick: DANCING MEN

Cummings, Joyce: THOR BRIDGE

Cunningham, Justice of the Peace: REIGATE SQUIRES

Cunningham, Alec: REIGATE SQUIRES

Cusack, Catherine: BLUE CARBUNCLE

Cushing, Susan: CARDBOARD BOX

Cushing, Sarah: CARDBOARD BOX

Cushing, Mary, AKA Mrs. Mary Browner: CARDBOARD BOX

D d

Damery, Sir James: ILLUSTRIOUS CLIENT

Derbyshire, William, AKA John Straker: SILVER BLAZE

Davenport, Mr. J.: GREEK INTERPRETER

David, King: CROOKED MAN

de Merville, General: ILLUSTRIOUS CLIENT

de Merville, Violet: ILLUSTRIOUS CLIENT

Dennis, Tom: STUDY IN SCARLET

Dennis, Sally: STUDY IN SCARLET

Dixie, Steve: THREE GABLES

Dixon, Jeremy: MISSING THREE-QUARTER

Dobney, Susan: LADY FRANCES CARFAX

Dodd, James: BLANCHED SOLDIER

Dorak, Mrs.: CREEPING MAN

Doran, Hatty, AKA Hatty Moulton: NOBLE BACHELOR

Doran, Aloysius: NOBLE BACHELOR

Douglas, John: VALLEY OF FEAR

Douglas, Mrs.: VALLEY OF FEAR

Dowson, Baron: MAZARIN STONE

Drebber, Enoch J.: STUDY IN SCARLET

Dunbar, Grace: THOR BRIDGE

Durando, Signora, AKA Miss Burnet: WISTERIA LODGE

Durando, Victor: WISTERIA LODGE

E

Eccles, Scott: WISTERIA LODGE

Edmunds, Police Official: VEILED LODGER

Etherege, Mrs.: CASE OF IDENTIFY

Elise (no last name); ENGINEER'S THUMB

Elman, Vicar J. C.: RETIRED COLOURMAN

Emsworth, Colonel: BLANCHED SOLDIER

Emsworth, Lance-Corporal Godfrey: BLANCHED SOLDIER

Ernest, Doctor Ray: RETIRED COLOURMAN

Evans, Killer, AKA John Garrideb, James Winter, and Morecroft: THREE GARRIDEBS

Evans, Mr., AKA Beddoes: GLORIA SCOTT

F

Fairbairn, Alec: CARDBOARD BOX

Falder, Lady Beatrice: SHOSCOMBE OLD PLACE

Farquhar, Mr.: STOCK-BROKERS CLERK

Ferguson, Master Jack: SUSSEX VAMPIRE

Ferguson, Mr., AKA Doctor Becher: ENGINEER'S THUMB

Ferguson, Robert: SUSSEX VAMPIRE

Ferguson, Mrs.: SUSSEX VAMPIRE

Ferrier, Doctor: NAVAL TREATY

Ffolliott, Sir George: WISTERIA LODGE

Forbes, Inspector: NAVAL TREATY

Forrester, Inspector: REIGATE SQUIRES

Forrester, Mrs. Cecil: SIGN OF FOUR

Fournaye, M. Henri, AKA Eduardo Lucas: SECOND STAIN

Fournaye, Mme. Henri: SECOND STAIN

Fowler, Edward: COPPER BEECHES

Fowler, Alice, AKA Alice Rucastle: COPPER BEECHES

Fraser, Mrs., AKA Mrs. Shlessinger: LADY FRANCES CARFAX

Fritz, AKA Col. Lysander Stark: ENGINEER'S THUMB

G

Garcia, Aloysius: WISTERIA LODGE

Garrideb, Nathan: THREE GARRIDEBS

Garrideb, John, AKA James Winter, Morecroft, and Killer Evans: THREE GARRIDEBS

Garrideb, Alexander Hamilton: THREE GARRIDEBS

Garrideb, Howard: THREE GARRIDEBS

Gibson, Maria: THOR BRIDGE

Gibson, Senator J. Neil: THOR BRIDGE

Gilchrist, Sir Jabez: THREE STUDENTS

Gilchrist, young: THREE STUDENTS

Gorgiano, Giuseppe: RED CIRCLE

Gorot, Charles: NAVAL TREATY

Green, the Honorable Phillip: LADY FRANCES CARFAX

Green, Admiral Phillip: LADY FRANCES CARFAX

Gregory, Inspector: SILVER BLAZE

Gregson, Tobias, Inspector, AKA Police Detective Gregson: STUDY IN SCARLET, GREEK INTERPRETER, RED CIRCLE, and WISTERIA LODGE

Gruner, Baron Adelbert: ILLUSTRIOUS CLIENT

H

Hammersmith Wonder, the, Vigor: SUSSEX VAMPIRE

Hardy, John: EMPTY HOUSE

Hardy, Mr.: CASE OF IDENTITY

Hargrave: VALLEY OF FEAR

Harker, Horace: SIX NAPOLEONS

Harringby, Lord: WISTERIA LODGE

Harrison, Annie: NAVAL TREATY

Harrison, Joseph: NAVAL TREATY

Hatherley, Victor: ENGINEER'S THUMB

Hayes, Ruben: PRIORY SCHOOL

Hayes, Mrs.: PRIORY SCHOOL

Hayling, Jeremiah: ENGINEER'S THUMB

Hayter, Colonel: REIGATE SQUIRES

Hayward, Mr.: RESIDENT PATIENT

Heidegger, Herr: PRIORY SCHOOL

Henderson, Mr., AKA Don Murillo, and Marquess of Montalva: WISTERIA LODGE

Holder, Mary: BERYL CORONET

Holder, Alexander: BERYL CORONET

Holder, Arthur: BERYL CORONET

Holdernesse, Duke of: PRIORY SCHOOL

Holdhurst, Lord: NAVAL TREATY

Holmes, Mycroft: GREEK INTERPRETER, BRUCE-PARTINGTON PLANS, FINAL PROBLEM, and EMPTY HOUSE

Hope, Lady Hilda: SECOND STAIN

Hope, the Right Honorable: **Trelawney**: SECOND STAIN

Hope, Jefferson, AKA Mrs. Sawyer: STUDY IN SCARLET

Hopkins, Ezekiah: RED-HEADED LEAGUE

Hopkins, Inspector Stanley, AKA Police Detective Hopkins: BLACK PETER, MISSING THREE-QUARTER, ABBEY GRANGE, and GOLDEN PINCE-NEZ

Horner, John: BLUE CARBUNCLE

Horsom, Doctor: LADY FRANCES CARFAX

Howells, Rachel: MUSGRAVE RITUAL

Hudson, Mr.: GLORIA SCOTT

Hudson, Morse: SIX NAPOLEONS

Hunter, Violet: COPPER BEECHES

Huxtable, Thorneycroft, Doctor: PRIORY SCHOOL

Hynes, Justice of the Peace: WISTERIA LODGE

J

John, Spencer: THREE GABLES

Johnson, Sidney: BRUCE-PARTINGTON PLANS

Johnson, Shinwell: ILLUSTRIOUS CLIENT

Jones, Athelney, Police Official: SIGN OF FOUR

Jones, Peter, Police Official: RED-HEADED LEAGUE

K

Kemp, Wilson: GREEK INTERPRETER

Keswick, Mr.: STUDY IN SCARLET

Khan, Abdullah: SIGN OF FOUR

Khartoum, Khalifa of: EMPTY HOUSE

Kirwan, William: REIGATE SQUIRES

Klein, Isadora: THREE GABLES

Kratides, Paul: GREEK INTERPRETER

Kratides, Sophy: GREEK INTERPRETER

L

La Rothière, Louis: SECOND STAIN and BRUCE-PARTINGTON PLANS

Lanner, Inspector: RESIDENT PATIENT

Latimer, Mr.: GREEK INTERPRETER

Leonardo, the strong man: VEILED LODGER

Lestrade, Inspector: STUDY IN SCARLET, NOBLE BACHELOR, CARDBOARD BOX, HOUND OF THE BASKERVILLES, SECOND STAIN, EMPTY HOUSE, NORWOOD BUILDER, BRUCE-PARTINGTON PLANS, CHARLES AUGUSTUS MILVERTON, SIX NAPOLEONS, and LADY FRANCES CARFAX

Lesurier, Madam: SILVER BLAZE

Leverton, Pinkerton detective: RED CIRCLE

Lexington, Mrs.: NORWOOD BUILDER

Lomax, Sub-Librarian: ILLUSTRIOUS CLIENT

Lopez, Senor: WISTERIA LODGE

Lucas, Eduardo, AKA Henri Fournaye: SECOND STAIN

Lucas, Senor, AKA Senor Rulli, and Lopez: WISTERIA LODGE

Lucca, Emilia: RED CIRCLE

Lucca, Gennaro: RED CIRCLE

Lynch, Victor, the forger: SUSSEX VAMPIRE

M

Maberley, Douglas: THREE GABLES

Maberley, Mary: THREE GABLES

MacDonald, Alec, Inspector: VALLEY OF FEAR

MacKinnon, Inspector: RETIRED COLOURMAN

MacPherson, Constable: SECOND STAIN

Marker, Mrs.: GOLDEN PINCE-NEZ

Martin, Inspector: DANCING MEN

Mason, John: SHOSCOMBE OLD PLACE

Mason, White, Police Official: VALLEY OF FEAR

Mathews, Mr.: EMPTY HOUSE

Maudsley, Mr.: BLUE CARBUNCLE

Maupertuis, Baron: REIGATE SQUIRES

Milverton, Charles Augustus: CHARLES AUGUSTUS MILVERTON

Mitton, John, the valet: SECOND STAIN

Morcar, Countess of: BLUE CARBUNCLE

Moffat, Mr.: RESIDENT PATIENT

Montalva, Marquess of, AKA Mr. Henderson, and Don Murillo: WISTERIA LODGE

Moran, Colonel Sebastian: EMPTY HOUSE

Morecroft, AKA John Garrideb, James Winter, and Killer Evans: THREE GARRIDEBS

Moriarty, Professor: VALLEY OF FEAR, FINAL PROBLEM, EMPTY HOUSE, and NORWOOD BUILDER

Morris, William, AKA Duncan Ross: RED-HEADED LEAGUE

Morrison, Miss: CROOKED MAN

Morstan, Captain: SIGN OF FOUR

Morstan, Mary, AKA Mrs. Mary Watson: SIGN OF FOUR

Mortimer, Doctor James: HOUND OF THE BASKERVILLES

Morton, Inspector: DYING DETECTIVE

Morton, Cyril: SOLITARY CYCLIST

Morton, Ralph: SOLITARY CYCLIST

Moulton, Francis Hay: NOBLE BACHELOR

Moulton, Hatty, AKA Hatty Doran: NOBLE BACHELOR

Mount-James, Lord: MISSING THREE-QUARTER

Munro, Grant: YELLOW FACE

Munro, Effie: YELLOW FACE

Murcher, Harry, Constable: STUDY IN SCARLET

Murdock, Ian: LION'S MANE

Murillo, Don, AKA Mr. Henderson, and Marquess of Montalva: WISTERIA LODGE

Munro, Colonel Spence: COPPER BEECHES

Murphy, Major: CROOKED MAN

Murray, Mr.: EMPTY HOUSE

Musgrave, Reginald: MUSGRAVE RITUAL

Musgrave, Sir Ralph: MUSGRAVE RITUAL

N

Neill, General: CROOKED MAN

Neligan, AKA John Hopley: BLACK PETER

Neligan, the Elder: BLACK PETER

Norberton, Lady Beatrice: SHOSCOMBE OLD PLACE

Norberton, Sir Robert: SHOSCOMBE OLD PLACE

Norlett, Mr.: SHOSCOMBE OLD PLACE

Norlett, Mrs.: SHOSCOMBE OLD PLACE

Norton, Godfrey: SCANDAL IN BOHEMIA

O

Oakshot, Sir Leslie: ILLUSTRIOUS CLIENT

Oakshott, Maggie: BLUE CARBUNCLE

Oberstein, Hugo, AKA Pierrot: BRUCE-PARTINGTON PLANS and SECOND STAIN

Oldacre, Jonas: NORWOOD BUILDER

Openshaw, Colonel Elias: FIVE ORANGE PIPS

Openshaw, John: FIVE ORANGE PIPS

Openshaw, Joseph: FIVE ORANGE PIPS

Overton, Cyril: MISSING THREE-QUARTER

P

Parker, (a garroter): EMPTY HOUSE

Paganini, the violinist: CARDBOARD BOX

Patrick, Elsie, AKA Mrs. Elsie Cubitt: DANCING MEN

Patrick, the Chicago gangster: DANCING MEN

Prendergast, Jack: GLORIA SCOTT

Perkins, Mr.: HOUND OF THE BASKERVILLES

Perkins, young: THREE GABLES

Peters, Henry (Holy), AKA Doctor Shlessinger: LADY FRANCES CARFAX

Peterson, Commissionaire: BLUE CARBUNCLE

Phelps, Percy: NAVAL TREATY

Pierrot, AKA Hugo Oberstein: BRUCE-PARTINGTON PLANS

Pike, Langdale: THREE GABLES

Pinner, Arthur, AKA Beddington: STOCK-BROKERS CLERK

Porlock, Mr.: VALLEY OF FEAR

Presbury, Miss: CREEPING MAN

Presbury, Professor: CREEPING MAN

Prescott, Roger: THREE GABLES

Prosper, Francis: BERYL CORONET

Pycroft, Hall: STOCK-BROKERS CLERK

R

Rance, John, Constable: STUDY IN SCARLET

Ras, Daulat: THREE STUDENTS

Ronder, Eugenia: VEILED LODGER

Ronder, Mr.: VEILED LODGER

Ross, Duncan, AKA William Morris: RED-HEADED LEAGUE

Ross, Colonel: SILVER BLAZE

Roundhay, Vicar: DEVIL'S FOOT

Roylott, Doctor Grimesby: SPECKLED BAND

Rucastle, Alice: COPPER BEECHES

Rucastle, Edward: COPPER BEECHES

Rucastle, Jephro: COPPER BEECHES

Rucastle, Mrs.: COPPER BEECHES

Rufton, Earl of: LADY FRANCES CARFAX

Rulli, Senor, AKA Senor Lucas and Lopez: WISTERIA LODGE

Ryder, James: BLUE CARBUNCLE

S

Saltire, Lord: PRIORY SCHOOL

Sandeford, Mr.: SIX NAPOLEONS

Saunders, Sir James: BLANCHED SOLDIER

Savage, Victor: THE DYING DETECTIVE

Sawyer, Mrs., AKA Jefferson Hope: STUDY IN SCARLET

Selden: HOUND OF THE BASKERVILLES

Sherman, Mr.: SIGN OF FOUR

Shlessinger, Doctor, AKA Henry (Holy) Peters: LADY FRANCES CARFAX

Shlessinger, Mrs., AKA Mrs. Fraser: LADY FRANCES CARFAX

Sholto, Major: SIGN OF FOUR

Sholto, Thaddeus: SIGN OF FOUR

Sholto, Bartholomew: SIGN OF FOUR

Sigerson, AKA Sherlock Holmes: EMPTY HOUSE

Simpson, Baker Street Irregular: CROOKED MAN

Simpson, Fitzroy: SILVER BLAZE

Sinclair, Admiral: BRUCE-PARTINGTON PLANS

Singh, Mahomet: SIGN OF FOUR

Slaney, Abe: DANCING MEN

Small, Jonathan: SIGN OF FOUR

Smith, Culverton: DYING DETECTIVE

Smith, Mordecai: SIGN OF FOUR

Smith, Mrs.: SIGN OF FOUR

Smith, Ralph: SOLITARY CYCLIST

Smith, Violet: SOLITARY CYCLIST

Smith, Willoughby: GOLDEN PINCE-NEZ

Soames, Hilton: THREE STUDENTS

Southerton, Lord: COPPER BEECHES

Spaulding, Vincent, AKA John Clay: RED-HEADED LEAGUE

Spender, Rose: LADY FRANCES CARFAX

St. Clair, AKA Hugh Boone: TWISTED LIP

St. Clair, Mrs.: TWISTED LIP

St. Simon, Lord: NOBLE BACHELOR

Stackhurst, Harold: LION'S MANE

Stamford, young Doctor: STUDY IN SCARLET

383

Stangerson, Joseph: STUDY IN SCARLET

Stapleton, Miss, AKA Mrs. Vandeleur: HOUND OF THE BASKERVILLES

Stapleton, Mr., AKA Mr. Vandeleur: HOUND OF THE BASKERVILLES

Stark, Colonel Lysander: ENGINEER'S THUMB

Staunton, Godfrey: MISSING THREE-QUARTER

Staunton, Mrs.: MISSING THREE-QUARTER

Steiler, Peter: FINAL PROBLEM

Sterndale, Doctor Leon: DEVIL'S FOOT

Stewart, Miss: THE CROOKED MAN

Stewart, Mrs.: EMPTY HOUSE

Stimson, Mr.: LADY FRANCES CARFAX

Stockdale, Barney: THREE GABLES

Stockdale, Susan: THREE GABLES

Stone, Reverend Joshua: WISTERIA LODGE

Stoner, Helen: SPECKLED BAND

Stoner, Julia: SPECKLED BAND

Stoner, Major General: SPECKLED BAND

Stoner, Mrs.: SPECKLED BAND

Stoner, Miss: COPPER BEECHES

Straker, John, AKA William Derbyshire: SILVER BLAZE

Straubenzee, old Mr.: MAZARIN STONE

Summer, Mr.: BLACK PETER

Sutherland, Mary: CASE OF IDENTITY

Sutro, Lawyer: THREE GABLES

Sutton, Mr., AKA Blessington: RESIDENT PATIENT

Sylvius, Count Negretto: MAZARIN STONE

T

Tangey, Commissionaire: NAVAL TREATY

Tangey, Charwoman: NAVAL TREATY

Toller, Mr.: COPPER BEECHES

Toller, Mrs.: COPPER BEECHES

Tregennis, Brenda: DEVIL'S FOOT

Tregennis, George: DEVIL'S FOOT

Tregennis, Mortimer: DEVIL'S FOOT

Tregennis, Owen: DEVIL'S FOOT

Trevelyan, Doctor Percy: RESIDENT PATIENT

Trevor, Justice of the Peace, AKA James Armitage: GLORIA SCOTT

Trevor, Victor: GLORIA SCOTT

Turner, Alice: BOSCOMBE VALLEY

Turner, John: BOSCOMBE VALLEY

U

Underwood, John: STUDY IN SCARLET

Uriah, the Hittite: CROOKED MAN

V v

Van Seddar, Mr.: MAZARIN STONE

Vandeleur, Schoolmaster, AKA Stapleton: HOUND OF THE BASKERVILLES

Vandeleur, Mrs.: HOUND OF THE BASKERVILLES

Venucci, Lucretia: SIX NAPOLEONS

Venucci, Pietro: SIX NAPOLEONS

Verner, Doctor: NORWOOD BUILDER

Vernet, M., the French artist: GREEK INTERPRETER

Vigor, AKA the Hammersmith Wonder: SUSSEX VAMPIRE

Vittoria, AKA the circus belle: SUSSEX VAMPIRE

Von Bork, Herr: LAST BOW

Von Herder, Herr: EMPTY HOUSE

Von Herling, Baron: LAST BOW

Von Kramm, Count, AKA Wilhelm Gottsreich Sigismond von Ormstein: SCANDAL IN BOHEMIA

von Ormstein, Grand Duke and King, AKA Count Von Kramm: SCANDAL IN BOHEMIA

W

Walter, Colonel Valentine: BRUCE-PARTINGTON PLANS

Walter, Sir James: BRUCE-PARTINGTON PLANS

Walters, Constable: WISTERIA LODGE

Warren, Mr.: RED CIRCLE

Warren, Mrs.: RED CIRCLE

Watson, Mrs. Mary, AKA Mary Morstan: SIGN OF FOUR

West, Arthur Cadogan: Bruce-Partington Plans:

Whitney, Isa: TWISTED LIP

Whitney, Kate: TWISTED LIP

Wiggins, Baker Street Irregular: STUDY IN SCARLET and SIGN OF FOUR

Wilder, James: PRIORY SCHOOL

Williams, Mr., AKA James Baker: WISTERIA LODGE

Williams, the coachman: SIGN OF FOUR

Williamson, Mr.: SOLITARY CYCLIST

Wilson, Jabez: RED-HEADED LEAGUE

Wilson, Police Sergeant: VALLEY OF FEAR

Windibank, James, AKA Hosner Angel: CASE OF IDENTITY

Windibank, Mrs.: CASE OF IDENTITY

Windigate, Innkeeper: BLUE CARBUNCLE

Winter, Kitty: ILLUSTRIOUS CLIENT

Winter, James, AKA John Garrideb, Morecroft, and Killer Evans: THREE GARRIDEBS

Wood, Corporal Henry: CROOKED MAN

Wood, Doctor: VALLEY OF FEAR

Woodley, Edith: EMPTY HOUSE

Woodley, Jack: SOLITARY CYCLIST

Woolwich, Violet: BRUCE-PARTINGTON PLANS

Y

Youghal, Inspector: MAZARIN STONE

NAMED CHARACTER STATISTICS

Two Kings (The Biblical King David, and von Ormstein, Grand Duke and hereditary King of Bohemia)

One Khalifa (Khartoum)

One Prince (Colonna)

One Princess (Colonna)

Three Dukes (Balmoral, Belminster and Holdernesse)

Two Earls (Maynooth and Rufton)

One Marquess (Montalva)

Two Counts (Sylvius and Von Kramm)

One Countess (Morcar)

Four Barons (Dowson, Gruner, Maupertuis, and Von Herling)

Ten Lords (Backwater, Balmoral, Prime Minister Bellinger, Cantlemere, Harringby, Holdhurst, Mount-James, Saltire, Southerton, and St. Simon)

Twelve Knights and Baronets (Charles Baskerville, Henry Baskerville, Brackenstall, Burnwell, Damery, Ffolliott, Gilchrist, Musgrave, Norberton, Oakshot, Saunders, and Walter)

Eight Ladies (Adair, Blackwell, Brackenstall, Carfax, Falder, Hope, Maynooth and Norberton)

One Don (Murillo)

Five Constables (Anderson, MacPherson, Murcher, Rance, and Walters)

One Senator (Gibson)

Three Professors (Coram, Moriarty and Presbury)

Two Vicars (Elman and Roundhay)

Four Police Sergeants (Coventry, Gregson, Hopkins and Wilson)

Five Police Detectives, including one Pinkerton Detective (Gregson, Forbes, Hopkins, Lestrade and Leverton) Forbes, Gregson, Hopkins, and Lestrade were later promoted and identified as Inspectors.

Fourteen Inspectors (Baynes, Bradstreet, Forbes, Forrester, Gregory, Gregson, Hopkins, Lanner, Lestrade, MacDonald, MacKinnon, Martin, Morton, and Youghal)

Seven Police Officials Several must be Superintendents or other senior ranks, because they assigned duties to Inspectors (Algar, Bardle, Edmunds, Peter Jones, Athelney Jones, Mason, and Merivale)

Four Detective/Inspectors in more than one adventure (Lestrade 12, Gregson 5 Hopkins 3, [Gregson and Hopkins started as detectives], and Bradstreet 3)

Eighteen Doctors, MD, DD and PHD (Agar, Armstrong, Barnicot, Barton, Becher, Ernest, Ferrier, Horsom, Huxtable, Mortimer, Roylott, Saunders, Shlessinger, Stamford, Sterndale, Trevelyan, Verner, and Wood)

Three Justices of the Peace (Cunningham, Hynes and Trevor)

Three Generals (de Merville, Neill, and Stoner)

Two Admirals (Green and Sinclair)

Four Sea Captains (Basil, Calhoun, Carey, and Crocker)

Nine Colonels (Barclay, Emsworth, Hayter, Moran, Munro, Openshaw, Ross, Stark, and Walter)

Two Majors (Murphy and Sholto)

One Army Captain (Morstan)

One Sub-Lieutenant (Charpentier)

Two Corporals (Emsworth, and Wood)

One Soldier (Uriah, the Hittite)

One Pageboy (Billy)

Also from MX Publishing

Close To Holmes

A Look at the Connections Between Historical London, Sherlock Holmes and Sir Arthur Conan Doyle.

Eliminate The Impossible

An Examination of the World of Sherlock Holmes on Page and Screen.

The Norwood Author

Arthur Conan Doyle and the Norwood Years (1891 - 1894)

www.mxpublishing.com

Also From MX Publishing

In Search of Dr Watson

Wonderful biography of Dr.Watson from expert Molly Carr. Now fully revised and updated 2nd edition.

Arthur Conan Doyle, Sherlock Holmes and Devon

A Complete Tour Guide and Companion.

The Lost Stories of Sherlock Holmes

Eight more stories from the pen of John H Watson – compiled by Tony Reynolds.

www.mxpublishing.com

Also From MX Publishing

Watsons Afghan Adventure

Fascinating biography of Watson's time in Afghanistan from US Army veteran Kieran McMullen.

Shadowfall

Sherlock Holmes, ancient relics and demons and mystic characters. A supernatural Holmes pastiche.

Official Papers of The Hound of The Baskervilles

Very unusual collection of the original police papers from The Hound case.

Also From MX Publishing

The Sign of Fear

The first adventure of the 'female Sherlock Holmes'. A delightful fun adventure with your favourite supporting Holmes characters.

A Study in Crimson

The second adventure of the 'female Sherlock Holmes' with a host of sub-plots and new characters joining Watson and Fanshaw

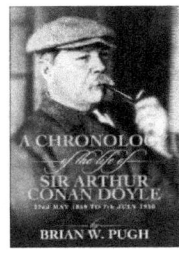

The Chronology of Arthur Conan Doyle

The definitive chronology used by historians and libraries worldwide.

www.mxpublishing.com

Also From MX Publishing

Aside Arthur Conan Doyle

A collection of twenty stories from
ACD's close friend Bertram
Fletcher Robinson.

Bertram Fletcher Robinson

The comprehensive biography of the
assistant plot producer of The Hound
of The Baskervilles

Wheels of Anarchy

Reprint and introduction to Max
Pemberton's thriller from 100 years
ago. One of the first spy thrillers of
its kind.

www.mxpublishing.com

Also From MX Publishing

Bobbles and Plum

Four playlets from PG Wodehouse 'lost' for over 100 years – found and reprinted with an excellent commentary

The World of Vanity Fair

A specialist full-colour reproduction of key articles from Bertram Fletcher Robinson containing of colour caricatures from the early 1900s.

Tras Las He huellas de Arthur Conan Doyle (in Spanish)

Un viaje ilustrado por Devon.

www.mxpublishing.com

Also From MX Publishing

The Outstanding Mysteries of
Sherlock Holmes

With thirteen Homes stories and
illustrations Kelly re-creates the
gas-lit, fog-enshrouded world of
Victorian London

Rendezvous at The Populaire

Sherlock Holmes has retired,
injured from an encounter with
Moriarty. He's tempted out of
retirement for an epic battle with
the Phantom of the opera.

Baker Street Beat

An eclectic collection of articles,
essays, radio plays and 'general
scribblings' about Sherlock Holmes
from Dr.Dan Andriacco.

www.mxpublishing.com

Also From MX Publishing

The Case of The Grave Accusation

The creator of Sherlock Holmes has been accused of murder. Only Holmes and Watson can stop the destruction of the Holmes legacy.

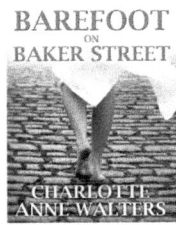

Barefoot on Baker Street

Epic novel of the life of a Victorian workhouse orphan featuring Sherlock Holmes and Moriarty.

Case of Witchcraft

A tale of witchcraft in the Northern Isles, in which some long-concealed secrets are revealed including about the Great Detective himself.

www.mxpublishing.com

Also From MX Publishing

Murder in The Library

Modern day thriller set in Chicago with a Sherlock Holmes theme.

No Police Like Holmes

Hilarious thriller where all the murder suspects are Sherlockians at a Sherlock Holmes event in South Carolina.

And coming in the fall of 2011:

Sherlock Holmes and The Affair In Transylvania

I Will Find The Answer (Holmes vs Dr. Jekyll)

www.mxpublishing.com

www.ingramcontent.com/pod-product-compliance
Lightning Source LLC
Chambersburg PA
CBHW071148020726
47502CB00002B/319